Under the
Rainbow

Also published by Poolbeg

Ebb & Flow

As Easy As That

Parting Company

Inside out

Under the
Rainbow

MARY O'SULLIVAN

POOLBEG

Published 2010
by Poolbeg Press Ltd
123 Grange Hill, Baldoyle
Dublin 13, Ireland
E-mail: poolbeg@poolbeg.com

Typesetting, layout, design © Poolbeg Press Ltd.

1 3 5 7 9 10 8 6 4 2

A catalogue record for this book is available from the British Library.

ISBN 978-1-84223-385-6

Typeset by Patricia Hope in Bembo 11/14
Printed by
Litografia Rosés, S.A., Spain

www.poolbeg.com

About the author

Mary O'Sullivan lives in Carrigaline, Co Cork, with her husband Seán. Her bestselling novels *Parting Company*, *As Easy As That*, *Ebb & Flow* and *Inside Out* are also published by Poolbeg.

You can visit Mary's website at **www.maryosullivanauthor.ie**

Acknowledgements

This is the nicest part, where I get to thank people who helped me along the way with *Under the Rainbow*.

First Paula Campbell and all the staff in Poolbeg. Thank you for the support and your faith in my work. A special word of appreciation to Gaye Shortland for her editorial skills and advice.

A warm thanks to Susan and Paul Feldstein of Feldstein Literary Agency for practical advice, admirable patience and perpetual optimism.

Thanks to the stalwarts Karen Kinsella, Mary Lynskey and Jo Kinsella, who bravely read first drafts without complaint. I am grateful to Carmel Barry for help with research.

To my husband Seán and my family, both here and abroad, my love and thanks. To the many friends who have encouraged me, your support has meant a lot.

And to the readers who have read my books, I am very grateful.

For more information go to my website:
www.maryosullivanauthor.ie

For Claire Vickery

"I believe that true friends are quiet angels who sit on our shoulders and lift our wings when we forget how to fly."

AUTHOR UNKNOWN

Chapter 1

He accidentally spilled my drink in a Dublin club one wet February night. Not a very auspicious beginning but that's how I, Adele Burke, met Pascal Ronayne. He ticked all the boxes. He was tall, dark-haired, at twenty-six the same age as me and, I guessed instantly from his cultured accent, wealthy too. I was almost right. Pascal, like his father, was an architect. A very successful one. He worked in his father's company designing prestigious new buildings in Dublin city. Some day, Pascal would inherit the company and then he too would be rich. This was a man with dark brown eyes, broad shoulders and prospects.

I believed, on that wet February night, that Pascal was the man I had spent my life waiting to meet. I still believed it two years and three weeks later when I came home early from my teaching job. I had picked up a tummy bug from my seven-year-old pupils. Feeling nauseous, I turned the key in the door to the apartment Pascal and I had shared

1

for the past year and wondered if I'd make it to the bathroom before being sick.

I stood in the open doorway, unable to move. From where I was, I had a perfect view into the kitchen. A girl was lying across our kitchen table and Pascal was leaning over her. Neither of them was wearing clothes. My first thought was how inappropriate it was for them to have sex where I ate my cornflakes in the morning and my pizza in the evening.

Pascal turned towards me and I tried to see shock and embarrassment on his face, even some sign of apology. His expression was blank. Calmly he stooped and handed the girl her clothes from the floor. She was young. Maybe about twenty and very beautiful. Blonde and blue-eyed. A slut who looked like a virgin. It must have taken her minutes to dress but it felt like hours to me as I stood in the doorway, unable to leave or to speak any word of condemnation or disgust or anger. When I looked away from her, I noticed that Pascal too had put on his clothes. His jeans which fitted so snugly and his expensive cashmere sweater.

He kissed the slut-virgin on the cheek and murmured something into her ear. The girl walked towards me, sneering. "Loser!" she muttered. The only word I ever heard the girl speak. An ending to my relationship with Pascal Ronayne which was even more inauspicious than the beginning had been.

I rang Carla and Jodi. We had always been best friends, Carla, Jodi and me. Born within three months and three miles of each other in the seaside town of

Cairnsure, we had been destined by fate to share whatever life had in store for us.

Carla, pregnant with her second child, and Jodi, wearing a designer suit and a laptop as accessory, came to Dublin to help me curse Pascal Ronayne and the blue-eyed blonde. I had by now discovered that the girl had been his regular bit on the side, or on the table, for the last six months of our relationship. The three of us sat around that same table while Jodi and I got very drunk and Carla sipped orange juice and patted her bump.

"You must get out of this apartment straight away," Carla advised. "Don't be under any compliment to him."

"No! Stay as long as you need to," Jodi insisted. "Let him wait. In fact, just squat here for ever."

It was a messy situation and thinking about it now still makes me shiver. It was Pascal's apartment and I'll have to acknowledge that he was gentleman enough to allow me to stay there until I found somewhere else to live. Until I crawled away in disgrace, humiliated. Which is exactly what I did two weeks later.

This time I bought a property. A one-bedroom apartment which the estate agent described as bijou. Probably because he was too embarrassed to call it a shoebox with plumbing, but it was what I could afford. It was mine. Just me and the hurt I carried from Pascal Ronayne.

I then entered my celibate period. I had been deeply hurt by Pascal. I was twenty-eight, single, the proud owner of a mortgage and teacher by now to a group of eight and nine-year-olds who thought they already knew it all.

3

There were many bleak evenings. Just me and my books and television in my little apartment. Some hectic evenings too, rushing to night class for Russian or chess, tai chi or art. Whatever the interest of the moment happened to be.

In London, Jodi was promoted by her accountancy firm again and this time became head of her own department. She never mentioned any romantic interest in her life. Neither Carla nor I asked. It was obvious that Jodi's first and only love was work. It was equally obvious that Carla's first and only work was love. Four months after her second baby was born, Carla fell pregnant for the third time. She and Harry decided to move to Cairnsure, our home town, to live. They bought a site and built a house so big that I thought they were definitely aiming for a score of Selby babies. The birth of their twins, Lisa and Dave, confirmed that notion in my mind.

Somehow, Carla, Jodi and I had managed to pass through school, college and most of our twenties in the blink of an eye. Here we were, Carla no longer nursing, married to Harry Selby and mother to a nursery full of babies, Jodi married to her work . . . and me – I was drifting. My apartment seemed to be getting smaller, the children I taught more demanding, the city streets meaner. There were men. A few. Adele Burke was not made for permanent celibacy. Nothing serious though.

I went to London to visit Jodi and spent a week luxuriating in the clean, white space of her waterside apartment. She took me to the theatre and parties and shopping. I came back to Dublin with the same unsettled, uneasy, dissatisfied feelings as when I had gone away. My world consisted of my small apartment, evening classes, precocious children and solitary nights. It was time to face the truth.

I, Adele Burke, was almost thirty. My life was halfway through and I had to admit Part One had not lived up to expectations. I was not over-enthusiastic about facing into Part Two. I was at a crossroads.

Chapter 2

Jodi and I went back to Cairnsure for the Easter holiday. We met up in Carla's house. After the children had been admired Carla brought the conversation around to our birthdays.

"We'll be thirty soon. We must do something special. A huge party. Go for it. The works."

"But when?" asked Jodi. "Our birthdays are spread over the summer. Do we tot up and go for an average?"

Stumped by that question we were all quiet then as we sat in Carla's conservatory, looking out on the landscaped gardens. For an instant I envied Carla. This was a beautiful house full of beautiful babies and Harry Selby was a surgeon with a beautiful bank balance. So much beauty. Granted, Harry had come to the marriage with baggage. An ex-wife to be exact. A very small minus for so many pluses.

I wondered why Carla looked tired. She had an au

pair to help her. A Hungarian girl. But yet four babies in quick succession, two boys, then twins, would tire someone far stronger than Carla. She had always been slight. Delicate. Her very fair colouring and petite frame lent her an ethereal quality. I was the one with child-bearing hips. My mother called me big-boned. She usually did see the upside to everything. I was comfortable with my curvy figure and had no intention of letting it slide towards either skinny or fat. Maybe that's what started my new-found interest in cooking. I was trying to ban quick and convenient from my menu.

"Well, what do you think, Del?"

"Can't you see she has the vacant look?" Jodi asked. "She's not listening again. Spit it out, Adele Burke. What's on your mind?"

"Food."

I watched as both faces registered understanding. They thought comfort-eating was the focus of my life. They would never say that of course. But I knew what they were thinking.

"Not eating it," I said defensively. "Cooking it. From scratch. Using herbs and spices. Mixing, blending, kneading, braising. I've joined a new class and I'm really enjoying it. I think I went into the wrong profession."

"Not you, Del. You're a born teacher."

I looked at Jodi, so self-assured, so very chic with her glossy dark-haired bob and perfect make-up. So slim. Nobody doubted that she had always been meant for business success. Her thin genes were intertwined with promotion genes. I shrugged my shoulders now as I looked at my two friends, trying to impart a casual impression. Truth was, I felt anything but relaxed about my teaching career.

"I don't know. I love children and I'm passionate about giving them a good start in education but somehow lately I feel – I feel less enthusiastic than I should."

Carla leaned forward, her blue eyes narrowed. "You're serious, Del, aren't you? Are you really fed up with teaching?"

"Not fed up with it, no," I answered, more to explain to myself than to Carla. This was the first time I had allowed myself to examine the uncomfortable thoughts which had been niggling ever since the start of this school year. "It's just that I haven't the same love of teaching that I had. The children are getting more cheeky by the year and I find I'm spending less time educating and more time trying to control their low boredom thresholds."

Jodi tapped her fingers impatiently on the table. "Stop complaining! How hard can it be to get the little whippersnappers to tow the line?"

"You should try it sometime, Jodi," said Carla. "See how long you can stand it."

Jodi turned her attention back to Carla. She was peering closely at her. "You're not in the best of form, Car. Do you have anything to tell us?"

Carla laughed. A sort of don't-be-so-silly laugh. "Jesus, no! I'm not pregnant if that's what you mean. Give me a break. The eldest is four and the twins are just over a year. Plus a two-year-old in between. Never again. That's my family now. If Harry wants more he can . . ."

Carla stopped talking abruptly but not before we understood what she had tried not to say. Could it be that Harry wanted more children and Carla did not?

"You might see it differently in a couple of years' time," I said, hating my own matronly tone but feeling I needed to utter some reassuring words. "You had them all very quickly one after the other. You're bound to be tired."

"I'm not just tired. I'm overwhelmed."

"How come you've so much to do?" Jodi asked sharply. "Aren't you paying an au pair to help you?"

"That's what Harry says too. It's not that I don't trust her. I do. Brigitte's fantastic with the children. It's just that . . . Shit! I don't know what it is."

"Post-natal depression?"

"No. I'm fed up. Not depressed."

"Snap!" I said quickly, knowing exactly how Carla felt. I too was walking that very narrow line between grey and utter black. I almost fell off my cane chair when Jodi said "Snap" at exactly the same time.

"You?" I gasped. "Never! How come? Why?"

Jodi poured water for herself and swirled it around in her glass. Ice cubes tinkled against the glass while the shouts of the children drifted in from the garden accompanied by Brigitte's strongly accented tones as she encouraged the twins to toddle. But not a sound from Jodi who continued to stare into the swirling water.

"It's a man," Carla said. "It must be. Tell us about him, Jodi. Have you just met him or just finished with him?"

Jodi looked up then and laughed. "I wish it was. Men

are easy to manage. It's all about letting them think they're in charge and then getting them to do as you want."

I squirmed a little bit at that comment. If men really were that easy to manage how come I'd failed so miserably at such a simple task?

"I feel something like you do about teaching, Del," Jodi continued. "A bit stale. The cut and thrust has gone flat for me."

"What about starting your own business? You always said that was your ambition."

"Would you start your own school? Take on private pupils instead of national-school kids?"

I shook my head. I saw what she meant. Teaching was teaching and accounting was balancing books whether you were doing it for yourself or an employer. But this was a Jodi I had never seen before. A Jodi without ambition. Or was it just that her drive to succeed was taking off in another direction? Carla obviously had the same thought.

"I think you must have something else in mind, Jodi," she said. "Am I right?"

"You're wrong, Carla. I know what I don't want but I'm damned if I know what I do. I'm – I'm . . ."

"At a crossroads?" I suggested.

Jodi smiled at me and leaned across the table to pat my hand in a way I found patronising.

"Good old Del! That's where I'm at. A crossroads and I don't know which turn I should take. So I've decided to take time off. A year out."

I sat staring at Jodi and wondering why I hadn't

thought of that. A sabbatical! Why not? Get my head together, maybe travel a bit, do some cooking, come home to Cairnsure for a while. Mom would be glad.

"What are you going to do for the year?" Carla asked.

"I'm going to come back to —" I began to answer before I realised the question was meant for Jodi and not me. I laughed. "Me too! I'm going to take a year out. I'm supposed to have sixth class next year and I really can't face the thought. I think I'll come home to Cairnsure. Recharge the batteries."

Carla leaned back in her chair and stared at us both, a puzzled frown on her face.

"What is it with you two? Here I am thinking if I had a career my life would be so much easier and both of you are opting out."

So! That's what was wrong with Carla. Was she crazy? Why should she even think of a career, with a houseful of children and a husband who was a surgeon? Hardly for the want of something to do and certainly not for the want of a pay-packet.

"Are you talking about going back to nursing?" I asked. "As in bedpans, long shifts and short pay?"

"Well, I'm at a crossroads too," Carla answered sulkily. "And I was a good nurse."

Identity crisis, I thought. Carla couldn't decide whether she was wife, mother, nurse or all of them at the same time. And wasn't that my problem too and maybe Jodi's? We had each gone along the routes we had planned for ourselves and now, at almost thirty years of age, we had each lost our way.

Chapter 3

Before leaving Cairnsure at Easter, the girls and I agreed on July the second as the date to have our joint thirtieth birthday party. School would by then be over for me. Jodi, due to begin her year off on the first of July, would be back from London. Carla of course was firmly planted west of Cairnsure, on hand for organising the myriad party details which would need sorting before July.

It took me two days before I had the courage to go to the school principal and tell him of my plans. He hemmed and hawed. "You've left it late, Miss Burke. You know how slowly things move in the Department. You should have applied for leave months ago."

I knew he just hated the thought of all the bureaucracy involved and of course the extra work in recruiting a replacement. Tough, I thought as I put my application in writing. His problem, let him deal with it. That thought was immediately chased by hours of shivering self-doubt. What was I thinking? What was I going to do with myself for a whole year? Float about Cairnsure on my mother's coat-tails, playing whist, singing in the choir and going on day trips for the active retired? The idea that none of these activities involved anybody under the age of sixty began to make them seem quite attractive. Not a six times tables, an Irish reader or a runny nose in sight. Well, I could be sure of the first two anyway. Two out of three wasn't bad.

In London Jodi was busily, and with a lot more assurance, tidying up her affairs before coming home. I was about to advertise my apartment for rent when the school secretary asked me about it. The deal was struck over coffee in the staff room. She would move in as soon as I had hightailed it back to Cairnsure.

By the last day of term, my official leave was granted, my apartment rented out and nothing more left to do except pack my notes and books away and say goodbye to staff and pupils. I had anticipated sadness, a little lump in my throat as I left the school. Instead I was engulfed in a huge wave of relief. Whatever happened, however boring or dissatisfying my sabbatical turned out to be, at least I would not have the responsibility of trying to indoctrinate mostly reluctant pupils with the basics of numeracy and literacy.

Leaving my apartment brought the same type of surprising relief. Maybe it was that my toe-hold on the property ladder was forever linked in my mind to Pascal Ronayne and the awful way he had betrayed my trust. It had been the bolthole to which I had fled to lick my wounds. The walls, the ceilings, cups, plates, even the microwave seemed to have absorbed some of my hurt. Hopefully the school secretary might exorcise those melancholy demons when she moved in.

And so it was, on the first day of July, a warm, balmy day, I left Dublin, my Fiat Uno packed to the roof with clothes and things I had not been able to leave behind. Things like my collection of novels and cookery books and my Simpson's mug – coffee didn't taste the same out of anything else.

The approach road to Cairnsure meanders along the coastline. It climbs in places, skirting black-faced cliffs and an ocean hundreds of feet below. At other times it dips into valleys where little villages nestle. The road widens several miles outside Cairnsure and a big welcome sign announces to anyone who needs to know that Cairnsure is twinned with Vladysburg. I remember reminding myself on that July morning to find out where Vladysburg was. I forgot about it as I drove through the town centre, busy with native and tourist trade, and headed back towards my own home. Or rather my mother's home.

At one time we used to live in the countryside. Now the town had spread out to meet us. New builds had sprung up all around our once isolated house. Keeping tabs on arrivals entertained Mom. She had been shocked at first when I told her about my sabbatical. "You've a good pensionable job," she had pointed out. "Don't get any ideas about giving it up. It's not as if . . ." We had that conversation very frequently on the phone in the weeks before I came home. It always tailed off with the same words – "it's not as if . . ."

Of course she meant it's not as if you've a man to support you financially or look likely to have in the future. I think she had given up by then on the idea of being mother-of-the-bride. The fact that Jodi had not married either didnt help. Another "it's not as if . . ." situation. Although I sometimes found my mother's attitude annoying, it never really angered me. It hurt a little, maybe. Mom wanted the best for me and to her that meant having a man at my beck and call, just as Dad had been at hers until that awful day when his heart suddenly decided to shut down. Equality, independence, the freedom to make choices and the concept that not every woman actually wanted a man in her life didn't enter into my mother's thinking. She had been in her mid-thirties when I was born but my arrival had done nothing to relax her firmly held beliefs. I had learned as a child that nodding and appearing to agree was by far the easiest way to cope with Mom's ideas which are as stiffly lacquered as her hair.

She was standing at the door as I pulled into the driveway. Apron on and hands joined sedately together. I waved at her as I poked around the car, trying to find my bag in the mounds of clutter. She walked towards me in the busy-little-step way she had when she was bursting with news.

"Carla rang. She said you must have been out of range on your mobile. I told her you were probably driving through Glengorm at the time because the reception is bad there."

She took a breath just as I found my bag and stepped out of the car. Leaning towards me she offered her cheek for a kiss. I stooped down to her, careful not to injure myself on the barbed hair.

"You're pale," she said, her tone like an accusation. "Plenty of red meat, that's what you need."

"What did Carla say, Mom?"

"Oh! Yes. The tent is being delivered today. She was wondering if you could go over to her house to help decorate it. Jodi will be along later she said."

"It's a marquee."

My mother sniffed and turned to go into the house. As far as she was concerned, size didn't matter. A marquee was just a big tent and she was none too pleased that her daughter's, her only child's, thirtieth birthday was going to be celebrated under canvas. I remember not feeling too pleased myself either. Not about the marquee. That had been Carla's idea and both Jodi and I had gladly gone along with it. Carla's garden was more than big enough to accommodate "the tent" and I was really looking forward to our birthday party. But I had wanted some time alone today. A few hours to stroll barefoot along the beach, feel the wind in my hair. Just a little space to let the city blow away and the calm of Cairnsure seep into my soul.

"I was going to ask if you wanted to come to the gardening club with me but I s'pose you'll be busy with the tent."

I had an instant's preview of the year ahead, full of gardening-club meetings, and I almost choked with panic. What in the hell had I done? I parked myself at the kitchen table and I think I went into shock. Mom put a plate of shepherd's pie in front of me and then reached out and stroked my hair like she used to do when I was a child.

"I'm so happy that you're home, Adele. I'm looking forward to having you around for a while."

"Me too, Mom," I answered and to my surprise I found that I meant it.

* * *

The marquee was visible from a mile down the road, a big white blob on the Selbys' lawn. Harry and Carla had built their house eight kilometres outside town in an area that was, as yet, populated by more cows than people. Although it seemed possible then the rapidly expanding Selby family would soon redress that imbalance. For now, at least, there would be no neighbours to complain about noisy parties. Or about children, I thought, as I parked in front of the house and got out. The noise being made by the four mini-Selbys rivalled a school playground.

Finn, the four-year-old, ran towards me, waving a balloon on a string and trailed as he always was by his younger brother, Liam. I don't think at that stage I had ever seen Liam step out of his older brother's shadow. Liam was two and a half and quietly occupied his place between his very extrovert older brother and the eighteen-month-old twins.

"Adele!" Finn squeaked. "C'mon, we'll show you the marquee! We're going to have a party too. Coke and crisps and ice-cream. C'mon! Mum's in there."

Finn grabbed my hand just as Brigitte approached with the twins. She was carrying Lisa and holding Dave by the hand. My eyes were immediately drawn to Lisa.

She was dressed in denim dungarees over a pink frilly blouse and on her blonde curls was a matching pink floppy hat. I needed to hold her so much, I let go of Finn's hand. As I was about to reach out my arms, I felt a tug at my leg. I looked down to see Liam, tears clinging to his long curling eyelashes. I stooped down to him.

"Balloon broke," he said, his bottom lip puckering. He held out his hand which clutched the piece of string and shrivelled plastic. I looked into the child's face and saw a very adult-sized heartbreak there.

"Baby!" Finn mocked.

"Never mind, Liam. We'll find another one for you," I said just as Carla appeared, clipboard in hand and a frown on her forehead.

"Finn! What have you been up to? I warned you to leave Liam alone. Brigitte, would you put the twins down for their nap now, please."

Brigitte grunted a reply and walked away with the babies. Carla lowered her head then and raked her fingers through her hair. There was something in the gesture, something very tense and even angry, which made me stare at her. When she looked up her smile was in place. The one I knew so well. Broad and welcoming.

"Hi, Del. Welcome back to Cairnsure. I hope you're in form for decorating our marquee. What do you think of it?"

"It's great. But first I must find a new balloon for Liam."

"He's always whinging. Take no notice."

I had to bite my words back. I had seen pain in the child's eyes. He was heartbroken about his balloon. I also

18

saw the stress in Carla. Whatever was going on with her, she wasn't coping with it very well.

Inside the marquee, I stood and gawped. The interior was vast, so much more floor space than I had expected from looking at the outside. Underfoot was springy timber flooring and dotted all around a central platform were groups of tables and chairs. Sunlight filtered through the domed canvas bathing the whole space with a warm glow.

"This is fabulous, Carla. How are we going to fill it? Who's coming?"

"Half the hospital staff and you know the size of Jodi's family. The Walls could fill a concert hall on their own. I told you several times to invite whoever you wanted. So far you've just mentioned your mother."

A little tug at my leg again reminded me that I had yet to get Liam's new balloon. On a table opposite I saw a box of balloons and an air pump. Taking Liam by the hand I headed towards the table and was almost there when Finn's piercing voice reached me.

"Why does Adele's chest wobble when she walks, Mum? Yours doesn't."

Too late, Carla shushed him. I tried not to resent the child. He was just making an astute observation but I felt the old familiar blush begin to creep up my face. Little brat! Spoiled! Precocious. Bullying his small brother and his mum's well-built friend. After that, I kept a close eye on Liam and the new red balloon I had blown up for him.

Brigitte came back and took the two children away, leaving Carla and me to pump up balloons, hang streamers and put little vases in the centre of each table which we would fill with flowers tomorrow. Jodi arrived, svelte in close-fitting jeans and a T-shirt which had taken less material to make than a table napkin.

"Hi, girls! This is super! You must be exhausted from all the organising, Carla."

Carla looked exhausted all right but I had my doubts if it was from organising the party. The tiredness she exuded seemed far more mental than physical to me. Carla, always the one with secrets, was very worried about something. The fact that she seemed to have been a bit heavy-handed applying her fake tan added an extra dimension to her appearance, which for once seemed to be falling short of perfection.

"God! I need a drink!" said Jodi. "Bloody airports make me thirsty."

I was thinking tea or coffee when Jodi reached into one of the many cardboard boxes scattered around the marquee and took out a bottle of wine. Another search produced glasses and a corkscrew. Glasses full, we sat at one of the tables, Carla and Jodi and I raised a toast to our friendship. In each of us I saw the children we had been. In the glow of filtered sunlight I could also see the older women we would become. At least I could see embryo wrinkles and frowns on my friends' faces and I felt them on my own. Jodi, head bent, pen in hand, was checking the clipboard which Carla had been holding on to so tightly.

"We're doing well money-wise," she announced. "Still inside the budget."

"What about the catering?" I asked. "Do you want us to do something, Carla, or is the catering company handling it all?"

Carla took the clipboard from Jodi, flicked through the pages and pulling one from the bottom, handed it to me.

"You're the foodie," she said. "Check this and see what you think."

I glanced at the heading on the page. The catering firm was from Cork city. Twenty miles away.

"Wasn't there anyone nearer? Twenty miles seems like a long journey for cocktail sausages and bits on sticks."

"Why didn't you organise the catering if you think you could have done better?"

I don't know which of us was most shocked. Carla for having snapped at me or Jodi and I for the peevish tone we had never before heard from Carla. She put her elbows on the table and wearily lowered her head onto her hands.

"I'm sorry, Del," she muttered.

She stopped talking then. Just sat there while both Jodi and I stared helplessly at her bowed head. We knew from experience that there would be no point in asking her what was wrong. She would tell us when she wanted us to know. If ever.

An electrician came and did things with cables and power lines. The upshot was electricity in the marquee. We had a turning-on-the-lights ceremony for the children before they went to bed. The child in me reacted as they did. The Selbys' garden was a wonderland of fairy lights strung on trees and looped along the inside

21

of the marquee so that overhead resembled a star-studded sky.

By the time we had finished organising the marquee, the sun had set, the children were in bed and we three were exhausted. But at least most items on the clipboard were ticked off. We were almost ready for our thirtieth birthday party.

I did wonder though, as I drove back home to where I knew Mom would be waiting up for me, just how much of a celebration tomorrow's party was going to be. Carla was obviously stressed. Jodi less so but I had been surprised over the course of the day to catch her sometimes staring into the distance with a very vacant, most un-Jodi-like expression on her face.

As I drifted off to sleep in the room I had slept in since infancy, I was tormented by the idea that the comfort and security I had come back to Cairnsure to find was no longer here.

Chapter 4

The second of July, party day, dawned. When I woke, disoriented for a moment by the vastness of my Cairnsure bedroom in comparison to my cramped Dublin sleeping space, the sun was high in a blue sky. Mom was already out in the garden. I smiled when I saw the table set for my breakfast. Cereal bowl, cup, saucer, plate and egg cup. It was nice, even at thirty years old, to feel cared for. Especially at thirty years old. I knocked on the window and she came in to join me, looking as if she had just come back from the hairdresser.

"Have you been downtown, Mom?"

"I might have been. Why?"

"Your hair's nice. That's all."

"Oh, it's all right. The young girl did it. I'll have to fix it myself before the party."

I made a mental note to be well out of the way before the lacquer-spraying began.

"The party," Mom said again and this time I noticed she was in position for an announcement. The hands were folded, lips pursed. "I'd like to bring a guest if that's all right."

I was intrigued. "Of course, Mom. Who?"

"Tom. Tom Reagan. He's in the gardening club. He gets lonely since his wife died, poor man. I just thought it would be nice for him to have a night out."

As I put my egg on to boil, it dawned on me, with a painful dart of self-pity, that my widowed mother had more of a social life than I did. Whatever drivel she was spouting about pitying this man, I knew by the way her eyes were darting from me to the floor and back again that her dealings with him were not all motivated by altruism. The thought of Mom in a relationship put me off my boiled egg. I showered and dressed quickly and headed towards the beach.

I admired all the new bungalows as I walked along our road, losing count of arches, pillars, decking and conservatories. Cairnsure East seemed to have become the place to build your four-bed bungalow with master-bedroom en suite and dormer windows. The sameness of the bungalows made me like our own solid, sensible, three-bed, cottage-type house all the more. Our slate roof and leaded windows had character and the garden was lush with trees and shrubs Mom and Dad had planted when they had moved in.

The town too, had lost some of its individuality. As I walked along Main Street, I saw many of the high-street stores I knew from Dublin. Just small branches but a presence and an influence in Cairnsure all the same.

Hearing the surf pound on the strand, I speeded up my pace. When I turned the corner by the Catholic Church, there it was: the broad sweep of the Atlantic, the pier, the promenade and beneath it the waves of full tide lapping against the sea wall. I practically ran the last hundred yards. Cairnsure beach curved in a semi-circle around the town, the arc easing back to the prom before arching gracefully towards sand dunes on either side. I would have to walk the full length of the prom and get to the dunes before I could feel sand beneath my feet.

Ahead I saw families, rugs spread, parasols open, occupying every available space, sandy or grassy. Children called out as they dipped their toes in the ocean or tossed Frisbees to each other. Some of them were throwing sand. I had to remind myself to leave teacher mode behind and let the parents deal with the offending little aggressors.

"Adele Burke! It is, isn't it?"

I turned to see Kieran Mahon standing behind mc, a camera slung around his neck. In the blink of an eye I was taken back to my early teens. My God! I had stalked this man for a while. My face blazed now as I remembered my obsession with him during my early teens. That was when I had been thirteen and he a very sophisticated sixteen. Or so I had thought then. I had always made sure to sit behind him on the school bus, arrive at the school gates at exactly the same time as him, even made excuses to walk past his house about five times a day. I got over my painful crush when he told me to scram and leave him alone. That day had been a low point in a burgeoning love-life which hadn't since risen much above that nadir.

"How are you, Kieran?" I asked, manoeuvring myself so that the breeze was to my back, blowing my long dark hair around my face and hopefully covering my blushes.

"Great. Still with the *Cairnsure Weekly*. We hear all the latest there. I'm told you're coming back to us for a while."

"I'm taking a year off school but I'm not sure yet what I'll do with it. I might travel a bit."

"Your mother probably won't want you too much under her feet now anyway. Where are you thinking of going?"

What in the hell did he mean about my mother? That was a ridiculous thing to say. I looked at Kieran Mahon again, through my thirty-year-old eyes, and wondered what I had seen in him. It could have been his height. He had been a tall teenager and must be six foot two inches now. Or maybe it had been his green eyes. I had always thought they were very special. Cats' eyes that gazed with utter concentration. Or maybe it was the cleft in his chin. A softness on the otherwise angular face. Or it could have been the long eyelashes . . . I suddenly realised I was gaping at him.

"I - I haven't decided yet," I stuttered, feeling as overawed in his company now as I had back then.

"Maybe you and Jodi Wall should team up and go trekking to the Amazon jungle."

"You really have your finger on the pulse, don't you?"

"Sure do," he grinned. "See you tonight at the party.

26

I'm going in my official capacity as photographer and roving reporter for *Cairnsure Weekly*. Have the glad rags on, Adele! You'll be on page 3 next week."

He winked then. A saucy, or was it mocking, drop of his eyelid over one crystal-clear green eye. I turned and continued my walk, forcing myself not to look over my shoulder at his retreating figure.

Five yards on I had put a few things together. Well, two, to be exact. My mother and the widower with an interest in gardening. Tom Reagan. That must be what Kieran Mahon meant by his enigmatic remark about being under my mother's feet. The pratt! What made him think I didn't have interests of my own, none of which involved getting in the way of my mother's apparent renewed interest in men? Having no answer to that question, I walked quickly and breathed the ozone-laden air very deeply. Anyway, I needed to get over to Carla's house. We had a lot to do before party time.

* * *

At first glance I thought Jodi had dressed early for the party until I remembered that casual for her was not wearing a bracelet to match her earrings and neck chain. I gave a sigh of pure envy. Jodi, in short skirt and a lacy top looked ready to glide down a catwalk, even without a bracelet.

"C'mon, Del. Lazy bones! Carla and I have been slaving in this marquee for the past two hours. Where were you?"

"Walking. On the beach. So what's to do? Just tell me. I'm ready for work."

"Jesus! You'll have to tell her, Jodi. In fact tell me too.

I don't know where to turn next. The bar thing. Do we put glasses out on that or will the people we've hired to run the bar do it?"

"Calm down, Carla! They'll do it of course. They're charging enough. Everything's under control. We're supposed to be enjoying our day."

"Under control? Is that what you think? Do you know, the caterers —"

A scream, long and loud rippled around the marquee. Jodi and I were rooted to the spot where we stood but Carla ran like an Olympic sprinter. When we got our breath back we ran after Carla and towards the direction of the awful sound. I slowed down as soon as I saw Finn on the ground, kicking his legs and screaming as loudly as he possibly could. Brigitte was standing over him. The girl looked ready to cry.

"What have you done to him?" Carla was demanding, almost as hysterical as her son.

"Nothing. Nothing, Mrs Selby. Finn, he take Liam's bike and I say no."

"She hit me! She hit me!"

"My God! Did you hit my child? Tell me the truth!"

Brigitte was crying now, tears rolling down her cheeks. She was shaking her head and muttering but I couldn't hear what she was saying because Finn was screaming again. Then she turned and walked away, her shoulders still shaking, as she cried her way back to the house.

I walked over beside Finn and stooped down. His eyes were screwed shut and his face red with the effort of shouting.

"What's going on, Finn?" I asked quietly.

He opened his eyes and looked up at me with calculation way beyond his four years. He began to scream louder. "Take her away! She hit me too. Adele hit me!"

I stood and faced Carla. Her eyes were wide. "Attention-seeking," I said. "I don't think Finn wants your time taken up with the party."

"I'm sorry, Del," she whispered. "He gets these tantrums. I don't know how to handle them. I don't know how to handle anything."

Carla's eyes filled with tears. I couldn't quite believe what I was seeing. This was supposed to be a celebration day and I was surrounded by tears. Finn's piercing screams were quietening now. I think he knew he'd got his quota of attention.

"No need to apologise to me," I said to Carla. "But what about Brigitte? You know she didn't hit him any more than I did. I don't believe so anyway."

"I know. Brigitte wouldn't do something like that. I shouldn't have doubted her. She'll leave now. What am I going to do?"

"Take control of him for a start," said Jodi. She was standing beside Finn who was still thrown on the ground. "Get up, Finn. Apologise to Adele for telling lies and to your mother for ruining her party day. Stop behaving like a baby. You're four."

I held my breath as Jodi glared, Finn stared and Carla just seemed to go into a trance. In the battle of wills with Jodi, Finn lost. He stood up and came over to me.

"Sorry, Adele. You didn't hit me. Brigitte didn't either."

"And your mother," Jodi reminded him. "She deserves an apology too."

Before Finn could say any more Carla caught his hand. "I'd better talk to Brigitte. Apologise to her. Try to persuade her to stay. Even just for today."

As Carla, with Finn skipping happily along beside her, crossed the lawn towards the house, Jodi and I looked at each other and shrugged.

"Do you know what's going on with her?" Jodi asked.

"No. Except that there's something wrong. But she was always one for secrets, wasn't she? I wonder if she's pregnant again, even though she said she's not? She looks peaky."

"I don't think so. But I wonder if that's the problem?"

"What? You mean, she wants to be? Don't be daft, Jodi, she has four children between the ages of –"

"No. That's not what I mean at all. Have you seen any sign of Harry Selby since we came home?"

"We just arrived yesterday."

"Right. But did we see him at Easter?"

I thought about that. We had seen a lot of his wife and children then and nothing of Harry Selby.

"He works long hours at the hospital," I offered by way of a defence I felt was needed.

"He didn't use to. Anyway, none of our business. Let's get back to the marquee. Start the party early. I need a drink after all that drama."

I gladly joined her. I was thinking back from the time the twins were christened right up to today. I had visited this house many times, day and night, in that eighteen months. I could not recall having met Mr Harry Selby, not even once, since the christening. I needed a drink too.

* * *

By the time Carla had Brigitte placated and the children organised, Jodi and I had finished decorating the marquee. I was drained. Jodi was a slave driver and a first-class delegator. I should have drawn the line at changing the big heavy tables around to suit her aesthetic sensibilities but of course I just dragged and hauled where she ordered. This meant Jodi was still svelte, Carla, when she arrived back was tense but cool and I was dishevelled and hot. Good old Del!

"I'm going home," I said. "I need a bath and a miracle to make myself presentable for tonight."

"Be here at eight, girls. I know we probably won't have guests until around nine but I want you both here to organise the caterers with me."

I nodded at Carla just as Jodi started her "you're paying them to do the work" speech. I decided to leave them to it.

As I turned to go I remembered my mother. "Oh, Carla – you'll be glad to hear that Mom is bringing a friend."

"Tom Reagan?"

"How did you know?"

She glanced at me and looked quickly away again but not before I had seen the puzzled expression in her eyes. "Just a guess," she said and I left it at that, but I knew that before my bath and before my miracle makeover, Mom and I would need to have a serious talk.

* * *

31

There was a note on the kitchen table when I got home. *"Gone to whist drive. Will see you in the tent later. Mom."* I had to smile. Such a raver, my Mom. I still needed to have a chat with her though.

I then got down to the demanding business of overhauling the untidy mess that was Adele Burke. Glancing at my watch I noticed I had just an hour and a half to make the transformation. Taking a deep breath, I dived into the bathroom and began my campaign.

One hour and ten minutes later, I emerged smooth-skinned and straight-haired. With my strappy dress, black of course, high heels and chunky beads, I felt unusually good about myself. Good enough to closely examine my reflection in the mirror. Hazel eyes, dark hair, high cheekbones, full lips and an impressive bust. I wasn't Carla or Jodi-beautiful. Not many women were. But I was happy with the thirty-year-old Adele Burke reflected in the mirror. I locked up the house and left to go to my birthday party.

Chapter 5

The sky had lost its daytime intensity by the time I got back to Carla's house. The marquee glowed in the dimming light. Several cars were there already, and one bus with *Sound Bytes* written in huge letters all over the body of the vehicle. The band had arrived. I didn't have to see the bus to know. I heard them, as I'm sure, every person and animal within a five-mile radius did. They were obviously tuning guitars and tweaking the sound system because twangs and squeaks and repetitive "One two testing – one, two" echoed around the whole of Cairnsure.

I headed for the marquee, tottering as my heels dug into the Selbys' lawn. Sound Bytes' noise was deafening when I got inside. I watched as Jodi strode towards the improvised stage, flapping her hands. Two seconds later the volume was reduced to tolerable levels. Jodi got things done quickly. She looked stunning. My jaw dropped when I saw what she was wearing. Her dress was black and strappy and her heels high. The cut of her dress was different to mine, I'm sure hers cost five times more money for five times less fabric, and she had no chunky beads, but nevertheless at first glance we were wearing the same outfit. Except of course that Jodi seemed waif-like inside hers and I was barely contained within the strappy confines of mine. The confidence I had felt leaving home was more than a little dented.

Carla on the other hand had opted for a blue sparkly top and a floaty print skirt. Judging by all the flat planes on her body, nobody could have guessed that she had produced four children in four years. I sucked my stomach in, tugged down my skirt which was riding up and decided to hell with insecurity. I was going to enjoy our party.

"What about the caterers?" I asked, remembering that Carla had wanted Jodi and me here to check them out.

Carla glanced at her watch. "They're late. I'll go ring them."

As soon as Carla had left, Jodi leaned towards me. "She's gone to ring Harry again. This is the third time in the last half hour."

"No, she said the caterers were late."

Jodi nodded her head in the direction of the entrance. A team of girls, all carrying covered trays were on their way in. So if Carla wasn't ringing the caterers . . .

"Why should she be ringing Harry like that? Is he delayed at the hospital or something?"

"I'd say 'something'," Jodi whispered just as the team of caterers reached us.

34

The next hour whizzed past as we supervised the organisation of the food and greeted guests as they began to trickle in. I knew most of them but had to add years of growing and ageing on to the faces in order to put names to them. They were probably doing the same with me. I wondered if they were thinking to themselves that Sissy Burke's daughter had aged a lot. Fearing that I was about to slip into a mood of self-pity, I threw back my shoulders and smiled until my face ached. I noticed Carla and Jodi were doing the same. I saw it in the way their eyes were wary and untouched by the warmth of their smiling mouths. Lack of confidence was at the heart of my cosmetic smile. Just what, I wondered, was clouding the eyes of the beautiful Jodi and Carla?

* * *

The party was in full swing before my mother arrived in, a tall grey-haired man by her side. There was something about the way they seemed to fit together, he protective of her and she nestled by his side, that made me realise Mom and Tom Reagan shared a close relationship. How long had this been going on and why had she not told me? Their progress across the marquee towards where I stood was like a biblical parting of the waves. People stood aside and pretended not to stare.

"Adele, you look lovely. Black is very flattering," Mom said.

I smiled, knowing she meant it as a compliment. Backhanded, but a compliment none the less.

"You do too," I answered, glancing at her galvanised

hair and her pale-lilac silk suit which was her standard wear for weddings, dinner dances and any other social occasion she considered worthy of her most precious item of clothing. I raised an eyebrow and she turned casually towards the man by her side, almost as if she had forgotten he was there. I wasn't fooled. I had seen the nerve tic beneath her eye.

"This is Mr Tom Reagan. Ex-Garda and now retired to Cairnsure. Tom, meet my daughter, Adele."

He moved forward a step and offered me his hand. A good firm handshake. I liked that.

"Nice to meet you, Tom. I believe you're interested in gardening?"

"Yes, I am. It's good to have the time to indulge my hobby now. I've been told you're taking a bit of time off work yourself."

My mother shuffled her feet a little. Just enough to confirm my suspicion that she had told Tom Reagan every detail of my life from my first tooth to the time I robbed apples from the convent orchard. I did a bit of foot-shuffling myself before I answered him.

"Yes. A year off to recharge the batteries. How long have you been in Cairnsure?"

"Nearly two years now but it's just a year since I met your mother."

"A year and two months," Mom corrected him. They smiled at each other and I looked away in embarrassment. I had not thought my mother capable of such coquetry.

"I'd like to have a proper chat with you, Adele. It's impossible here with that din," Tom said, nodding his head in the direction of the stage where the band was belting out what sounded like the same tune over and over again. To be fair they varied the rhythm. But never the volume.

I smiled at him. "I agree with you on both counts, Tom. We do need to talk but certainly not here. How about —"

"Just hold it there, Adele! Turn slightly towards me. That's it! Mrs Burke, a little closer to your man. Right! Smile!"

Before I had time to pull in my tummy, Kieran Mahon had taken his photo.

"A lovely family shot," he laughed and I saw a rash of smiles breaking out around the marquee. The whole town must know that my mother and Tom Reagan had been keeping their affair secret from me. Worse still, Jodi and Carla would have learned from their families that Mom was enjoying a lot more than horticulture at her gardening club and they had never thought to warn me. Kieran Mahon was laughing at me, his eyes glinting with amusement.

"Now that introductions are over, Adele, I want to get you three birthday girls together for a shot. I see Jodi over by the bar. Where's Carla?"

Glad of the excuse to turn away from him, I began to look around the marquee. I didn't need a mirror to know that my face was mottled with red patches of embarrassment. The band had downed the tempo on their tune and were announcing a slow set. Mom was off like a greyhound out of a trap, dragging Tom in her wake. I couldn't see Carla anywhere. The lighting was dim, the crowd seemed like hundreds but I knew it was ninety, most of them Walls. Jodi was one of a family of nine. Two brothers, six sisters and an army of aunts, uncles and cousins. A big crowd had come from the hospital as well. People Carla had worked with until she had gone full-time into having babies. But no sign of Carla. Harry Selby was sitting at a table just inside the door, deep in conversation with the red-haired woman he had been talking to since he had arrived here, late and suave and very handsome. In fact, I thought he and the red-haired woman had come in at the same time.

"Would you like to dance, Adele?"

Kieran Mahon's question caught me by surprise. It was seventeen years too late.

"I'd better find Carla. Besides, you're working, aren't you?"

"I was going to interview you while we danced."

He was laughing at me again and something in the lift of his eyebrow and his grin reminded me of Pascal Ronayne. Sardonic. I had done handsome and sardonic and I had the scars to show for it. To hell with that.

"I'll get Carla and Jodi," I muttered before wending my way across the dance floor towards the bar, barely avoiding a collision with my mother and Tom Reagan as they twirled and dipped at a furious pace.

Jodi was surrounded by cousins. I tapped her on the shoulder. "Kieran Mahon wants to take a photo of the three of us for the *Cairnsure Weekly*. Do you know where Carla's gone?"

"I haven't seen her for a while. Maybe she's in the house with the children. Ask Harry."

"Who's that woman he's been talking to since he came in?"

As soon as I asked the question I noticed Jodi and her cousins exchange glances. Just the merest little peek but it alerted me. Jodi leaned close to me. "That's his ex-wife."

I stared at her in disbelief. "What's she doing here?"

"You may well ask. I'm not even sure that Carla knew she was coming. Well, you wouldn't expect your husband to do that, would you? I could be wrong. Maybe Carla knew. She's a close one."

"And you too," I accused. "Why didn't you tell me about my mother and Tom Reagan?"

"It was up to your mother to tell you when she was ready. We all have things we prefer to keep to ourselves."

She was right of course. I had never told anybody about my blind date with the guy who had turned out to be a priest or about how I sometimes still missed Pascal Ronayne even though I knew he was a cad. Yes. We all had secrets.

"I'll check in the house. It's time to bring the cake in anyway."

"Let the caterers do that. They're —"

"Don't say it! We know at this stage they're being paid enough! You've made it your mantra."

I walked quickly away, surprised by how annoyed I was with Jodi. And Carla. And Mom. Kieran Mahon too, and especially Harry Selby.

I hesitated near the entrance. Harry was no longer there, nor was the red-haired woman. Stepping outside the marquee, I took a deep breath of the night air. The noise of the Sound Bytes boomed around the garden but out here the sharp edges of guitar and keyboard were blunted by the soft lowing of frightened animals in neighbouring fields.

I walked quickly over the lawn, conscious that my spiky heels were ploughing up the turf. As I approached the wide tarmac area in front of the house, I slowed my pace, admiring the fleet of very expensive cars parked there. My Fiat Uno looked like a Dinky toy sitting as it was between a BMW and a Merc. Glancing back over my shoulder I saw that the long driveway was strewn with the cars of latecomers. I stood as my attention was caught by a scarlet low-slung sports car. It shimmered in the diffused light of the marquee and the sparkle from the fairy lights strung on the trees. I turned towards the driveway and peered. I wasn't an expert on cars, and especially not luxury models, but I was almost sure the scarlet car with the roof rolled back was a Ferrari. More at home on the streets of Monaco than in Cairnsure. I took a step towards it but stopped when I noticed a couple sitting in the car. They were locked in an embrace so close that they were almost like one. Feeling like a voyeur, I had begun to turn away when something stopped me in my tracks. The woman's red hair was glowing in the dim light. I peered at the couple. When my eyes adjusted to the available light, I clearly recognised Harry Selby and his ex-wife. Snogging. Right here in front of the house he shared with Carla and the children. Under her very nose. As I watched, Harry's head bent towards his ex-wife's. I turned, feeling physically sick at the thought of seeing them together. Harry Selby was a prick! A low-down, two-timing, deceitful . . .

I had just taken a couple of wobbly steps when I heard a car door open and then slam, quickly followed by the sound of a powerful engine revving up.

Puffed up with anger, I began to walk more quickly towards the house. Suppose Carla had been watching? Suppose she had been at a window and seen her husband with the former Mrs Selby? It was easy to imagine what Harry and Ruth Selby got up to in private since they were so blatantly demonstrative in public. As I pounded along, I began to understand Carla's obvious stress. The man she married would appear to be a serial adulterer. Footsteps sounded behind me on the tarmac.

"Happy birthday, Adele! I haven't had a chance to talk to you all night."

I turned to glare at Harry Selby. "No. You've been busy, haven't you?"

He caught me by the arm. His fingers, the long fingers of a surgeon, bit into my soft flesh. "I hope that wasn't sarcastic. Not your style, I would have thought."

"You don't know anything about me, Harry."

"Ditto. So don't go making any assumptions. Understood?"

I understood all right. I was to keep my nose out of his grotty little affair. I must never tell Carla that I had seen her husband and his ex-wife together in a way which said that their relationship was still alive and passionate. What an arrogant sod! How had I ever thought Harry Selby to be a gentleman? Why had I envied Carla her surgeon husband?

"I've known Carla a lot longer than you have," I said angrily. "I don't want to see her hurt. And how do you know she didn't see you canoodling with your ex-wife? You're just outside the front door for heaven's sake!"

Harry's grip on my arm loosened and he laughed. A mocking laugh. "How quaint! Canoodling. You've never really left Cairnsure behind, have you? Do you honestly think if I had anything to hide with Ruth, my ex-wife's name by the way, that I'd bring her here?"

I looked up at him. Tall, his dark hair streaked with silver, his features even. A perfectly balanced face. A handsome man. A man in control of himself and his life. And yes, I did think he would do whatever he considered best for himself. But he was right in implying his marriage, or marriages, was none of my business. I shrugged my shoulders as nonchalantly as possible and still stinging from his jibe about my provincial attitude, I strode ahead of him into the house.

Carla was coming down the stairs as we entered the hall.

"Kieran Mahon wants to photograph the birthday girls," I said quickly.

"Women surely," Harry remarked. "You three have left girlhood behind a long time ago."

"Whatever. He wants to photograph us with our birthday cake. Are you ready to come out now, Carla?"

"The children?" Harry asked.

"Asleep," Carla answered. "Even Finn. Brigitte's keeping an eye on them in case the music disturbs them again."

Harry nodded and then stood between Carla and me, offering us an arm each. I glanced at Carla and thought for a moment that she had been crying. Her eyes were perfectly made-up but slightly puffy. As I watched, she smiled up at her husband. The first real smile I had seen on her face all night. She linked her arm into his. I linked onto his other arm. If Carla could do it, so could I.

Together the three of us walked out to the marquee, to the blowing out of the candles, the photo session, the increasingly frenetic dancing, the conga and rock-the-boat. At some stage my mother and Tom Reagan slipped away. Mom must have told me she was going but details were getting hazier with each gin and tonic. I do remember seeing Carla and Harry Selby dancing so intimately that when they disappeared I knew they had gone to bed.

Jodi and I joined forces with a crowd from the hospital. I tried to match them drink for drink but began to feel dizzy while they were still just warming up. The idea of getting some fresh air seemed appealing. I began to make my way out of the marquee. It took some careful negotiating to get to the entrance. When I reached there, I took a step outside and meant to take a deep breath.

Instead I found myself breathless as I watched Jodi and this person, whose name I did not know, stagger along the pathway leading to the back of the house, their arms wrapped tightly around each other, their heads really close together.

Through my fuzzy thoughts and alcoholic stupor I began to remember things, significant pointers, signs I should have seen a long time ago. I put it all together and then got dizzy again. Somebody dragged me back from the door and put a drink in my hand. Drunk as I was, and I have never before or since been so drunk, I knew I should not tell anybody what I had seen. Not until I had spoken to Jodi first. But then, like with my mother and Tom Reagan, maybe everyone already knew.

It was after that I began on the shots of tequila. That's most probably why I have no idea how I came to be in Kieran Mahon's car at four thirty in the morning. If he's to be believed, I insisted on turning towards the lightening eastern horizon and singing the national anthem before going in home.

As I lay my head on the pillow, one very clear memory floated free of all the noise in my head. It was of Jodi and the girl from the hospital as they headed towards the darkness and privacy of the Selbys' back garden. I blanked out the memory as quickly as I could. I was exhausted and drunk. A clear head would be needed to come to terms with Jodi's sexual orientation.

Chapter 6

I woke to the racket of Sound Bytes playing their one tune outside my bedroom window. As I got up, I realised they were playing it in my head. By the time I had showered and dressed, the truth became apparent. The birds were chorusing and Mom was singing in the kitchen. My tender head was amplifying the sound of birdsong and mother-twitter. Worse still, I could smell fry. The thought of sausages and rashers sent me racing back to the bathroom.

Pale and shaken, I braved the kitchen and the major-domo.

"Morning, Mom."

She turned around from the cooker, spatula in hand. She had what she called her "slacks" on – brown trousers with elasticated waistband. That meant she was ready for an action-packed day. A walk along the beach or even a day trip with the over-sixties club.

"Good morning, Adele. Sit yourself down and get this inside you. Your father always said a good fry-up was the best cure for a hangover."

"I don't think so. Thanks, Mom but I'll just have coffee."

"Do what you're told now. Eat first and then tell me what you thought of Tom Reagan. No. That's the wrong way round. Did you like him? Tom, I mean."

"I've barely met him. How could I say whether I like him or not? And anyway, you're the one who should be doing the talking. Why didn't you tell me about him? From what you said last night you two have been an item for over a year."

Her back to me, Mom continued to poke and prod at whatever was on the pan.

I was sitting at the table, coffee made for both of us and some bread buttered, before she finally turned towards me and decided to answer.

"I'm going to marry him."

My stomach churned again. I thought of Dad, how patient he had been with her, how loving. I felt like crying. I remembered little things, like the way he used to bring her breakfast in bed every morning and hold an umbrella over her in the rain in case a drop of wet fell on his precious wife. The way he had died in her arms, here in this very kitchen, his last words ones of love for Sissy Burke. For a moment, I was my Daddy's little girl again, my small hand in his big, gnarled one. I swear, in that instant, I smelt his pipe tobacco, saw his overalls hanging on the hook at the back of the kitchen door, heard him chuckle in that warm and funny way he used to do. Of course, I was badly hungover. Maybe still a little drunk. But even today, I believe my father came back to sit with Mom and me in the kitchen the morning she told me she was going to marry Tom Reagan.

"When?" I asked.

"In a few months."

"Why did you keep him such a secret from me? Everyone in the town seems to know except me."

"I didn't want to hurt your feelings."

"What do you mean? Why should your relationship with Tom hurt my feelings? I'm glad for you. I know you've been lonely and it's ten years since Dad died."

Something spluttered on the pan then and she turned back towards it, busying herself with taking up the fry. By the time she put the two plates on the table and sat herself down opposite me, I was wondering if she was ever going to talk to me again.

"Mom, what is it? Why didn't you tell me about Tom?"

Putting down her knife and fork, she reached her hand across the table and caught mine.

"I was very happy with your father, Adele. He was a wonderful man. I don't have to tell you that. I don't want you to think that Tom Reagan will ever replace him. I know how close you and your father were. I was worried you would be upset."

I looked at her fragile hand in mine and noticed the wedding and engagement rings Dad had put on her

47

finger. I noticed too, brown splotches on her crêpey skin. The harbingers of old age. I squeezed her hand, clinging on as I tried to obliterate the thought that my gentle little mother with her outmoded hairstyle and moral values would one day be no more. In a way I became my father, wanting nothing but her happiness. I smiled at her.

"Can I be your bridesmaid, Mom?"

She was off then, relentlessly. I listened as she talked on and on about Tom and his family of two sons and a daughter. Reading between her pauses, I knew she was very disappointed that both Tom's sons were already married and had families of their own. What a let-off that was for me. I gave a shiver at the thought of the heavy-handed matchmaking Mom would have engaged in had there been a glimmer of hope for a double wedding. She spoke and I nodded occasionally, glad to see the youthful sparkle in her eyes.

I cleared off the breakfast ware after she had left to meet Tom. Then I looked around the empty house and wondered how I was going to fill the day ahead.

* * *

Deciding that my main reason for coming back to Cairnsure was to be near the sea again, I put on my shorts and blue cropped top with my flip-flops and headed for the beach. My body clock felt all out of sorts. Today was Sunday and I should be planning a programme for the week ahead in the classroom, correcting tests and doing my washing and ironing. My routine seemed to have seeped into my bones and it weighed heavy on me as I headed towards the strand.

I quickened my pace. Thinking about anything except my next breath became impossible as I swung my arms and pounded along the road. I knew how silly I looked. I had observed power-walkers for long enough, always with a smile at their striding legs, swinging arms, baseball hats and earphones, faces blank of any expression except determination to walk further and faster.

The sun was high in a cloudless sky. Sweat began to trickle between my shoulder-blades. By the time the sea came into view, my pores were oozing alcohol and my mind was gloriously blank. I sat on the sea wall, gasping, and deciding to invest in a baseball hat and MP3 player.

I was still in the relax zone when my mobile rang, almost causing me to fall off the wall with fright. It was Jodi.

"God, Del, how I'm suffering today! This house is bedlam and very loud. I must get out. Where are you?"

"Sitting on the sea wall."

"Stay there. I'll be with you in ten minutes."

I did as Jodi said. I sat and waited. And wondered. What was I going to say to her? Should I admit I had seen her and another woman sneaking off to the Selbys' back garden last night, their arms around each other? Maybe she would want to talk about it. It might be a relief to her. I still had not reached a decision by the time she came to join me, perfectly made-up and stunning in shorts and a bikini top.

"You don't look hung over," I greeted her, trying to keep the resentment out of my voice.

She pushed her sunglasses up on her forehead and leaned towards me. "Look into my eyes. You'll see unbearable suffering there."

I did. Her eyes were bleary. I realised she had not yet sobered up fully.

"I'm going for a swim," she announced. "Are you coming?"

"I've no togs and you've no towel."

"My bikini's on and I'll drip-dry. I'm going for a dip anyway. Come on. Nothing but the Atlantic will cure this pounding head of mine."

She began to stride along the prom, drawing admiring glances from every man she passed. I felt like telling them they were wasting their time as I trotted in her wake. I caught up with her before we reached the dunes.

"Did you enjoy the party?" I asked.

"Mostly. It was a bit of a slow start, wasn't it?"

"You mean with Carla continuously disappearing back into the house and Harry chatting up his ex-wife?"

"I'd be surprised if chatting up was all that was going on."

I slowed my pace, wondering if I should tell Jodi that I had seen Harry and his ex-wife in the car last night. In no fit state to make a decision, I took a few long strides to catch up with her and walk abreast.

"What do you mean?" I asked. "Do you know something about Harry Selby?"

Jodi waved her hand dismissively. "Just gossip from my mother so that may not be too reliable. She said he's been spending a lot of time travelling recently. He's often away from home. And not alone either."

"Are you saying his travelling companion is his ex-wife? That's a big leap."

"Well, one of the hospital staff told me Ruth and Harry were in London together for the past few days. That's why they were late getting to the party last night. They were supposed to be checking out some new medical equipment but who knows what they got up to."

I felt as if someone had kicked me in the stomach. Sure, I didn't know Harry Selby much and didn't like what little I did know of him but I loved Carla like a sister. I understood the pain of being rejected. And though the evidence was circumstantial, little doubt remained in my mind now that Carla's downbeat mood was due to her feckless husband and his ex-wife, who obviously had not learned by experience.

By the time I got my breath back, Jodi was well ahead and I had to run to catch up.

"Wait up," I called. "I thought you were supposed to be in agony with a hangover."

"I am," she groaned. "I can remember very little of last night. I went overboard with the vodka. My dad gave me a right telling off this morning. I'm regretting coming back here already."

So, Jodi didn't remember last night. The trouble was I couldn't forget it.

The tide was out. Already the dunes were packed with day-trippers. Mothers, fathers and their two-point-two children camped in the humps and hollows carved out by wind and water. The air was reeking with the scent of sun lotion and seaweed. I stopped to kick off my flip-flops. Jodi hopped impatiently from foot to foot.

"You go on," I said. "Have your swim. I'll wait here."

Quite unselfconsciously, Jodi stepped out of her shorts. I, and almost everyone else, watched as she walked towards the sand still damp from the receding tide and headed into the sea. I knew I had prejudiced ideas of what a stereotypical lesbian should look like but, by any standards, Jodi was not butch. Dainty, and pretty, even beautiful, Jodi seemed like the essence of heterosexual femininity.

I sat and curled my toes into the warm grittiness of sun-heated sand. Jodi was swimming out to sea now, going against all the rules of safety. She was a very strong swimmer. Always had been. Swimming against the tide was her speciality.

My headache was completely gone. Rolling up Jodi's shorts, I made a pillow of them and lay down, turning my face to the sun. The wash of tide on shoreline hissed softly, background to children's yelps and screeching gulls. A lullaby if I had not been so confused by my Jodi thoughts. I had seen her wrapped around a woman. So what? But the other thoughts would not go away, the ones which last night had seemed to fit so well with the sight of Jodi's head so close to another woman's.

Try as I might I could not remember Jodi ever

having a boyfriend. Not for any length of time anyway. She'd had the same initiation as Carla and I. Stolen kisses in the back row of the cinema, a little fondling at the discos. She had always, always, spoken of her disgust afterwards and made fun of whichever boy had tried to become the latest to conquer the beautiful Jodi Wall. Kieran Mahon had been the one to come nearest to breaching her defences. A bitter pill for me to swallow at the time.

It seemed that Jodi had made career her focus and brushed off any mention of boyfriends as Carla and I were falling in and out of love. Then there were her comments about men, getting increasingly more acerbic with age. Jodi, never one to suffer fools gladly, did not suffer males at all. Sometime in our early twenties, I had stopped asking Jodi about the men in her life. I had pretty much figured at that stage that there were none. None that she was willing to speak of anyway. Even that time, that post Pascal Ronayne time, when I had gone to visit her in London, I had noticed that her circle of acquaintances seemed to be mostly man-free. Now, at last, I thought I knew why. Did her family know? The Walls considered themselves pillars of the community and were devout Roman Catholics to boot. They'd had nine children rather than use contraception, or so Jodi had confided at a time when we used to confide in each other. And why was I lying here trying to second-guess the Walls' attitude to homosexuality when it was my own I should be questioning? Would I feel differently towards Jodi now that I suspected her sexual orientation? Would I be uncomfortable around her, wondering if she was ogling me?

Too many questions for my tired mind to answer. I felt myself drifting off to sleep. Sun warm on my face, breeze gently caressing my hair, I went with the soothing drift. A sharp prod in the midriff woke me up abruptly.

"My sunglasses are in the pocket of my shorts. If they're squashed, you're dead, Adele Burke!"

I opened my eyes to see Jodi, sleek like a seal and dripping salt water, glaring at me. I sat up and frantically shook out her shorts, listening for the tinkle of broken lens. With shaking fingers, I drew out her sunglasses, whole and entire. Not a scratch. I sighed with relief. They were probably worth a month's salary.

"Was the water cold?" I asked, hoping to distract her from the near-catastrophe.

She didn't answer. She was peering in the direction of the dunes.

"Isn't that Carla and the children over there? Brigitte too."

I looked in the direction she was pointing and saw Finn throwing sand, Liam crying and the twins sitting on a rug. Brigitte was trying to stop Finn while Carla sat beside the twins. No Harry. Unless he was in swimming.

"C'mon, Del. We'll go over to join them. Looks like that little brat Finn could do with another talking to and I'm the one to give it to him. I don't know why Carla lets him get away with it."

"Harry's not with them today either."

"He should be around more to control Finn. Carla just doesn't seem to be able."

Liam saw us first. He came running towards us, a big grin on his face. Carla had a bikini on. I was shocked when I noticed just how thin she was. She had always been slim but she was bony now. She must have exercised and starved herself half to death to get her figure back after the babies. Or else she was sick. I shook that thought off quickly. Carla was, after all, a nurse and her husband a doctor. It would be unlikely that she would be fading away from an undiagnosed illness. No, she was either worrying or dieting herself into this bony state. My money was on worry and I knew the source of that.

"Hi, girls. I wasn't expecting to see either of you surface until mid-week. I heard ye both went a bit over the top last night after I left."

"Oh my God! Were we that bad?" Jodi asked. "My father told me I disgraced the Wall name. He claims a nurse from the hospital had to take me outside and walk me around to prevent me passing out. He was pretty pissed off with me this morning."

I flopped onto the sand beside Carla. Jesus! How near I had come to having a heart to heart with Jodi about her lesbian tendencies! She had been getting medical attention from that nurse last night. Not sneaking off behind the house for – for sex with a woman. Our friendship might not have survived my stupid, misjudged, interference.

Impatient with adults, Jodi seemed to have no

tolerance at all of children. Especially Finn and on that one I could go along with her. She had gone over to where Finn was throwing sand. I couldn't hear what was said but a chastened Finn and a relieved Brigitte trailed back to sit with us. Finn stood in front of me and stared until his mother told him to stop being rude. He stuck out his bottom lip and began to sulk.

"I was just wondering why she has only half a T-shirt," he said, pointing to my cropped top. "It looks silly."

"That's enough, Finn," Carla said irritably. "If you don't behave yourself, I'll tell your father."

"Where is Harry?" Jodi asked. "Is he working?"

Carla nodded. "He's on call at the hospital and when his duty's over he has some work to do for himself. This is confidential as yet but he's setting up a private practice with a partner. He's been rushed off his feet for the past few months getting it organised."

"Really? In the private clinic?"

"Yes. It's in the hospital grounds so he won't have too much travelling to do."

"Who is he going into partnership with?"

Carla looked directly at me when I asked the question and even though she had sunglasses on I noticed a shadow dull her eyes, a defensiveness about her mouth.

"His partner is Ruth Selby. An endocrinologist. It just happens that she's his ex-wife."

My eyes opened wide but I clamped my mouth shut. Lesson learned with Jodi, I was not going to second-guess the state of Carla's marriage.

Jodi apparently, had made no such promise to herself.

"Carla! How could you let him do that? Isn't there someone else he could go into practice with? His ex-wife for God's sake! How do you feel about it?"

"It's a business arrangement and one that I've given my full support to," Carla answered, an angry edge to her voice. The "mind your own business" was not spoken but it was certainly implied in the sharpness of the reply.

When Liam caught my hand and whispered that he'd like to go for a paddle, I gladly jumped up.

"Okay if I take him down to the water?"

Carla nodded. Liam and I had just taken a few steps when we were joined by Brigitte and the rest of the children.

"Will we all go with you, Adele?" the girl asked. There was a plea in her voice. Like me, she seemed anxious to run away from the tension between Carla and Jodi.

We chatted as we herded our brood towards the sea.

"Where are you from, Brigitte?"

"Hungary. The Balaton area. You heard of it?"

"Balaton, the thermal lake? Yes, I've heard of it. It must be beautiful. Do you miss home?"

"Yes, sometimes. But I go back soon. I come here just to improve my English."

"Well, your English is very good. Will you continue on with child-care work?"

Brigitte looked at me and smiled. I understood. She'd had enough of looking after other people's children.

"So what will you do then?"

"I'm interested in cooking."

Finn had reached the water by now and was scooping up fistfuls and throwing it at us as we approached. I went back into teacher mode. Firmly, I told him to stop. He heard the authority in my voice and responded. Easy. Except for the very base urge I felt to dig a hole in the sand and bury him up to his neck. I wanted to talk to Brigitte about what was fast becoming my first love too. Cooking. The conversation had to wait as we herded the young Selbys along the shore and gave Carla and Jodi a chance to settle their differences.

* * *

When Brigitte and I with our caravan of children arrived back to the dunes, Carla and Jodi seemed to be on friendly terms. At least they were talking. I sat down beside them and decided now was as good a time as any to make my announcement.

"My mother is going to marry Tom Reagan."

They both chorused "Aaaah!" together. I suppose they were right. It was a touching "love in the winter of life" romance. But . . .

"You're all right with it, aren't you, Del?" Carla asked.

Jodi decided to answer for me. "Of course she is. Why not? It must be a relief to know your mom won't be your sole responsibility now, Del. It gives you a lot more freedom to do whatever you want."

That was true and yet I couldn't at that stage get the thought of Dad out of my mind.

"Of course I feel happy for her," I agreed. "I keep

thinking of my father though. I wonder how he'd feel about it."

Jodi whipped off her probably expensive, and thankfully undamaged, sunglasses and glared at me. "Surely you don't begrudge your mother her happiness? Don't you want her to enjoy the time she has left?"

"You know, I do. It'll just take a while to get used to the idea. Remember I only met Tom Reagan for the first time last night."

Carla, smoothing sun-block onto Lisa, stopped what she was doing and began to laugh. "Talking of last night, you're a sly one, Adele Burke. I heard you went home with Kieran Mahon."

My arch-enemy Finn saved me the trouble of explaining that before she left "the tent", my mother had asked Kieran to drive me home.

"I need a coke and an ice-cream too," Finn was demanding.

Immediately Brigitte went to a cool box and took out some orange juice.

"No! I want Coke. And ice-cream!" Finn's lip was beginning to wobble. Another tantrum was imminent. We had ignored him for five whole minutes.

Jodi stood up and brushed off the sand which had clung to her wet bikini. "You've given me a longing for ice-cream now too, Finn. How about both of us go to the shop and get some for everyone. You can help me bring it back."

Carla got her bag and poked around until she found her car keys. She handed them to Jodi.

"Here, take these."

"I'm walking. It's not far."

"You'll have to go into town. Didn't you notice The Cabin is closed?"

"No! Since when?"

"Since last week. You know Mrs Elliot died a year ago and Gussie, her big lazy son, took over the shop. He ran it into the ground in no length of time. He's put it up for rent now and rumour has it that he's spending his days between the bookies and the pub."

I was amazed that I hadn't noticed. The shop known as The Cabin had been synonymous with Cairnsure strand for generations. It was a splash of colour on the prom with all the spades and buckets and swimming tubes hanging outside the door in the summer months. Mrs Elliot had lived and died behind the counter. She had survived winters by selling fruit and veg and raked in the money during the summer by supplying every item a day-tripper could possibly want for a visit to the seaside. And now, it seemed, you would either have to bring what you wanted with you or else go back into town.

I stood and looked around me. From dune to dune and all along the length of the beach, children played, adults sunbathed and almost every available inch of space was occupied. On the prom I noticed a queue snaking from behind a mobile chip van. Hungry people, appetites whetted by sea air and a swim in the ocean.

Jodi was standing beside me, jangling the car keys in her hand. We looked at each other. I believe we got the idea at exactly the same time. I was thinking food and Jodi was thinking numbers but we arrived at the one conclusion.

"A café!"

"On the prom!"

"With a kid's menu too!" Carla added.

Finn began to tug at Jodi's hand. As she pulled on her shorts over her damp bikini she had a look of fierce concentration on her face. I knew she was mentally calculating start-up costs and capital investment. I was planning menus and even Carla seemed to be thinking café thoughts.

And that was how Carla, Jodi and I began to consider going into the café business.

Chapter 7

I was up and dressed next morning before Mom had even stirred. It was another sunny day and I was buzzing with energy. I wasn't due to meet Jodi and Carla until eleven o'clock but there were things I needed to do before then. On my own.

Hair tied back in a ponytail, slip-on shoes on my bare feet, I headed towards the beach at a pace which was for me impressively fast. I was really getting the measure of this stride-walking. After ten minutes my shoes began to pinch and after fifteen I knew I was developing a blister. I would have to grit my teeth and buy trainers if I was going to stick with my promise to exercise daily for the next year. I had every intention of being ultra-fit and toned by the time I got back to Dublin.

The strand was already dotted with people. Even on a Monday morning. I watched as cars were parked and hordes of children released, followed by parents carrying rugs, towels and cool boxes. All of them potential clients for a café on the prom. The chip van was still parked there, a greasy smell wafting around it though it was locked up now.

Turning my back on the sea I looked towards Elliots' shop. It had the forlorn appearance of all abandoned things. The one-storey building was dominated by a large front window overlooking the beach. The window was blanked out by some type of white cream smeared on the glass. An albino eye. I remembered what a jumble of colour that window had been when Mrs Elliot had piled it high with souvenirs, sweets and always an array of straw hats. The most interesting thing there now was the sign which said "To Let". I closed my eyes and imagined the door opened, the window cleaned, tables and chairs inside the newly painted shop, the smell of freshly brewed coffee and home-made apple-pie . . .

"Excuse me. Are you all right?"

My eyes opened to see a tanned, well-built man staring curiously at me. I blushed. I had by that time cornered the market on hot, splotchy blushes which flooded north of my neck at lightning pace.

"I'm fine, thank you. Just getting my breath back after a long walk."

"Not in those shoes," he remarked, glancing down at my slip-ons.

"Why, what would you expect me wear? High heels?"

"Trainers or walking shoes. Not little pumps like those."

I looked down at my size-eight slip-ons and wondered how he could ever call them little. But they would be to him. He was a very big man, broad-shouldered and muscular. The type who would probably fall into fat in middle age.

"I haven't seen you around here before," I said. "Are you visiting?"

"Well, yes and no. My family was originally from Cairnsure. I was born in New Zealand but my mother was pregnant with me before she left here. I was made in Ireland, so to speak."

So that would explain his accent, a very attractive mix of Irish and British with undertones of Australian thrown in for good measure.

"Eoin," he volunteered. "I'm pleased to meet you. And you are?"

"Adele," I muttered as I shook the hand he offered. It was a huge hand, engulfing mine in a firm grip.

"My father had a small construction business here before he left. He was contented in New Zealand but his heart was always in Cairnsure."

"Is the family thinking of moving back, then?"

"My father died last year. He was considering retiring to Cairnsure when he got sick."

"I'm sorry. So you're just here on a visit? Tracing your roots?"

"I haven't decided yet."

Glancing at my watch I noticed it was after ten o'clock. I had something else to do before I met Carla and Jodi.

"I must get going, Eoin. It was nice meeting you."

"Likewise. We might bump into each other again. Not many places to hide in Cairnsure."

He smiled at me and I noticed that he had even,

white teeth. I always notice teeth. It was a nice smile, touching his brown eyes with a glint. I wondered why he would want to hide anyway and dismissed the fleeting thought that hiding was exactly what I was doing back here in my home place. I smiled back at the man from New Zealand then headed off to my next stop.

* * *

Cairnsure cemetery overlooked the sea. High on a hill, generations of Cairnsure families had followed coffins up the steep slope. My father's grave was underneath one of the granite stone walls, sheltered from wind and the excesses of our temperamental Irish climate.

From a distance, I saw the red slash on the green of his plot. Nearer, the bouquet of roses was still almost fresh, their delicate petals just beginning to curl at the edges. I knelt on the kerbstone, tears in my eyes, my question answered. Only Mom would have put those roses there, testament to a love that would never die. How could I ever have thought that she would forget Dad? She was about to marry another man, yes, but Dad would never be replaced in her life. Just as she had said. Head bowed, I tried to pray but soon gave up. I talked to Dad instead, told him about Tom Reagan and what a decent man he seemed to be. I told him too about Elliots' shop and how the girls and I had the idea to open a café there. He would have smiled at that.

Thinking about the girls brought my contemplative period to an end. The clever thing about Cairnsure cemetery was that the way back to the town was downhill.

I allowed gravity do its work and sped to where I was due to meet Carla and Jodi at the estate agent's.

* * *

Potter Auctioneers and Estate Agents was on Main Street. Old Man Potter had run the business there ever since Main Street had been the only street in Cairnsure. It was now the main artery in the growing town, veiny offshoots spreading along its length and breadth. Potter's eldest son, a replica of the old man, had inherited the business. Even the glasses he wore, perched on his nose, resembled the round specs his father had always worn. Never, as far as I can remember, to look through but to peer over in an intimidating way. I smiled as I followed Carla and Jodi into Potter's office. No amount of over-spectacle peering would intimidate either of those two women.

Jodi, as I knew she would, took the initiative. She immediately approached Seán Potter's desk and shook his hand.

"Mr Potter. How are you? Thank you for seeing us so quickly. As I told you on the phone, we want details please on the Elliot property."

Wordless, Seán Potter waved us to seats and handed each of us a printout of the details.

"Read them. Then we'll talk."

I looked at him in surprise. How had the business lasted so long if his manner was always this brusque?

As I glanced down the page, I realised we had not thought our idea through. Rates, water charges, refuse and electricity were just a few of the items I had not considered. I had been too busy thinking apple-pie and bread-and-butter pudding. In fact I had not taken running costs into account at all, preferring to leave that to Jodi.

"Two thousand euro a month is a ridiculous sum for these premises," said Jodi. "It's too far from the town centre to justify that."

"It'll be right in the centre of everything when the marina development goes ahead," said Seán Potter.

Carla and I exchanged puzzled glances. What marina development? Jodi showed no such surprise. She leaned towards Seán Potter.

"You know better than I that the new marina depends on planning and EU grants. It may never happen and certainly not within the next few years. Not until the economy picks up again."

"But it will happen, Miss Wall. And when it does, Elliots' shop will be at the hub. By the way, what do you intend doing there?"

"Does that matter now?" Carla asked. "We'd prefer keep our business plan confidential until we've made a final decision."

"You can't just open up whatever you like."

He eyed each of us over his specs and his attitude was reflected in his down-turned mouth and lowered brows. He considered us to be three silly women who wanted to play shop. Big, spoiled children without a scrap of common sense. I heard Jodi's impatient sigh. I sat back and waited for her to set Seán Potter straight. She leaned towards him and he automatically leaned back from her angry glare.

"Do you really believe, Mr Potter, that we're making this enquiry without having our homework done? We know Mrs Elliot had got council permission for change of use of the premises just before she died."

Seán Potter was surprised by Jodi's announcement but not near as taken aback as Carla and I. Jodi had been a very busy girl this morning. She must have been onto the Planning Department in the Council offices as soon as they opened.

"Well, yes. She had been thinking of opening a café there and had set the wheels in motion. Is that what you three intend to do – open a café?"

The patronising tone of the "you three" annoyed me enough to answer him back.

"We've already told you that our business plans are confidential, Mr Potter. Now could you please arrange for us to see the premises?"

He slid a little black leather-covered notebook towards him and flipped it open. I was certain it must be a replica of the black notebook his father had always used. Seán Potter was obviously a man who revered tradition and disliked change. Especially women involving themselves in business.

"What about tomorrow afternoon?" he asked.

Carla shook her head. "I'm away tomorrow. I'm going to Dublin for the day."

"The day after then?"

"What's wrong with today?" Jodi asked.

"Another client is viewing it today. You should know there's a lot of interest in Elliots'."

"Surely you, with all your experience can manage to have two viewings on the same day? Four o'clock? How would that fit in with your schedule, girls?"

Carla and I nodded at Jodi. Four o'clock would suit us fine and it would have to suit Seán Potter too.

"I'll meet you there. Four sharp," he said, his tone far from gracious.

We confused him totally then. We smiled at him and shook his hand. He was shaking his head as we left the office.

Out on the street we looked at each other and laughed out loud.

"I can't believe it," Carla said. "We're actually going to do it."

"We've started the ball rolling," I cautioned. "But do we have any idea of the expenditure involved?"

Carla and I both looked at Jodi, waiting for an answer. She was, after all, an accountant and a natural leader to boot.

"It's significant," she said and I immediately went on alert.

"What do you mean by that?"

"We'll have to comply with a plethora of expensive catering regulations. Staff training in safe handling of food. Specific requirements for kitchen appliances. Millions of rules and regulations, environmental, health and safety . . ."

With a sick feeling in the pit of my stomach, I raised my hand to stop Jodi.

"Jesus! We don't have a clue what we're getting ourselves into, do we? And how are we going to fund it? Two thousand a month for Elliots' old shop before we even bake a scone. Maybe we should just forget it."

"Like hell! We're going all around the town now to size up the opposition. Ready for coffee, girls?"

"What about the children?" I asked Carla, puzzled that she seemed relaxed about leaving them totally in Brigitte's care.

"Do you remember Vera?"

I nodded. Vera was Carla's youngest sister, an afterthought in the family, born when the others were already going to school.

"She's just finished a child-care course. She'll be taking Brigitte's place at the end of the month. So they're both looking after the children until then."

I made a silent wish that Vera could handle Finn's bullying tactics a bit better than Brigitte. Or indeed Carla.

"Sounds like a good plan," I said.

Carla smiled. Her sad smile again. I noticed the dark circles underneath her eyes. Then I forgot about how she seemed to be oozing sadness as we three visited coffee shops, cafés and carveries in downtown Cairnsure.

Chapter 8

We had seven catering outlets to call on in Cairnsure before our spying mission was complete. The lunch-time trade was certainly thriving here. A nice symbiosis between the new industries and the town caterers. The industries fed clients into the town and the cafés and carveries fed the workers.

Carla and Jodi seemed to be able to cope with the gallons of coffee we had sampled much better than me. By the time we were making our way towards the prom for our four o'clock appointment with Seán Potter, I was lagging behind, slowed down by the sheer weight of coffee I had drunk.

"C'mon, Del. Get a move on. We're going to be late."

I did as Jodi ordered and walked more quickly. I was only slightly out of breath as we approached the Elliots' shop. The door opened and Seán Potter emerged, dwarfed by the big man beside him. Eoin! The man from New Zealand! What was he doing here?

"Ah! One of the interested clients," Jodi whispered.

"No. He's just here on holiday. Well, maybe. He's deciding."

"You know him?" Carla asked in surprise.

"No. Not really."

Just to prove me a liar, Eoin walked straight towards me and flashed those lovely white teeth.

"Adele! I knew we'd meet again. I didn't think it would be this soon though."

"And I didn't think it would be in Elliots' shop," I answered before I had time to put a softer slant on my annoyance.

"I did warn you that there's a lot of interest in this premises," Seán Potter said. He looked over his specs, evil satisfaction glinting in his eyes. I knew he was itching to tell us that this Eoin was a proper client while we were just wasting his time.

"Clever marketing ploy this," Eoin remarked, looking down at the estate agent. "Letting us all know the competition is sharp."

"You bet," Carla said, glancing at her watch. "You'll have to excuse us now. I believe it's time for us to view Elliots'. It was nice meeting you, Mr . . .?"

"Kirby. I've seen all I need to for now anyway. Good luck, ladies."

Seán Potter looked a bit panicked, wondering whether to follow Eoin Kirby or keep a close eye on us women as we inspected the shop. He decided on compromise.

"Go on in and have a look around," he ordered. "I'll be in as soon as I've finished talking to Mr Kirby."

Jodi flounced ahead, trailed by myself and Carla. I couldn't resist a glance over my shoulder. Eoin Kirby was grinning. He gave me a wave and I gave him the beginnings of one of my splotchy blushes.

Even though the door to the shop was open, the air inside was musty. The shelves were mostly bare but some items still sat forlorn. Here a box of lollipops with faded labels and there a heap of sticky fly-papers which I had not seen on the market for years. Things not even the unpaid suppliers wanted back.

"It's bigger than I remember," Carla said, glancing at the measurements on her printout.

She was right. Emptied of most of its stock, The Cabin seemed to have the proportions of a ballroom. I squinted my eyes in the dim light which filtered through the smeared window and imagined the counter gone, shelves ripped off, walls painted white, tables with checked cloths, a vase with a rosebud on each table. And me, efficient and gracious, serving grateful customers with plates of lemon meringue pie, smothered in cream. No. That image was wrong. I peered harder and saw that the cream was served in a separate bowl . . .

"Del! Stop daydreaming. C'mon through to the back."

I shook myself out of my fantasy and followed the girls through the door behind the counter, remembering that as a child I had often wondered what lay beyond that door. The reality was far removed from the treasure trove of sweets and toys I had imagined then. We had to hold our noses as a horrible smell engulfed us. I flicked the light switch but the bulb remained unlit.

"The electricity's been cut off," Seán Potter said from behind me.

He shone a torch and immediately the beam focused on a sack of putrid potatoes thrown in one corner of the very large storeroom. Brown liquid oozed from the bag, forming an odorous puddle on the floor, while green leaves from the sprouted vegetables poked through the top. Another corner was piled with sun hats and swimming tubes, while stacks of papers were scattered everywhere. Mrs Elliot must have been an uneasy spirit if she was witness to what her lazy son had done to her always pristine shop.

"Are there rats here?" Carla asked and I could hear the disgust in her voice.

"The Elliots always had cats. They run wild out the back now but they keep the vermin at bay."

I gave Seán Potter what I hoped was a filthy look. Why had he not removed the sack of rotting vegetables before showing the property for letting?

"Seen enough here?" he asked. Not waiting for an answer he walked to the back door and opened it up.

We followed him out, each of us taking in a gulp of pure air. I had always known that Elliots' shop had a bit of ground behind it but I was stunned by the length and breadth of the back garden. It was overgrown now. A tangle of brambles and weeds.

"A patio with wrought-iron tables and parasols.

Maybe a barbeque in summertime," Carla whispered and I knew that she and I were dreaming the same dream. The shop front would be just to entice people in. And for rainy days.

"A smoking area and fire exit," Jodi, ever practical, added.

"Anything else you want to see?" Seán Potter asked, not bothering to hide his impatience.

"We would like to see a plan of the building, a copy of the letting agreement and a realistic rental for this rundown premises," said Jodi.

Seán Potter glared at her. "I told you. Two thousand euro a month is the asking price and I'll have no trouble getting that."

Jodi laughed into his face. I thought his glasses were going to pop off. She reached out her hand to him. "Thank you for showing us around, Mr Potter. We'll be looking elsewhere. I believe there's a new estate agency after opening up in town."

He shuffled his feet and pushed his glasses higher up on his nose. "I'll talk to Mr Elliot. See what he says. How much are you willing to pay?"

"One thousand euro a month."

Seán Potter shrugged and led the way back inside. We were assailed by the horrible smell again and walked quickly through the storeroom and back into the shop. Reluctant to leave so quickly, I looked around me. The potential here was huge. The renovation bills would be equally gigantic. This shop needed to be gutted, every worn and dirty surface replaced. Then I remembered something.

"Water?" I asked. "I didn't see any water supply."

"There's a kitchenette in the back."

We trooped behind the counter again and Seán Potter opened up another door we had not noticed in the dimness. Only one of us at a time fitted into the space but I was happy to see a sink there. I turned the tap and a trickle of water came through.

"Mains supply. Toilet's at the other side of the store and it's connected to the main sewage scheme."

Another problem solved. Our dream was still alive and well as we left Seán Potter on the prom and arranged to meet up again in two days' time.

"Enjoy your trip to Dublin," I said to Carla as she got into her jeep. "Are you driving up?"

"Flying from Cork. See you two Wednesday. Text me if there's any news."

As she drove off, I noticed again how tiny she seemed in the driver's seat of her four-by-four.

"Can you believe she left the children for so long?" Jodi asked.

"It seems like she intends spending more time away from them if our café goes according to plan. Do you really think we'll get it for one thousand a month?"

"I hope so. I haven't all the costings finished yet. That dump of a shop needs some serious renovations before we could open up as a food outlet."

"Shit! Are you saying we can't afford it?"

"Del! Would you get real? We haven't discussed yet where and how we could finance it or even how much it would cost. I'm going to spend the rest of today and all tomorrow working on a business plan. We'll discuss it then and see where we stand."

We went our separate ways. Jodi off to do her spreadsheet work and me back home to my mother. Leaving practicalities aside, I thought of the café as I walked along. I saw it shining and bright and full of customers. The journey home seemed short.

* * *

Mom had been busy. I sniffed her steak and kidney pie even before I set foot in the kitchen.

"I hope you have a good appetite, Adele. I made your favourite dinner."

"I'm starving," I lied. There was something about Sissy Burke that made everyone, including me, want to protect her from the harsh realities of life. Such as a daughter too full of coffee to eat the steak and kidney pie she had spent hours preparing.

"I went to Dad's grave," I told her. "I see you put a lovely bouquet of roses there."

"No, I didn't. Not recently anyway. Maybe Lily Burke put them there. Your father's sour-faced sister must have finally discovered her heart."

I nodded, a little disappointed. I had imagined that the bouquet had been Mom's way of saying that she still loved Dad even though she was about to marry another man.

"Well, tell me all about Elliots'," she said, her head tilted to one side as it always did when there was a bit of gossip involved. I had figured out long ago that her hearing was better in her right ear than her left. By angling her head to the left she was more confident of not missing a detail.

"It's very rundown. I don't know how that yob of a son managed to get it into such a state in just one year."

"Gussie has problems, the poor boy. He'd bet on two flies crawling up a wall and he's very fond of his drink. His mother spoiled him. She should have made him work for a living."

"It's way roomier inside than I expected. Did you know the back garden is really big?"

"That's because the Elliots bought the adjoining garden when the family in the house behind them moved. They went to New Zealand years ago. Before you were born."

New Zealand? Just how many families from Cairnsure had emigrated to the furthest corner of the globe? Surely that man Eoin's family couldn't be the only one? Maybe this was just coincidence. What had he said his surname was? Kirby. Yes, that was it. Eoin Kirby.

"Would that family have been named Kirby? The father had a construction business."

On her way to the table with my heaped plate of steak and kidney pie, my mother stopped mid-stride. Like a wind-up toy whose spring had unwound, she stood there plate in hand, mouth slack, eyes staring straight ahead.

"Mom? Are you all right?"

She shook her head, as if waking up from a long sleep, and smiled at me. "Yes, I'm fine. Just fine. Here, have your dinner while it's hot."

"You didn't answer my question. Did the Kirbys live behind The Cabin?"

"They did. They sold the house to Mrs Elliot when they left. She sold it on to developers some years ago but she kept the garden. Now eat. Your dinner will be going cold."

"Their son seems like a nice person."

Mom flopped onto the chair opposite me and there was no mistaking her expression now. She was shocked.

"What do you know about their son?" she asked in a tone which for her was sharp.

"I met him. He's here in Cairnsure. He says on holiday but he was viewing Elliots' shop today too."

She went pale, her years very suddenly etched on her face. I was puzzled. What was it about the Kirbys that robbed my mother of her perpetual calm and her lovely pink glow?

"Did you know them well?" I asked.

"Your father worked for them as a carpenter before he went into business for himself."

"The son told me his father died a year ago."

"Dead! Michael Kirby? Are you sure?"

"Well, the man I met said his father was dead, anyway. I don't know if his name was Michael. Was he a friend of yours?"

She didn't answer me. She was staring out the window but I was pretty sure she wasn't seeing anything. She had a glazed look in her eyes. I touched her hand and she jumped with fright.

"And this man's mother. Is she still alive?"

"As far as I know. Eoin didn't really say."

"Eoin?"

79

"Yes, Eoin Kirby. What's the matter, Mom? Why does mention of the Kirbys upset you?"

"I don't want to talk about those people any more. I'm warning you to have nothing to do with any one of them." She stood up and began to untie her apron. "Tidy up when you're finished. I'm going out. Over to Tom. I'll see you later."

She left the kitchen before I had a chance to ask her any more questions. I had wanted her recipe for steak and kidney pie but more than that I needed to know just what the Kirbys had done to upset her so badly. Whatever happened in the past was obviously still seething. And hurting.

Chapter 9

The next day was grey and windy. Even though the temperature had dropped by only a few degrees, it felt chilly. My bed was cosy. I pulled the duvet up around my ears and had a debate with myself. Cuddle into bed, be lazy. Get up, showered, dressed and go pounding the roads. The lazy me lost. Looking out the window at the summer storm, I noticed that the clouds were so dark rain couldn't be far off. I didn't envy Carla her trip to Dublin. A sunny, vibrant city had a certain attraction, an ability to infuse energy. Damp, puddly paths crowded with umbrella-brandishing pedestrians and streets crammed with traffic were the stuff of depression.

Mom seemed to be taking a rest so I wrote a note for her before I left the house. I headed off in the direction of town with no particular plan other than to walk as quickly as possible. Despite the wind it was a lot warmer out than I expected. In minutes I was regretting the sweater, jeans, laced shoes, thick socks and rainjacket I had thought necessary. By the time I reached the prom I felt like I was in a sauna. I stood at the wall panting and looking out over the ocean.

The sea looked angry, waves white-capped and slapping against outlying rocks before curling onto the shoreline. Opening my jacket and throwing back the hood, I lifted my face to the wind. A gull wheeled overhead. I followed the bird's swooping, gliding course. What freedom! What abandon! I envied the bird as I watched it rise and fall with the vagaries of the air currents. No decisions to be made. Just go with the prevailing wind, dive for food when hungry, make a nest and find a mate when broody. At that moment I wanted, more than anything else, to be a seagull.

Head down from the clouds again, I went to the strand and, turning left, began to walk towards the rocky part of the eastern shore. I remembered a cavern there, a secret place where I used to hide as a child. A place to lick wounds and allow healing to begin. Soon sandy beach gave way to rocky shoreline. The rocks by the cliffs were jagged and daunting. Nearer the sea, where I was walking, they were slick with seaweed but easily negotiable. I scrambled along until the sandy dunes were far behind me and ahead I heard the deep growl of the tide as it rushed into the mouth of the cavern, then swirled and ebbed. No hiding place today, the tide was too far in, but I still had wounds to lick and healing to begin.

Near the cliff face I found a rock formation eroded into a semi-circular shape, the open end facing towards the cliff. Not as enclosed my cavern but yet it had the same inviting quality. Like a big stone armchair. I went inside and sat down on a patch of wet sand, my back supported by the cold, hard slabs. I smiled as it dawned on me that my surroundings reflected my dilemma. I was between a rock and a hard place. I no longer wanted to be in Dublin teaching but now I was not sure that I wanted to be in Cairnsure either. The warm glow of homecoming and freedom from routine was already beginning to pall.

The worst thing was that I didn't know what had brought on this mood of uncertainty. Just last night, I had been excited, looking forward to the café, working with Carla and Jodi, the challenge of starting a business, the joy of cooking, the pleasure of meeting all the new people I expected would be our customers when we opened up. Of course it was still just an idea, an impulse. The prospect of the three of us working together remained exciting but reality was beginning to dull the shining ideal. Serving food to the public was far more than just throwing a few ingredients together and garnishing them with parsley or luscious sauces.

Maybe it was Mom and realising how little I really knew about her. Why had she kept Tom Reagan a secret from me and why had she reacted so strangely to the name Kirby? Why was Carla so wan, so very stressed? And Jodi. Could I really work with her? Could I just sit back and allow her to take control of our business? The truth was that all three, Mom, Carla and Jodi – the people I loved most in the world – were not as I remembered them to be. I had been lonely in Dublin, sometimes isolated from the life of the city, the excitement I felt bubbling in the streets around me. But I had been in charge of my own life. I had a place there. A status in the school, refuge in my little apartment. Adele Burke, primary school teacher and property owner. Here, I was Sissy Burke's daughter and since I didn't really know Sissy Burke, I didn't really know Adele Burke either.

I stood up and tried to shake wet sand from the back of my raincoat. It was cemented on. I was allowing myself to spiral into a real down mood. Knickers to that! All I had meant to think about was the café and our impulsive idea to commit ourselves to a business none of us knew anything about, without ever stopping to think how much it would cost or even if we could cope with it.

I came out from between my sheltering rocks. With a sense of shock I noticed how far in the tide had come while I had been sitting there, trying to sort out my life. A wave came rushing towards me. I scrambled up on a rock and watched the wave curl and foam around the back of the stone armchair I had just left. I stood still for a moment and took a deep breath. Behind me the cliff loomed and ahead was the grey, swollen ocean. Spray drenched my face as a wave crashed against the rock I was standing on. My heart began to pound with fear. I turned to my right and peered towards the distant sand dunes. My path back to them was under water except for a narrow ridge of rock near the cliff face. Here where I stood, the rocks were battered by myriad storms into easily climbable shapes. About two hundred feet ahead the rocks got steeper. There they towered into sharp peaks, How had I not noticed the rapidly incoming tide? I should have heard its angry rumble. Panicked, I began to scramble forward along the narrow rock path between cliff and sea, trying to keep my focus on the sand dunes in the distance and not the tide which was taunting me by pushing closer with every wave. I struggled from rock to rock praying more sincerely than I ever had in my life.

Driven by fear, I made progress. The dunes were nearer. I paused to catch my breath. A quick peek behind told me the rocks I had just crossed were now almost submerged. I knew I had reached the end of the easy climb. Ahead the tall rocks loomed dark, water swirling at their base, their peaks jutting up against the cliff face. I looked up, wondering if scaling the cliff would be a better option. A shiver of dread rippled through me as my eyes travelled the height of the cliff face. I could never scale those sheer heights.

Knowing without any doubt now that my life was in danger, I took a few steps forward towards the first towering rock. It was wide at the base, or what I could see of the base. Maybe about twelve feet in diameter it rose, many feet above, to a jagged plateau. I looked for a path between cliff and rock. There was none. The rock was solidly embedded in the cliff face, the front of it jutting out into the tide which slapped against it with a deep rumble. If I was ever to see home again I would have to find a way past this rock, even if that meant hanging on by my fingertips and circling around it while the tide raged beneath me.

I scanned the rock surface and noticed a roughness, a ledge about two feet up. Narrow but enough to step on and bring myself forward. Then I looked more closely and saw little crevices that would serve as handholds. As panic subsided I saw more and more irregularities on the stone I had thought so smooth. It was mapped with juts and nooks. All shallow but deep enough to allow me cling on.

I lunged at the rock, my right foot scrabbling for the ledge. My foot found purchase. With all my strength I hauled my body up, finding space on the ledge for my left foot too. Gripping tightly into my handholds, I moved my left foot forward until I found another ledge. Inch by inch, I made my way along the rock face until I knew that one more step would bring me around to the other side from where I would be able to see the dunes.

I rounded the rock face and all thoughts of the sand dunes were banished. I stood there on a little ledge, clinging onto my shallow handholds and staring down into a vicious swirl of water which lay between me and the next rock. The tide roared as it swept between the rocks and growled as it ebbed. I watched as seaweed and driftwood were first lashed into the channel, then drawn back by the powerful tide. I was a strong swimmer but saw quite clearly how I would be tossed against the rocks and then dragged out to sea if I attempted to swim this channel. It was no more than twenty feet in breadth yet it was much too wide to jump and had too strong a current to swim. Trapped.

I cried then and made no attempt to check the tears. I was about to die, to be swept away. And just as I was starting on my year's leave. Had fate brought me back to Cairnsure just to die in the sea I had loved all my life? What about Mom? She had lost Dad and coped. She would not survive losing her daughter, her only child.

I was not yet ready to surrender to this awful fate.

I dragged my eyes away from the hypnotic rhythm of the tide and, carefully balancing myself, leaned my head back and looked above me. If I could climb higher and cling on until the tide went out, then I could survive. A careful inspection told me that the rock got smoother as it got higher. The footholds and handholds were all at the level I was on now. I turned my head and looking over my shoulder caught a glimpse of the beach and the edge of the sand dunes. They were deserted.

I began to shout. To my father, to God, to anybody who would help me. My cries became increasingly desperate as my fingers and toes began to cramp from clinging on to the narrow supports. I knew I should try to move, to keep my circulation going but by now I was too terrified to do anything but yell for help.

When I heard an answering voice on the wind I thought I was hallucinating. I shouted and then held my breath. I heard it again. Someone was yelling at me to hold on. A man's voice. As the voice got closer, I recognised it. He was very near now. I glanced around and almost lost my balance. I had just caught a glimpse of him and the lifebuoy he was holding. He was standing on the rock across the deep channel.

"Are you hurt?" Kieran Mahon called across. "Can you move from there?"

"I've got nowhere to go," I answered, noticing that my voice was now hoarse from all the shouting I had done.

"You'll have to swim across – I'm going to throw the lifebuoy over to you!"

I glanced down again at the maelstrom beneath me. It was getting nearer my feet. Ready to whip me away and pound me against the rocks. The undercurrent was so strong that I could hear the scrape of boulders against the rock base. How could a little buoy protect me against that elemental power? And how was I going to be able to catch it anyway with my numb fingers?

"Reach out your hand!" Kieran called.

I tried to free my right hand from its hold on the rock face. My fingers held rigidly on to their support. I didn't know at this stage whether they were numb with fear or cramped from clinging on so desperately. I was afraid to let go.

"Do it! Now!" Kieran ordered.

My hand and arm responded to the urgency in his voice. I shifted my weight to the left for balance and stuck my right arm out as far as I could. I heard Kieran grunt with effort as he flung the buoy, then a splash as it and the attached rope landed in the water.

"We'll try again," he shouted. "Be ready to grab!"

After two more unsuccessful efforts to catch the buoy, I was in despair.

"Del! You'll have to jump!" shouted Kieran then. "You'll be able to catch the buoy more easily once both hands are free! Go on – jump!"

My terror reached a new level. I glanced quickly beneath me and knew I would never have the courage to launch myself into that cauldron without a safety device. Suppose I couldn't reach the buoy? Suppose a wave swept me out to sea before I could grab it?

I was so terrified all I could manage was to scream a long, loud "No!" at Kieran. My fingers clung so desperately into my handholds that my arms trembled with the strain. I leaned my face against the cold rock and knew without any doubt that I was about to die.

A deep whooshing sound struck a new note of terror. It was a vicious, I'm-coming-to-get-you sound. Water swirled around my feet as the huge wave thundered into the channel. The wind rose in sympathy, whipping at my rain-jacket. The rain, anxious to show willing, began to fall in big, cold drops. I felt the drag of the undertow on my feet as the wave curled over on itself and began to race back to sea. Eyes closed, I whispered a prayer to my father. My ears registered a change in the sound of the sea. A flash of silence. Without giving myself any more time to think, I released my hands from the holds, bent my knees and threw myself back into the water. For a panicky second I couldn't breathe as salt water closed over my face. I surfaced, gasping for air, my rain-jacket billowing around me. I kicked my legs against the rock and surged backwards into the channel.

"Grab the buoy!" Kieran roared. "It's to your right. Grab it!"

I flipped over in the water, better able to gauge my position now that I was facing the opposite wall of rock.

With relief I saw the red and white of the buoy bobbing beside me. I grabbed the buoy and with both hands pulled it over my head and worked my arms and shoulders through. Then I began to kick my legs as hard as I could. A scissors kick. A desperate struggle to power across this narrow cauldron of swirling water. I kicked more frantically as I sensed rather than heard the turn of the tide, the gathering of another wall of water out at sea.

"You're nearly there. Come on!" Kieran shouted.

He was pulling me towards the rock now at an increasing pace. He must also have noticed another big wave on the way. My kicks got weaker as my shoes began to drag my feet down. My clothes too felt like anchors pulling me towards the bottom.

I almost swam into the opposite rock. Terrified, half-drowned, I felt my face break into a beatific smile. I had made it! I was across.

"Grab the rope. I'll haul you up as you climb!"

I looked up at the wall of rock over my head. It was as high as the one I had just left but it was pitted with holes and ledges. The thundering sound of another wave reached me. I scrambled onto the rock, then picked my steps, my speed boosted by Kieran's upward tug of the rope attached to the lifebuoy I still wore.

At last I planted my feet firmly on the broad ledge on which the pale-faced Kieran Mahon stood. Tears began to stream down my face, joining in with the rivulets of seawater and the rain which was by now falling heavily. I was thoroughly waterlogged and shivering with shock and cold.

Kieran moved towards me and I took a step forward, anticipating the comfort of his arms around me. I shivered even more when I heard his angry tone.

"What in the bloody hell were you doing over there? Surely you haven't been gone from Cairnsure so long that you forgot how deadly the East Beach is at high tide?"

I understood his anger. I had put both our lives at risk by my carelessness.

"I'm sorry, Kieran. And I'm very grateful to you. I don't know what would have happened if you hadn't come along."

"You would probably have drowned."

He was right. There was nothing to add to that. I wriggled my way out of the lifebuoy as he began to coil the rope.

"Come on," he said. "We'd better get back or both of us will end up in the sea."

He took off his coat and wrapped it around my shoulders. It did nothing to lessen my shivering which was convulsive. He smiled at me.

"Sorry if I was brusque with you. I react like that to shock."

I could do nothing more than offer him a weak smile. He led the way down the rock and onto a very narrow path between the rock and the cliff. In less than ten minutes we were back near the sand dunes, right beside the lifebuoy stand. Kiernan hung up the buoy and gave it a little pat as if to reward it for dragging me through the water.

"You stay here," he said to me. "I'll drive my car over and take you home."

"No. No, I'll be fine. Just ring Mom for me, please."

"And give the poor woman the fright of her life? Stand here, Adele. Don't move until I come back."

I did as he told me. I had to. I could barely walk in my sodden shoes. My legs too were shaking. The horror of what had almost happened held me firmly anchored in place. I kept seeing the water in the channel swirling around. Even when I closed my eyes, the image was still there. I jumped when I heard a car horn hoot. I looked out towards the road leading to the dunes and saw Kieran's car there. My stubbornness gone, I was very glad to accept his offer of a lift home. He came down the path to meet me and took me by the elbow.

"We'll go by the doctor's surgery. You need to be checked over."

That I wouldn't hear of. I was shocked, yes, and very embarrassed about putting myself and Kieran in such danger but I didn't need medical care.

"I just need a warm bath and dry clothes. Take me home, please."

"If you're sure."

I was. I trudged on towards his car. Before I got in I stood and looked back at the rocks. Only the tops of the tallest ones were above the tide now. I shivered and clambered into his eco-friendly Prius. My nose was assailed with the unique scent of new car. I hated sitting on the seats with my wet clothes.

"I'm sorry," I muttered. "I'm ruining your car. And I'm sorry I put you to all this trouble. And danger. I'm sorry . . ."

"Stop apologising. Just don't do it again."

He started the car and fiddled with the heating controls. By the time we reached the prom glorious waves of heat were wafting around my frozen body.

"I hope you realise how very grateful I am to you," I said.

He took one hand off the steering wheel and waved it in a dismissive gesture. "Forget about it. I'm just glad I arrived along when I did."

"Yes, why did you? What were you doing down on the beach at this hour of the day? And such a miserable day too."

"I wasn't on the beach. I was on the prom when I saw someone scrambling over the low rocks on the East Beach. I knew that person would be trapped when they got to the high rocks. That's why I grabbed the buoy and brought it with me. You should have known that too."

I had known it. I had stored the knowledge in the back of my mind with all the other useless facts and figures that came my way. Except that my knowledge about East Beach had not been useless at all and forgetting that had almost cost me everything. I owed Kieran Mahon my life.

"I wish there was something I could do for you, Kieran. Something to show you how grateful I am."

"There is something you could help me with."

"Anything. Just tell me."

As soon as I had said "anything", I realised how rash that promise was but I was taken aback by what he actually wanted.

"Tell me about Jodi Wall. Why is she home? What happened?"

"I don't know what you want me to tell you. She's taking a year off. Just like me."

"Come on, Adele! Everyone knows that teachers suffer burnout. They need a break. But Jodi's different. She was flying up the corporate ladder and now suddenly she's taking time out – in Cairnsure of all places."

For an instant all my gratitude was forgotten. Kieran my rescuer was once again Kieran the smug man who had always, since we were children, managed to upset me. I saw then that my future relationship with him was going to be a very delicate balancing act. I tried to keep the sharpness from my tone but I don't think I succeeded very well.

"What's wrong with Cairnsure? You work here, don't you? How come you're here reporting on football matches and town planning instead of being some big-shot reporter in the city?"

He laughed. A hearty, fulsome laugh. I kept staring straight ahead but I knew if I looked I would see lights glinting in his eyes. I was relieved when we turned into my mother's house. I slipped off the coat he had lent me and grabbed the door handle. Before the car was fully stopped I had one leg out.

"This is so different to the night of your birthday party," Kieran said. "I had to practically drag you out of my car that night."

"I can't really remember but I'm sure you're

exaggerating. Thank you again, Kieran. I appreciate what you've done for me today. I'm very grateful."

"I'm taking you in home."

There was no point arguing. He was determined. He held me firmly by the arm and led me into the house. Mom was in the kitchen. In her dressing-gown. She was covered in virgin-blue fleece from chin to the tips of her furry slippers but judging by the shock on her face and the way she grabbed the lapels of her dressing-gown it was as if she had been caught in the nude.

"Oh, my God! I apologise for not being dressed, Kieran. What happened, Adele? What have you done to yourself?"

I felt a sharp stab of resentment. Mother's first assumption was that I had caused the catastrophe. That's what she always thought. "Your own fault, Adele." It just happened that this time she was right.

"I got stranded on rocks in the East Beach. Kieran rescued me and drove me home."

"You were walking the rocks in a storm?"

"Exactly what I thought, Mrs Burke," said Kieran, his voice thick with gloating.

"Get out of those wet clothes at once," Mom ordered. "Now Kieran, would you like a cup of tea?"

I gave up. Kieran had parked himself at our kitchen table and Mom was going into her hostess mode. I knew the good china was about to be brought out and the cake tin would be opened. I left them to it and went to soak in the bath.

* * *

Hair washed, dry jeans and sweater on, I made my way back to the kitchen. They both had their elbows on the table, Kieran Mahon and my mom, heads close together, voices low. Kieran looked up as I came in the door.

"Ah! How are you now?"

"Fine, thank you. I told you I just needed a warm bath."

"That will teach you not to climb the rocks when the tide is in," my mother added unhelpfully.

Kieran stood up and smiled at my mother. "Thanks for the tea and the chat, Mrs Burke. And I'll be delighted to take photos at your wedding. Just let me know the date. I'll hold a front page for you."

He winked at me. I was annoyed with myself but I couldn't help responding to his saucy smile.

"Kieran, I know you told me not to mention it again but thank you for rescuing me and apologies for putting you to all that trouble."

"Stay off the rocks, okay?"

I nodded agreement but he was already on his way out of the kitchen. Mom, apparently at ease now about being seen in her dressing-gown, walked to the front door with him. I had a sudden fear that she would tell him about our plans for a café. I had forgotten to warn her about secrecy. I listened as they chatted easily and thought no female, no matter what her age, was immune to Kieran Mahon's charm. My smile lasted until I heard Mom ask Kieran about his daughter. Daughter? Wife? Since when?

The front door closed and Mom came back into the kitchen.

"He has a daughter? Why didn't you tell me? I didn't know he was married!"

"He's not. He and his girlfriend, the little girl's mother, are no longer together. She's better off. He's a great man for the ladies."

"So why did you ask him to drive me home after the party?"

Mom sat down opposite me and stared until I felt uncomfortable. As if she was trying to see inside my head. Eventually she clasped her hands together and spoke.

"I saw the way he was looking at Jodi Wall. I knew you'd be safe with him."

For a treacherous moment I wondered how naïve my mother's incisive remarks really were. Could it be possible that she didn't know she was battering my already bruised ego? She smiled at me.

"He's a good catch, you know. He owns *Cairnsure Weekly* now, lock, stock and barrel! He has four staff there as well as himself."

So. Now I knew why he stayed here rather than work for a bigger publication. He would much rather be boss here rather than fight his way up the ladder elsewhere.

"Anyway," Mom added. "You're far too good for him."

I took that thought to bed with me and stayed there for the rest of the miserable day.

Chapter 10

Jodi was on the phone next morning before I had even got out of bed.

"I don't believe you're still in the sack, Adele Burke. Get up! We've loads of work to do today."

"It's only seven thirty," I muttered, squinting at the time display on my mobile.

"I'll collect Carla and we'll come around to yours. Is that okay? Our house is chaos and Carla's is like a crèche. Yours is the only quiet space. See you around nine."

I had no option but to agree. I heard Mom moving around. The phone must have woken her. I was glad. Her lie-in yesterday had worried me a little. She had never been a woman to take a rest. By the time I got to the kitchen she had a pot of porridge bubbling on the hob and ready to serve.

"Carla and Jodi are coming round. We're having a

meeting about Elliots'. That won't interfere with your plans, will it, Mom?"

"I'll be leaving early. I meant to tell you that Tom and myself are going to visit his eldest son in Kerry. We'll be staying a few days. Don't worry about your dinners. I cooked them all last night. They're in the freezer."

I nodded my thanks. We both knew I could look after myself so it would be useless labouring the point. Like Jodi, Sissy would do what she wanted to anyway. Yet again, I felt an empathy with my father. Life was so much more pleasant when my mother got her own way. Mom was chopping strawberries now, freshly picked from the garden, and sprinkling them over my porridge.

"That'll build you up for the day. How are you feeling? Any after-effects from your rock-climbing adventure yesterday?"

I was fine. So good that I had not thought about my almost-disaster until now. "I'm great, Mom, thanks."

"You were always healthy. Red meat, you know. It builds you up. His wife's a teacher too, Tom's son."

"Really?"

"Yes. About this Kirby person. You're not seeing him again, are you?"

She caught me off-guard. I had only been half-listening, waiting for her to go into minute detail about Tom and his family.

"Eoin Kirby? What about him?"

"I'd prefer you had nothing to do with him."

She sat down across from me and folded her hands on the table. I put my spoon down and stared at my mother.

The prissy pursed lips and cute head–tilt to one side were gone. Mask dropped, there was vulnerability in her slack mouth and glittering eyes. Were those tears I saw?

"Mom! What is it about the Kirbys? Tell me. Why are you so upset?"

Her hands clasped and unclasped. Her eyelids dropped to cover her eyes. She was hiding. From what? From me, from the past?

"Well, Mom?"

She looked up as a tear slowly trickled from the corner of one eye and began to track along the soft folds of her cheek. I dashed to her side, not caring now what the Kirby mystery was about. Gathering her small frame into my arms, I held her tight.

"I just bumped into Eoin Kirby once, Mom. You needn't worry. I'll probably never see him again."

"Please don't."

"If it means that much to you, I'll promise – but you should tell me why."

I felt her stiffen in my arms. She pulled away from me. When I looked at her face again, she had her mask back in place. Prissy, sedate. She stood up.

"I must go to the shops for a present to take with me to Kerry and I'll have to get your lunch ready before I go."

I was angry. Hurt. She was pushing me away, assigning me to my unending role of child who needed protecting.

"I'll get my own lunch, thank you. I'm quite capable of feeding myself. I'm capable of handling the truth too.

Why do the Kirbys upset you so much? For Christ's sake, whatever happened must have taken place over thirty years ago!"

"Adele! Watch your language, please! I'll have none of that kind of talk in my house."

Her house. Her rules. Her mystery.

"I'm sorry. I don't want us to fall out, Mom, but I wish you'd realise I'm thirty years old and no longer a child."

"You'll always be my child and I'll always protect you."

She turned then and walked out of the kitchen, leaving me with a bowl of strawberry-strewn porridge and a feeling that life in Cairnsure was about to get a lot more complicated.

* * *

Jodi came dashing in the front door at ten minutes to nine. She was laden down with files.

"Carla will be along soon," she announced, unloading everything onto the table. "She told me go ahead."

I could see why. Jodi was wired. Not the person you'd want around if you were trying to dress and feed your children.

"I can't believe how grown up Carla's baby sister is now. Vera's brilliant with the children. She's trained of course. They're all lined up at the table. A proper little Von Trapp family. Even Finn seems to be behaving for her."

"That's great," I said. "It should give Carla the break she badly needs. Did you notice how thin she's got?"

"Can't be too thin, Del."

I was about to argue the point about bony size zero when I realised Jodi wasn't listening to me anyway. She was looking out the kitchen window into my mother's fruit and vegetable garden.

"Oh! Strawberries! Do you think your mom would mind if I had a few?"

By the time we had picked and washed the fruit, Carla had arrived. She looked tired with dark circles underneath her eyes, emphasised even more by the tan which had deepened on the beach Sunday.

"How was Dublin?" I asked, leading her into the kitchen where Jodi was tucking into strawberries and cream.

"Awful."

After saying that one word, Carla plonked herself down at the table and began to stare into the distance. The cold feeling in my stomach which had started earlier dropped another few degrees. Carla was in trouble. Big trouble. I didn't need proof. I knew in my heart that Harry Selby was the root cause of her haggard appearance and distant manner. The pig!

"Did you buy much? Anything exciting?" Jodi asked. Carla didn't answer. "Carla? Come back to us. How did your shopping spree go?"

Carla shook her head as if to shake off an annoying insect and stared directly at Jodi.

"Who told you I was going shopping? Not me."

"Why else would you go to Dublin?"

"Maybe just to escape Cairnsure."

The tension between the two women was so intense that I could almost put out my hand and touch it. I laughed, as I usually do when I'm nervous.

"It works in reverse too," I volunteered. "I came to Cairnsure to escape Dublin."

Neither woman was too impressed by my contribution. They continued to stare silently at each other. I thought of telling them about my episode on the rocks yesterday but felt neither would be interested in their present moods. How were we going to run a business together if we couldn't even hold a meeting without tantrums and sulks? Annoyed, I put on the kettle for coffee. By the time the coffee was made Jodi had the table covered with papers.

"Stop fussing around and sit down, Del. We've a lot to discuss. Money first."

"I'm not fussing! I'm making coffee. I think we'll need it. We've a lot more than just money to sort out."

"We sure have," Jodi agreed. "We haven't even touched on décor, menus or any of the day-to-day practicalities of running a café yet. We –"

Jodi and I jumped as Carla thumped the table with her fist.

"Stop! This café notion has gone far enough. It's time we began to act our age instead of the teenagers we wished we still were."

We both turned to stare at Carla. It wasn't so much what she said. It was her tone. Disparaging, as if having a hare-brained idea to open a café was somehow disgusting.

"That's harsh, Carla," I said. "I must admit I'm having

doubts too but I think we should hear what Jodi has to say first. Maybe it is viable."

"Exactly," Jodi agreed. "I've put a lot of work into this business plan for the bank. I think you should at least have the manners to listen."

"Bank?" Carla asked. "I'm not borrowing any money."

"Me neither," I added.

"Great then," said Jodi. "So you both have fifty grand to invest? Because that's what we're going to need."

Carla stood up and pushed her chair back. "This is crazy. What were we thinking about? It would take months to get that stinking shop into shape and probably a few months more to fit it out with catering equipment. In the meantime we'd have to pay rent on the premises. None of us has the first clue about running a café or preparing food —"

"For heaven's sake! How difficult could coffee and baguettes be?" said Jodi. "There are grants. And courses. Health and safety courses and government departments who would advise us. I've been in contact with them and —"

Carla leaned across the table until she and Jodi were almost nose to nose.

"Think, Jodi! Best scenario, we have the café up and running in four or five months' time. What do we do then? Run it for six months until you go back to London and Adele to Dublin? If you think you're going to land me with it, you're making a big mistake."

"Maybe we could sell it then as a going concern," I suggested. "We might even make a profit."

"And what if I wasn't going to go back to London?" asked Jodi. "Suppose I said I intend staying at home?"

Carla and I stared at her in disbelief.

"Then I'd say you were lying," Carla answered and I nodded agreement. Jodi Wall had outgrown Cairnsure by the age of thirteen. She most certainly would not stay here now. In fact, I began to wonder why she was here at all and I remembered Kieran Mahon's curiosity about that too.

Carla sat down again. "I don't want to argue, girls. It's just that opening a café on the prom seemed like a good plan on a nice sunny day. And I'll agree that it's a great idea for the right person. Someone who knows catering, someone with training and a track record in the business. But for us, it's a non-starter as far as I'm concerned. Count me out."

Jodi threw down the pen she had been holding in her hand. It hit the table with a sharp rap and then rolled onto the floor. "Bloody great! I stay up all night getting this shit together, spend hours on the phone to one department after another and now you decide to pull out even before you've seen my proposals!"

"Maybe we all need a little more time to think it through," I suggested.

Carla glanced at her watch. "Sorry, I've got to go now. I'm taking Finn to the dentist for a check-up. And I don't need any more time to think. Good luck to both of you if you want to go ahead with the café but I won't be part of it."

She got up then and quickly left the kitchen. I walked

to the door with her, wanting to ask her what was wrong, wanting to tell her I was there if she needed to talk. But somehow I knew the words would be unwelcome. I saw it in the proud way her chin was lifted and in the way she avoided any eye contact.

Quite unexpectedly at the door, Carla turned and hugged me. She felt like a child in my arms, fragile and needy. "I'm so sorry, Del," she whispered and then she was gone.

I stood on the doorstep and watched until her four-wheel-drive had disappeared from view. My heart ached with pity for Carla while my gut burned with venom against Harry Selby. I knew with every instinct of my being that the desperation I had felt as Carla had clung to me was his fault. I had seen his ex-wife in his arms and it was a small step from there to imagine that she was back in his bed too. He had broken Carla's heart and I hated him for it. I took a deep breath before going back to face the inevitable tantrum from Jodi.

Jodi was pacing when I got back. Cooker to table, table to cooker, she was firing herself with manic energy around the confined space of our kitchen, all the time ranting.

"This is all Harry Selby's fault. Carla knows he's fucking around with his ex-wife and she can't handle it. Why should our business plan be thrown out just because he can't keep his pants on?"

While that was the conclusion I too had come to, I felt I should say something in the interest of balance.

"You don't know that, Jodi. It's not fair to say."

She gave a particularly violent twirl at the cooker and glared at me.

"I should have known you'd be on her side. Of course that's the problem! If everything in the Selby mansion was hunky dory, I bet Carla would still be all on for the café. Like she was Monday. What do you think happened? Did she catch her husband and the first Mrs Selby at it?"

That was exactly what I was thinking but I wasn't going to admit it. The sheer brazenness of Harry smooching with his ex-wife at the party made me wonder what he had got up to yesterday when he knew Carla was in Dublin. Unless he had gone there with her. Maybe he had. Jodi was right about one thing though. Carla's attitude towards the café had done a complete U-turn in one day.

"Adele! Will you answer me! Is Carla pissed off with us or is her tantrum just about Harry?"

"She's not having a tantrum. That's your area. Can't you see? She's frantic with worry. I'll be straight with you, Jodi. At this minute I'd don't give a flying shit about the café."

"Great! Two down, one to go! What do I do now? Go ahead on my own? It's too good a chance to let go just because Carla can't control her man and you haven't the brains or the courage to make a decision on your own!"

My worry about Carla was instantly replaced by a huge wave of anger against Jodi. White hot, quiet, rage.

"Who do you think you are, Jodi Wall?" I almost whispered. "How dare you insult me like that! I may have far more control over my life than you have."

"Ah! So Kieran Mahon has been putting ideas about me into your head."

"It might surprise you to know that I have plenty of ideas of my own! Besides, why would I be talking to Kieran Mahon about you anyway?"

"C'mon, Del! He told me about the way you threw yourself at him yesterday on the rocks. Pretending to be marooned so that he could come to your rescue."

I walked over to the kitchen door and held it open. "I think it would be better if you left now, Jodi. While we still have some shred of friendship left."

"Don't take your disappointment about Kieran Mahon out on me. I've no interest in him. He's not my type."

"I'm sure. Who is your type? Or is that another question you'd rather not answer?"

"Oh, fuck off, Adele! You and Carla too. I'll open the café myself. I would have been doing most of the work anyway."

In one swoop, Jodi gathered all her papers and tucked them under her arm. She swished past me, leaving a trail of perfume in her wake. An expensive brand, no doubt.

I stayed where I was and watched as she strode through the hall. The front door opened before she reached it. My mother, shopping bags in her arms, stood there, Tom Reagan just behind her.

"How are you, Jodi?" Mom asked. "Is your meeting over already?"

"It never really started, Mrs Burke."

With a nod to Tom, Jodi rushed past, leaving my

mother and her husband-to-be staring after her. In less time than seemed possible we heard Jodi rev the engine of her mother's Mini and then the spit of gravel against the bodywork as she sped down the driveway.

"What did you do, Adele?" Mom asked.

I took a deep breath before answering, reminding myself that the happy pair would very soon be heading off to Kerry. "I told her I'm not going to open a café with her. So did Carla."

"Proper order. 'Twas a daft idea. I didn't say anything to you before now because you know I never interfere."

Tom winked at me from behind her back. We smiled at each other and in that moment an understanding was born between us. It was a silent acknowledgement that we both loved Sissy Burke despite her foibles.

Convincing Mom that there was no need to cook my lunch before she left took another while. Then her suitcase had to be packed and her hair done to her own liking with the help of almost a full can of hairspray.

I walked out to her car with them, just to be sure that she would really go. "We still didn't get to have a proper chat," Tom said. "We must sit down together when I get back."

I had to shout my agreement to Tom because Mom switched on the engine and revved up with her usual enthusiasm. Just as I thought she was ready to go, she opened her window.

"Don't go climbing the rocks," she called.

I waved them off, then went back into the gloriously silent, empty house.

Chapter 11

Our garden seat was over twenty years old. Maybe twenty-two or three. I must have been about seven when my father had made it, crafting it so carefully and skilfully from teak. I had helped him, or at least he had allowed me to believe I was helping. I loved that seat. Over the years I had done some of my deepest thinking, made most of my life-changing decisions while sitting on its smooth, weathered slats. On that day, when Carla, Jodi and I had had our first ever serious row, the seat under the branches of the oak tree in our back garden was the only place for me to go.

It was a very hot day, any residual damp from yesterday's storm burned off in the heat of the sun which climbed higher in the sky as I sat and tried to come to terms with the very changed relationship between me and my best friends.

It had been foolish to expect a seamless return to the

type of friendship we had. The last time we had been together, really together as an inseparable unit, we had been teenagers. Maybe that was the problem. We had gone from being dependent on each other to being independent adults. We had certainly changed. But not enough. Carla remained secretive, Jodi arrogant and I continued to tag along. Characteristics we had accepted when we were young had suddenly become unacceptable flaws. Why couldn't Carla tell us what was wrong? I was worried about her. She knew that, yet she was making no effort to put my mind at rest. And when had Jodi's bitchy streak turned from amusing comment into vitriol? And I, who had always been happy just to belong – where was my willingness to tag along now, my gratitude at being allowed into the inner circle of the two most attractive girls in Cairnsure?

I closed my eyes and turned my face towards the sun. It filtered through the wide oak leaves and gently warmed my skin. Bees buzzed as they flew from lupin to nasturtium, feeding happily on the full-blown blooms.

I knew that of the three, I had changed the least. I still smarted from Jodi's comments. I squirmed as I imagined the conversation between her and Kieran Mahon. I felt hurt too by Carla's lack of trust. So, Harry Selby had done the dirt on her. Tough, especially since she had four children, but she had witnessed my humiliation when Pascal Ronayne had done the same to me. I had shared every grotty little detail with Jodi and Carla and I'll have to say their support was instrumental in helping me move on. Why wouldn't Carla let us do the same for her now? Did she think it inevitable that a man cheated on me but unbelievable someone should do it to her?

And then there was Jodi and her waspish tongue. Why did she repeat the lies Kieran Mahon had told her about my rescue off the rocks? It was as if she had to make herself feel better by making me feel worse. A cold sweat prickled my skin as I thought about what she had said. Kieran Mahon knew I didn't deliberately maroon myself on the rocks so that he could do his knight-in-shining-armour act. It was he who had followed me across the rocks. I hadn't even been aware he was in the vicinity. On the other hand, it was a good story for him to tell if he wanted to make himself look better in Jodi's eyes. Which he obviously did.

I was hurt and confused but certain of one thing. The café, fun and all as the idea had seemed, was a non-starter. Opening it up would take money and skill which we did not have. I loved cooking but as a hobby. We didn't have the time to devote to it either. In just a year I would be back teaching, Jodi would be succeeding and Carla would probably be pregnant again. Carla was right. We had behaved a bit like teenagers. We want a café so we'll open one and to hell with the details.

A flutter of wings close by made me start. I opened my eyes to see a magpie settling onto the bird-table. I never have got over my superstition about lone magpies. "One for sorrow." When the doorbell rang my superstition went into overdrive. It was the police calling to say my mother and Tom had had an accident! It must be. They were here to escort me to the hospital. And it was all the bloody black and white bird's fault! It was still perched on the bird-table, its feathers shot with steely blue glints. A beautiful creature. A harbinger of death and destruction.

I dashed into the house to open the front door. My feet stuck to the ground and my eyes widened in a mixture of disbelief and relief.

"You're not the police," I announced.

"No. I admit that. Are you hiding from them?"

I blushed. He must have thought I was crazy. At that moment I was. I was shaking like a leaf, torn between relief that my mother was not injured in a horrific car crash and dread that she would ever find out that Eoin Kirby had stood on her doorstep. What in the hell was he doing here?

"What do you want? How did you find me?"

"Seán Potter told me where to find Burke's cottage. It's your mother I've come to see. That's if Sissy Burke is your mother."

I nodded and blushed deeper. What had possessed me to think that he had come to see me? Why would he?

"My mother's out. Driving. I thought she'd had an accident. I was in the garden and I –"

Realising I was babbling, I stopped mid-sentence and looked down, not wanting to see the mockery which I knew must be on his face. He was wearing navy boating shoes. A lovely soft leather with raised stitching on them. Expensive. Huge. Must be size twelve.

"That's a pity. I'll call when she's back."

My head snapped up. "You mustn't! You can't!"

"Why ever not? I just want to pass on a message to her. I've no evil intentions against your mother, Adele."

"But she wouldn't want to see you. She doesn't even want me to –"

Again I stopped mid-sentence. This was descending into farce. I was thirty years old and afraid my mother would find out I had been talking to this man. But I had promised her. She had manipulated me into promising her. I looked at his confused expression and the puzzlement in his eyes. I made up my mind.

"Come in, Eoin. I was just about to have a cup of coffee. Would you like one?"

I stood aside and waited as he seemed to hesitate.

"Are you sure?" he asked. "You seem a bit jumpy. I could always call back when your mother's here."

"No! That's not a good idea. Come in and I'll try to explain. Or maybe you can tell me."

Like Sissy the Second, I opened the cake tin while the kettle was boiling and began to cut chunks of cake. The kitchen filled with the rich fruity aroma of my mother's Dundee. Eoin Kirby sat on the edge of his chair, watching me curiously as if he couldn't decide whether I was a threat to his safety or not. Desperate to shift his unwavering gaze away from me I said the first thing that came into my head.

"Why don't you go look at the garden? I'll bring coffee out."

He stood and walked towards me. His approach showed a certain foolhardiness. I had a knife in my hand.

"Would you prefer if I left? You seem to be very nervous."

"It's just that – that – well, my mother doesn't want me to speak to you."

He made a sound that was halfway between a snort and a laugh.

"That's ridiculous on several levels. I never met the woman in my life. This is my first time in Ireland. How could she have anything against me? Besides, how old are you? Why should she tell you who you can and can't talk to?"

"She didn't tell, she asked. She seems quite upset at any mention of your family. Do you have any idea why?"

"I think more clearly with coffee and cake. I'll give you a hand with this and then we'll try to figure out what your mother's problem is."

"Maybe she has a good reason."

"Maybe."

We were silent then as we gathered plates and mugs and took them out to the garden seat. Eoin lifted the picnic table closer to the seat and we settled down to enjoy Sissy's cake and the peace of the garden. I was beginning to relax. My mother was by now safely in another county and Eoin Kirby was a restful companion.

Eoin rubbed his hands together to rid them of crumbs and sat back with a satisfied sigh.

"I hope I can convince your mum to change her mind about me. I'd sure like to have a steady supply of her fruit cake."

"You said you had a message for her. I'll pass it on if you like."

"It's from my mother. She said I should call and say

hello to Sissy. Tell her that Irene Kirby sent her best wishes. It would seem now from what you say that your mother wouldn't want to hear that message."

"She's adamant, Eoin. She's very upset. Did your family and mine have a row?"

"All I know is that your father worked for my dad for a while. Dad never stopped talking about Ireland. He was always on and on about the old country. New Zealand was never home to him."

"Why did he not come back so?"

"He often spoke about coming back but Mum wouldn't hear of it."

"But you said he was thinking of retiring here."

For the first time, Eoin seemed uncomfortable. Less sure of himself. He shifted on the seat, then gazed up into the canopy of the leafy oak overhead. He sighed and lowered his head to look directly at me.

"The truth is I think Dad might have come back but probably Mum would not. She loves the life we have in New Zealand."

"You mean they would have separated? After all their years together?"

Eoin shrugged his shoulders. I saw sadness in his eyes and it struck a chord with me. Eoin was still mourning his dad as I was mine. Without thinking, I reached my hand out and laid it on his arm.

"So you came here to make the journey your father could not. Is that it? You're visiting his home-place for him."

"Something like that. It feels a bit like a homecoming

for me too. I know every stick and stone in Cairnsure from the stories he told me."

My hand still lay on his arm and suddenly I noticed how strong his biceps were, how warm his skin. I withdrew my hand.

"Maybe your father and mine had some disagreement about work. Mom doesn't forgive easily, especially if she thinks her family has been offended."

"On the other hand, Adele, I have to admit my mother can be . . . how should I put it . . . very assertive. She has made enemies from time to time. If there has been a row in the dim and distant past it's more likely to be between the two women than the men."

He glanced at his watch and stood up.

"I'd love to stay. This garden is so peaceful. I must go though. I've an appointment and I'm running late."

I wanted to ask him if the appointment was with Seán Potter and was he really interested in renting Elliots' shop but didn't want him to think I was nosey. I was. Why had he gone to view it in the first place? I stood up too and began to lead the way towards the front door.

"So have you decided what to do, Adele? Are you going to tell your mother I called?"

"I'll think about it," I answered as I held the front door open for him.

"Maybe we could discuss it again. Over dinner. We could talk about our mutual interest in the shop on the prom too. Are you busy tonight?"

"I'm sorry. I am. Some other time."

"Ah! The brush-off. Let me know if you change your mind. I'm staying at the Grand Hotel."

He smiled at me. A smile that bathed me in a warm glow. He walked away and I felt an urge to run down the path after him and tell him I had already changed my mind about the dinner date. An image of my mother's tear-filled eyes was enough to keep me on the doorstep. Sissy, underneath her frail exterior, was a strong woman. Whatever reason she had for asking me to stay away from Eoin Kirby must be serious. A crime. A betrayal. An unforgivable insult.

I went back into the garden and sat on the seat again but the sun seemed less bright and the colours of the flowers less intense. I fell into a restless sleep surrounded by the litter of the coffee and cake I had shared with Eoin Kirby.

* * *

When I woke I had a crick in my neck. I had somehow managed to sleep with my head tilted back and I was paying the price in tender muscles and sinews and whatever else was in there to hold my head on my shoulders. A quick shower sorted it out pretty well but I rubbed in some liniment just to be sure. Stinking of menthol and eucalyptus, I headed for town. The sales were on and I needed new trainers.

Cairnsure had three shoe shops. After visiting the first two, I almost gave up hope of finding anything. It was as if they had never heard of size eight in a woman's shoe. Annoyed and a bit embarrassed, I headed for the third and last shop, wondering if I would have been better off going the twenty miles to Cork city. As I passed the cinema, children were pouring out from the matinée. I was just thinking what a waste of a beautiful day for them when I noticed Brigitte and Carla's eldest son coming towards me. Finn's face was flushed and his eyes shining. He ran to my side.

"Adele! I've been to see Shrek! He's so ugly but he's very funny."

"Really? He's an ogre, isn't he? Aren't you scared of him?"

"Don't be so silly. He's just an animation."

Put in my place by the four-year-old, I stood and waited for Brigitte to reach us. I noticed that she seemed a lot more relaxed than I had ever seen her. Obviously sharing the work of looking after Carla's children was suiting her very well.

"You must be relieved to have Vera with you," I remarked.

"Yes, it's very good for all of us. I do the cooking now. I like that."

"Brigitte and me made Rice Krispie cakes," Finn piped up.

I looked down at the child and he was calm and smiling. He seemed content. A miracle.

"How did you get on with the dentist this morning?" I asked. "Were you brave?"

"I was at the dentist last week," he said and I read the annoyance on his face.

Finn thought I was a moron. So too, evidently, did his mother. I raised an eyebrow to Brigitte.

"It's true," she said. "He was with me all day."

So why had Carla said she was taking her son to the dentist this morning? Just to get out of the overheated café-or-no-café debate? Why couldn't she have just shagged off? She didn't have to lie to us.

"Will you call to see us while Mum and Dad are away?" Finn asked.

More eyebrow-raising in Brigitte's direction.

"They're gone away for a few days," she explained. "Alone. The two of them."

"They're going to bring back surprises for us," said Finn. "I asked for a computer but I don't think they were listening."

I smiled at the four-year-old who wanted a computer and had no doubt that he would be able to master it. The more I saw of Finn, the more I realised the child needed stimulation, not calming down.

"Tell you what, Finn. How about I bring my laptop to your house some day and we can practise on that until you get your own computer?"

"Cool! When?"

"How would tomorrow suit, Brigitte? How long will Carla and Harry be away?"

Brigitte shrugged her shoulders. So she didn't know either.

I smiled at Carla's eldest son. "Tomorrow after lunch, young man. Be ready for your first computer lesson."

Finn skipped happily away with Brigitte while I stood on the street looking after them. I was glad that Carla and Harry were together and I hoped that they could sort out their problems but I was furious that Carla had lied to me. Was that why she had apologised? Well, apology not accepted. She had broken our code of honour. There were many times, and rightly so, that we didn't tell each other the truth. Those were the silent times, things nobody wanted to share even with best friends. But we had never before blatantly lied. At that moment I felt the Carla, Jodi and Adele circle had been broken. Never again to be re-joined.

With my heavy heart and big feet, I headed to see what the last shoe shop in Cairnsure had to offer. It must have been the upset, the sale prices, or maybe it was just lack of concentration. Whatever the reason, I bought two pairs of trainers, a pair of high-heeled boots, purple Wellingtons with white spots and, even more inexplicably, blue, stiletto-heeled, sandals. I cleared the shop of its stock of size eights. Laden with bags, I struggled back to my car, anxious to get home now and change into my trainers. A good long walk was the only antidote to my blue mood.

As I pulled out of the car park onto the main street, a familiar car slowed down to let me out. Seán Potter the auctioneer waved me on. I raised my hand to acknowledge his unexpected politeness. My hand stayed airborne for what seemed like forever. Beside Seán Potter sat Eoin Kirby and from the back seat Jodi Wall grinned at me. What in the hell was going on? Had Jodi already found herself a partner for the café on the prom? Were she and Eoin Kirby about to go into business together? And why had he not mentioned Jodi to me?

Seán Potter tooted the horn of his car impatiently. I

dropped my hand, managed a half smile and shot back as I mistakenly put the car into reverse. They were gone by the time I had the gears sorted. How very apt, I thought. Adele Burke was going backwards while all around everyone else was full throttle ahead.

* * *

I had never liked Aunt Lily. The antipathy was mutual. She saw me as an unsuitable heir for her younger brother and I saw her as the intimidating maiden aunt she indeed was. I always felt I was a disappointment and an annoyance to her. Nevertheless, I would have to see her now. If anyone could solve the Kirby mystery for me it would be Aunt Lily. She had a memory like an elephant and a viper's tongue. In fact Aunt Lily was a menagerie from the top of her poodle-like perm to the soles of her elephantine feet which I unfortunately had inherited.

As soon as I got home from town, I took my new footwear out of the boxes and put them all away except the trainers with the pink laces. With precautionary plasters on my heels, me and my pink-laced trainers set out to walk the three miles to Aunt Lily's home at the foot of the hills. My father's parents used to farm sixty acres there. I barely remember my grandparents but I recall each and every fluffy lamb on their farm. One in particular. A little orphan that I had been allowed to feed from a baby's bottle. I christened her Mandy because at the time that was the name I would have liked to be called. Aunt Lily christened her Chops and that most probably was how poor Mandy ended up.

I glanced at my watch as I approached the farm. I had made good time. The house was set back from the narrow road, sheltered by a belt of rowan trees. It was a house of shadows. A collie barked as I approached the door. I waited for the net curtain on the window to twitch. I didn't have to wait long. Aunt Lily peered at me and then did that thing with her face like as if she had got a bad smell. She dropped the curtain and came to the door.

"So, I hear you're back from Dublin. Are you in trouble?"

"Hello, Aunt Lily. No, I'm just taking a little while off. How are you?"

"Why are you asking? It's not as if you care. I haven't heard from you since Christmas. I could be dead and buried for all you know."

"You look fine to me. Can I come in?"

She stood aside and allowed me to precede her into the kitchen which had changed very little since my father had been a child there. Apart for the addition of indoor plumbing and electricity everything was much as it had been. The dresser still groaned with willow-pattern ware and the grandfather clock still ticked in the silences.

"Where's your car?" Lily asked.

"I walked."

"I hope you're not at that silly dieting."

"No. I'm perfectly happy with my weight. I just want to be healthier."

"Your Uncle Noel was big-boned too. You take after him."

Noel, my father's elder brother had lived on the farm here with Lily and worked the land until he was sixty years old. Then one spring morning, he had gone out to the barn, slung a rope from the rafters and hung himself. I thought I understood. I would probably have done the same if I had to live with Aunt Lily. She was pottering around now, putting on the kettle and getting out cups and saucers. I waited for her to mention Tom Reagan and my mother's forthcoming wedding. She surely must have some caustic remarks to pass about that. When the silence dragged on, I guessed Mom hadn't told her yet. It was time for me to get going on what I had come here to do.

"Aunt Lily, I want to ask you something."

"Well, I didn't think you came just to see me."

"Do you remember a family named Kirby who lived in the town? The father was a builder. Dad worked for them for a while."

She put down the tea caddy and came to stand in front of me. The bad smell look was on her face again. "What do you want to know about them for? They left Cairnsure a long time ago. Went to New Zealand, I think. And good riddance to them."

"Why? Were they not nice people?"

"She was a nasty piece of goods. I don't want to talk about her."

What in the name of God had Eoin Kirby's mother done that was still unspeakable so many years later? So bad that not even Aunt Lily would say.

Lily had gone back to her tea-making. It was a major

production of scalding the pot, spooning in exactly the right amount of leaves and then brewing. No tea bags for Aunt Lily. I listened to the clink of spoon on saucer and wondered how I could get the information I needed. Maybe if I volunteered some she might loosen up a bit.

"The Kirbys' son is in town. Eoin. I met him."

Lily dropped one of the willow-pattern cups which had been in the Burke family for generations. It smashed on the tiled floor.

"He's here! In Cairnsure?"

"Yes. And he seems like a nice man."

Stooping down, Lily began to pick up the pieces of broken ware. I went over to help her and was reminded, when I noticed her hand shake, that she was now in her seventies.

"Sit down. I'll tidy this up and pour the tea," I ordered. "You just tell me about the Kirbys."

She allowed me to help her to her feet and lead her to a chair. I felt her body tremble and didn't know if it was from the weakness of old age or shock. But why should she be shocked?

"Did you talk to Sissy Roberts about the Kirbys?" she asked.

Never once, not in my hearing anyway, had Lily ever referred to my mother by anything other than her maiden name. Just my aunt's way of showing that she did not accept Mom as her sister-in-law. Ignoring that, I smiled at Lily in a sneaky effort to get her to talk about the Kirbys.

"I tried to talk to Mom about them. She's as reluctant as you to mention them."

"Have you no respect for your elders? If you're asked to stay quiet, it's for a good reason."

"Exactly. So I think I should be told the reason."

The rhythmic ticking of the clock marked the passing of time as I poured the tea. Aunt Lily had gone so quiet that I jumped when she shouted at me.

"Stop! Use the strainer unless you want tealeaves in your cup. For all your education, you know nothing."

She was back to herself again. I gave up then. Tea and two cream crackers later, I was ready for the walk back home, no wiser about the Kirbys than when I had arrived.

The road was lonely and the sky darkening. I walked quickly. In fact I bounced along on the cushioned soles of my new trainers. I think they must have had turbo boosts because there was still some remnant of light in the sky when I arrived at the front gate of our house.

There were several phone messages from Mom. "Don't forget" messages. Put the rubbish out for collection; your dinner's in the freezer; make sure the doors and windows are locked before you go to sleep. Just normal Mom stuff. When I checked my mobile which I had left at home there were three text messages from Jodi. Or rather the same message sent three times. **"Must talk. Urgent."**

I switched off my mobile and took the phone off the hook. My feet which had sped over country roads were burning now and my head felt muzzy. I had the very disturbing idea that I was living in a parallel universe. Everybody in my circle – Mom, Aunt Lily, Carla, Jodi

126

and even Eoin Kirby – seemed to know things I didn't. It was as if I was outside looking in while they lived their secret lives beyond my reach.

I climbed on a stool before getting into bed and took down Barry Bear from the top shelf of the wardrobe. He was tattered now, his ears frayed and his once-red paws a faded pink. I hugged him close to me as I curled up in bed. My childhood teddy bear felt like the only friend I had in the increasingly isolated space in which I found myself.

Chapter 12

The next morning was so full of sunshine, butterflies and summer scents that I decided to have my breakfast in the back garden. I planned my day as I ate. Pick gooseberries from the overladen bushes in the fruit garden, wash and clean fruit and jars, go for a walk to the beach, go to Carla's with laptop, come home and make gooseberry jam. I buried the uncomfortable thought that I was becoming Aunt Lily.

The fruit was picked, topped and tailed before I switched on the phones again. No word from Mom. She must be settling into her holiday. But my mobile had a new text from Jodi. I had forgotten about her. **"Will I come over this morning? Urgent."** I didn't want to see her. Was I now supposed to forget that she had insulted me and that when last I had seen her she had been leering from the back seat of Seán Potter's car? Annoyed, I texted back. **"Busy today. Call over tonight if suits you."**

I put new plasters on my heels, donned trainers, the

blue-laced ones this time, and headed for the beach. Shoulders back, chest forward, I strode past the new builds on our road and soon reached the prom. Seán Potter was just coming out of Elliots' shop. The keys still in his hand, he walked across to me.

"You'd want to take driving lessons, Miss Burke. You're a danger on the road."

I stared at him in surprise until I remembered my reversing incident.

"I've got a full licence and no penalty points."

"Didn't look like that to me yesterday. Anyway, it's the shop I wanted to talk to you about. Have you three ladies made up your minds? Are you going to up your bid?"

Now I was really surprised. Bid! What bid?

"I don't know what you're talking about, Mr Potter. I assume you must be referring to Elliots'. I most certainly have not put a bid on it. In fact I'm no longer interested in renting it."

His features took on an even more pinched look and his glasses slipped another notch down his nose.

"Gussie Elliot has changed his mind about renting. It's for sale now. Surely you know that since you and your partners offered to buy it?"

I glanced at the window then and saw the new *"For Sale"* sign Seán Potter had just put up. He was getting more agitated by the minute, tapping his foot as he sprayed words and spittle into my face.

"Sort things out with your business partners, please. I have a genuine client and I want to close the deal with him as soon as possible."

This mess had the imprint of Jodi Wall's arrogance all over it. She had gone too far this time.

"I've no interest in either renting or buying Elliots' shop, Mr Potter. Neither has Carla Selby."

"But Miss Wall said that she was speaking on your behalf. She —"

I knew it! Whatever Jodi's plan was, it had to be stopped here and now. I was outraged at her presumption.

"Nobody speaks on my behalf. I'm telling you now, I've no interest in either buying or renting Elliots'. Is that clear?"

Seán Potter decided against saying whatever else had been on his mind. His mouth snapped shut and he stormed off across the road, the keys jangling in his hand. In a perfectly synchronised movement, I stormed off in the other direction, murderous thoughts jangling in my head.

* * *

I went to Carla's house with the intention of calming Finn down. Things turned out to be the opposite way around.

I was still fuming, angry Jodi-Wall thoughts thumping around my head, when I arrived at the Selbys' with my laptop. I was met at the door by Vera, so like her older sister, yet different too. Vera had a glow about her. Her eyes shone and her skin was radiant. She was that rarest of creatures, a contented person.

"Come on in, Adele. Finn can't wait to start his computer lesson."

The four young Selbys scampered along the hall to greet me. Lisa had a pale-blue frilly dress on and matching

130

slides in her blonde curls. I scooped her up in one arm and, in the interests of fairness, picked Dave up in the other. I began to understand Carla's frustration as Liam tugged at my leg and Finn tried to catch my hand.

Smiling, Vera took the twins from me and stooped down to Liam. "Why don't we go and have a game of football? The twins need a big boy to teach them how to score goals."

Liam puffed up with pride. He threw Finn a smug grin and then ran out to the garden. I smiled at Vera, liking the wise person she had grown up to be.

"Brigitte's in the kitchen, cooking up a storm. You and Finn go into the study to do your computer stuff."

I had my suspicions about Finn before then. They were confirmed that day. The child had an almighty IQ. Without the appropriate tests to hand I could only guess, but I estimated his reading age at nine. By the end of the first computer lesson, I had exhausted my not very extensive computer skills.

"You'll be teaching me soon, Finn," I said.

"Do you think you could tell Mum and Dad I need a computer of my own?"

"I certainly will. Of course it will be up to them but I'll explain how good you are and how much better you would be with practice."

My little Einstein became a child again as he threw his arms around my neck and hugged me. I must admit that was the first time I warmed to him. His frustration was that he had a brain which appeared to have had a lot more life experience than his scant four years of life explained. At the risk of being told to mind my own business, I decided I would talk to Carla about getting Finn professionally assessed and providing him with the stimulation he needed to stave off tantrums.

"I'm going out to play with the others now. Thanks, Adele."

"Thank you, Finn," I said as he ran off and I realised I had enjoyed the past hour and a half more than any time since I had come home.

I followed the delicious aroma then and found Brigitte in the kitchen. She was humming to herself as she worked. Obviously in her element. She looked up when she saw me and smiled.

"Hi, Adele. Finn was so excited about learning computer. Did he do good?"

"Very well. He knows his way around the computer already. He must have a chip in his brain."

I was just about to ask Brigitte how soon she intended going back home when the whole troop of Selby children, led by Vera, came tumbling into the kitchen.

"Stay for dinner, Adele," cried Finn. "Please, please, please!"

Finn's plea was taken up the other children. I must say I was flattered. I looked at Vera.

"Do stay, Adele. Brigitte cooks enough to feed an army."

"In that case I'd love to stay, thank you," I answered just as I noticed Vera nodding her head in the direction of the door.

"I'm showing Adele the new plasma screen in the

lounge," she told the children. "You lot wash your hands before dinner and we'll be back in a few minutes."

I followed Vera into the lounge, wondering why she wanted to see me alone. She closed the door behind us as we stepped into the huge room which was approximately the same area as the entire ground floor of our cottage. When she turned to face me, a frown creased her forehead and there were shadows in her blue eyes.

"What's wrong with Carla? Do you know?"

I flopped onto the nearest leather upholstered settee. What was I supposed to say? That I suspected Harry Selby was having an affair with his ex-wife, that I believed Carla's marriage was pretty much on the rocks? I couldn't possibly say the words to Carla's sister when I had nothing much to go on other than instinct. Obviously Carla hadn't confided in her young sister either. Vera came to sit beside me, her eyes glittering with tears. I touched her hand. It was trembling.

"The honest answer, Vera, is that I don't know. Carla hasn't said anything to me."

A little smile crossed Vera's troubled face. "That's our Carl. She doesn't share, does she? I thought she might have told you and Jodi. Well, you anyway. She seems to be angry with Jodi for some reason. They had a row."

"Really! When?"

"The other morning when Jodi called to bring her to a meeting in your house."

So! The days for Adele, Jodi and Carla sharing were truly gone. They'd even had a row behind my back. I swallowed the little lump of hurt and turned my attention back to Vera.

"Do you think Carla might be pregnant again?" I asked. "That surely would upset her. She said she's not but maybe it's something she'd prefer keep quiet for a while."

"God no! Carla wouldn't allow herself to get pregnant if she didn't want to. You know she's a bit of a control freak."

I nodded agreement. Nothing much happened in Carla's life unless she had planned it. She had always been the same.

"She's very thin, did you notice?" Vera asked. "To be honest, I had been worried for a while that she was bulimic or anorexic so I watched her like a hawk."

This was a possibility, wasn't it? Carla, devastated by Harry's treachery, deciding to control her weight if not her husband.

"Anyway," Vera continued, "I'm sure now that she's not gone overboard on dieting or laxatives or anything like that. But there's definitely something wrong. It's as if – as if . . ."

Since Vera didn't seem to be able to put words to her fears, I spoke them for her.

"Could it be that things are difficult between herself and Harry?"

Vera surprised me by throwing back her head and laughing. "God, Adele! Whatever else I suspect, it's not that! Those two idolise each other. I'll be honest, I envy them. They're so in love."

I teetered on the brink of interfering. Should I tell Vera about my suspicions of Harry and his ex-wife or should I mind my own business? Adoring husbands don't go around cuddling other women in sports cars, accompanying them to conferences and opening up private clinics with them. Especially ex-wives. Had he done the same to Ruth when he decided to swap her for Carla? Vera saved me the trouble of having to make a decision. She jumped up from the couch.

"We'd better get back to the gang. And thanks for spending the afternoon with Finn. He really needs grown-up time."

I followed Carla's young sister back to the kitchen and enjoyed the chicken dinner Brigitte had cooked. I laughed and played with the children but all the while a dull ache sat in my throat and refused to shift. Things got even worse when I went home and saw the magpie back on his bird-table perch again. I shooed him away but couldn't shake the feeling that his bad karma remained behind.

* * *

Mom rang as I was in the middle of making my jam. I made a big mistake. I told her what I was up to. I spent the next three quarters of an hour with the phone cradled between my ear and shoulder, trying to measure, pour, stir and listen to her instructions on proper jam-making at the same time. I reminded her several times that Tom's son might not like her hijacking his phone line but she turned her deaf ear to that particular comment. There was no getting away from her until the last pot was sitting on the counter full of warm jam and sealed with a wax disk and cellophane cover.

"Now, Mom, maybe you should tell me how you're

getting on in Kerry, unless of course you want to instruct me on washing up the pots and pans here?"

"No need to be sarcastic, Adele. I'm only trying to help. I'm having a grand time."

Ouch! I knew what "grand" meant in Sissy-speak. It was her way of saying that her holiday was bearable, just about. Like when I wore a top or dress she considered too revealing, or got my hair cut in a way she didn't like, she would tell me I looked "grand". "Lovely" was a step up and "wonderful" was at the top of my mother's likeability scale.

"Are you feeling all right, Mom?"

"It's very cold here near the mountains and anyway I'm worried in case you meet that person again. You promised me. Remember?"

She could only be talking about Eoin Kirby. Hot and sticky from my steamy bout of fruit-boiling, worried about Carla and angry with Jodi, I felt my temper rise. When was this woman going to realise I was thirty years of age and could talk to whomever I chose? When was she going to trust me enough to tell me what her Kirby secret was? I closed my eyes and counted slowly to five.

"Adele? Are you there? What's going on?"

"Yes, Mom, I'm here. And that's my question too. What's going on? I asked Aunt Lily about the Kirbys and she wouldn't tell me either."

"Sweet Mother of God! What did you go asking her for? Why did you let her know our business?"

"Your business. Remember? I don't know what's so bad about the Kirbys because you haven't told me."

"You didn't say anything to that old biddy about me and Tom getting married, did you?"

"No. I guessed early on that you had kept your husband-to-be secret too."

I heard a sniffle and immediately my temper cooled. Was she crying? I thought of her standing in a strange hallway, her small frame hunched over the phone and tears running down her soft face. I felt like a heel.

"Mom, I promise you I won't be seeing Eoin Kirby. For all I know he could already be gone back to New Zealand. Now does that make you happier?"

"You're a good girl, Adele. I know you wouldn't lie to me. And yes, I'm happier now. We'll have a chat about it when I get home. Be sure to dry the big saucepan properly before you put it back in the press."

It was only when I put down the phone that I realised I could have been duped. Again. Had she really been crying? At least she had said we would talk about the Kirby saga when she got back.

Just to assert myself, I only half-dried the big saucepan.

* * *

I had barely sat down with my book when the doorbell rang. The contented mood which had descended on me after my jam-making splurge disappeared as I saw Jodi Wall on the doorstep.

"We must talk, Del."

"Bloody sure we must," I answered hotly. "What in the hell did you mean by telling Seán Potter I wanted to buy Elliots' shop? You don't speak for me. Nobody does."

She hung her head and her shiny hair fell like a satin curtain in front of her face. She had a sleeveless top on and I noticed goose bumps on her arms.

"Come in," I said begrudgingly and led the way into the kitchen. I waited for her to sniff the freshly made jam and order me to put on the kettle. Jodi always had an amazing appetite for one so slim. I used to convince myself she had worms until finally admitting she was blessed with a five-star metabolism.

"Coffee?"

"Strong and black, please."

She sat in silence as I pottered around with mugs and spoons. Every time I glanced at her she seemed to be shivering. When I looked closer there were little beads of sweat on her forehead. So! She had flu from going around half-dressed. Good enough for her. My guilt complex kicked in again as I put a mug of coffee in front of her and noticed how she seemed to be shrivelling into herself.

"Well, Jodi. I'm still waiting for an explanation. What did you say to that creep Potter? What made him think we're going to buy Elliots'? Not even rent, mind you. Buy."

She looked up at me. Her eyes were huge in her face. Pleading eyes.

"We can't let it go, Del. Don't you see? It's a fantastic opportunity. We should grab the building and that big back garden. It's going for a song now. It'll be worth three times more once the Marina development is up and running."

"Three times more than what?"

"Eoin Kirby has offered four hundred and eighty thousand euro."

I almost spilled my coffee. Nearly half a million euro for Elliots' old wreck of a shop. Eoin Kirby must be a very wealthy man.

"Are you crazy, Jodi? Jesus! It was daft enough when we were thinking of renting, but this! How could you raise that kind of money? Especially now that the banks are so stingy with credit."

"Not me. Not just me. The building itself would be collateral and I was thinking you own an apartment in Dublin and Carla has a half share in that mansion she lives in."

The cheeky little bitch! I almost asked her to leave then but hesitated. I still wasn't sure that she hadn't committed me to something I might have to honour against my will. Her shivering was making me even more annoyed. I went into my bedroom, got out my blue woolly favourite cosy cardi and handed it to her. She slipped it on and immediately looked like a little girl lost in its folds. I should have made myself feel better by giving her the pink cardigan I had shrunk in the wash.

"I told Seán Potter neither Carla nor I are interested in Elliots' and that you don't speak on our behalf. Confirm that to him, please. You make your own decision about The Cabin but leave me out of it. And Carla too. Understand?"

When she reached out to pick up her mug, her hand was shaking.

"Do you want some aspirin? Or maybe a brandy to heat you up?"

She shook her head. "I can't. I'm driving to Cork."

I glanced at the clock. It was ten thirty. "Now? So late? Are you going clubbing?"

"I'm meeting someone. A friend from London."

"That's another thing. I didn't hear you volunteer your own apartment as collateral. It's all right to play money games with my home and Carla's but not yours."

"I sold it. Got an offer I couldn't refuse."

I thought I had misheard. The apartment she prattled on about endlessly – and with good reason. It was *Ideal Homes* perfect. All glass frontage onto the river and so lofty that it came with an echo all of its own.

"Your London apartment? You told me you had it rented out."

"I had. Sort of."

"How could you have it 'sort of' rented, for heaven's sake! You lied to me. Anyway why do you need a partner for Elliots' with all that money in your back pocket?"

"I had to clear my mortgage, didn't I? How much do you think I have left after that?"

Wrapping the cardigan tightly about her, she got up and began to pace the kitchen. I don't think she was aware of me sitting there.

"Jodi! Sit down for feic's sake! You're making me dizzy watching you."

Her back to the wall she slid down along it like a raindrop on a windowpane, landing in a puddle on the floor. Her head dropped onto her knees and she began to cry. Jumping up, I ran to her and tried to get my arms around her but she was curled up into a defensive ball.

"Jodi! Ah, Jode! Tell me what's wrong. It can't be that bad. We'll sort it out."

She looked up then, her white face streaked with tears and dissolving make-up, mucousy tracks dribbling from her nose to her mouth. I flopped onto the floor beside her. I could have fought the brazen Jodi, the one with perfect hair and figure and a smart one-liner to answer everything. But looking at this vulnerable bundle of tear-stained blue cardigan robbed me of fight. I felt tears well in my own eyes. I hauled myself up and got a box of tissues, then helped her to her feet and over to a chair. I sat down opposite her.

"Talk. And tell the truth. I'm listening."

She lifted her head. My breath caught in my throat when I saw her eyes burn dark over the wad of tissues she held up to her face. For an instant, Jodi Wall looked like a madwoman.

"You and Carla can't mind your own business, can you? You were both always jealous of me and now you're gloating."

"What in the fuck are you talking about?"

"I know Carla told you. You two were always closer to each other than to me."

"I heard you and Carla had a row but she said nothing to me about you. Not behind your back anyway. She's not like that."

"How do you know what she's like? She keeps her business pretty much to herself, doesn't she?"

True. Carla was secretive but she hadn't a gloating bone in her body. And she most certainly had never been jealous of Jodi. She had no reason to be. That was my territory. Jodi was trying to sidetrack me and she had nearly succeeded.

"So are you going to tell me what you and Carla know and I obviously don't?"

Jodi stood and I thought she was going to start her pacing again until I saw her come to stand in front of me. She was shaking with temper, jagged flashes which I could only think of as hatred sparking in her eyes.

"You smug bitch! Miss Teacher-butter-wouldn't-melt-in-her-mouth! I know you, Adele Burke. I know all your faults and weaknesses. Don't you dare criticise me!"

The person screaming at me looked a bit like Jodi Wall, even sounded like her but she was not the Jodi I had known since childhood. In fact, I was afraid of this raving woman.

It was with relief I saw her sag and heard her anger dissipate with a sharp hiss. Like a rag doll, she folded onto a kitchen chair and arms on table, head on hands, began to cry again, all the while muttering between sobs.

Just as I thought it would be safe to speak to her, she suddenly leapt from her chair. "Shit! Look at the time. I must be in Cork for eleven thirty. Mind if I hang onto your cardi? It's nice and warm."

"Sit down, Jodi. You're obviously very upset. You're not fit to drive."

Already as far as the kitchen door, she stopped and turned towards me. Her tear-stained face softened and I saw a flash of the Jodi I thought had gone for ever. "Thanks, Del. And I'm so, so sorry for the things I said to you. I'm not myself. I'm – I'm worn out from all the stress of London living. I need home right now."

My head was beginning to spin trying to keep up with her mood swings. "Well, stay in Ireland then. You'll easily get work as an accountant."

"I don't want to. Accounting's too boring. That's why the café's so important to me. It would give me a reason to stay. A challenge. It must happen. I'm sorry for making the offer to buy without your permission or Carla's. I'll square that with Seán Potter. I can't let the idea go though. I'm working on Eoin Kirby. He might give me a partnership. A job at the very least."

She turned then and went. My mind was so shocked the only thing to register was that my blue cardi, that shabby, woolly thing worn only in the privacy of home, somehow looked sexy on Jodi Wall.

I warmed some milk and sipped it slowly, went into the garden and inhaled heady night-scented stock, watched a TV programme on tornados and tried to read a chapter of my book. Then, tired and confused, I went to bed and followed the curving trail of my thoughts. As they unwound, they led me down many paths I would rather not have travelled. Was Jodi Wall having a nervous breakdown? Had the cost of her high-flying lifestyle been her mental health? Whatever the reason, I was certain of one thing. Jodi was not behaving rationally. I would talk to Carla about it except that she too seemed so very preoccupied and anyway she was away with

Harry. To add to the problems, Mom would not tell me about the Kirbys.

By the time I fell into a troubled sleep, I was longing for the simplicity and solitude of my shoebox apartment in Dublin.

Chapter 13

I was woken by a loud knock on the front door the following morning. Squinting at my watch I saw it was ten thirty. Shit! The day was half over. The knock sounded again, louder and more impatient this time. Maybe someone to read the electricity meter or the postman with a parcel. I tumbled out of bed, grabbed my dressing-gown and hurried through the hall. I was just about to open the door when the knock sounded again, sharp in my ears. I cursed softly and flung the door open.

Kieran Mahon was standing there, a newspaper in his hand and a very smug grin on his face. For a moment I forgot that this man had saved my life.

"Do you always thump on doors like that?" I asked crossly.

"Only when I'm trying to wake the dead."

"What do you want?"

"A smile would be nice. And maybe a cup of tea."

He handed me the newspaper he was holding.

"Hot off the presses, Adele. You're front-page news. The photos of the thirtieth party are in there too."

I took the copy of *Cairnsure Weekly* from him and was hit right between the eyes by the banner headline on page one. "Near Tragedy Averted." I didn't have to read the text to know it was an article about my escapade on the East Beach. Colour and temper rising in tandem, I scanned through the article, looking for my name.

"Don't worry. I didn't say you were the rock climber or that I was the rescuer. No names."

"And did you print the same lies you told Jodi Wall?"

"I don't know what you're talking about. Why should I lie about it?"

"I didn't deliberately maroon myself on the rocks so that you could rescue me. How dare you say that!"

I had expected a smart reply, a sardonic grin, even a mocking denial. Kieran just stood there, silent, a worried frown on his forehead.

"Can I come in, Adele? We need to talk."

I hesitated. He had indeed rescued me so at the very least I owed him courtesy. But I needed an apology for the story he had told Jodi and maybe the rest of the town too. "Apologise first and then we'll see."

"For feic's sake, Adele! I've nothing to apologise for. We'll have to talk. But, all right, I'll say I'm sorry if that's what it takes."

I was stuck then. I had got an apology of sorts. I stood aside to let him in and quickly ran my fingers through my hair as I followed him into the kitchen. I filled the kettle and read the article as I waited for the water to boil. I shivered a bit when I learned that eleven people had drowned off those very same rocks in the past twenty years. The article called for a warning sign to be erected and lifebuoys to be installed on the East Beach. At least he told the truth in print. The "thirty-year-old woman" had been unaware of the danger and if "the man with local knowledge" had not come to her rescue there could have been a tragedy. The incident should serve as a warning. Putting the paper down, I turned to look at him.

"Did you write that?"

He nodded. I was even more furious now.

"How come you wrote the truth in the paper but told Jodi Wall a heap of lies just to make me look pathetic?"

"You have that the wrong way around, Adele. Ask yourself why Jodi told you lies."

I didn't like this. But I felt that Kieran was telling the truth. He was letting me know that Jodi had lied to me. Why not? So had Carla. It was hurtful to realise that neither had any respect for me. At the same time it was a consolation to know that Kieran hadn't been making a mockery of me. Ironic that Jodi, the woman I considered to be one of my best friends, had been the one to do that. I busied myself cutting slices of Mom's soda bread which I had defrosted last night.

"Do you like gooseberry jam?"

Kieran glanced at my jam pots lined up like little soldiers on the counter and smiled at me. "Been a busy girl, I see."

"I have. Want some?"

We both tucked in and I was relieved to find that my gooseberry jam was every bit as good as Sissy's. Halfway through my first slice I realised that I had never before been in Kieran Mahon's company for so long without hearing him pass a smart comment. He was so quiet I would have called him withdrawn if I had not known better. I felt uncomfortable.

"I didn't realise you had a daughter," I blurted out. "How old is she?"

He put his cup down and I could see light glint in those beautiful green eyes.

"Amy is four now and a right little madam. She looks like her mother but personality-wise she takes after me. She has a nose for a story already."

"Does she . . . Are you and . . ."

"Her mother has custody but I get to see Amy most weekends and some weekdays if Norma is away."

Norma? That must be Norma Higgins. Solicitor. Daughter and granddaughter of solicitors. I had known Kieran Mahon and Norma Higgins had been an item some time ago. In fact they had been much more than that without my knowledge. They were parents to this little girl.

"So you and Norma Higgins . . . ?" God! I was making such a mess of this. Prying into his private life. Being an interfering old biddy. "I'm sorry," I muttered. "I don't mean to be nosey."

"Don't be silly. Of course you can ask me questions. We go back a long way, don't we? Norma and I tried to make a go of it for Amy's sake. I'm afraid her career and my lack of commitment to monogamy made things difficult. We had a civilised parting by mutual consent. Now it's my turn to ask questions. Do you have any children? Ex-husband? A partner?"

"No, I don't have any children. Yes, I was living with someone for a year or so but that too ended by mutual consent."

I had the grace to blush as I lied about how mutual and consensual my parting from Pascal Ronayne had been. I don't think Kieran noticed. His head was bowed and he was fiddling with a spoon, twirling it round and round and making a very irritating scrapey sound on the table. When he looked up, he seemed older, graver. Not a sneer in sight.

"I asked you why Jodi Wall was back here. Are you going to tell me?"

"Speak to her."

"I did. She told me some cock-and-bull story about opening up a café with you and Carla Selby."

"That's not cock and bull. At least it wasn't. We had been tossing the idea around. Looking at renting The Cabin. But that's hit on the head now. At least for Carla and me, it is. Jodi doesn't seem to be able to let the idea go."

"Gussie Elliot told me a New Zealander wants to buy the old shop. And that somebody else put in a bid too. Gussie's drooling at the thought of all the money he's going to have. Why would you have been interested in starting a business here if you're going back to your job in a year's time?"

"Just an impulsive, ill-thought-out idea. It was fun while it lasted."

Kieran leaned across the table towards me, his eyes boring into mine. I felt speared to my chair by the clear, green gaze.

"How do you think Jodi is? Have you noticed how much she's changed?"

I was tempted for an instant to tell him what a bitch Jodi Wall was. How she had lied and insulted me and even frightened me with her irrational behaviour. Something about Kieran's expression stopped me. He seemed vulnerable, an anxious frown on his forehead as he waited for my answer.

"I think she seems upset. Edgy. Even a bit desperate. To be honest, I feel I don't know her any more."

He stood and walked to the window overlooking the garden, his back to me. The kitchen grew darker with his bulk blocking daylight. He spoke so softly I had to strain to hear him.

"I contacted Jodi's workplace in London. They told me she left there six months ago."

"What! Are you sure? She never said . . ."

I stopped myself there. Of course she hadn't said. Everything she had told me was untrue, from renting her apartment to taking a year's break from her job. I was angry with her and with myself but mostly with Kieran.

"You had no right to contact her employers! What did you do that for? Another story for your rag of a paper?"

"I had every right. I care about Jodi. I care what

150

happens to her. Can't you see she's in trouble? She needs her friends now."

I remembered her tear-stained face last night. Her waif-like appearance as she had gone out the door smothered in my blue cardi.

"So what if she changed jobs? That doesn't mean she's in trouble, does it?"

"For heaven's sake, Adele! She didn't change jobs. She was fired."

Kieran turned around slowly to face me. I noticed the way his shoulders were hunched and his forehead puckered in a frown. A little shiver went down my spine as I waited for him to continue.

"She embezzled money from client accounts. The charges were dropped when she paid the money back but she had to sell her apartment to cover her debts."

Jodi Wall, embezzlement and criminal charges did not to belong in the same sentence. I felt like hitting Kieran Mahon, slapping the mouth that dared speak such treachery. Such slander. Yet I sat where I was, staring silently at the pale-faced man in front of me and letting two facts trickle slowly and painfully into my consciousness. One, that Kieran Mahon cared deeply about Jodi and two, that he spoke the truth.

"So what did she do when she . . . when she was fired? You said that was six months ago."

"She worked as a waitress for a while."

Ah! So that's where she got the idea for opening a café. I could well imagine Jodi sulkily serving coffee and rolls and planning on how soon she could take over the whole business. But not in London, of course. Not with her tarnished reputation. Kieran had come to sit opposite me now and up close I could see the pain in his eyes.

"I know journalists have their methods, Kieran, but how did you get all this information from her employers? Her ex-employers."

"I had met her colleagues several times when I was over to visit Jodi."

"I didn't know. I never guessed. . ."

"It wasn't like you think. I just dropped by to see her any time I was in London on business."

He didn't fool me. I knew he had gone just to see her and found a convenient excuse. I felt a base pleasure at the thought of Kieran Mahon pining after her. I was ashamed but not enough to dim the satisfaction. Now he knew how much it hurt to want someone who didn't care. Justice!

"She obviously doesn't want anybody to know, so I'm trusting you not to say anything, Adele. I just want you to be there for her if she needs you."

"Of course. But she's impossible to talk to now. She was here last night and she made it clear that I'm not one of her favourite people. In fact, she was downright scary. I was glad when she went to meet her friend from London."

"From London?"

"Yes. She went to Cork. It was late though. She must have been going to a club."

Kieran stood then and pushed his chair back under the table. I looked at his cold tea and unfinished bread and jam.

"Will I make another cup of tea for you before you go?"

"No. I must be off. There's more to the Jodi story but it's her business and she'll tell you if she wants to. I'm just asking that you'll be there for her. No matter what she says now, her friendship with you and Carla Selby is very important to her."

I nodded but didn't answer. I didn't see him to the door either. I waited until I heard the front door close and then I opened the *Cairnsure Weekly* to page 3 and spread the pages out on the table. I spent a long time staring at the picture of Jodi, Carla and me, our hands joined on the handle of the knife which was slicing into our birthday cake. We were laughing, Carla and Jodi either side of me, the three of us so close together, so happy. I thought of the adage that every picture tells a story and I knew that it did not apply to this picture. We all looked content, successful, in control of our lives. I eventually folded the paper and put it on the top shelf of the wardrobe where Barry Bear used to live until I had reinstated him in my bed. I knew I wouldn't look at the photo again for a long time. Not until I had figured out exactly what was behind those smiling faces.

I put on my trainers with the pink laces and pounded the roads until my mind was blank and my legs aching.

* * *

There was a strange car parked on our driveway when I got home. Eoin Kirby was standing on the doorstep. I was too exhausted to be angry but I was certainly annoyed.

Why was he here when I had made it clear that my mother didn't want him near her house? Maybe I hadn't made it clear enough. As I approached him I was ready to attack. That was until he smiled. He really had the nicest smile in which I had ever had the privilege to bask. It was impossible not to respond.

"Good morning, Adele. I was just beginning to think you had gone off with your mother."

"Lucky for you she's not here. I warned you."

"How else am I supposed to contact you? You forgot to give me your phone number."

"How careless of me. I suppose you'd better come in."

"Any fruit cake left?"

I grinned. A discerning man. Mom's Dundee cake was superb. I got the key from my sweatsuit pocket and opened the door, noticing the scent of his aftershave as he stood beside me. It was very subtle. Musky.

I went through the routine of coffee making and cake cutting while Eoin gathered mugs and plates. By tacit agreement we had our coffee in the garden again. Finally, picnic table in place we sat under the oak tree. I felt the quiet of the garden begin to work its magic. The sharp edges of my shock about Jodi's alleged criminal activities blurred. I felt safe enough to let my mind drift. For some reason I began to think about the day we three, Carla, Jodi and I, had decided to put blonde streaks in our hair. We must have been around fourteen at the time. We had spent hours in Carla's house darting between bathroom and bedroom, applying peroxide and waiting with bated breath for our highlights to develop. We got it very wrong. It had taken a long time for the frizzy straw-coloured streaks to grow out. Mom had been furious.

"I need to talk to you about the Elliot property."

I jumped when Eoin spoke. Dragging my mind back to the here and now I turned to look at him. That was the first time I really saw Eoin Kirby. I noticed his dark brown eyes, his long lashes, the stubble shadow on his chin, a tiny scar on the right-hand side of his forehead just at the hairline. An open face: kind, patient, strong.

"I've made an offer on Elliots'," he said. "I know you and your friends did too. Not much sense, I reckon, in us getting into a bidding war. I was talking to your friend, Jodi. She told me about your café plans."

Jesus! Jodi was certainly making waves. I made up my mind to talk to Carla as soon as she got back. Carla was stressed, yes, but Jodi Wall was a danger to herself and to us too. How could I tell this stranger that Jodi had told him lies without completely betraying the friendship I had shared with her since childhood?

"What plans do you have for Elliots' shop?" I asked.

"Initially, just an investment. Part of the back garden belonged to the house where my parents once lived. I suppose you could say my interest is nostalgic too."

"So, you're saying you just intend to let it sit there?"

"For the time being. I have some big decisions to make."

I made a big decision of my own then. I couldn't leave him under the impression that we were serious contenders for the old shop.

"We've withdrawn our offer on Elliots'," I said. "Jodi and I are on career breaks for a year. It would be impossible for us to get the café up and running in that length of time. And Carla has her hands full with her children. So the field is clear for you to go ahead."

"Really? That's not the impression I got from Jodi."

"Check with Seán Potter if you like. Carla and I have withdrawn. I doubt if Jodi is in a position to go it alone. When were you talking to her?"

"Last night. In Cork. I was visiting some relations of my father's. I bumped into Jodi as we were leaving the pub where they brought me to have a drink. I must say I was surprised by her."

"Surprised. Why?"

Eoin seemed to think carefully before answering. "Let's say she seemed a little the worse for wear. I offered to drive her back to Cairnsure but she said she was meeting someone."

"Do you mean she was drunk?"

"I don't think so but she wasn't herself. I don't know her, of course, but she had given me the impression that she's a very capable woman. Glamorous too."

"And you're saying she was neither last night?"

"Well, she was wrapped up in a dowdy woollen thing and she seemed excessively anxious. So yes, I'd say she was neither capable nor glamorous."

I disappointed myself again. My first reaction was to be defensive about my precious blue cardi when of course it should have been concern for my friend. Thankfully, my phone rang before I had a chance to expose my shallowness. I excused myself and went into the house, following the elephant-roar ring-tone I was always meaning to change until I at last found my phone hiding underneath a tea towel. It was Kieran Mahon and he sounded frantic.

"Have you heard from Jodi yet?" he asked without any preamble.

"No. I haven't been talking to her since last night."

"She didn't come home. I've been to her house looking for her. Her parents haven't seen her since yesterday morning. You said she went to Cork, didn't you?"

"Yes. As a matter of fact Eoin Kirby is here, the New Zealander. He met her in Cork last night."

"Was she all right? Did she say where she was going? Was she with someone?"

"Hey! Hold on, Kieran. Jodi is thirty years old and you're carrying on as if . . ."

"Shut up and just listen. Jodi could be in danger. Tell me anything you know about where she went and who she was with."

"Don't talk to me like that! You're such a drama queen! Calm down. She only went to town to meet a friend."

"Adele, would you open your eyes. Wake up, girl! I wasn't going to tell you but I'll have to because you're being so dense. Jodi could be in danger because I'm pretty sure she went to meet a drug dealer. Now, are you going to tell me what you know?"

Snippets of a Drugs Awareness Conference I had attended last year began to filter through my shock.

Warning signs. Personality change, money problems, mood swings. Jesus! I should have known. Me of all people. A teacher, someone charged with the welfare of young people. I would have seen the signs in a student. I know I would. But in Jodi, never.

"I assume you've tried ringing her," I said to Kieran because I didn't know what else to say. Maybe I should have screamed and shouted at him, called him a liar and a fool, defended Jodi's reputation against such a slur, but deep down I knew he had spoken the truth and that I was the fool not to have seen it before now.

"It's switched off. I'm going to ring around the hospitals in case . . . in case she had an accident. She was driving her mother's car. That yellow Mini."

An image of the types of accident Jodi could have had if she was in Cork trying to score a hit made my legs weak. I flopped onto the hard kitchen chair, landed with a heavy thump on my backside and yelped in pain. Eoin Kirby came rushing in, fussing, offering to help. I shook him off, too concerned about Jodi to be embarrassed.

"What was that scream?" Kieran asked when I had breath enough to speak again.

"Nothing. I'm going to put you onto Eoin Kirby now. He'll tell you where he met Jodi last night. I'm just dashing to change out of my sweatsuit and then I'm going to Cork. Keep in touch."

Before Kieran could say anything else, I had handed the phone to Eoin, quickly explaining who was on the other end of the line and why he should tell anything he knew of Jodi's last sighting. I ducked into the shower and tried to think of nothing but the needles of hot water prickling my skin. Wrapped in my dressing-gown, I ran barefoot to my bedroom to dress. No jeans. In a fit of domesticity I had washed them all yesterday. They were in the utility room off the kitchen. I pattered through the kitchen and grabbed the first pair of jeans I could find in the ironing basket. They were wrinkled but at least they were clean and dry. As I rushed back past Eoin, I heard him tell Kieran that he would meet him in Cork later on. So Eoin was joining the posse too. We were all going to look pretty odd galloping around Cork city, searching for a little woman in a big cardigan.

I heard a noise. The unmistakable sound of a key being fitted into a lock. The click as it engaged. The rattle as the door opened and the keys jangled against the timber. I thought of warning Eoin to run out the back door. I thought of running out the back door myself. I thought of shrivelling up and floating away on a breeze. I thought of many ways to avoid what was coming but I could not move. My feet were stuck to the floor in pure shock.

Mom came bustling into the hallway, Tom trailing behind carrying her case. She had her greeting-guests face on. The one with chin and eyebrows slightly raised, a welcoming smile hovering about her lips. She had seen Eoin's hire car in the driveway so I could not deny that there was somebody here. Why in the hell hadn't she rung to say she was coming home today?

She stood still when she saw me. I could see how disapproving she was of me entertaining in my dressing-gown. I remained standing there, hair dripping wet, feet bare, my jeans in my hand and a very deep, male voice in the background. Mom and I just stared at each other. I saw realisation dawn as she listened to Eoin's unmistakable New Zealand accent. Mom's smile, no longer hovering, slipped off her face, leaving a shocked expression in its wake. She opened her mouth to speak but no words came out. Eoin's bass boomed around the hall as he finished his conversation with Kieran Mahon.

"Right, Kieran. As soon as Adele has some clothes on, we'll be on our way."

The sound galvanised Mom. She took a step towards me, her eyes blazing.

"You promised me! How dare you bring him into my house. How dare you!"

"I - I . . ."

"My good God! How could you behave like this?"

The penny began to drop. She thought I had been having sex with her arch enemy. Considering that I was obviously nude underneath my dressing-gown and that I had my pants in my hand, it was a fair assumption to make.

"It's not what you think, Mom. Eoin just came by to . . ."

Eoin chose that moment to come into the hall and quite unnecessarily introduce himself to Mom.

"Eoin Kirby. Great to meet you at last, Mrs Burke. My mother sends her best wishes. She told me you and your husband were good friends of hers when she lived here. I believe you shared many good times together."

Eoin held his hand out and Mom shrank back as if he

had been about to hit her. Her eyes were terrified as she craned her head back and stared up into Eoin's face. Tom came to stand beside her and I saw her hand shake as she reached out to him. Then without another word, my mother and Tom Reagan turned and walked out the front door, banging it firmly shut in our faces. I needed to run after her but found myself unable to move.

"Blast! I'm sorry, Adele. I thought you were exaggerating your mother's antipathy towards me. In fact, I even suspected you were using it as an excuse to get rid of me."

"Then why in the hell didn't you take the hint and stay away? Look what you've done now!"

"I've done sweet damn all. I don't know what your mother's problem is but I can see she's passed on some of her prejudice to you. You're both judging me by my family name and for some reason finding me wanting."

"My mother's not prejudiced," I answered stoutly, conveniently ignoring all Mom's biases against people with piercings or tattoos, smokers, nail-biters, gum-chewers, those who holidayed in Spain and especially those who had plastic surgery or Cockney accents. She was a woman of strong and not always fair opinions. But her dislike, and even hatred, of Eoin Kirby was on a different level.

"So you think it's all right for her to treat me like that?"

"Of course not! But she must have a reason. And I did promise her not to see you any more."

"Jesus! Why? What have I done to either you or your mother?"

I didn't have an answer to that question. Nor did I want to think about it now. Jodi could be in trouble and I needed to find her. I also needed to put on my bra. Quite illogically, in the midst of all this angst, I became aware of my breasts, heavy without the uplift of underwiring. I folded my arms underneath them to apply an emergency anti-gravity measure.

"Eoin, I apologise for the way my mother treated you. I don't know why she's being this way. She's extremely courteous and I've never seen her behave so rudely before. Now you'll have to excuse me. I need to go look for my friend."

I left him standing in the hall, went to my bedroom and shimmied into underwear, un-ironed jeans and T-shirt in seconds. Running back to the hall to grab my car keys, I saw with relief that Eoin had gone. My relief was short-lived. He was waiting for me in the driveway, sitting in his car with the driver's window down, the engine already running.

"Jump in. We'll go to where I saw Jodi last night. We'll work from there."

Hands on hips I stood glaring at him. "Eoin Kirby, why can't you just go to blazes? Haven't you caused enough trouble already?"

In one very swift movement for such a big man, he opened his door, leapt out of his seat and stood in front of me.

"This isn't about you! From what Kieran Mahon told me, Jodi could be in need of help. Will I show you where to start looking or not?"

He had a point there. I hadn't a notion where to start.

"Why didn't you bring her home last night? You said she looked unwell."

This was obviously the last straw for Eoin. He sat into his car and closed his door. I knew that had been an unfair comment. I had also seen that Jodi wasn't well last night and had done nothing to help her. She hadn't been very receptive to a helping hand then and had probably been less so later on. Especially from a relative stranger.

I walked around to the passenger door of Eoin's car and got in. He didn't even look at me as he put the car into gear and drove out through our gate. In strained silence we headed off towards Cork city in search of the missing Jodi Wall.

Chapter 14

It was a measure of my upset on the journey into Cork city that I didn't care about my hair drying into a curly mop. Still shocked by my mother's behaviour and the revelations about Jodi, I had to fight rising resentment too. Against my mother for her refusal to discuss the Kirby issue, against Jodi for lying to me, and Carla for the same reason. And especially against Eoin for not staying away from my mother's house when I had asked him to. I stole a peep at him and gathered from his tight mouth that he had resentment issues of his own. The silence between us was so intense that we both jumped when my phone trumpeted its elephant call again. It was Kieran.

"She hasn't been admitted to any of the Accident and Emergency units. I asked a cop friend of mine to do a discreet check and she wasn't picked up by the Gardaí either."

"That's good," I answered, "but it doesn't tell us where to find her. Do you think she's still in Cork?"

Kieran was quiet for a moment. I sensed that he gave a helpless shrug. "I don't know where else to look, Adele. I suppose she could be gone back to London. Her passport is at her parents' house but she wouldn't need it to travel to the UK anyway. I don't know."

"Eoin and I are about twenty minutes from the city. We'll ring you as soon as we get there. Where are you now?"

The reception bars on my phone faded and the line went dead. I looked up and noticed that we were dipping into Glengorm valley. There would be no reception until we had driven out of this low-lying area again.

"Good news from what I heard," Eoin remarked.

Snappy answers immediately came to mind. Things like none of your business and who asked your opinion. That was before I remembered he was kind enough to help with the search for a woman he didn't really know. Or did he? He and Jodi had looked pretty cosy in Seán Potter's car. Maybe . . .

"Why are you doing this? You don't know Jodi Wall. Not really. Or do you?"

"What in the hell do you mean by that? Are you asking in your very tactless way if there's something going on between Jodi and me?"

Shit! He was astute. And direct. Yes, that's exactly what I had been wondering.

"Of course not!" I answered, injecting as much

indignation into my reply as possible. "In the first place that isn't anything to do with me and in the second place I happen to know Jodi is very choosy about men."

"Bloody great! What is it with you Burke women? First your mother insults me and then you. What have I ever done to either of you? Jesus! No wonder my mother doesn't want to come back here."

"Changed your mind quickly, haven't you? Just an hour ago you were talking about buying property here."

"That's business. It doesn't mean I have to like the place. Or the people."

I took a deep breath then. Getting involved in a tit-for-tat argument with Eoin Kirby wasn't going to help the situation. We were leaving the valley behind now and beginning to climb again. I looked ahead as we approached the forest road, thinking how eerie and shadowed the passageway through the trees was. Great oaks towered on each side, blocking sunlight and somehow making this half-mile stretch seem like it belonged in another landscape, another era. I always imagined horses and carriages clip-clopping along this section of road. I used to picture myself in a beautiful crinoline, or maybe an Elizabth Bennett type dress, sitting in a carriage, a pretty bonnet on my curls and, of course Mr Darcy by . . .

"Stop! Now!"

Eoin had very good reactions. He pressed the brake the instant I shouted.

I jumped out almost before the car had stopped. As I raced towards the woods on the left-hand side, I glanced back over my shoulder and saw Eoin staring after me.

"C'mon, follow me!" I called out as I ran.

I had caught the merest glimpse of yellow but it had been enough to set my heart thumping. My ankle twisted as my feet struck the roughly hewn path through the trees. I felt the pain for an instant and then ignored it as I rushed towards the turn in the path. And there it was. The bright yellow Mini which belonged to Jodi Wall's mother. Abandoned where the path narrowed too much to drive any further. I slowed my pace, afraid now of what I might find. Heavy thuds sounded behind me. Eoin caught my arm.

"Is that Jodi's car?"

"Her mother's. It's the one she was driving last night."

"Stay here. I'll check."

I didn't argue with him this time. My mind had suddenly gone blank but I knew it was to protect me from horrors which lurked in my subconscious. They tried to surface, the Jodi-is-dead thoughts, but I wouldn't allow them. Eoin was walking around the car now, peering in windows and trying to open the doors. They were locked. I began to walk slowly towards him. He looked up as I approached.

"She's not here," he told me. "Maybe her car was stolen from the city."

"Joyriders would have crashed it or burned it out. Jodi must have parked it here herself."

"That blue blanket thing she was wearing last night is on the back seat."

"That 'thing' is my favourite cardigan! I lent it to her because I thought she had flu."

"Sorry."

I shrugged. An insult to my cardi seemed trivial now. "She may have just gone for a walk and got lost in the woods," I suggested.

Eoin peered through the thick forest growth. "Maybe. Let's split up and search. We'll swap phone numbers and keep in contact."

I checked my phone. The reception bars were full. Phone numbers exchanged, Eoin went right into the densest section of woods while I continued along the path towards the heart of the forest. The path got narrower, the trees taller and the daylight dimmer as I trod the track which was springy with seasons of decay. Creaks and sudden cracks made me jump. I heard gurgles and knew that somewhere nearby a stream was trickling over stones and fallen timbers. A wood pigeon cooed and high above my head wings fluttered. I called Jodi's name and the sound echoed through the treetops. The path was even narrower now, overgrown with brambles and sweet woodbine. I felt sweat pepper my forehead and heard my own heartbeat loud in my ears. I was terrified. Afraid to go on. Suppose there were vicious wild animals here or worse still vicious people, psychopaths who camped out in the woods waiting for a lone woman to fall into their clutches?

I took my phone out of my pocket, clutched it tightly in my hand and scrolled through until Eoin's name came up on the screen. I felt braver then. He wasn't that far away and I could contact him in seconds. I took a deep breath and a step forward. I stopped, my eye caught by something. It was a fern. Once tall and feathery, now bent to the ground. Trampled underfoot. Very recently. It was still fresh, sap glistening on the broken stem. I looked along the path which was now no more than a narrow aisle between the vigorous vegetation on either side. As far as I could see ahead, brambles and ferns had been pushed aside and snapped. Somebody had walked through here. Could it have been Jodi?

Without allowing myself time to speculate further I began to run along the passageway, all the time calling out to Jodi. The path suddenly curved to the left. When I rounded the corner, I stood stock still. I had come to a clearing. A magic place full of sunshine, buttercups, daisies and lush grass. It was almost a perfect circle, protected all around by towering trees. And there, in this warm heart of the forest lay Jodi, sprawled on her back, one arm across her face. She was motionless. Her shiny dark hair which I so envied glistened, her slim body was graceful but Jodi Wall was not moving.

I opened my mouth to call her name. It echoed loud and desperate in my head but no sound passed my lips. A little breeze shivered through treetops and gently touched my face. I lifted my hand and stroked my cheek. I felt my skin, warm and smooth. This surreal scene could not be denied its reality. I was awake. The bee which buzzed from flower to flower, the peaty smell of decayed vegetation, the gurgle of the unseen brook, were all real. So too, was the body of Jodi Wall, lying so still in this woodland grotto.

I moved. So slowly at first, right foot forward, then as if trawling through viscous mud my left followed suit. Four tentative steps later, I was close enough to notice the deep pink varnish on Jodi's toenails. Another step and I saw sun refract rainbow hues from the stone on her neck chain.

I stopped noticing when I heard the noise. Loud and threatening in the stillness, twigs snapped and birds rose in terror from their secret hiding places. The rhythmic noise grew louder and nearer by the second. I looked at Jodi's prone body and had a premonition of my own sprawled beside her, a companion in death. I lifted my phone and frantically pressed Eoin Kirby's number. How far away was he? Would he get here on time? Should I run? Where to? Help!

A phone rang to my right-hand side. The sound reverberated through the clearing. It was still ringing as Eoin emerged from the trees, big and brawny, a twig comically entwined in his hair. I heaved a huge sigh of relief, then wordlessly I pointed in the direction of Jodi's prone body. His face paled.

"Have you checked for a pulse?" he asked.

I shook my head. "I was just going to when I heard noises and rang you."

He walked away from me, stooped down beside Jodi and placed his fingers on her neck. Turning around, he held his hand out to me. I walked slowly towards him and took his outstretched hand. I knelt on the ground beside him and allowed myself to really look at Jodi. To see how beautiful her face was, how still her body. How shallow her breathing.

"She's breathing!" I said, my relief evident in my triumphant tone.

Eoin checked Jodi's pulse again and frowned.

"Do you think she took an overdose?" I asked, now wondering if we could get her to a hospital on time.

"Could be. But her colour's good, her breathing even. From what Kieran told me it's more likely she's sleeping off a high. Crashing. We must try to wake her. You do it. She might be frightened if she saw me first."

So! He did know about the drugs. I knelt down beside Jodi and gently shook her. Her eyes remained firmly shut. I shook her more vigorously. "Jodi! It's Adele. Wake up!"

Jodi's eyes flickered open. They were dazed and dull. She stared at me and then recognition sparked. She smiled and weakly lifted her hand to touch my face. "Good old Del," she muttered and her eyelids closed again.

I put my arms around her, cradled her close to me and cried tears of relief onto her shiny hair. Eoin was talking about getting her up on her feet, of helping her back to her car, of bringing her to a doctor but I just held on to Jodi and cried. Leaning close to her ear, I told her I was sorry I had not seen how deeply troubled she was and that I would always, always be there for her. Her eyes opened again and this time she sat up, blinking as she looked around her.

"How in the fuck did I get here?"

"We were hoping you'd tell us," Eoin said. "But that doesn't matter now. Up on your feet. It's not far to where you left your car."

While Eoin was helping Jodi, I rang Kieran Mahon. He was ecstatic. "Oh, thank God! Thank God for your sharp sight and thank God for her mother's outrageously bright yellow Mini. I'd better let her parents know she's safe. I'll just say she's with you. Are you sure she's okay?"

"We'll bring her to a doctor as a precaution but, yes, I think she's fine."

"Thanks, Adele," Kieran said, his voice breaking. "Thank you so much. You're a good friend to her."

That was the first time I realised that Kieran Mahon didn't fancy Jodi Wall. He loved her. With all the passion and pain of unrequited love.

* * *

I drove Mrs Wall's car while Eoin followed on behind in his rental. Jodi sat silently beside me, her head dropping every so often. Our house was the only place she would allow herself be taken but I was dreading going there. If Mom was back she would be stroppy and make a big fuss and if she wasn't I'd feel guilty. Either way the mother problem would have to wait until Jodi was looked after. I turned into the town, making my way towards the doctor's surgery. Jodi suddenly came alive.

"Where are you taking me? I'm not going to the doctor if that's what you're planning."

"Just a quick check-up, Jode. To put my mind at rest. It won't take long."

Out of the corner of my eye I saw her snap open her seatbelt and grab the door handle. I jammed on the brakes.

"What do you think you're doing, Jodi? How many different ways have you of trying to kill yourself?"

"I'm not going to the doctor. I refuse to be poked,

prodded and lectured. There's nothing wrong with me a shower and a sleep won't cure."

I could see from the fear reflected in her eyes how terrified she was. I decided then to play along with her. I could always call the doctor to the house if needed. I smiled at her and turned the car back towards our house.

I had a question to ask her. Not sure how to phrase it properly, I just blurted it out.

"Since you can't remember how you got to the woods, how do you know what happened to you last night? Are you sure you weren't . . . that you weren't raped?"

"Oh, Del, stop! I couldn't remember when I woke up but I know now. You needn't worry. I was alone all night."

As I turned the car onto our road, I saw that our driveway was empty except for my car. Mom was not there and I couldn't decide whether I was relieved or not. Glancing in the rear mirror, I noticed that Eoin Kirby was flashing his lights at me and indicating for me to pull in to the side. I stopped Mrs Wall's car and got out, watching him as he parked and walked towards us.

"Will you be all right now?" he asked. "Kieran Mahon said he'll call to see you both soon."

I had a moment of clear thinking. I was thirty, in shock, in need of support and afraid of what my mother would say if she saw me talking to Eoin Kirby. The man who had been so kind to me and to Jodi too. He was a good man and whatever notion Mom had about him was wrong.

"Won't you come in with me, Eoin? You need a drink after all that drama."

"No, Adele, I'll go away. I don't want to upset your mother again."

"She's not here."

"The days when I went sneaking around behind parents' backs are well gone for me. They should be for you too. I don't care whether she's there or not, I don't want to go where I'm not welcome."

I had no answer to that. Mom had made it very clear that she didn't want him to set foot in her house again. And it was after all, her house. I looked up at Eoin and saw hurt and anger in his dark brown eyes. On impulse I stood on tip-toe and kissed him on the cheek. His bristly skin tickled my lips and the warm, musky scent of him gave me a mad urge to snuggle into him. I took a pace back, afraid that I might act on instinct. He was smiling at me.

"So do I take it we're friends then? Maybe you'd find the time now to have dinner with me. Tonight?"

"I'd love to, Eoin, but Jodi . . ."

I stopped then. Jodi, Mom. Two stubborn women behaving exactly as they chose. Why should I not go out for a few hours with a man I was finding increasingly more intriguing? Kieran would probably keep an eye on Jodi, or maybe she would have gone back to her own home by then. Eoin was staring at me, one eyebrow raised. I smiled at him.

"I'd love to, Eoin. On condition that dinner's on me. Just to say thanks for all your help today."

"We can argue about that later. See you at eight then. In the lobby of The Grand Hotel – unless you'd prefer to go somewhere else."

"No. The Grand is lovely. See you at eight."

My step was lighter as I walked back to my car. The euphoria lasted until I sat in beside Jodi and saw that she was again wrapped in my cardi and had a half-full bottle of vodka in her hand.

"What in the hell are you doing with that? Jesus! Jodi! You haven't even eaten yet."

"You're right. And I'm starving. I'll have to eat something before I do anything else."

Whatever about the ethics of drinking neat vodka before her breakfast, her slug from the bottle had certainly improved Jodi's mood.

"Any sausages here?" she asked as she followed me into the kitchen. "I really fancy a fry-up."

That sounded like the Jodi I knew. I opened the fridge and got out sausages, rashers and eggs and then put on the pan. While it was heating, I filled a bowl with muesli and brought it over to the table to Jodi. She dived in while I picked up the note I had just seen propped against the saltcellar. I too sat as I read the unfamiliar handwriting:

"Adele, your mother is going to stay with me for a few days. I live at No 6 Willbury Lawn near the Community Centre. You are very welcome to call if you want to see Sissy although I would advise waiting a day or two before talking to her. I know this is difficult for you but I assure you she does have good reason to be upset. I'm sure you'll understand when she explains. See my phone number below and feel free to ring anytime. Tom Reagan."

Bloody hell! Mom could tell Tom Reagan why she

was behaving like a shrew but she couldn't tell me. How unfair was that! And she was running away rather than face me. My temper was rising to titanic proportions and would have exploded except that the fire alarm went off because I had forgotten to switch on the extractor fan. The pan was puffing out clouds of blue smoke. I ran about, switching off the cooker, lifting the pan out to the back garden, opening windows and doors, flapping a tea towel under the alarm while Jodi serenely continued to eat her muesli. I had to remind myself that just a short while ago I would have sold my soul to see Jodi Wall alive. To kill her now would be hypocritical and a waste of our rescue efforts so I worked around her instead.

The pan was on again, this time with heat low and extractor on, when Kieran Mahon knocked on the front door for the second time that day. He barely glanced at me as I opened the door to him. "In the kitchen," I said and stood aside as he dashed past me. When I got back in Kieran and Jodi were sitting across the table from each other, she smiling and he pale and grim-faced.

"You gave us all a terrible fright, Jodi. Your parents were just about to report you missing. Don't ever pull a stunt like that again."

"I'm sorry to have inconvenienced you all and I'm very grateful to you but there was no need for all the fuss. I can look after myself."

"Really?"

"Yes. Really. I'm fine now. In fact I'm bloody fine. Never better."

Kieran put his elbows on the table and leaned across

towards Jodi. I looked away. I had got over Kieran Mahon seventeen years ago — well, almost — but I was not yet ready to see him kissing Jodi. I busied myself filling plates and waiting to hear the soft smacks and sucks of a passionate kiss. When Kieran shouted I almost dropped the fried egg I was transferring to a plate.

"How in the hell could you do that, Jodi? When? Where? In your mother's car? Here in this kitchen?"

I twirled around to see Kieran staring into Jodi's eyes. She was laughing at him. A hysterical laugh, rising with each gasping breath she took. She was high.

For some reason, I continued on getting breakfast. Maybe I couldn't handle the fact that Jodi had taken drugs while in my company. It must have been during the time I was out of the car talking to Eoin. She had played me for a fool again. I walked over to the table with the food and placed it front of them. Jodi immediately pushed her plate away and wriggled on the chair like a small child wanting to use the bathroom.

Peering closer, I saw what Kieran had noticed. Her pupils were huge.

"She drank vodka as well," I told him.

"Stop talking about me as if I can't hear," Jodi spluttered. "I just took this fucking stuff to clear my head. I can see everything now. I even know what ye're thinking."

Kieran pushed his plate aside and leaned towards Jodi again.

"What is it this time?" he asked in almost a whisper. "Are you still on cocaine or have you graduated?"

"One line. That's all. You're talking as if I've a drug

habit. As if I snatch purses and prostitute myself for drugs. For Christ's sake! Everyone's on coke."

"Not everyone loses their job and gets sent to a rehab clinic. Stop bullshitting, Jodi. I know all that's happened."

That piece of information seemed to have penetrated Jodi's defences. She stared at Kieran.

"How? Who told you? Were you sticking your nose into my private business?"

In a flash she was on her feet and pacing in the manner I had found so annoying last night. She was mumbling to herself as she strode, cursing everyone from her work colleagues to a London traffic warden who had apparently issued her a parking ticket two years previously. Whichever drug she had taken was certainly ploughing very deep furrows in her mind. She suddenly stood still in front of me.

"My parents. Did you tell them? I'll kill you if you did. It's none of your business. Not Carla Selby's either. Why don't you go away and find yourself a man? Maybe you'd stop interfering in my life then."

I can't say I wasn't hurt by her words. I was. But I chose to believe that Jodi wasn't fully aware of what she was saying. A little voice in my head told me that her line of cocaine had removed her inhibitions and allowed her to say what she really thought but I ignored that idea.

"I'm not interfering, Jodi. I'm trying to help. I didn't know you had been in rehab. How long were you there? Why didn't you let me know? I would have gone to see you."

"I'm sure you would. You and Carla too. How good that would have made you both feel, lording it over me. I'm sure you would have helped me clear out my apartment too and pretended to be concerned. Well, I don't want your sympathy or pity. I don't need it."

"From where I'm sitting," Kieran said, "sympathy and pity are the last things you need, Jodi Wall. You must take a good long look at yourself and see what you're doing to your health. To your life. Enough, Jodi. Give me whatever else you bought in Cork last night. What have you left?"

I was shocked when I saw Jodi's hand go to the pocket of my cardigan. My God! She was using my cosy cardi as a drug mule! Kieran held his hand out towards her. Her eyes got huge. I saw real fear in them as her hand dug deep into the woollen pocket, clinging on tightly to whatever she had in there. Kieran stayed perfectly still, his hand outstretched, his gaze never leaving Jodi's face. There must have been sounds, background noises, but all I can recall now is a profound silence as Kieran and Jodi tested each other's strength. Slowly, as if walking in a dream, Jodi moved towards Kieran and stood in front of him. "Will you help me?" she asked in a little-girl voice that didn't seem to belong to her at all.

"Of course. But you must first want to help yourself."

"And you, Del?" she asked turning towards me. "Can you still be my friend?"

I nodded, unable to speak because a knot of sadness was blocking my airways. She drew her hand out of the pocket. Her fist was so tightly closed around the little plastic packet that her knuckles were white. She raised her arm until it was hovering over Kieran's outstretched hand. Then with a cry, her fingers opened and the bag of cocaine powder dropped onto Kieran's palm. Jodi's face crumpled and she folded onto the floor, her head in Kieran's lap. He began to tenderly stroke her hair and murmur soothing words to her. I looked around the kitchen from the congealing fry on the plates to the couple united in emotion so intense that it was like a barrier around them. I needed to get out of there.

"I must go out for about an hour or so, Kieran. Is that okay?"

He nodded without looking up so I crept silently away, knowing instinctively that it would have been wrong to make any noise in that pain-filled room.

As the front door closed behind me, I stood and took a deep breath. Without any clear idea of where I was headed, I jumped into my car and did a very creditable wheel spin as I shot down our driveway and away from the place I used to consider my sanctuary.

Chapter 15

An urge to assure myself that innocence and openness still existed led me to Carla's house that day. I knew Carla was probably still away with Harry but it was the children I needed to see. I wanted to hear them laugh and giggle and to share in their sense of awe and wonder. No drug addicts or big dark secrets shadowed their world and I needed to slip into that safe place if only for an hour.

All the children were in the garden, crowded around Vera. They each, even the twins, had little trowels in their hands and the path where they stood was strewn with containers of bedding plants. Finn raced towards me, so excited his words were tripping over each other.

"Guess what! Guess what! We're making our own garden. A surprise for Mum and Dad. I'm planting marigolds. C'mon, c'mon!"

Dragging me by the hand he rushed back to where Vera was kneeling. The children were all talking together, laughing, excited and once again I marvelled at how wonderful Vera was with them. Lisa and Dave, blonde curls and dimpled smiles, were so covered in soil that it seemed like the twins themselves were planted. Lisa held a scrunched-up pansy in her hand.

"Flower," she said, holding it up for me to admire. I stooped to kiss her on the cheek and it was then I noticed that Vera hadn't raised her head or even saluted me. I cringed. Maybe she thought I was interfering. Keeping an eye on her. Being the nosey old bag that Jodi too must believe I was. A wave of self-pity washed over me as I momentarily wondered if there was any place in the whole wide world where I could go and feel I belonged. Vera looked up at me then and I forgot my bout of introspection. Her eyes were puffy and the sides of her nose were red. She must have cried buckets to get her face into that state.

"Vera! What . . ." I began but she frowned at me, rolling her bloodshot eyes at the children.

"I'm going to make sunflowers," Liam said, showing me the seeds he had in his hand. I picked up a seed and admired it but all the while I was thinking about Vera and why she was so upset.

"Did you bring your laptop?" Finn asked.

"No. I knew you'd be too busy to practise. I'll bring it next week."

"No need. Mum and Dad are bringing me one home. They'll be here soon."

Shit! I had to get out of there before Carla and Harry arrived. I made a point of looking at my watch. "Must dash. I'm very busy today."

Vera stood up. "I'll walk you to your car."

"Will you come back to see our flowers growing?" Liam asked.

"Of course. I'll bring my giant beanstalk seed with me next time." Finn sighed and rolled his eyes. I tousled his hair and smiled at him. "Don't be too smart, young man. There is magic, you know."

Finn gave me a very cynical smile for one so young, then turned his attention back to his gardening while the other children contented themselves with digging huge holes for their tiny plants.

Vera walked along beside me in silence, her head bowed. I was tempted to say that I knew what was wrong, that I had guessed the Selby marriage was in trouble despite Vera herself telling me that Carla and Harry were the perfect pair. But I kept my mouth firmly shut. It wasn't my place to bring up the topic. By the time we reached the car, Vera still hadn't spoken.

"Is there anything I can do to help?" I asked. "You seem very upset, Vera."

"Actually, Adele, there is. I was just about to ring you and Jodi. Carla and Harry want you both to come to dinner tomorrow night. Here. Can you organise that with Jodi?"

So, Mr and Mrs Selby were going to make a joint announcement. Could it be about their divorce? How civilised. I hesitated now. What should I say about Jodi? Reluctant to mention anything of today's drama, yet unsure about committing her to an appointment she might not keep, I said nothing.

"Please, Adele. It's very important to Carla."

A car drove in through the front gates. It was Carla's parents. If body language was anything to go by, they were as upset as Vera. I turned to her and smiled.

"Of course I'll be here. I'll let Jodi know too."

"Thanks, Adele. Tomorrow night, eight thirty. The children should be well asleep by then."

I got into my car and waved at Vera and her parents as I drove away. Nobody waved back.

* * *

I had meant to drive straight home to check that Jodi was all right. I got sidetracked. Somehow I found myself passing the Community Centre and searching out Willbury Lawn housing estate. Just to be sure where it was. Just to see the place where my mother was choosing to hide from me. Her car was parked outside number six. It was an end house on the front row.

I sat in my car for ten minutes staring at the white PVC door and tiny front garden of number six. And fuming. Debating with myself, making first one decision, then another. Suppose I walked up to that door and Mom refused to see me? Suppose she was waiting for me to make the first move? In the end I decided there were too many supposes. Squeezing my eyes shut I pictured the note Tom Reagan had left on our kitchen table. I have a photographic memory so I mentally read his phone number. Opening my eyes again, I keyed in the number on my phone. He answered after two rings.

"Tom, this is Adele Burke. How's Mom now?"

"Hello, Adele. She's fine. Just resting. She had a terrible shock. It'll take her a day or two to be herself again."

"I'm sorry that she's upset, Tom, but I wish I knew why. If she won't tell me, I can't do anything about it, can I? What has she got against the Kirbys?"

"That's for her to tell you. I don't want to interfere."

"Don't you think allowing her to hide in your house is interfering?"

Tom's laugh took me by surprise and really annoyed me. I failed to see any humour at all in my mother's upset and the man she was about to marry should not either.

"Since when did Sissy need anyone's permission to do what she pleased? Your mother, as you well know, does things in her own time."

"For God's sake! She's given me all these dire warnings about the Kirbys and then won't say why. You can tell her that until somebody gives me a reason to think otherwise, I'm proud to say Eoin Kirby's my friend."

I heard him sigh. Tom Reagan sounded as tired of the whole saga as I was by now.

"Your mother will talk to you when she can."

I had always known Mom was stubborn. Spoiled by her parents and by Dad in his turn, her world turned on a what-Sissy-wants axis. But she was going too far this time. Such fuss and drama. Tom wasn't helping either, encouraging her in her swoons and weaknesses. I was angry with them both.

"Just tell her I called, please, and ask her to ring me, or better yet, tell her to come home."

I switched off my phone and this time I headed straight for home.

* * *

The clock on the dash read five as I left the town to drive towards my mother's house. A different and more immediate problem came to the fore now. What was I going to wear to my dinner date with Eoin Kirby? My mind wandered through my wardrobe and rejected most of what it found there. I should have gone shopping. The Grand Hotel was hardly the Ritz but I still felt dinner there, especially with Eoin Kirby, should be a skirt occasion. I did have a favourite turquoise sundress which I had bought in Turkey a few years ago. The colour was a bit strong for my pale skin but I could always slap on some fake tan. And I had a light blue cardigan, one of those little bolero things which tied underneath the bust. The blue sandals I bought on impulse only a few days ago would complete the look which I hoped would be dressy yet casual.

Happy with my plan, I was calmer than I had been all day as I opened the front door and went into my house. Kieran was still sitting at the kitchen table in the same position I had left him. There was no sign of Jodi.

"Ah! Adele! Jodi rang you ten minutes ago but your phone was engaged."

"Where is she? Did something else happen?"

"She's fine. Just gone to shower. That's why she was trying to contact you because —"

"I hope you don't mind, Del. I had to change and I found these in your wardrobe."

186

I turned around to look at Jodi. She was like a different person to the down and out sprawled on the forest floor this morning. In fact she was stunning. A vision in my turquoise sundress and my pale blue cardigan, the ties on both doubled around her slender figure.

"I tried to ring you but . . ."

"I know. I know. I was on the phone to Tom Reagan. No problem, Jodi. Keep them. They look nice on you and I'll probably never wear them again anyway."

"I wouldn't either. Not my style."

Up yours, I thought and then I began to panic about the "what to wear" dilemma all over again.

"I'm going home now," Jodi said. "Just in case my folks happen to ask, I've told them you and I went to Cork yesterday, went clubbing last night and hit the shops today."

"Really? What did we buy?"

"This," she said, twirling around in my sundress and laughing as folds of material flapped around her legs. At least she was wearing her own shoes. There are advantages to my size eights.

"You look much better, Jodi. How do you feel?"

She walked across and threw her arms around me. "Del. How can I ever thank you enough for what you've done for me? I feel grateful to have a friend like you. And Kieran too. I don't feel alone any more now. That makes a big difference."

I hugged Jodi close to me. Making that little speech must have cost the proud Jodi Wall a lot.

"I'm always here for you, Jode. You know that."

"And me too," Kieran added, getting up and coming to join us in a group hug.

"You don't have to go, Jodi," I said. "Stay here if you want."

"No. Thanks. I'd better face my parents. I'll have to tell them the truth sooner or later but I'm a bit fragile yet. I'll pick my time. Kieran's coming home with me to break the ice. At least I know my mother will be pleased to have her car back."

I exchanged a look with Kieran over Jodi's head.

"I'm going to drive Jodi home in Mrs Wall's car," he said. "I'll send one of the lads to collect my car later. Okay?"

He winked at me. It was a relief to know that Jodi wasn't getting behind the wheel of a car and heartening to see a return of the saucy Kieran Mahon.

As they walked away, Kieran with his arm protectively around her, I thought they looked the ideal couple. Which is what reminded me of dinner with Carla. I ran after them and caught up with Jodi just as she was about to get into the passenger seat of her mother's Mini.

"Harry and Carla want us to go to theirs for dinner tomorrow night. I promised Vera I'd bring you along. Will you be up to it?"

"I don't know. I've been through this before, Del. I'll have some good days and some bad ahead."

"They want to tell us something. I think . . . Do you think maybe Carla and Harry are splitting up?"

"It wouldn't surprise me. At least he seems to keep in contact with his ex-wives."

"That's cruel, Jodi. Carla deserves our support at a time like this."

Jodi had the grace to bow her head and look ashamed.

"Well, Jodi? Eight thirty at their house tomorrow night. Will I pick you up?"

"Do, please. And I'll try to keep my tongue under control. I'd be genuinely sorry if Harry and Carla are having problems. And all those children. What would they do?"

I shrugged. I was all out of solutions to problems and on top of that I had curly hair and nothing to wear tonight.

I waved at Jodi and dashed back into the house. I had a hectic few hours ahead.

* * *

It had been a long time since last I had been in the Grand Hotel. Landmark occasions had always been celebrated there by Cairnsure natives. I remember lunching in The Grand the day I made my First Holy Communion, Mom and Dad sitting proudly either side of me and Aunt Lily opposite, glaring and complaining that her roast beef was tough.

A flight of steps led up to the very impressive double front door. I stood at the bottom of the steps and tugged at the hem of my burgundy dress. Well, I called it a dress but it was just a sleeveless tube really. I worried that it was too short but vanity had made me choose it to wear. It showed off my long legs to the best advantage, especially with my grey high-heeled sandals. I was satisfied that it was more flattering than the turquoise dress would have been. Jodi was fully forgiven. The day was still bright and the air warm so I just carried my grey shrug to wear later when the evening cooled. My feet were aching already and I had yet to negotiate the steps in the perilously high heels. Just as I reached the top step, it crossed my mind that Eoin Kirby might not be there. I almost lost my footing. He could have changed his mind or forgotten. Or just plain decided to not turn up.

The lobby was deserted. I glanced at my watch. Shit! I was early. It was just gone five minutes to eight. I turned in a panic to go out again. My ankle, the one I had twisted in the woods that morning, turned at an impossible angle on the stiletto heels. I bent over and grabbed it, dropping my bag and my shrug in the process. That, of course, was the moment Eoin chose to appear in the lobby. He rushed towards me asking the most obvious, but superfluous, question possible.

"Are you all right, Adele? Have you hurt yourself?"

I gritted my teeth and tried to grin at him but the pain was sharp and sickening.

"I need to sit down a minute. I've twisted my ankle."

"Come over here," he said, taking my arm and helping me towards one of the plush seats near the window. I glanced around, horrified at the thought of someone I knew seeing me being led along like a doddering old lady. I plopped onto the seat, very glad to take the weight off my foot and even happier that, for now at least, Eoin and I were alone and unobserved. He knelt in front of me and took off my sandal. As I watched in stunned silence, he took my foot in his hand and began to massage my ankle, his strong fingers kneading and rubbing. I stared at the foot he was holding. It didn't look like mine. The size of his huge hands lent my Yeti-like foot a delicacy and femininity which was completely novel.

"Wriggle your toes," he ordered.

I did, glad that my toenails were painted a pale pink. They looked cute as they did a little dance on the palm of his hand.

"Put your weight on your foot now."

I stood and gingerly lowered my shoeless foot onto the ground. It felt perfect. Better still it felt small. Sitting again, I strapped on my sandal.

"That's amazing, Eoin. Thank you. Are you a physiotherapist?"

He laughed and I frowned. I had chased through an isolated woods with this man, sliced Mom's Dundee cake for him and had my foot in his hand and yet I knew nothing about him.

"I picked up so many injuries in my rugby days that I learned to manipulate bones and muscles. My work has nothing at all to do with physiotherapy."

"What do you do, then?"

"I'm a director in the family construction company."

"So who's running the company while you're here?"

Just as I asked the question, it hit me that I might not like the answer. Of course he was married. Why wouldn't he be? How had I not realised before now? And why did it worry me? What if he was? We were just having dinner. A chat. It wasn't as if . . . Even though my mother was entombed in No 6, Willbury Lawn, I could hear her finish that sentence for me. "It's not as if he's interested in you anyway. You saw the way he combed the woods for Jodi Wall."

"My brother," Eoin answered. "My younger brother."

"So what would he think of you investing in Elliots' shop here in Cairnsure?"

"Nothing to do with him. That's a personal investment. Are you comfortable enough now to walk to the dining room?"

He offered his arm and I gladly took it as he escorted me to dinner. No doubt about it, married or single, Eoin Kirby was a lady's man.

The dining room of The Grand Hotel had changed a lot since I had made my First Holy Communion. The thick carpet had been replaced by parquet flooring. White walls, abstract art, potted plants and red chairs around tables with gleaming white cloths completed the transformation from country hotel to urban chic. We were led to a corner table overlooking the garden and I wondered if Eoin had ordered it specially. He seemed to like gardens.

As the waitress lit the candle on our table and fussed with menus, I glanced around. All tables were occupied but I didn't recognise anybody. Maybe that's what made my friendship with Jodi and Carla so precious. Cairnsure had changed so much with the influx of new people. It was possible, and probable, to walk the full length of the town and not see a familiar face. At least we three knew each other. Or rather, we were all part of each other's history. We knew who we had been. The people we had become seemed to be a different matter altogether. Especially Jodi.

"How is Jodi now?" Eoin asked, as if he had read my mind.

"Fine. She went back to her own home this evening. Kieran Mahon went with her."

"I feel guilty. I knew there was something wrong when I met her in Cork but I never guessed that she had a such a serious problem. I should have at least offered to bring her home."

"How could you guess? I didn't either and I know her a lot better and for longer than you."

Our starter was served then. Delicately flavoured lobster bisque. I chose salad as main course while Eoin opted for rack of lamb which brought us neatly to talk of New Zealand. I discovered that the Kirbys lived in Auckland on the North Island.

"My parents were very lucky," he explained. "They emigrated at a good time. There was plenty of work for Dad and it didn't take him long to build up his business. Although, as I told you, he never forgot Cairnsure."

It struck me as odd that if Eoin's father had missed Cairnsure so much he had never come back, even for a visit, but I thought better of saying so.

"So you have relations in Cork. Cousins, uncles, aunts?"

"No one that close. Third cousins, I think. I'm not

very good with these complicated family relationships. From what I can gather, your mother and father were far closer to my parents when they lived here than any of their blood relatives."

"That's obviously not true now. Not on my mother's part anyway. She walked out today after you left and hasn't come back since."

I noticed his mouth tighten and I was immediately sorry I had told him about Mom's flight to Willbury Lawn. It had sounded as if I was blaming him. Sissy was blaming him but for what? With relief I saw the waitress cross the room with our plates balanced cleverly on her arms. We were both silent as we ate.

Eoin cleared his plate and then sat back with a satisfied sigh.

"That was good," he said. "Almost as good as your mother's fruit cake."

I put down my knife and fork and leaned towards him. "Mom's a terrific person, Eoin. I've never seen her behave like this before. I'm annoyed at her but I know she must have a good reason. Or a valid reason anyway. It can't be good. She's genuinely upset,."

"I rang my mother tonight and asked her what it was about."

I sat up straight now, holding my breath. At last I could find out what Sissy was so unwilling to say. Eoin was looking out into the garden, a frown on his forehead.

"And?" I prompted. "What did she say?"

He turned back towards me and smiled. "I forgot

about the time difference between here and New Zealand. She read me a lecture about ringing her so early in the morning. Mum never did like to see the sun rise."

"What did she say about Sissy Burke?"

"Nothing much. Just that there had been a misunderstanding. She said she doesn't want to talk about it. And when Irene Kirby says no, she means it."

Eoin waved at the waitress, beckoning to her to take our empty plates and bring the dessert menu. I chose crème brûlée while Eoin decided on chocolate gateau.

"So what do you think happened?" I asked when we were alone again. "What's it about?"

"I have no idea. All I know is that it has nothing to do with us, so let's drop the subject. We have more interesting things to talk about."

I agreed. There was so much I wanted to know about Eoin. Starting with his age.

"How old are you, Eoin?"

"Thirty-four. Can't call myself a young lad any more!"

I was surprised. He had given me the impression of being older than that. Maybe it was his air of self-assurance or the apparent fact that he had already achieved so much in life.

"Of course your age is no secret," he said. "I read in *Cairnsure Weekly* about the joint thirtieth party you and your friends had."

My stomach, until now feeling well fed and looking forward to more, did a summersault. If he had been reading that issue of our local rag, then he could have read the article about the rescue of the "thirty-year-old woman" off the rocks on East Beach. I had been forced to share the story anonymously with the town but I was damned if I wanted to share it with Eoin Kirby. I waited for him to say something about the East Beach article while he was obviously waiting for my comment on the birthday party.

The arrival of dessert broke the awkward moment's silence. My crème brûlée was delicious. A crisp coat of caramelised vanilla sugar over the smoothest of custards, topped with swirls of clotted cream. I spooned every last delicious mouthful from my bowl and saw Eoin do the same with his dessert.

"That was so good," he said. "I usually grab something to eat on the run. It's great to sit and enjoy my food."

Did that mean there wasn't a domesticated little woman in his home, preparing gourmet meals for him? Or maybe his woman was a high flier? Immersed in a demanding career of her own. How was I going to find out without appearing predatory or gauche? He made it easy for me.

"Tell me about yourself, Adele. I know you're a teacher on a year's leave and that you're a caring friend and loyal daughter. I don't know if you're involved in a relationship. Anyone special in your life?"

I invoked the spectre of Pascal Ronayne again.

"Actually, there was but it's over now."

"Ditto. I was living with someone for a long time but we split up just before my father died. I'm a free agent again."

I tried not to smile. Not openly anyway. Eoin Kirby was single and available! I sat back in my chair and let a feeling of satisfaction wash over me. I had not realised how much I had hoped to hear him say those words. Granted, I was by this stage frustrated. I needed the strength of a man's arms around me, the touch of powerful hands, the scent of aftershave, the prickle of beard against my skin. The warmth of being wanted, if only for a small while. But Eoin Kirby was by far the most interesting man I had met for a long time. I wanted to know his favourite colour, what movies and music he liked, which authors he read. Everything about him, especially what he looked like first thing in the morning, his fair hair tousled, his brown eyes sleepy . . .

"I seem to have lost you, Adele. Would you like to go for a walk or not?"

I glanced out through the window. A splash of daylight still shimmered in the darkening sky. A perfect night for a stroll along the prom, maybe arm in arm. I smiled at him and nodded. When I stood my twisted ankle was painless. I remembered then what I had said to little Finn Selby. Magic did indeed exist.

* * *

The tide was out and there was a faint whiff of sewage in the air as we walked along the strand, my grey, vertigo-inducing sandals in my hand. With my heels off, the top of my head barely reached Eoin's shoulder. My free arm was linked into his and, unpleasant smell aside, I felt like I was walking through a scene from a romantic film. The sea hissed softly in the background and the sand, still holding warmth from the day's sun, tickled the soles of my feet.

"They'll have to do something about this," Eoin said, sniffing the air. "Bad planning to allow all this development without putting the proper infrastructure in place first."

"You're right," I agreed. "Cairnsure as it is now seems to have sprung up overnight. The population has trebled in ten years and every year brings a new housing estate. At least it used to until that kind of development crashed. Yet the facilities are still geared towards the smaller population."

"I've an appointment with the Planning Authority in Cork. I must see what they intend doing here before I make my final decision."

"I understood you had already made an offer on Elliots'?"

"I have. And since mine is the only offer now it will be accepted. That's not what I have to decide on."

He didn't add anything to that curious statement. We walked along in silence, my right-hand side all cosied into Eoin's body heat, my left cooled by the increasingly nippy sea breeze. Nippy enough for me to have thrown on my shrug. We turned at the point where the East Beach loomed dark and threatening.

"I read an article in Kieran's newspaper about a near disaster on those rocks," Eoin said as he peered into the darkness. "Some silly person climbed over there when the tide was coming in."

I deliberated for just a second longer. "That silly person was me and the rescuer was Kieran Mahon. That's why the article made front page."

Eoin stood in front of me and I stared defiantly up at him, squirming when I heard his deep belly-laugh.

"What were you trying to do? Impersonate a mermaid?"

He was mocking me! This wasn't part of my plan. We'd had such a lovely evening. I had been anticipating a kiss before I went back home tonight. A gentle touch, a hug, even a little admiration.

"I – I got stuck," I protested. "I was thinking and didn't notice the tide come in."

He laughed louder. I was hurt now, the butt of the joke he was enjoying so much. I turned and began to walk back towards the prom, the cool breeze suddenly cold, the tepid sand gritty and uncomfortable. I hadn't wanted Eoin Kirby to remember me because I had become marooned. Or because I had a friend who turned out to be a drug addict and a sixty-five-year-old mother who ran away from home rather than reveal her secret. I had convinced myself that he too had felt something of the growing attraction I felt towards him. I should have known better.

I didn't turn when I heard his footsteps behind me. I just wanted to get to my car now and drive home. I felt his hand on my arm but kept my eyes firmly focused ahead.

"I'm sorry if you thought I was being insensitive, Adele. You must admit you've managed to get yourself into some pretty weird situations, though."

I could give him that. His arm slid around my shoulder and I let the last of my resentment go. It floated off on the tide as Eoin turned me towards him and lifted his hand to my face. His fingers gently trailed through my hair and slipped to the back of my neck. I felt a shiver run through me as he lowered his head. My sandals fell from my fingers just as his lips met mine. I tried to live in that moment, to savour every thrill, the warm excitement, the tender touch of his lips, but something told me I should be filing it all away in my memory. I knew, as my knees shook and I nuzzled my face into his neck, that this was a moment I would treasure when I was a very old woman, scrunched up in an armchair in a nursing home, wearing incontinence pants and thinking about the night my heart almost jumped out of my chest when Eoin Kirby kissed me.

He was stroking my hair now and murmuring. I closed my eyes and listened to his deep voice. "You're a funny girl, Adele. And beautiful too."

I must admit, for only the second time in my life, I did feel beautiful that night wrapped in Eoin's arms on Cairnsure Beach. I'm not coy about my attractiveness, especially to the opposite sex. I get my share of admiration for my dark hair, hazel eyes and curvy figure. But being beautiful is an altogether more exclusive category into which Jodi and Carla fitted naturally and I did not. The other time I felt I too belonged to the beautiful group had been when Dad had bought me my red coat with the black velvet collar. I was ten at the time. I had been lusting after the coat, going by the drapery store just to see it in the window. When Dad arrived home with the coat, I dived into it. My father had said I looked like a beautiful princess and that's exactly how I had felt. My growing spurt started shortly after that. I quickly outgrew my red coat and any residual feeling that I could be beautiful. Until that night on Cairnsure Beach with Eoin Kirby.

Hand in hand we strolled back to The Grand Hotel. "How about a nightcap?" Eoin offered.

I hesitated. It had been a perfect evening except for the newspaper-article glitch. I didn't want to risk spoiling it. I just had one more question to ask and then I could go home to dream.

"How long will you be staying here, Eoin? When are you due to fly back?"

"I haven't decided yet."

And that, I thought, was the next best answer to hearing him say he was about to apply for Irish citizenship. I smiled at him.

"I'll skip the nightcap, thanks. I'm driving home. It was a lovely evening. Thank you very much."

"I'd like to see you again, Adele. Are you busy tomorrow night?"

"I am, yes. I'm going to visit Carla Selby and her husband."

"How about daytime tomorrow then? Are you interested in going for a swim?"

"I'd love that," I answered too quickly. I hadn't really thought of the consequences of exposing bits of me that probably looked better covered up. I could have kicked myself but it was too late now. Eoin was already making plans to meet me at the prom tomorrow afternoon at one o'clock. He walked me to my car and kissed me again before I drove away. I floated home, quite independently of my Fiat Uno.

Chapter 16

Typical Irish summer, I thought, as I looked out the window next morning. The sun shone during the weekdays and, come Saturday, when factories and offices closed for weekends, the rain fell on the unlucky work-force. Although it wasn't raining yet, the clouds hung low with bellyfuls of moisture ready to spill.

Frustration gnawed as I stood at the kitchen window. I must go see Mom, check on Jodi, do some grocery shopping, put on washing and yet be ready to meet Eoin at one o'clock. Unable to decide where to begin, I plumped for the next best option. I put on my trainers, the ones with the blue laces, and went out for a walk.

Even though it was dull, it was still warm. I was hot by the time I reached Willbury Lawn. Mom's car was not there. Not giving myself time to dither, I went to the door of number six and rang the bell. There was no reply.

I rang a second time and kept my finger on the bell for longer. I heard footsteps approach. Tom opened the door to me.

"Adele! Sorry. I was out in the back garden. Were you waiting long? Come in."

He led the way through a long narrow hallway into the kitchen at the back of the house. A cake of soda bread sat cooling on a wire rack on the windowsill so I knew Mom couldn't be far away.

"You've just missed Sissy," Tom said. "She's gone to the supermarket."

Ah! So Mom was in recovery mode. I wondered now if she would at last be well enough to talk to me.

"That sounds like good news then. I notice she's been baking too. Are we seeing the return of Sissy Burke to normal?"

"There's no call for glibness, Adele."

This was too much for me. Having Mom treat me so badly was one thing. I loved her and could accept a lot of eccentricity, even unfairness, from her. But I didn't know this man, nor he me, and yet he had taken it on himself to lecture me.

"I really don't think you have any right to judge me, Tom," I said coldly, trying to keep my anger under control. "If Mom had a shock, it's not my fault. I think at the very least —"

Tom put up his hand to stop me talking. "Sit down, please." He waved me towards an armchair and sat himself down opposite me.

"You're right, Adele, of course. I apologise. It's just

that I hate to see your mother so upset. I didn't mean
that you don't care or that it's your fault."

"Who's fault is it so? Do you know what it's about?"

"You know I do but Sissy has sworn me to secrecy.
She insists on telling you herself."

"Then I wish she bloody would!"

I stood up. I wasn't comfortable discussing this with
Tom.

"Could you tell Mom I called, please? Ask her to ring
me and tell her I'll be in Carla's house tonight in case
she's looking for me."

Tom stood too and walked to the front door with
me. Just as I was leaving he caught me by the arm. "I
think the world of your mother, Adele, but that doesn't
mean I believe she's always right. I wish I could say more
to you now but I can't. I have to respect her wishes. Do
you understand?"

"No, Tom, I don't. And I really don't think it's any of
your business. Goodbye."

I walked back home at Olympic pace, black clouds
hanging over my head and red-hot anger sizzling inside.
The first drops of rain fell just as I opened the front door.

* * *

Eoin rang at twelve o'clock. I was wearing leg-wax and
a face mask at the time and thanking my stars that video
phones were not yet the norm.

"How do you feel about swimming in the rain?" he
asked.

I weighed my options. This could be an escape route

for me. A cop-out. Keep my imperfections under wraps. My face mask was drying and beginning to shed pale green flakes. It needed to be taken off and Eoin Kirby needed an answer. I needed an answer.

"Adele? Are you there?"

"Yes, sorry, Eoin. I was just thinking about swimming in the rain. I love it. And you?"

"Can't wait. See you at one."

As soon as the mask was peeled and my legs smooth, I rang Jodi. She was in bed. I heard a profound tiredness and depth of sadness in her voice. "I feel like staying here for the rest of my life," she said. "I can't get up and face people. An object of pity. That's me now."

"Concern isn't pity, Jodi. And talking of concern, I'm worried about Carla. Don't forget she and Harry want to tell us their big news tonight."

"Oh, yes. The pathetic 'it's all over but we'll stay good friends for the sake of the children' announcement. What a surprise. Where were they anyway?"

I shrugged. I didn't know where Carla and Harry had been nor did I know if Jodi should go to Selby's tonight. She was obviously emotional at the moment and very much centred on her internal battles. Carla must be devastated and in need of support. A backlash from Jodi's drug withdrawal could only make her situation worse.

Glancing at the clock I saw it was almost half past twelve. I yet had to decide between my moss-green swimsuit with the support bra and high-cut leg or the black one with more coverage but less support. Jodi spared me the trouble of wondering whether she should go to Selby's or not.

"I'll see you around quarter past eight so, Del. Promise I'll be in better humour by then. Kieran is taking me with him this afternoon. He's covering some match or other for the paper."

"Enjoy. See you later."

I went with the moss green. It gave more definition to my curvy shape, a little more confidence. I stuffed a beach towel into my duffle bag and rushed to my car, glad that I had little time to think about where I was going.

Eoin was waiting on the prom when I arrived. Leaning his elbows on the wall, gazing out to sea, he didn't see me approach. I tapped him on the shoulder. He turned to smile at me.

"I like your hair curly," he said, looking over my already drenched head. I smiled in a way I hoped would convey the impression that the compliment didn't impress me much.

The rain, finding its rhythm after a gentle start, was pelting down. It seemed that we might not even have to go into the sea to get thoroughly wet.

Together we walked towards the dunes and found a hollow in which to change out of our clothes.

Sitting on the sand, I fiddled with my shoelaces, nervous about revealing all. Eoin showed no such hesitation. His shoes, jacket, sweater and jeans were stripped off in seconds and shoved into the gear bag he had brought along. Like me, he was wearing his swim togs underneath. I tried not to stare but my eyes were drawn to his broad chest and strong thigh muscles. An ex-athlete's body with the hint of a pot belly.

"C'mon, Adele," he grinned. "I'm suffocating here trying to hold in my stomach."

Laughing, I quickly took off my clothes, put them into my duffle and looked around for a place to shelter my bag from the rain. Noticing an overhang of reeds I shoved the bag underneath and Eoin put his one alongside. Then I stood there, feeling naked. Eoin's eyes skimmed over my body as mine had his. I tried to pull in my tummy too but my breath was shallow. I examined his face for signs of rejection or disappointment. Then I remembered I was thirty years of age, a teacher, a woman who owned her own apartment. I had no business feeling these adolescent pangs of insecurity.

I turned my face to the sea and began to run. The sand felt cold underfoot, the rain stung my skin, the breeze raised goose pimples on my arms but yet I ran. I was entombed in greyness. The sea and sky were the same dark grey hue. It was as if the sky had fallen or maybe the sea had risen towards the clouds. I heard Eoin approach, his footfall making slapping sounds in the wet sand. He grabbed my hand in his. His touch gave me strength and speed. It was like I was flying, the wind blowing my hair back, his hand warm in mine. We plunged into the sea together, gasping as the cold Atlantic water went knee-deep, thigh-high, up to our armpits and finally buoyed us as we both struck out towards the grey horizon. He too was a strong swimmer. We matched stroke for stroke as we swam. After ten minutes I had reached the limit of my journey towards the open sea.

"Far enough!" I shouted at him. "I'm going to float for a while now."

Turning on my back with my head directed towards the shore, I relaxed into the tumbling water and stared into the greyness of the sky. Rain dimpled the surface of the sea and pattered onto my face. My head was full of the sound of water, splashing, curling, hissing. Beside me Eoin floated too. In tandem we rose and dipped with the swell and trough of tide. There was no Sissy, no Carla or Jodi, no decision to be made about the year ahead or the future of my teaching career. There was nothing but Adele, Eoin, the sea and a deep inner calm I had not felt since I was a child. A flash of fork lightning streaked through my calm. I gave a little yelp and rolled over onto my stomach.

"We'd better head in," Eoin said.

I began to swim just as a clap of thunder shook Cairnsure.

"That was close," I gasped.

"Are you afraid?"

"No."

I had always liked the elemental power of thunder and lightning from the safe shelter of indoors. But today was different. Eoin Kirby was the only safe shelter I needed. And with that thought, the little warning voice in my head insisted on being heard. I had trusted Pascal Ronayne too, hadn't I? Look how that had ended up.

The beach was deserted as we waded ashore and back to our hollow in the dunes. Just us and a few seagulls. Dragging out our towels from our bags we quickly wrapped them around us and began to rub our cooling bodies. My teeth were beginning to rattle and I knew, even without a mirror, that my lips were turning an unflattering shade of blue. Eoin took a step towards me, opened up his very large beach towel and wrapped both of us into it.

"Nothing better than body heat to stop your shivering," he said.

I didn't contradict him. He couldn't know that my shivers were now caused by the nearness of him, the weight of his body against mine, the warmth of his arms around me. I laid my face on his chest and realised I had wanted to do this since the moment I had first seen him near Elliots' shop. His chest hair tickled my cheek and I giggled with a childish joy.

"So you find me amusing do you, Miss Burke?"

"I find your chest hair tickly. I suppose you can be funny too," I answered, surprising myself by giving him a very flirtatious smile. Eoin Kirby was unleashing a latent vamp in me.

He responded by lowering his head to mine. His lips were warm against my cold mouth. My arms snaked around his neck and his hands gently pressed my lower back until we were so close together that I could feel his heart beat and he, I'm sure, could feel the tremors which shivered through my body. Saturated in sensation, from the top of my head to the tips of my toes, I suddenly panicked. Another few seconds of this close contact and we would end up having sex on the beach like a pair of randy teenagers. I stepped back and glanced around the strand just to be sure we were still alone.

"I must get back home, Eoin," I said in an unsteady voice. "I have a lot to do. I enjoyed this swim so much. Thank you."

"I was hoping we could go for a drive somewhere tomorrow afternoon. Maybe have a spot of lunch."

I smiled at him, my new teasing smile. "You're tempting me. That sounds good. I'll meet you at the hotel around one. OK?"

Self-conscious now, we both quickly put on our clothes over our wet swimsuits and headed back across the dunes. My car was parked near the prom. I sat in and drove home without noticing the discomfort of cold, wet clothes or gritty sand poking into sensitive areas of my body. I was happy and excited at the thought of meeting Eoin again. All that welter of anticipation evaporated in one puff as I turned the car into our driveway and almost collided with a slate-grey Fiesta. Mom was home.

* * *

The first thing I noticed when I went into the kitchen was that it was still messy. I had left it in a bit of a state this morning and had promised myself that I would tidy it up later. I was taken aback to see Mom sitting in the middle of the clutter, her coat still on. Why had she not gone into her usual perfect-housewife mode? It was against her nature to leave as much as a teaspoon out of place. She had a vacant look on her face, as if she didn't notice her surroundings or even care that I had broken some of her cardinal kitchen rules.

"Hello, Mom. Are you feeling all right? You look tired."

"I am. And you're very wet. How did you get that drenched? Surely you weren't climbing the rocks again."

"I was swimming."

211

Sissy's mouth tightened with disapproval. "In this rain? That's daft. Go change your clothes."

Ignoring her curt order, I sat opposite her. She had dark circles underneath her eyes. Her hair was as meticulously arranged as ever but her face seemed to have shrunk over the past couple of days.

"Are you ready to talk to me, Mom? Would you care to explain why you were so rude to Eoin Kirby?"

"You're soaked to the skin. You'll get pneumonia."

"I'm going to sit here until you tell me what went on between you and the Kirbys and why you ran away rather than talk to me."

"I didn't run away. I just didn't want to be here while there was a Kirby in the house. You're a very stubborn girl, Adele."

"I'm a woman or haven't you noticed? I'm all grown up, Mom, so stop treating me like a child."

I had just begun to regret my curt tone when she spoke again and made me sorry I hadn't been even harsher.

"Did you bring that man into your bed, Adele? Was there immoral behaviour here in my house?"

I had to make a huge effort to control my temper before I answered her, further riled by the expectant look on her face as if she had a right to a reply.

"That, Mom, is my business but I'll have to tell you I'm very, very, insulted that you think I'd jump into bed with a stranger. You don't think much of me, do you?"

She began to fiddle with a button on her coat and I had a terrifying recollection of a television programme I had seen about Alzheimer's disease. Despite the wet and cold and my outrage at her lack of respect for me, a sweat broke out on my back. My God! Vacant expression, altered mood, irrational behaviour. Could it be?

"John Burke was a fine husband to me and he was a good father to you too."

"He was the best," I agreed, really frightened now. "Nobody said he wasn't, Mom."

Convinced by now that my mother had, at the very least, a touch of dementia, I got up from the table and put on the kettle. I had an inbred belief that a cup of tea would help sort all problems. When I turned back, Mom was standing by the kitchen door, her handbag sedately held in the crook of her arm, her mouth pursed.

"Are you going away again? Where to? Back to Tom, is it?"

"Yes, for another day or two. We're going on a pilgrimage to Knock Shrine tomorrow with the over-sixties group. I'll pray for you."

"When you're done talking to God, you might consider talking to your daughter too."

"Cynicism doesn't suit you, Adele. Your father would be very disappointed to hear you talk like that. I am too."

I stood open-mouthed as she sailed through the hall and out to her car, still carrying her secret with her. I ran after her. She was standing by the door of her car, raindrops bouncing off her lacquered hair.

"That's just typical of you, Mom. Rather than answer the question I asked about Eoin Kirby, you start criticising me. And using Dad to get at me too. That was low."

She turned around to face me. Her eyes were

troubled, so very sad, Her mouth worked but no sound came out. I ran to her and put my arms around her. She felt slight in my arms and I was overcome by an urge to hold onto her forever.

"Mom, will you stop upsetting yourself like this. I know it'll turn out to be a thing of nothing – like the time you couldn't eat for a whole week because you were convinced a harmless mole was cancerous. Just spit out whatever it is about the Kirbys and have done with it."

"I wish it was that easy, Adele. But it's not."

She slithered out of my hold then and sat into her car leaving me no wiser but a lot more concerned. I wondered if she should be driving, if Tom realised that she was not well, if I should insist on her seeing a specialist.

As I stood and watched her drive away my thoughts travelled treacherously in the opposite direction. Suppose there was nothing at all physically or mentally wrong with Mom? What if the Kirbys were really bad people? If they had done something terrible to my family? I felt resentment begin to rage against people I didn't know, who might have committed an offence I couldn't identify against my parents. Against those I always had, and always would, love most. Something so bad that it still cast a shadow more than thirty years later. An idea stirred somewhere in the back of my brain. It was fuzzy, not fully formed and unacceptable. A thought I could not allow myself to examine.

I immediately went back inside and began to scrub, polish and shine. I did grocery shopping, washing and ironing. The welter of activity did nothing to clear my mind of suspicion and the uneasy sense that if I knew the truth, if I allowed the embryo thought at the back of my brain to develop, I would hate Eoin Kirby as much as my mother seemed to do. In fact, I almost rang him to say I couldn't go tomorrow. I'd think of an excuse. After a long time thinking I couldn't come up with an excuse strong enough. The fact was, despite my misgivings and my mother's warnings, I needed to see Eoin again.

Chapter 17

Jodi was ready and waiting when I called to the Walls' house at quarter past eight that evening. Mrs Wall dived on me the minute I set foot inside the door.

"You two should have more sense at your age. Out all night in one of those club places in Cork and not even letting us know where you were. It's not proper."

I bowed my head and tried to look suitably contrite.

"I bet Sissy Burke had plenty to say about it," she said.

"Yes, she's very angry with me," I agreed.

Jodi caught me by the arm and led me towards the door. "Must rush, Mother. Carla will be waiting for us. I'll be late home so don't go having another hissy fit."

"That skirt is too short on you, Jodi. You're not a teenager any more."

"I never was," Jodi answered and I gasped at the bitterness in her reply.

"Why can't you wear sensible clothes like Adele?"

216

"Thanks, Mother. You've now insulted us both. I'm going before you think of something else to say."

Jodi continued muttering about her mother as we drove out to Selbys'.

"I've got to get out of there, Del. It's bad enough trying to get back on my feet after — after everything but coping with her constant carping as well is too much. And my father isn't any better. They make a big display of going to the church, praying and doing penance. Hypocrites! They haven't a charitable bone in their bodies."

I allowed her to rant and made no comment. I didn't know her parents very well. By tacit agreement, as children we had always met in either my home or Carla's. Seldom Jodi's. The Walls had always seemed to be busy organising their big family with military precision and, as Jodi rightly said, running off to church. It wasn't a comfortable house to visit. I had never understood how much Jodi craved her parents' approval. Nor how disapproving the Walls were of their daughter.

I parked my car beside Carla's four-wheel-drive in Selbys' and then reached across to catch Jodi's hand.

"I'm sure, like my Mom, they mean well. It's just that they can't understand us. Our generation has so much more independence and personal freedom than they had."

"Sissy's a pet, Del. The perfect Mom. You're lucky to have her."

I got out of the car without replying to that remark. A pet Sissy was, but not an altogether tame one. Just because her remarks were more softly spoken than Mrs Wall's didn't mean they hurt less.

217

"I knew it!" Jodi said as she got out of my car and pointed to the empty space on the other side of Carla's jeep. "Harry's not here! He's leaving Carla on her own to tell us about their break-up."

I shushed Jodi. Unlikely that they would hear her from the house but just in case. "We're only guessing. Maybe they're not splitting up at all."

"Of course they are. Why else would he have paraded his ex-wife here at the party? Do you think he's going back to her? The rat!"

I could see that Jodi was working herself up into a right tantrum. Maybe she was craving a fix. I grabbed her arm and hauled her towards the door of Carla's house. Whatever fit she was about have would be a lot more containable indoors.

Carla answered the door on the first ring. She had obviously been waiting for us. I was glad that Carla's attention seemed to be taken by Jodi. She didn't see me gape at her and notice her puffed-up eyes. She had been crying and had done nothing to try to disguise it.

"All bright-eyed and bushy-tailed, I see," she said to Jodi, peering into her face.

"No need for code," said Jodi. "Adele knows about me."

Carla turned to smile at me and I noticed her eyes were not just swollen. They were dulled with sadness too.

"How are you, Del? Come on in. We've a big treat in store. Brigitte's cooking for us."

We followed Carla into the spacious dining-room. The lights were dimmed and candles glowed. Three places were set at one end of the huge oval table. Jodi and I sat ourselves either side of the top carver while Carla went to the kitchen to let Brigitte know we were ready to eat.

"She looks terrible," Jodi whispered. "I could happily string Harry up. Bloody men!"

"Kieran Mahon's a man. You seem to be pretty cosy with him."

"That's different. He's a friend. A very good friend."

"Are you sure that's all?"

Before she had a chance to answer, Carla came back into the room and flopped onto the carver.

"Well, tell me the goss," she said. "I caught a little bit of that. Who's just a good friend?"

"Kieran Mahon," I answered. "I'm trying to find out if he's had any better luck with Jodi lately than he had in the cinema years ago."

"Feic off, Del! You know we're just friends. Granted, he chased all over the county to find me but I'm not so far down yet that I have to depend on a man."

Jodi stopped then, the look of shock on her face mirrored on mine.

"I'm sorry, Carl," she said. "I didn't mean anything about Harry. You know I'm just shooting my mouth off as usual."

Carla smiled and I breathed again. "If you weren't talking out of turn, Jodi Wall, I'd think there was something very wrong with you. But that reminds me, Harry sends his apologies. There's an emergency at the hospital and he's on call. He had to go because he's had so much time off lately."

"I bet," Jodi muttered and I saw by the frown on Carla's face that she had heard.

In the tense moment's silence which followed, I spluttered out the first thing that came into my head.

"How did your holiday go? Did you and Harry enjoy it?"

"Not really."

I looked down at the beautiful place settings. Newbridge cutlery and linen napkins. I looked at the flickering candle flame and then at the arrangement of freesias in the Waterford crystal vase. I looked everywhere except at Carla. How could I have been so stupid as to ask that question? Shit! One look at Carla was enough to show that whatever had happened wasn't enjoyable.

Brigitte spared my blushes. She came bustling into the room carrying a tray with our starters. They smelled delicious as she placed the individual onion quiches in front of each of us.

"Brigitte has agreed to stay on with us as our cook," Carla announced.

"So, you're going to be doing what you love best, Brigitte," I said.

She smiled at me and winked. "I leave the children to Vera and Mrs Selby. I stay in the kitchen in future. After my trip home."

Jodi and I exchanged glances. So, it seemed like Carla would be staying on in this house whatever happened. In some luxury too by the sound of things. Provided with a cook and a nanny.

"What's this about Kieran Mahon chasing you around, Jodi? What did I miss while I was away?"

"Kieran's been very, very busy," Jodi said. "I'm not the only one he rescued. Haven't you read the *Cairnsure Weekly*?"

By the time we had Carla brought up to date about the rescues in the woods and off the rocks, Brigitte was back with our main course of Beef Bourguignon and sour cream. Jodi's prodigious appetite seemed to have faltered, Carla pushed her food around her plate and I felt too full of tension to eat much.

When we had finally put our cutlery down, Carla sat back into her chair and looked towards Jodi.

"Sorry about the row the other morning, Jode. You needed talking to but I went a bit over the top."

"You were right, Carla, as I proved by meeting the supplier in Cork. I was starting down the slippery slope again. It's being back home. Jesus! My parents!"

"There are plenty of people here to help you, Jodi. What about counselling? Harry could arrange an appointment for you. Discreetly."

"No. No, thank you. The clinic and all the counsellors I had in London didn't work. Not for long anyway. I must do this myself. And at least I don't owe money now. All my debts are paid."

"How did it start?" I asked. That had puzzled me and I hadn't felt comfortable asking until now. Jodi had always had such control over her life I would have thought her the last person to develop a dependency.

"The usual way. A line of coke at a party. It was an

accepted part of the social scene with my set. It stayed like that, just a social thing, until I got my promotion. I was under huge pressure because there were people, men need I say, who were jealous of my position. I had to prove myself better than them. Every day, every hour of every day was a challenge. That's when I remembered the euphoria, the optimism, the energy I got when I snorted coke. It helped me work around the clock. It quickly became a daily habit and one line became three."

"I know you can fight physical dependence," Carla said softly, "but you realise better than anyone how very difficult the emotional and psychological effects of withdrawal are to handle. Won't you even consider getting professional help?"

Jodi's face flushed red and I thought she would leap from her seat. Brigitte saved the day again, arriving in with chocolate fondue and little bowls of chopped-up fresh fruit. Despite my edginess my mouth began to water. Strawberry and pineapple dipped in chocolate sauce are my idea of a near-perfect dessert.

Jodi collapsed back onto her seat and sat there sulking until Brigitte had left with our dinner plates.

"How in the fuck do you think I could afford a shrink, anyway?" she asked then.

"I told you Harry can arrange it. Just say the word."

"Bloody marvellous, isn't he?"

"He is. Absolutely bloody marvellous."

I examined Carla's face for signs of a sarcastic grin or even a sneer. She was serious. So serious that her eyes glittered with tears. I put the chunk of pineapple I had been just about to dunk in chocolate down on my plate.

"What's wrong, Carla? You asked us here to tell us something? What is it?"

Her mouth opened and then shut again. She fiddled with her dessert fork and then took a deep breath.

"The café," she said. "Elliots' old shop. I would have loved that. It would have been great for us to work together, if only for a year."

"I wanted to make it my livelihood," Jodi said. "And it could have been a money-spinner. Too late now anyway. Eoin Kirby has bought it. Gussie Elliot told Kieran."

"The New Zealander? The same man who found you in the woods?"

"That's right," I explained to Carla. "You saw him that day we went to see the shop. Don't you remember?"

She nodded and I don't think either of them noticed my discomfort at the mention of his name.

"It would have been fun, wouldn't it," Carla said wistfully. "It used to be a dream of mine that the three of us would end up working together. I'm sorry to have spoiled our plan."

Jodi opened her mouth to say something but I frowned at her and leaned towards Carla. "Why did you change your mind about the café so quickly, Carla? It seemed that one day you were all enthusiasm, planning menus and décor and the next you wouldn't even consider the idea."

"Things changed."

"Things?"

She reached out a hand to each of us and gripped our fingers tight. "I have something to tell you both. It's not easy. I was hoping Harry would be here."

"The bastard is leaving you!" said Jodi. "I knew it!"

Carla looked at Jodi and smiled. "No, Jodi. You have that the wrong way around. I'm leaving him."

"Good on you! I hope you catch him for a fortune in alimony. Leave nothing for that red-haired, weasel-faced ex-wife of his!"

"Shut up, Jodi!" I hissed as I saw Carla's face crumple.

Carla withdrew her hands, buried her head in them and sobbed. I jumped up and went to her, wrapping my arms around her thin body. I knew then. The bones were too sharp, the sobs too profoundly sad.

"Are you sick, Carla?"

She looked at me and close up I noticed that the whites of her eyes were taking on the same sickly yellow as her skin. Not sun-bed, not badly applied fake tan. Carla was drowning in a vicious yellow wave.

"What is it?" I whispered but I didn't want her to answer. I didn't want to hear the words.

"Cancer. Pancreatic cancer."

"No!"

"Yes. Inoperable. Metastasised."

"Don't talk that medical shit, " Jodi said angrily, an edge of hysteria in her voice. "What does that mean for God's sake?"

"It means I'm dying, Jodi. The cancer has spread to my liver and bones."

"But there must be something they can do!" said

Jodi. "Harry's a surgeon for God's sake! How could he let this happen to you?"

Carla laughed then. The sound was so inappropriate in the emotion-charged room that it raked across my nerves and set my teeth on edge. How could she laugh in the face of this tragedy? She was grinning at Jodi now.

"This is one thing you can't blame on Harry. I'm too young to have this disease. No family history of pancreatic cancer. Nothing at all to indicate that it was there."

"You've lost a lot of weight," I pointed out. "Didn't that concern you?"

"That's why I went to see Ruth Selby. You know she's an endocrinologist. The best there is. She referred me to a specialist in Dublin, a classmate of hers. I think she suspected what her friend confirmed after a scan. He booked me into his hospital for more scans and tests. Harry stayed there with me. That was our holiday, Del. So now you know why we didn't enjoy it."

I went back to my place and sat again, the sight of the chunk of pineapple speared on my fork disgusting me now. I pushed my plate away and asked the question I knew I must.

"Treatment?"

"Palliative. There will be no cure. It's too late. Chemo will hopefully give me more time. But not enough. The children . . ." Carla howled then, a sound wrenched from her very soul. "My babies! My babies!" she gasped between sobs. She slid off her chair and sat on the floor, arms wrapped tightly around her shrinking frame, rocking back and forth and all the time mourning for the children she would never see grow up.

Silently, Jodi and I joined her on the floor. Legs crossed, our arms slid around each other, our heads snuggled close together. A parody of the pose we had always adopted to share our childhood secrets. We were those three little girls again. It was as if life had not moved on. Nothing mattered but the sharing. Jodi and I clung tightly to Carla, willing our strength to flow into her and her pain to ebb back to us. Unwilling to let her go.

"Coffee and tissues here. You want them on the floor or the table?"

We turned our tear-stained faces towards Brigitte. Her mouth smiled but her eyes shone with unshed tears. She knew. So that's why she had decided to stay. What a comfort she would be to the children and Harry when ... when ... I dismissed the thought without bringing it to its conclusion. There were cures, weren't there? And miracles.

We laughed through our sobs as we helped each other to our feet. We were far too old now for sitting on the floor. But far too young for dying.

"You must go to bed soon, Mrs Selby. You look shite," Brigitte said and we all smiled.

"Your English is really coming on," I grinned, though tears still tracked down my face.

She was right. Carla looked exhausted. "You'd better do as you're told, Carla," I advised. "Save your strength. Jodi and I will see ourselves out. You get some rest."

She hugged us again and slowly, her hand on the small of her back, she left the room. I saw it then. The portent of what was to come. Jodi and I standing here, heartbroken, helpless, while Carla shuffled away in the clutches of her life-sucking disease.

* * *

We drove home in silence. What could we have said? Words did not have depth enough to express our feelings. I pulled up outside the Walls' house and turned to Jodi.

"I wish we had been right about Harry and Ruth Selby having an affair. At least Carla would still be here to get her life back together."

Jodi clapped her hands over her ears. "Stop! I don't want to hear this. And I don't want to go into that convent my parents call home."

She was shaking and I knew that Jodi needed some cocaine, cannabis, amphetamine. Anything to take the edge off her pain.

"Do you want to come home with me?" I asked.

"Take me to Kieran, please."

I drove to the centre of town where Kieran Mahon had an apartment. "I'll wait just to make sure he's there," I said as she got out of the car. After a few minutes, Kieran rang me to say Jodi was with him. In safe hands.

I drove around for a bit, reluctant to go back to my empty home. I passed Willbury Lawn and saw that number six was in darkness. Mom and Tom were in bed, though not, I was certain, together. They would probably be up at dawn to go on their holy pilgrimage to Knock Shrine. I needed to see Mom now, to have her hold me and say everything would be all right. Just like she used to do before she got obsessed with the Kirbys.

I almost hit a traffic cone in the square, so I decided to go home before I had an accident. I drove automatically, all my conscious thought concentrated on Carla.

The house was cold. I went straight to bed and Barry Bear came with me. I hugged him close and cried into his fur. I kept remembering. Snippets. Little cameos of childhood. A Carla, Jodi and Adele childhood. The big doll's house Dad had made for me and fitted out with beautifully crafted pieces of miniature furniture. We had spent hours playing with that in my bedroom. Carla had always been the Mammy, Jodi the Daddy and me the baby in that fantasy grown-up world we created then. A template for the lives we were to live. I saw us, twelve years old, all stooped down behind the wall of the graveyard, puffing cigarettes, coughing and pretending we liked them. Fourteen and experimenting with make-up and boys, giggling, sharing. Cutting our cake for our thirtieth birthday. Friends. More than that. Sisters.

"No! No, Carla, no!" I cried as the image of her sallow face and already wasted body superimposed itself on my memories. I sat up and turned on the light again. I ached. I felt cold inside and empty. And very afraid. Hands shaking, I picked up my phone and dialled. It rang for what seemed like a long time. A sleepy voice answered.

"Eoin? I can't be alone tonight. Will you come to see me?"

"Where are you?"

"At home. On my own."

"Be with you in ten."

I was at the door to meet him when he arrived. I threw myself into his arms. He stroked my hair and rubbed my back as I explained in gasps and gulps about Carla. Then I led him into our sitting-room where we sat on the couch, me crying and Eoin holding me, consoling me with his warmth and kindness. His nearness was not just physical. Our closeness was beyond that. More life-affirming, mind-numbing, grief-assuaging. More loving.

I fell asleep in his arms and dreamt of Carla, laughing, skipping about, healthy, young and with her whole life stretching ahead of her.

Chapter 18

We were both stiff and cold when we woke next morning. A glance down reminded me that I was wearing pyjamas and my dressing-gown that had gone all knobbly in the wash. I felt embarrassed and a little ashamed as Eoin stood up and massaged his left arm where my head had lain all night. What must he think of me now?

"God, I need a shower," he said. "I feel grotty."

"I didn't mean you to stay all night. I just needed a shoulder to cry on. I wasn't trying to lure you here or anything."

He sat down beside me again and swept my untidy hair back from my face.

"Adele Burke, last night you were a friend in need. How could anyone put a sleazy interpretation on that?"

"My mother could."

The instant I mentioned Sissy the warm atmosphere between the two of us cooled. He stood up.

"Excuse me, Adele. I really do need to shower now."

"I'll get a dressing-gown and towels for you."

Mom had kept Dad's clothes. Like a shrine to his memory they still hung in his side of their wardrobe. I brought Dad's dressing-gown and some towels to Eoin.

"What would you like for breakfast?" I asked and then laughed. "I can't believe I slept with someone without knowing whether they like Weetabix or Cornflakes. I've broken all my own rules."

"Guess."

I ran my eyes over his big frame. "Definitely a Weetabix man. And maybe a boiled egg or two."

"You're a witch. Could you conjure up some toast too?"

I was smiling as I went into the kitchen. I had some tidying up to do before starting breakfast. When Eoin came in he looked very cosy in Dad's dressing-gown which fitted him perfectly. While he got our cereal bowls and filled them up, I pottered happily about, putting on the kettle, getting out the saucepan to boil our eggs, popping bread in the toaster. There was a rhythm to the way we worked together, perfectly synchronised. No need for words. Just an instinctive understanding of each other. I sighed with deep contentment and there was a smugness too in the shuddering exhalation.

Glancing out the window I saw that it was still raining. A light drizzle. This morning I saw past the grey and knew the sun shone warm and bright above the blanket of clouds. Just as I was turning back to join Eoin at the table, I noticed the window box. Sissy had planted anemones in it this year. One bloom, vigorous and fully opened, leaned against the windowpane. Its delicate petals were a magnificent blue-violet shade. A deep rich hue. The colour of Carla's eyes. My smile faded. The full impact of her illness rushed at me. Carla was going to die! Too late. No cure. No future. No growing old with Harry, no attending her children's graduations, no holding her grandchildren. No being there for her friends. For Jodi or for me. Hot and hard, the grief stuck in my throat. I banged my fist on the draining board. Eoin started in fright.

"Jesus, Adele! You nearly gave me a heart attack!"

"My father died from a heart attack. Here in this very kitchen. You wouldn't have said that if you had known anything at all about me."

Frowning, he got up and came towards me. I saw the hurt in his brown eyes and I tried to find a logic in my muddled thinking. I had deliberately upset Eoin and felt satisfaction in his puzzlement. Did I want him to suffer as I was doing or was it just a reaction to my own guilt at feeling happy, even for a fleeting moment? What kind of friend was I? Selfish and shallow. I had forgotten Carla while I had been playing house with Eoin. I had actually forgotten her and, not wanting to blame myself, I was blaming him.

"I'm sorry, Eoin. It's just that I – I suddenly remembered about Carla's illness. I shouldn't have been nasty to you. You've been so good to me."

He drew me close to him. My tears fell on Dad's dressing-gown. "You must be strong for her, Adele. She'll need you so much over the next few months."

"Maybe years. She might have years yet. There must be a cure. Harry could get her into a research programme for a new drug. One that really works."

"And maybe her time is very limited. You must accept that. Remember Jodi too will need you. She's not as strong as you are."

I sighed again, this time devoid of smugness. "I'm not ready to give up yet. There's always hope. Carla's still here. But I don't know what I should do. Should I go to see her or should I let her have her time with her family?"

"I think you should sit down and eat your breakfast. We'll talk about it after. You'll be no good to Carla if you're sick too."

I smiled at him. He was so wise and it was nice, if mistaken, that he thought me a delicate flower which needed careful tending. We ate in silence and then, wordlessly, we both stood and together tidied up the kitchen. There was a clarity, a communion in our silence which words would have blurred.

Kitchen tidied, we went back to the sitting-room and sat side by side on the couch again. My head resting in the crook of his arm, I had more control over my earlier feelings of panic.

"I want to help Carla but I don't know how," I explained. "Vera is there to mind the children. Brigitte to cook. Harry will take care of her medical needs. I don't want to be a nuisance to them."

"You've told me that you and Jodi and Carla have been friends since childhood."

"That's right. Best friends. We grew up together. We

were inseparable. Even when we took different career paths, we still kept in touch."

"So, that's what you can give Carla. Your friendship. You three have unique memories. Share them with her. Remind her of the happy times."

"How? How am I going to look at her suffering and be all jolly hockey sticks and 'do you remember the time' when what I want to do is scream and rage and cry?"

Eoin sat forward and looked into my face.

"How much worse do you think Carla feels? She'll have to say goodbye to her children, her husband. To life. Just be there when she needs you. You owe it to your friendship."

He kissed me then. A tender kiss. I felt his strength flow into me.

He looked at his watch and jumped up. "Are you still on for the picnic we had planned?"

I hesitated for a moment. It felt wrong to be going out to enjoy myself today. Besides, it was raining.

"Is it really a picnic day?"

"Was yesterday a swimming day?"

I laughed at that. Yesterday had been the best swimming day ever and today could be the best picnic day.

"I must get back to the hotel to make a few calls. You get ready. Phone Carla and Jodi too. I know you'll be anxious unless you've spoken to them. I'll look after the food. Just bring yourself along to the hotel at one. Then we'll see where the day takes us. Okay?"

I walked to the door with him. Then, knowing that my mother was safely on her way to her shrine in Co Mayo, I stood on the doorstep in my knobbly dressing -

gown and kissed him. Feeling like a defiant sixteen-year-old, I waved him off and went to ring Jodi and Carla.

* * *

Harry answered the phone when I rang Selbys'. "She's resting," he told me. "I had to give her pain relief for her back. It's made her sleepy. Apologies for not being here last night to talk to you and Jodi. Couldn't be helped."

"Harry, I'm so sorry about the way I spoke to you at the party. Carla explained how Ruth helped her. I jumped to the wrong conclusion when I saw you and Ruth in her Ferrari. I thought you were, you know, cosy together. I'm so sorry."

"Not at all, Adele. That's a very little thing now, isn't it? It takes something like Carla's illness to make us all get our priorities straight. And of course the priority is to make Carla as comfortable and as accepting as she can possibly be."

I felt my legs go weak as I stood in the hall, the phone in my hand. There was no hope in Harry Selby's voice, no promise of new treatments or radical cures. Just the sound of defeat. I heard him take a deep breath and imagined him trying to take control of his shock and grief.

"Carla mentioned you this morning, Adele. She said she was very grateful to you for spending time with Finn. So am I."

"I enjoyed my time with him. Actually, I wanted to talk to you about him. I suspect he has a very high IQ. I think you should consider having him professionally assessed. There are programmes for children who need extra stimulation."

Harry laughed then. "Do you mean we should forgive the mayhem he causes because he's a little genius?"

"Not at all. But that behaviour would, at the very least, be modified if he had enough intellectual challenge."

"I'm more worried about him now than the rest of the children. The others will be upset of course. But what am I going to tell Finn about Carla's illness?"

"The truth. He'll figure it all out anyway. Just answer the questions he asks honestly."

"He's only four. I'm forty and I can't cope with this truth."

I heard the pain in Harry's voice and felt tears in my own eyes. I remembered Eoin's words. Be strong for Carla. I swallowed hard and blinked my tears away.

"He'll cope better when he has the facts. He's very logical."

"There's no logic to this. Thirty-year-olds don't get this disease. Not without a history . . ."

Harry's voice cracked with emotion. I think he was crying. I stood there, helpless, desperately trying to think of something comforting to say. Everything that came to mind was either patronising or pious. I waited silently until he was ready to speak again.

"I'd really appreciate it if you could keep an eye on Finn for me," he said. "Vera is marvellous with the children, Brigitte, too, but Finn seems to have bonded with you. Would you mind, Adele? Just a chat with him every now and then."

I jumped at his request. At last something positive I could do to help.

"Of course, Harry. It would be a pleasure. And if there's anything else, just let me know."

"Actually, there is. Carla will be admitted to hospital tomorrow. My hospital in Cork. We're doing a few more tests. We need to confirm if chemotherapy is viable. Maybe you and Jodi might drop by to see her. I know you two are like sisters to her."

"We'll be there, Harry. We'll always be there for Carla."

I put down the phone and cried very bitter tears for fear that Carla might not always be there for us.

When I got my breath back again, I phoned Jodi. I was worried at first. She sounded very down. Not just sad. The darkness of depression echoed in her low voice.

"I can't believe the news about Carla. It's shit. It's not fair."

"No, Jodi, it's not fair. I've just been talking to Harry and he wants us to visit Carla tomorrow. She'll be in hospital in Cork."

"I can't! I can't watch her dying. I couldn't look at our Carla all tubed up. No, I won't go."

I heard a muttered conversation and then Kieran came on the phone to me.

"Hi, Adele. Don't worry about tomorrow. Jodi will be ready to visit Carla by then. She's just going through a bad patch at the moment."

"Anything I can do to help?"

"Not now, thanks. She just needs a little TLC."

"You're quite the dashing hero, aren't you? Rescuing maidens in distress all over the place."

"I was born for the role," he laughed. Then his tone changed. "Awful news about Carla, isn't it? I'm so sorry, Adele. I know how close you three have always been."

"We still are, Kieran. Tell Jodi I'll ring her tomorrow. We can arrange about going to Cork then."

"Will do. And don't worry. I'll look after her."

As I put down the phone this time I was smiling and wondering how Jodi would react when she eventually realised Kieran Mahon was in love with her.

Chapter 19

The rain had stopped by the time I had parked my Fiat Uno at the Grand Hotel and sat into Eoin's car. We set out for our picnic, heading west, past the Selbys' grand house and back towards the hills. Eoin had changed into a navy sweater and jeans. Casual but classy. A look echoed, I hoped, by my best top and jeans. We came to a crossroads and Eoin slowed the car to a stop.

"You're the guide," he said. "Which way?"

"Left. The scenic route through the hills."

"You're quiet. Are you still thinking about Carla?"

I shook my head. In fact, I was thinking about him and how very little I knew about him. He was kind, considerate, a good swimmer, liked Weetabix, fruit cake and boiled eggs and bought grotty old shops in countries he was visiting. Other than that, Eoin Kirby was still a mystery to me. He gave me a quizzical glance and then concentrated on guiding the car along the increasingly steep hill road. The view would have been spectacular except that a heavy mist clouded the hills and distant mountain range. I felt the brooding presence of the mountains in the murk. Lurking, much like death lurked in wait for Carla.

I shook my head to rid it of gloomy thoughts. I was being unfair to Eoin, sitting here moping when he had gone to such trouble to entertain me. But maybe that's what he deserved. He was after all a Kirby. Shocked by that Sissy-thought, I flashed him a guilty smile.

Eoin pulled the car into the viewing area on the summit, which, on a clear day, afforded breathtaking views over hills and dales. Even today, it held a certain magic. I opened the car door and got out. The mist was rolling by in great fluffy wads. I closed my eyes and raised my face skyward. The drifting mist touched my skin with the delicacy of gossamer. I opened my eyes again when I heard Eoin leave the car and come to stand beside me. He put his arm around my shoulder and I instinctively cuddled close to him.

"Can we make a deal, Adele? Try to forget about Carla's illness. Just for a few hours. I admire your caring quality but you owe yourself a break too. Deal?"

Standing there, Eoin's arm around me, of course I wanted to say yes. It was just that I couldn't forget, could I? But maybe, if I tried very hard, I could push the thoughts of death and dying to the back of my mind for a little while. Eoin hugged me closer and my decision was made. I smiled up at him.

"You're right, Eoin. I'm sorry I've been such a misery guts."

"I've got something to cheer you up then."

Going to the back of his car, he opened up the boot, took out a rug and handed it to me.

"Just spread that on the seat there," he said, pointing to the hilltop picnic table and seat which the council had provided.

I did as I was told and watched as he took out a cloth and a picnic basket and put them on the table. He grinned at me.

"I'd like to claim credit but the hotel staff made it up for me. I hope you eat chicken."

I opened the lid of the wicker basket. Inside was a buffet of chicken breasts, cold salmon, Parma ham, cheese, crackers and oven fresh, crusty bread rolls. Nestling in there too, I saw flasks and the chocolates without which a feast would not be complete.

"No alcohol because we're both driving. I got flasks of coffee instead. Do you mind?"

Did I mind? I felt like telling him this was the nicest thing anyone had ever done for me. What girl wouldn't like to picnic in the clouds with this gorgeous hunk of a man? Putting a rein on my enthusiasm, I gave him a kiss on the cheek.

"It's absolutely perfect, Eoin. Thank you."

"Good. Let's eat."

As we sat there, side by side, enjoying our hilltop picnic, the sun poked dazzling rays through the mist. By the time we were eating our luscious handmade chocolates, a swathe of blue sky appeared above us. It seemed like a good omen to me. I stood and stretched. Sated. Satisfied like a cat. Maybe I purred.

"How about a walk, Eoin? Work off some of those calories?"

"Are you sure?" he asked, glancing down at my high-heeled shoes. "Will I have to massage your ankle again?"

I hit him a playful slap on his arm. Laughing, holding hands, we started our walk along the road which sloped gently down from the summit. The air smelled of rain-washed earth and heather. Rabbits scurried for shelter when they heard us approach, nothing of them visible except their fluffy white scuts as they bobbed away in fright. A curlew called. The breeze, gentle and now warmer, began to blow away the remaining mist. Eoin held me close to his side, the hills emerged, fresh and green, the sun shone. The moment made me think of my future and wonder if Eoin Kirby would have any part to play in it. He might quite possibly be going back to New Zealand next week, never to be seen again.

Shit! I stopped walking.

"Eoin, can you tell me yet how long you're going to stay?"

My blush started in my toes and sped facewards at supersonic speed. How rude! How gauche! I began to mumble and stutter and dig an even deeper hole for myself.

"I – I mean, do you have to get back to work? None of my concern, I know. I – I'm sorry."

"The answer, Adele, is that I still don't know. I'm not

trying to be mysterious but I'm checking out a few possibilities and haven't decided on anything definite yet. I'll certainly be around for a few weeks and I hope to see a lot more of you in that time. If you want to, that is."

"We'll play it by ear," I answered, hoping my casual reply betrayed none of the confusion I felt. Excitement at the thought of getting to know Eoin better fought for space with the fear of upsetting my mother even more.

"You mean it depends on whether I remain on your mother's black list or not?" he asked with uncanny perspicacity.

"Of course not. I'm quite capable of making up my own mind. But I am worried about Mom."

"I see. So she was waffling on again about some grievance, real or imagined, against my family."

"My mother doesn't waffle," I answered. "Besides, I'm beginning to believe her. Something very sinister did happen. She wouldn't be this upset otherwise."

I began to walk faster. My runaway mother and her secrets had no more place in this idyllic scene than did thoughts of Carla and cancer. Eoin lagged behind for a moment or two then fell into step beside me. He too seemed to have decided to drop the Burke-Kirby saga.

"What about your teaching career?" he asked. "Do you think you'll go back to it?"

"I haven't left it. I've just taken a break."

"Last I heard, you were going into the café business."

"I didn't stay long in that," I laughed but I felt more like crying, remembering Carla saying last night how important the café idea had been to her. It would have been so wonderful if only our plan had not been scuppered before it had time to fly.

"I know you said I shouldn't think about Carla but she told us last night that she had always dreamt of the three of us working together. Herself, Jodi and me all under the one roof. We could have done that in the café."

"You would probably have ended up tearing each other's hair out. It's not a good idea to go into business with friends."

"But you work with your brother."

"I didn't say we were friends."

"Oh!"

Eoin seemed to change then. Become more closed. We walked on side by side but I could see his mind was miles away. Probably in New Zealand and whatever life he had there.

"And what about you?" I asked. "Exactly what do you do in your father's company?"

"I'm an engineer by profession. I oversee all our projects."

I was immediately struck by "all our projects". Just how big was the Kirby company?

By the time we got back to the car, the mist had completely lifted. The mountain ranges, no longer threatening, shimmered in the distance and all around the land swooped and fell in a glorious pastiche of greens. We spread the rug on the picnic seat again and sat to drink the coffee from the second flask.

Eoin lapsed into silence, sitting there sipping his

coffee and looking off into the distance. Even though my first impression of him was of an open and honest person, I now sensed something guarded in his nature. He startled me by suddenly turning towards me and taking my hand.

"I don't like secrets," he said, his brown eyes so intense they seemed to bore in through me. "I want to tell you something about myself. Something very personal."

I nodded. I couldn't say anything. What in the hell was he about to reveal? A string of wives, a murder conviction, a boyfriend?

"I told you I was living with a woman for a long time. Five years. She left me. For my brother. They had been having an affair behind my back for two years. They treated me like an idiot. To be honest, for a time, I agreed with their opinion. I had trusted them both. I had no idea what was going on until she packed her case and left me."

I breathed a sigh of relief. The revelation could have been so much worse. I empathised with him. If Adele Burke knew anything well, it was rejection. I squeezed his hand.

"So that's why you said your brother's not your friend. It must be very difficult working together knowing . . . knowing that he cheated you."

"I managed for a while. Just kept my head down and worked, pretending not to hear the snide comments behind my back. I was a big in-joke in the company until the staff moved onto the next bit of gossip. But the wedding was too bitter a pill to swallow."

"They married? Your brother and your partner?"

"Last week. That's why I decided to come here. Not very noble. I ran away."

"Do you still love her?" I asked, knowing that it was an unfair question to ask but needing to know the answer.

He smiled, his lovely white smile, and I saw it touch his eyes. "That's the amazing thing. I had thought I really loved Trudi but I found that my pride, not my heart, was the most damaged after she left. Maybe that's how I managed to stay and work with my brother for the past year. The further removed I've become from Trudi and her God Almighty career as a PR consultant, the more I realise we should never have been together in the first place."

"Will you find it awkward when you go back? Trudi will be Mrs Kirby and maybe there will be babies soon. Your nieces and nephews."

"That doesn't bother me. Besides, I can't see her taking time out to have children. My problem now is that I came here to avoid the wedding and restore some pride. It was just an escape but I'm getting the feeling that I've come home. For whatever reason, I feel I have a place here."

"In Elliots' old shop?"

"Don't mock. That site has potential."

"You're not going to demolish The Cabin! You couldn't!"

He laughed. "The Cabin will probably fall down soon of its own accord. Anyway, my plans involve a lot more than just Elliots' property. Costings and feasibility studies must be done before I decide. But I must say I'm tempted."

"Or are you running away?"

"That's the big question, isn't it? And I'm not going to rush the decision. Now, that's my soul bared. How about you? Any deep and dark secrets you want to share?"

I smiled. How exciting it would have been to have lived a life full of intrigue and darkness! Of course there was the Pascal Ronayne incident. I was amazed how trivial it seemed now, sitting here on the hilltop with Eoin by my side.

"That man I lived with. He brought a girl into our apartment while I was at work and had sex with her on our kitchen table."

"Really! Was he an acrobat?"

"No, he was an architect. And an idiot!"

We laughed and held each other close. The sun sank westward. I leaned my head on Eoin's shoulder and thought I had never felt so content. Happiness, I could not contemplate. That would involve Carla's full recovery from cancer, Jodi's freedom from her drug addiction, the resolution of the Burke-Kirby family feud and a firm commitment from Eoin that he was going to stay in Ireland. But for that evening, as the setting sun flared orange and red, contentment was all I needed.

* * *

There was an awkward moment between Eoin and me

as we parted in the grounds of the Grand Hotel. I didn't want to invite him back to my home. I couldn't face another confrontation with my mother. I wasn't sure if he was expecting to be asked.

He walked with me to where I had parked my car earlier and his chat about his rugby-playing days was telling me nothing of his expectations. Every time I opened my mouth to tell him not to come near my house, I clamped it shut again. How pathetic it would be to say "I'm afraid my mother will see you." And how utterly unbearable it would be to have Sissy walk in on us for a second time. Her daughter and the man she had forbidden her to see.

"You're in one of your mysterious moods," Eoin said as I settled myself into my driver's seat and he stooped down beside me. "I'm almost afraid to ask now but can I see you again tomorrow?"

Problem solved! He was going to allow me to choose the where and when.

"I'll be going to Cork tomorrow afternoon to visit Carla in hospital. How about later? Here in the bar at around eight maybe?"

"Great. I'll look forward to that. I'm going to Cork too tomorrow. To the County Planning Offices. Our paths might cross."

"Thank you for the picnic. Thank you for . . . every-thing."

"My pleasure."

He looked at his watch then and stood up. "I'd better go. I'm meeting Seán Potter in Cooneys' soon."

"Doing business in a pub on a Sunday night? How Irish of you! You're one of our own."

"Maybe. We'll see."

With that enigmatic little comment, he smiled his glorious smile at me and walked away. I sat there, key in ignition and stared at his retreating back, at his height and breadth, his determined stride, his broad, straight shoulders. I closed my eyes and said a very fervent thank you to the fate that had sent this gorgeous, generous man into my life.

* * *

I meant to catch up on housework and some reading when I went in home. Instead I turned on the soft standard lamp in the sitting room, threw myself in Dad's armchair and daydreamed about picnics in the clouds with a handsome New Zealander. Tired from the emotion of Carla's illness and the intensity of the time Eoin and I had spent together, I dozed off to sleep.

I woke with a start when I heard a key in the front door. Rushing to the hall, I was in time to see Mom come in, Tom behind her carrying her suitcase.

"All the praying in Knock Shrine has turned her into a saint," Tom said. "She's not going to stay with me tonight."

His attempt at light-heartedness didn't fool me. He looked worried and Mom looked exhausted. She had been crying.

"Mom! Are you all right?"

She came to me and kissed me on the chin, a habit

she had developed when I grew too tall for her to reach my cheek. "I heard the news, Adele. Father Austin told us. I'm so terribly, terribly sorry. I know how much Carla means to you."

I folded my arms around her and hugged her to me. Tom nodded to me, placed her case on the floor and just slipped away, leaving us to cry in each other's arms.

When we finally got to the kitchen, I took Mom's coat and sat her down. She refused something to eat but we both decided to have hot chocolate. She spoke in a very subdued voice as I put on the milk to boil.

"We said a Rosary for her at the Shrine. I lit three candles. One for Carla and one each for you and Jodi Wall so that you might be strong for her."

"She's going into hospital tomorrow in Cork. Just keep praying. Miracles do happen."

"I know that. God spoke before man. It's hard to understand how a young mother could be taken like that. It would test your faith if you weren't strong."

I let that comment go. My faith had been tested and found wanting a long time ago. Mom's religious beliefs were very important to her. I envied her blind faith. She would pray for a cure for Carla but if her prayers weren't answered she would say it was God's will and accept it as such.

"How did Father Austin find out?" I asked as I handed her her hot chocolate and sat down at the table with her. "Carla only told us last night."

"Carla's parents. They wanted us to offer up Mass for her in Knock."

"She's going to have chemotherapy. Almost certainly. That's a good sign, isn't it?"

Mom didn't answer. She just caught my hand and squeezed it tight. I felt a sudden rush of despair. It seemed to me that everybody from Harry to the Knock pilgrims to Carla herself had accepted the inevitable. She was young, for God's sake! She had a husband and family. So much to fight for. Why was everyone assuming that Carla was going to die? I couldn't, I wouldn't allow that.

"I didn't want you to be on your own through this," Mom said. "That's one reason why I came back home."

"One reason?"

"The other reason is to apologise to you. I did a lot of thinking today and I prayed for guidance. I was wrong, Adele, and I apologise."

"Are you talking about Eoin Kirby and the way you've been talking about him and to him?"

"Partly. I made a big mistake not telling you the truth. I was trying to protect you but the truth is the best protection of all."

"Mom, will you stop going around in circles and just tell me!"

"I could do with a drink of water first. I'm parched after the journey and the hot chocolate is just making me more thirsty."

To my credit, I held my patience, got her the water and sat down again. She put on her very serious face and speared me with a stare.

"Your father and I grew up together. For as long as I

can remember, there was an understanding between us and our families that we would one day marry."

"I know, Mom. You've told me often enough and Dad told me how he used to pull your pigtails at school."

Her hand went automatically to her hair and she patted it. It didn't budge and she seemed reassured. "Yes. He always admired my hair, even when he was just tugging at it. Well, you know the rest. Your father served an apprenticeship as a carpenter when he finished school and I went into business."

I nodded. Mom always insisted that her job as counter assistant in the Cairnsure drapery store qualified as "going into business". I tried to fast-track the oft-repeated story.

"You saved your money, got married. Bought this house and eventually after years of waiting, I was born when you were thirty-six. What has this got to do with Eoin Kirby?"

Mom wriggled on her chair then and just when I thought she was about to unveil some uncomfortable truth she announced she needed to go to the bathroom. "I shouldn't have drunk so much this late. I'll be running to the bathroom all night now."

I put my head on my hands when she was gone. It seemed that my mother was going to turn this story into a saga. There was no option but to wait out the history lesson and bouts of bladder-control failure. But then at least I would know what was causing her antagonism towards Eoin.

I lifted my head and sighed with relief. Once I had

convinced Mom that the past was just that, a shadow on time, I would be able to explain to her what a good person Eoin was and how he had no responsibility for whatever his parents had done. I was smiling as I heard her head back towards the kitchen.

My smile faded when I saw her stand at the kitchen door, her face pale except for two angry, red spots on her cheeks, my father's dressing-gown in her hand.

"Where did you get that?" I asked to give myself time to think.

"In the bathroom. Who gave you permission to touch your father's things?"

Without missing a beat I told her Jodi had stayed over and had needed a dressing-gown.

"She had a bit of a row with her parents," I explained, warming to my tale. "You know what they're like. Very judgmental. Not understanding like you."

"Well, if Jodi wore her skirts longer they mightn't have as much to be judgmental about. Anyway that's all right. But you should have given her my dressing-gown. Not your father's."

"Sorry," I muttered though I felt anything but as I remembered how Eoin had filled out Dad's dressing-gown.

She draped the dressing gown over the back of her chair and sat again. "Back to our family history so."

"Mom! Would you ever tell me what this has to do with the Kirbys!"

"I'm getting to that. Michael Kirby was a big shot in this town."

"Eoin's Dad?"

"Don't interrupt me. I'll have to start over again."

Under that threat, I sat back, my lips tightly sealed.

"As I said, Michael Kirby owned half this town. He was a builder and he got all the big contracts. He built the National school and the new church and all the council cottages. He had everything except a wife. He offered your father a job. John was a first-class craftsman, you know."

"I know."

"At the time John went to work for Michael Kirby we had been married for two years and were living out on the farm with your Aunt Lily and Uncle Noel."

Jesus! What a nightmare start that must have been to the marriage. No wonder I wasn't born for a long time after they married.

"Michael Kirby paid good money and we were soon able to buy this house. And then . . ."

Much as I wanted to hear about the Kirby saga I felt my eyelids begin to droop. I was exhausted and had to make an effort to pay attention to my mother's solemn voice.

"Everything was fine until Michael Kirby went to Galway for his holidays."

"Really?" I asked sleepily. "It must have been one hell of a holiday."

"Don't smart-talk me, Adele. This isn't easy for me. And it won't be for you either, so just listen."

My wandering attention went on full alert. I sat up straighter.

"Michael Kirby came back from that holiday with a wife on his arm. Irene Kirby. She was very beautiful. Raven hair and dark-brown eyes."

So that's where Eoin had got his magnificent eyes. Not his hair though. He was fair, the type of dark blond which would have been golden in his childhood.

"She was twenty years younger than Michael. A slip of a thing. I'll be charitable and say she was strong-willed. She led Michael a merry dance."

"What do you mean? How?"

"Because she flirted with every man in the parish. Especially one. She flaunted herself at him. Irene Kirby was no better than she should be."

"But they stayed together, didn't they, Irene and Michael? I told you he died a year ago and she was still with him then. They had two sons together."

Mom leaned towards me and her voice was barely above a whisper.

"Irene was already pregnant with her eldest boy before she left Cairnsure. He is, I believe, the man you call Eoin."

"Yes, that's right," I agreed. "Eoin himself joked that he was made in Ireland but born in New Zealand. So what about it?"

Mom seemed to shrivel into herself, her shoulders raised, her arms folded tightly about her body. She opened her mouth but no sound came out. She tried again. Her voice was trembling.

"Michael Kirby might not be Eoin's father."

"What are you saying? Are you judging Eoin on his

parentage? And what has any of that private Kirby family business got to do with us?"

Mom didn't say anything. Despicable thoughts flashed through my mind. The ones which had been lurking there fuzzy and unacknowledged for several days now. I wasn't sure what they were about. Just that they were dark and dirty, left a trail of fear behind them and that I didn't want to confront them. Mom was staring at me as if waiting for my reaction. I tried to find a path through my confusion.

"Are you sure there's a doubt about who Eoin's father is, Mom? Really certain?"

"Irene Kirby herself told me. What better source could I have?"

"You must have been very close to her if she trusted you with that information."

"No. In fact we detested each other from the moment we first met."

This saga was getting more confusing by the minute. I began to wonder if Mom's memory of events had been distorted by time. Or even by the onset of the Alzheimer's disease I dreaded. The fact that Cairnsure of thirty-five years ago was so different to the bustling little town I now knew added to my difficulty. Back then, before residential and commercial development, it had been an agricultural community, a village steeped in tradition and Roman Catholic ethos. Not a place, I would have thought, where married women had affairs, even those who had been brought back from Galway as a holiday souvenir.

"I don't understand, Mom. Why did she confide in you if she hated you?"

"She thought it was my right to know."

We looked at each other then. I saw pain in her eyes, a pain which had dimmed over the years but was sharp and cutting now through reliving the past. She saw shock, denial and then realisation in my eyes. I had at last let my fuzzy thoughts escape from the back of my mind. Like a film on fast rewind, the past flickered by until the images stilled and focused on my father. A big man, kind, gentle. Caring.

"Please tell me I'm wrong, Mom! Please! It wasn't Dad, was it? It couldn't have been!"

She got up and came to stand behind me, gently stroking my hair.

"I'm so sorry, my sweetheart, but it's true. Your father had his head turned by Irene Kirby. I was his wife but she was the love of his life. It's possible that Eoin Kirby is their son. Named after his father. You know Eoin is the Gaelic for John. Of course you do. You teach the Irish language."

I remember screaming the one word, "No!" and then going into shock as my mother continued stroking my hair and crooning words which were meant to soothe. Instead each syllable she uttered was adding to my rising hysteria.

"You see why I couldn't tell you? I know how you adored your father. And he you. I didn't want to lessen him in your eyes. And I've never known for certain. Your father always vowed that they had never – you know –

had relations. He said he was just blinded by her glamour and behaved like a lovelorn idiot around her. But when I saw Eoin Kirby in this house it was like looking at your father as a young man, Adele. Except for the eyes."

My secret dreams of a future with Eoin Kirby mocked me. I hated myself, my gullibility, my neediness, my humiliating efforts to love and be loved. I was disgusted by Adele Burke and all she stood for. I had, quite unfairly, some hate left over for Eoin Kirby too. He was as much a victim of our parents' convoluted past as I was but yet I couldn't help but blame him for bringing this disaster into my life.

"I hope you understand now why I tried to warn you off getting close to Eoin Kirby and why I didn't want him to set foot in this house."

I wondered how Mom could be so controlled, so dignified, in the face of Dad's betrayal. Maybe the passage of time had blunted the anger and humiliation she must have felt. Had she howled and screamed, thrown things in rage, even lashed out at Dad and his bit on the side?

"Why did you stay with him, Mom?"

"Because John was a good man. And I wasn't going to let Irene Kirby ruin my life."

I laughed. A mixture of hysteria and admiration for my mother. The woman had an iron will. The Kirbys and Burkes must have been the talk of Cairnsure thirty-five years ago. A scandal like that would have kept the parish in entertainment for a long time. Where had she found the strength to ignore the whispers? And now Eoin Kirby was back to rake it all up again.

"Who knows about this?" I asked.

"Just us. And of course the trollop in New Zealand. There were whispers about her and your father. But they were just suspicions, rumours of them flirting and carrying on together. Michael took her away before her pregnancy showed. "

"So Michael Kirby knew then?"

"I doubt it. We certainly didn't tell him and I'm sure Irene kept her secret. She knew which side her bread was buttered on."

"What about Dad? I can't believe if there was any chance this child was his son he would have let him go just like that. Did he ever try to see him or contact him?"

"Your father always denied he could have been that child's father. As far as he was concerned all he had was a daughter – you. And you know how much he adored you." She shook her head. "I can't talk about this any more now. I think I'll go and have a lie down."

She picked up Dad's dressing-gown from the back of the chair, draped it over her arm and gently stroked it. "That's why I got so upset when I saw the dressing-gown. I feared the worst. I'm so glad that Jodi Wall was the one using it and not Eoin Kirby. I couldn't bear it if I had left it too late to tell you the truth. If you had been – compromised."

"No, Mom. You have nothing to worry about on that score."

But I did, didn't I? I didn't want to think about Eoin. Or lay eyes on him again. Nor would I ever willingly look in a mirror. How could I meet my own eyes and know that I had slept a night with a man who was possibly my brother, my half-brother? At my invitation. I could tell myself it had been just for comfort. To help me cope with Carla's illness, but who knows where it could have led? I stood up and faced my mother. There were so many other questions I wanted to ask her. About Dad, about how she managed to live with the betrayal. One glance at her vulnerable little face stilled my questions.

"Thank you for telling me, Mom. It must have been very difficult for you. And don't worry about Eoin Kirby. I'll be giving him a wide berth."

"Don't be harsh on the boy, Adele. He's not to blame any more than you. But I wish he had never come here to Cairnsure."

There was nothing to add to that. We went to bed. Sissy to the room she had shared with her errant husband. Me to the room I shared with my teddy bear and my shattered dreams.

Chapter 20

I woke slowly and reluctantly next morning. Without consciously knowing why, I realised that I was leaving a safe place behind. I struggled to slip back into peaceful sleep. I had forgotten to draw my bedroom curtains last night and the room was flooded with light which poked into drab corners and highlighted uneven plastering on the old walls. I had lain on my right hand. It was numb. I sat up and rubbed it. The memory of my mother's revelation about Eoin Kirby came back as painfully as the returning circulation to my hand.

My stomach muscles knotted and I jumped out of bed. I had kissed him, put my arms around him and he could be my half-brother. Words remembered from fire and brimstone sermons echoed fearfully in my mind. Knowing this was just superstitious nonsense did nothing to lessen the cold shivers of fear down my back.

It was not until I was in the shower that my self-disgust began to wane and anger took its place. Mom should have told me earlier. If she hadn't indulged in her juvenile running away instead of facing the issue this would never have happened. I grabbed the loofah and scrubbed until my skin hurt. I felt cleaner, on the outside at least, when I came out of the shower.

I tip-toed past Mom's room, not wanting to wake her for her sake but mainly for my own. How was I going to face her, to see the shadows of the pain my father had caused and know that, if only she realised it, I had hurt her even more? I had compounded my father's betrayal.

Putting on the first tracksuit which came to hand, I dressed quickly and gently closed the front door behind me. I wanted to go to the strand, to pound along the beach and watch the tide roll ceaselessly on.

I hesitated at the gate. Suppose Eoin Kirby decided to have an early morning run on the beach? What would I say to him if I met him? Curse him for coming to Cairnsure, hit him, spit into his face? Ignore him? I suddenly realised I hadn't considered Eoin's feelings in all of this mess. I remembered his puzzlement at Sissy's attitude to him, ringing his mother to ask her for an explanation of Sissy's antipathy. Thinking it through, it was obvious to me that Eoin was as ignorant of the events of thirty-five years ago as I had been until last night. He would feel as repulsed by me as I now did by him. Avoiding him seemed the best option.

I turned in the opposite direction. Back towards the hills. To where Aunt Lily lived. I remembered the bouquet of red roses on my father's grave. Had Lily left them there or were they a tribute to my father from his son?

I walked fast, building resentment against Aunt Lily with every stride I took. She too must know about her brother's fall from grace, about his being unfaithful with another man's wife and apparently fathering a child by her. I could understand – maybe – why Mom hadn't told me earlier but my crabby old aunt should have. By the time I was walking into her front yard my rage had reached epic proportions. I hammered on her door. There was no sound but the distant lowing of cows and the rustle of leaves in the trees. I knocked again, more controlled this time, and stood back to see if her net curtains twitched. The house was dark and glowering, a shadow on the sunny morning.

"You won't get an answer there. She's gone to Cork to the clinic."

I jumped with fright and turned around to see Ned Lehane, the man my aunt employed to do odd jobs around the small piece of land she had kept. The rest she had let out on conacre to a sheep farmer.

"She left at cockcrow this morning," he added, coming to stand beside me at the front door. He stared at me, his light blue eyes twinkling with curiosity in his weather-beaten old face. "You're her niece, the teacher, aren't you? I thought you were in Dublin."

"I'm home for a while. Just a year. Is Lily sick? Why is she gone to the clinic?"

"She goes every three months for a check-up. It's the ulcer on her leg. I think it's getting worse. Of course she's diabetic and she's a fair age now. But sickness is no respecter of age. I suppose you heard about Carla Gill, Carla Selby as she is now. Isn't it tragic?"

My breath caught as if he had hit me in the stomach. I leaned against the doorjamb of Aunt Lily's dreary house as the full impact hit me. Carla had cancer. Pancreatic cancer. Spread to her liver and bones. This time next year Carla would probably be dead. No!

"You look shook. Do you feel all right?"

I straightened myself up and smiled at Ned Lehane. "Yes. I'm fine, thank you. Would you tell Lily I called, please?"

"I will. I could go in and make a cup of tea for you before you go if you like. I have a key."

I shook my head, wanting now to get away from this dreary place.

"You're very like your father, God rest him. He was a fine man. A handsome devil in his day."

I stared into the age-worn face and with sudden insight realised that Sissy's secret might not be a secret at all. Ned Lehane was old Cairnsure stock. He and all the other newsmongers in the parish knew that my father, that laughing, smiling, kindest of men, had cheated on his wife with the bride Michael Kirby had brought back from his holiday in Galway. There had been no secrets in the old parish and maybe Cairnsure had not changed so much after all. The whispers still circulated. But did they know that Irene Kirby had gone to New Zealand with what might have been my father's son in her belly?

"Do you remember a builder named Kirby?" I asked before I could stop my runaway tongue. "My father used to work for him."

"Indeed I do. A decent man, Michael Kirby. I heard

264

his son is back here on a visit. Lashings of money by all accounts."

"What did Michael Kirby look like?"

"That's a very odd question. I can barely remember now. It must be over thirty years since he left here. As I recall he was small but wiry. You know the type."

I did. The exact opposite to my father who was tall and well muscled. Just like Eoin Kirby.

I tried to smile as I said goodbye to Ned Lehane but managed not much more than a baring of my teeth. I could feel his eyes boring into my back as I walked down the boreen and knew that the story of my visit to Aunt Lily and my questions about Michael Kirby would be passed on several times before the day was out.

For the first time my anger turned towards my father. Had people been sneering behind my back for years? And Mom. Dignified, gentle Sissy. Did she really believe that my father's dalliance with Irene Kirby was forgotten or was she just pretending in order to cope? Did everyone guess who the tall man from New Zealand really was? Did Jodi and Carla know? Just as they had known about Tom Reagan, Mom's new man-friend, long before I did?

As I walked back towards home again, my thoughts were more confused than ever but I knew one thing for certain. Cairnsure might have factories and housing estates now, even a shopping mall, but it was still as small-minded and back-biting as it had always been. I yearned for the anonymity of the city and each step towards home increased that yearning.

* * *

I arrived in just as Mom was making breakfast. She was placidly stirring scrambled eggs in a pot on the cooker as if nothing much other than a trip to a shrine had happened yesterday. She smiled at me.

"Have you been out walking already? I hope you ate something first."

"I'm not hungry."

"You must eat. Starving yourself won't change anything. You must be strong for Carla."

So, she was not going to talk about my father any more. Pretend it had never happened. Pretend it was history and nothing to do with our lives now. Just as she must have done with Dad. Lived with him day after day, slept with him night after night, and pretended that he didn't have an affair and possibly a son in New Zealand.

I sat at the table. "Does Aunt Lily know about Dad's son?" I asked.

Sissy stopped stirring and turned to glare at me. "I told you last night nobody but the people involved knew about the baby. It was none of Lily's business."

She turned back to the cooker where the eggs were beginning to stick to the bottom of the saucepan. Going to the press she got out two plates and busied herself filling them up.

"Was there contact between Dad and Irene Kirby after she went away?"

Mom walked over to the table and put the two plates down with a bang. She sat opposite me and I could see hurt in her eyes.

"What are you trying to do, Adele? Make me go

through it all again? I could have left this secret in the grave with your father, where it belongs, if only you had listened to me in the first place and had nothing to do with Eoin Kirby."

"For heaven's sake, Mom! Be fair! You should have told me. Eoin could be my half-brother!"

"Exactly. That's the only reason I told you now. It would be an even bigger tragedy if you – if you – well, you know what. You modern women are far more . . ."

She stopped talking then, her tight lips telling of her disapproval. My blush, that red tide of guilt, flooded my face. Mom leaned towards me, a proud smile on her face.

"It's a blessing to know that you're not like that, Adele. I know you wouldn't let yourself, or me, down by going to bed with a man you barely knew. You're too well brought up to behave like that."

"No. I didn't have sex with him, Mom. I told you that already. But I did consider him a friend."

I tried to smile back reassuringly but my lips refused to curl into anything resembling a smile. My mother chose only to believe what suited her. That's how she had managed to keep her marriage together. I envied her line of self-protective reasoning. And I was glad of it too. I didn't want to worry her more than I had already done. I made an attempt to eat some scrambled egg but it refused to slither down my gullet. I put my spoon down.

"How come Eoin believes that you and Dad were best friends with his parents? Irene even told him to convey her greetings to you."

"Greetings? From her? She was only having a joke on

me. And on her son too. New Zealand hasn't changed her much. I won't talk about it any more, Adele, so don't go asking questions. Just eat your breakfast," she said, pushing the sugar bowl and milk jug towards me. "What's done is done."

Wise words. How I wished for my mother's capacity to deny what I couldn't accept.

* * *

To my surprise, Jodi was ready and waiting when I went to collect her in Kieran Mahon's apartment. A black top tucked into her size-zero jeans drained her of colour. She seemed calmer than I had seen her for a long time. She walked and talked more slowly. I wondered if she had taken a tranquilliser. Transferred her addiction to suit her Cairnsure pace of life.

"You look tired, Del," she greeted me. "You should have put on some highlighter under your eyes."

I knew then that Jodi Wall was alive and well. Just paler. We didn't talk much on our way to the hospital. Neither of us wanted to put words on our reason for visiting Carla. Any mention of cancer was banned by tacit agreement. The nearer we got to the hospital, the more slowly I drove.

"Do you think she'll have tubes and needles stuck into her?" Jodi asked.

"I don't know."

"I can't stand the sight of them. They make me feel sick."

"Stop, Jodi ! For feic's sake! How do you think Carla

feels? Don't you go turning your nose up, no matter what you see. We're here to support Carla, not upset her more."

"I know, I know. Don't worry, Kieran has given me the lecture. I'll behave."

I swung the car recklessly into a narrow parking space in the hospital grounds and turned angrily towards Jodi. "Would you ever grow up! You're thirty, Jodi Wall, not thirteen. Nobody, not Kieran, not me, should have to tell you not to upset Carla. I know you have problems. So have I. So has everybody but none are as bad as Carla's. She needs us, so forget yourself for once. Think of someone else for a change."

Jodi leaned back from me and flinched as if I was about to hit her. She seemed to shrivel up until there was nothing more than a huge pair of eyes staring back at me. I felt like a bully.

"I'm sorry, Jodi. We're all upset but we've got to be strong for Carla. We'll both have to forget about our own problems until Carla is better again."

"Easy for you. There's nothing wrong with you a good . . ."

She stopped talking then. What had she been about to say? A good shag? My stomach did a churning motion again as I thought of Eoin Kirby and how close I had come to taking that drastic step with him. We walked in silence towards the hospital and made our way to the oncology unit. Outside the door of Carla's room, Jodi laid her hand on my arm.

"I'm sorry, Del. You're right. I'm selfish. Don't worry.

I'll be there for Carla. And for you too when you tell me what's wrong."

I looked at her and saw the old Jodi stare back at me. The one who could be snide and shallow on the surface but was loyal and generous at her core. At that moment I longed to tell her about Eoin. About my half-brother. To drag the secret out of the dark and burn it off in the light of day. I smiled at her.

"We'll look after Carla first. Then we'll sort ourselves out. Deal?"

"Deal!"

We both fixed our smiles and then went in to see Carla.

* * *

I don't know what I had been expecting to see. An emaciated Carla, a tragic Carla. A woman in pain. A dying Carla. She was sitting up in bed, hair done, make-up on, calmly reading her book. She lifted her head and smiled at us as we came into her room, both Jodi and I walking on tip-toe as if afraid the sound of our footfall would add to her pain.

"Hi, girls! Thanks for coming in."

We continued our creep towards her and, getting chairs, sat on either side of her bed.

"How are you feeling today?" I asked.

Carla laughed and looked from one to the other of us. "There's no need to whisper or creep. I won't shatter. I've had a busy morning of tests but I'm enjoying the rest now."

"I suppose it's too soon yet to have results. To know if . . ."

There was such profound sadness in Carla's eyes when she looked at me that I regretted asking the impulsive question. I tried without success to think of something to say that would wipe out the pain, something hopeful. Carla smiled at me.

"Don't look so uncomfortable, Del. I prefer to talk about it. I've nursed other people through terminal illness. I know how I want to handle my own."

"Stop! Don't talk like that. Don't you dare give up, Carla Gill!"

"I'm not giving up, Jodi. Far from it. I might be getting radiotherapy and I've already started on pancreatic enzymes."

"That's good news?" Jodi asked.

"By taking the enzymes before I eat, I'll be able to digest my food again and absorb some nutrition from it. Maybe get a bit more strength and energy. The radiotherapy will shrink the tumour on my spine so I'll have a lot less pain. So, yes, I think that's good news."

"Will you lose your hair from the radiation?"

I glared at Jodi. Trust her to be even more tactless than I had been. Carla laughed and ran her hand through her blonde hair.

"No. I'll probably keep my crowning glory, such as it is. I'll have some sore patches on my skin though where the radiation hits. Maybe some nausea. I'll cope. I'll have to. Now let's talk about something else. Any news?"

"Kieran Mahon has asked me move in with him," Jodi announced suddenly.

"I thought you already had," I said.

"That was just until I got my head together. No, he's interested in something more long-term."

Carla propped herself up higher in the bed and looked in surprise at Jodi.

"That's sudden. Last I heard you couldn't stand him."

"I couldn't stand men, full stop. I spent my days battling with them in the office. I certainly didn't want them invading my home or my nights."

"And you think Kieran Mahon's not a man?"

Jodi lowered her head and her silky hair flopped forward in the way I so envied. She was twisting her hands on her lap and looking more teen than thirty. When she raised her head, there was a smile on her face.

"Oh! Yes. Kieran Mahon's a man all right. But he's a rare one of the species. Not a domineering, patronising bone in his body."

"Jodi Wall! Are you in love?" I asked and as Carla and I leaned forward waiting for an answer, it was as if time had rolled back and we were young girls together talking about boys.

Jodi broke the spell. "Don't be ridiculous! You can't surely still believe in the mushy, stars in the eyes, forever-and-ever rubbish we talked about when we were teenagers!"

"I do," Carla said firmly. "Unfortunately my forever-and-ever is limited. I can't imagine saying goodbye to Harry . . ."

She began to cry then. Sobs wracked her thin body as I held her in my arms. I searched desperately for a phrase, a word, a pearl of wisdom, something comforting and very profound to say. My mind was blank of everything except the awful truth of Carla's terminal illness. I glanced at Jodi for help. There were tears in her eyes too. She reached out her hand and stroked Carla's hair. I don't know how long we three held on to each other and cried. It was a timeless sharing of grief.

A quiet knock sounded on the door. A nurse pushed it open and came in. She busied herself checking Carla's pulse and temperature as Jodi and I surreptitiously wiped our tears away. When the nurse left the room again, Carla slid down in her bed and closed her eyes for a moment.

"I'm sorry, girls," she murmured. "It was great to see you but I'm very tired now. I'll be home soon."

Her eyelids closed. Jodi and I stood either side of her bed and stared at the once beautiful, now gaunt face of Carla Gill. Carla Selby, wife, mother, daughter, sister and best friend. I stooped and gently kissed her forehead. Her skin was smooth and cold against my lips. I turned and ran from the room, almost knocking Harry Selby over in the corridor.

"Whoa! Take it easy, Adele. You'll end up in A&E at the speed you're travelling."

I looked up into his face and I saw the truth there too. "She's not going to get better, is she?"

His lips tightened as if he could not trust himself to speak and he shook his head. Jodi came along the corridor and joined us.

"Have you checked the tests yourself?" Jodi asked him. "Are you one hundred per cent sure of the results? Doctors do make mistakes, don't they?"

Harry nodded. "Indeed we do, Jodi, but unfortunately the biggest mistake with Carla's diagnosis was in not picking it up sooner. I should have known. I should have seen . . ."

My multiple layers of guilt, flowing uninterrupted from the cradle, empathised with the guilt I now sensed in Harry Selby. For some reason I hadn't figured at that stage in my life, I could not tolerate guilt in others. I wanted to protect them from the gnawing destructiveness, from the pervasive, energy sapping, uselessness of retrospective regret.

"Don't even think of blaming yourself, Harry," I said sternly. "If it had been possible to diagnose earlier, surely Carla could have done that herself. She's a nurse for heaven's sake!"

"They know more than doctors," Jodi stated.

To my relief Harry laughed. "You could be right, Jodi. A lot more. About everything. Thanks for coming to see her today. Hopefully, she'll be going home tomorrow."

"What about her treatment? The radiotherapy?"

"Her blood count is very low now. We'll build her up a bit. Give the enzymes a chance to work."

Despite my earlier feelings of doom, I felt hope in what Harry said now. So they had enough time to build Carla up! Time to delay her treatment. That must be good news. It had to be.

I smiled at him. "We'll see you at the house so, Harry."

"She's asleep," Jodi warned as she watched him turn towards Carla's door.

"I'll just sit with her a while," he said and immediately I pictured the scene: Carla, skin taut over her bones, lying there in a sleep so deep it looked like a rehearsal for her final rest, and Harry, wet-eyed, staring at his wife, the mother of his brood of babies, wishing her to continue breathing, to fight the cancer, to defy medicine. To live.

I grabbed Jodi by the arm and walked down the corridor as quickly as I could.

Outside the hospital, I took a deep breath of the disinfectant-free, illness-free, air. I felt grateful for my own health, for my strong body which resisted illness, for the long legs and big feet which carried me away from this place of dying. I was happy to be alive and well. Then I remembered Eoin Kirby.

Chapter 21

Preoccupied as I was, Jodi Wall sitting in the passenger seat of my car barely registered with me until we arrived back in Cairnsure.

"Where will I drop you off?" I asked, still not sure whether her stay with Kieran Mahon was permanent or temporary.

"Back at Kieran's apartment, please. I must change before I meet Eoin Kirby. Put on something classy. Make an impression."

I gripped tightly on the steering wheel, hoping Jodi wouldn't notice my white knuckles. "What are you meeting him for?"

"Oh, the green-eyed monster!" Jodi mocked. "Jealous, are we?"

"Why should I be jealous? Eoin Kirby is nothing to me."

"Really? One of my sisters works part-time in the

Grand Hotel. She saw you and the New Zealander sharing a very romantic dinner. You kept quiet about that, didn't you?"

"There's nothing to tell," I lied. "It's just that his parents and mine used to be friendly before the Kirbys emigrated."

"So I believe."

Luckily we had reached Kieran's apartment building by then. I stopped the car so suddenly that Jodi jerked forward in her seat.

"Hey! Del! What's the matter with you? Are you trying to kill me? You know how fragile I am at the moment!"

"No, I'm not trying to kill you but only because I'd have to go to jail if I did. I've had about enough of you and your self-obsession, Jodi. And you expect everybody to feel sorry for you. Well, I for one, don't. I'm keeping my sympathy for Carla. She deserves it."

"For God's sake, Del! What brought on this tantrum? I only asked you about Eoin Kirby."

We stared at each other in a silence broken only by the clicks of the cooling motor and the muffled sounds of town traffic. I didn't know what to say. There were no words to ease the hurt on Jodi's face, to tell her how much I regretted my bitter outburst.

Suddenly, inexplicably, she smiled.

"Ah! I think I understand now. Kieran's been talking to you. He's accused me of being selfish too. I admit I've been self-destructive. I hated myself enough to poison my body, to need the fleeting escape of a high. But no more, Del. I swear. I'm clean now and that's the way I'm going to stay. No clinics or counsellors, no tranquillisers, no substitute addictions. It's just me and my demons and I'm going to beat them. For Carla, for you, for Kieran but mostly for me. I promise."

I squirmed with shame. Here was Jodi, baring her soul to me and all the time I harboured the dirtiest secret of all. She was indeed clean. She'd had no control over the addiction which had cost her a career, an apartment and her independence. It was an honest falling from grace, a quirk of genetic pre-disposition to addiction and the circumstances of her life. I reached for her hand.

"I'm sorry, Jode. I didn't mean to be angry with you."

"I know that. But something's not right with you, Del. I thought it was because of Carla. I'm not so sure now after seeing the way you reacted when I mentioned Eoin Kirby . . ."

"Who told you his parents and mine were friends?"

"My sister said Mom mentioned it. Or maybe you told me yourself. Isn't that a long time ago? What has it got to do with now? What's wrong with all the parents being friends, anyway?"

"They had a big row."

"What about?"

My mouth was opened, my lips rounded but no sounds came out. I wanted to tell Jodi, to confess, to ask for help but the words could not pass the desert-dry, constricted area that was by now my throat. She was staring at me, a frown on her forehead. Why couldn't I ask her to enquire from her mother about the Burke-

Kirby scandal of thirty-five years ago? Was it that I was ashamed of my father or was I just ashamed of myself?

"I can ask Eoin today, if you want." she volunteered. "I'm meeting him to discuss his plans for Elliots'. I'm hoping that he offers me a job. He knows the truth about me now so I won't have to hide anything. I'm still a good accountant. I'd be an asset to a new business."

The idea of Jodi talking to Eoin Kirby on my behalf unleashed a flood of dammed-up words. "Don't even mention my name to him! Don't you dare! I do have a problem with him and our family history but I'll sort it myself. Promise, Jodi. Promise you won't say a word about me."

Her frown got deeper but she promised anyway. She swore on our life-long friendship and that was enough to ease my mind.

"So you think he's going to stay on here?" I asked.

"He seems to be considering it. I hope so. Cairnsure could do with a visionary developer. And I could do with a job."

"Good luck then. And remember your promise."

Jodi swore silence on the subject of the Burke-Kirby history again and got out of the car. She was still frowning though and I was still angry with myself as I turned the car and headed towards Willbury Lawn.

* * *

Mom's car was not outside number six but Tom Reagan's was. Just as I had hoped. Now the only thing left was for Tom to be at home and for me to have courage. I rang the doorbell and took a deep breath. And then another. I rang again and this time heard footsteps in the hall. Tom smiled at me and I glared back at him.

"Mom told me."

"Come in," he said calmly, holding the door wide open. I swept past him and went through to the kitchen-dining area where I had been on my previous visit.

"Sit down, Adele. Tea? Coffee?"

I felt like shouting at him. Didn't he realise this was not a social call? I shook my head. "No, thank you. I just want to talk."

"About Irene Kirby and her son, I assume."

"Yes. You should have told me."

Tom waved me to a chair at the table and then sat opposite me. He stared at me for a moment. In fact he stared through me. He had the probing, astute gaze I had always associated with policemen. Eyes which knew the shape of truth and saw the shadow of lies. I felt guilty as accused without knowing what my crime was supposed to be. "I think we'd better compare notes," he said at last. "What exactly has Sissy told you?"

I frowned. The story as I knew it was bad enough. A shiver of dread ran through me. Could it be possible that there was yet another layer of shameful history to be uncovered?

"She said Dad and Irene Kirby had an affair. Irene was pregnant with Eoin when she left for New Zealand and she claimed John Burke could be the father."

Tom nodded and then sat back in his chair staring at a spot on the wall behind me. When the silence got too

280

much for me, I spoke. "Well? Is that what she told you too?"

His gaze moved from the wall to look directly at me. "You know I think the world of your mother. After all, I'm going to marry her. But there are times when Sissy is blinkered. She jumps to conclusions."

"I know!"

"The devil and all wouldn't change her mind once it's made up."

"Too true. So what are you saying, Tom? That Sissy is wrong about Dad and Irene Kirby? Irene herself told Mom that the child she was carrying might be Dad's. The Kirbys and Burkes were certainly friends. Eoin said so."

"There's a big gap between friendship and adultery. All I'm saying is that we've only Sissy's word for what happened and we both know that can be very biased. I believe John Burke always denied that he could have been Eoin's father. You knew him. What do you think?"

I had to consider my answer very carefully. The Dad I knew – or thought I knew – would never have hurt Sissy by having an affair. My answer had to be that I hadn't really known my father at all.

"I don't know, Tom. I don't know what to think any more."

Tom nodded his understanding. "I get the impression that Sissy was very jealous of Irene Kirby. She would have put the worst interpretation on any situation involving Irene."

I thought about the way Mom had spoken of Irene.

Yes, there could be jealousy in her account or maybe it was understandable bitterness. Even Eoin himself admitted that his mother had made enemies. Irene might have been beautiful but she certainly did not appear to be a nice person.

"Sissy also claims Irene Kirby kept in contact with your father after she went to New Zealand."

"How do you mean? Mom never mentioned any contact between them after the Kirbys left. She said . . ."

I stopped, trying to remember exactly what my mother had told me. I couldn't recall her actually denying that Dad and Irene had stayed in contact nor did she confirm it either. But she did to Tom. My heart skipped a beat. If proof was needed, here it was. Why should Irene and Dad stay in contact if not to discuss their son?

"Letters from New Zealand were sent to your father care of your Aunt Lily at the farm. That's probably why Sissy hates the old woman. She found out about the letters but could do nothing to stop them."

I put my arms on the table and laid my head on them. Why in the hell hadn't Mom told me about these letters? And what else was she hiding from me? Eyes closed, I was safe for a moment in my little nest. I felt a rush of pity for my mother. How humiliating it must have been for her to know that, even though a world apart, my father and his fancy woman still loved each other. I thought of the way Dad had looked after Sissy, taking care of her every need, protecting her. Had that been guilt? Guilt because another woman was rearing his son in New Zealand. Had he stayed with Sissy just for my sake? No. That could not have been the reason. I hadn't been born until four years after the Kirbys had left Cairnsure. Now I felt even more confused. I lifted my head.

"I'm going to see Lily," I announced.

"She might tell you the full story. I don't believe Sissy has told us everything. Good luck to you. Lily's a tough old bird."

"Bad old bitch" seemed a more appropriate description to me. I smiled at Tom.

"Thank you, Tom. It's good to be able to speak about it without trying to hide the truth. My biggest dread is that people will find out. Cairnsure hasn't changed that much. I've been out with Eoin a few times and we're bound to have been seen. I'd be the laugh of the parish."

"Don't worry about other people, Adele. You did nothing wrong. If Sissy had told you the truth none of this would have happened. I really wanted to say something but I'd promised her and I'm a man of my word."

I knew instinctively he was indeed an honourable man. Mom had chosen wisely the second time around. He stood now to escort me to the door.

"How is Carla?" he asked. "It's sad someone that young is so sick."

"She's going to start treatment soon."

"Sissy is storming heaven. If prayers can cure Carla she'll be up and about in no length of time."

I nodded and said nothing. I still resented the fact that Sissy was praying for the strength to accept whatever fate decided. The thing she called "God's will".

"Let me know how you get on with Lily," Tom said as he opened the front door for me.

I would. I might have lost self-respect and maybe I would lose my Carla to cancer but today I felt I had found a true friend in Tom Reagan.

"I'm supposed to be meeting Eoin tonight," I told him.

"Are you going to?"

"I don't know."

I surprised him then, and myself, by kissing him on the cheek before I set out to tackle Aunt Lily.

* * *

Aunt Lily was home. I knew she was watching as I walked to the front door but yet she made me knock and wait for her to let me in.

"I heard you were looking for me this morning," she said. "What do you want?"

"I want to ask you some questions."

"I thought you young people knew it all."

"Can I come in?"

Without another word she turned her back and began to walk into the kitchen. I followed on, wondering how soon I could bring the conversation around to my father. I sat in the big rocking chair by the range. I would not have done so had I been thinking straight. That chair was Aunt Lily's designated throne.

"Make yourself comfortable, why don't you?" she said sarcastically.

"How's your leg? Ned Lehane said you were at the clinic this morning."

"He has a mouth as wide as Cork Harbour. The less he knows the better. My leg is fine. Will you have tea?"

I nodded yes because she already had the kettle on and had got two cups and saucers down from the dresser.

"So you want to know about the Kirbys?"

I was taken aback. Ned Lehane must have told her. Of course he would have. I wasn't ready, not sure how to ask the questions for which I needed answers.

"It's Irene Kirby I'm curious about."

"Curiosity alone wouldn't bring you to visit your neglected old aunt twice in the one day. Why don't you try telling me the truth?"

She shuffled her way across the kitchen and sat in the armchair opposite me, the one usually reserved for visitors. Her right leg was heavily bandaged. Looking into her face I saw tight lines around her mouth and smudges underneath her eyes. My father's eyes, dark blue but without the glint of humour his always had.

"Well?" she prompted. "Why did you come here?"

"To find out if Eoin Kirby is my half-brother or not."

The kettle began to bubble furiously. Lily hauled herself out of the chair and went to make the tea, ordering me to get biscuits and plates. It was five minutes before we were sitting down again, cups in hand, Lily in her rightful place in the rocking chair. She fixed me with one of her piercing stares.

"So Sissy Roberts told you Eoin Kirby might be your half-brother? I wouldn't expect much more from her. Bad-mouthing your father when he can no longer defend himself."

"Aunt Lily! Forget your vendetta against my mother for once. If you know the truth about Dad and Irene Kirby, please tell me."

"Your father never should have married Sissy. And that widower she has in tow now should run a mile."

"You know about Tom Reagan?"

"Of course I do. Only Sissy could believe I wouldn't know. Don't tell me you're as silly as her."

"Maybe you've got things the wrong way around. Mom might have had a happier life if she had never met Dad."

"You're quick to judge, aren't you? You don't know everything about your father."

"Then tell me! Did he have an affair with Irene Kirby and is he Eoin Kirby's father?"

When Lily picked up the poker and stooped over to stir the embers in the range, I thought I would burst with temper. Whatever she knew, if anything at all, it was going to be a monumental task to get her to speak. And she would not be coaxed. My only option was to sit and wait. She straightened herself up.

"Irene Kirby was a trollop. Michael Kirby should have left her on the streets where he found her."

"Do you mean she was a prostitute? I don't believe my father would have had anything to do with her if that's what she was like."

"I don't mean she plied her trade on the streets. She was more subtle than that. Turning men's heads. Ruining lives."

"So, did she have an affair with my father?"

"Your father and any man who would look crooked at her. And they all did. They flocked around her like bees around a honey pot. She was a beautiful woman."

"So what if she was attractive? That doesn't make her a whore."

Aunt Lily took in a deep breath and glared at me.

"Well, that's what you're saying, isn't it?" I said.

"I wouldn't go that far. But she did flaunt herself. She was a tease. Your uncle never got over her."

"Uncle Noel? You mean, that's why he . . . why he . . ."

"I don't know why he took his own life. I just know he was never the same after Irene Kirby left for New Zealand."

I was getting a picture of the beautiful Irene Kirby flirting with every man in Cairnsure parish but I still didn't know if she had been pregnant with my father's child when she emigrated. Aunt Lily prided herself on her directness but she was being very circumspect now. I would just have to be firm with her.

"Did my father and Irene Kirby have a child? That's what I want to know. My mother thinks they did."

"Why can't you let him rest in peace? God knows he needs it after a lifetime of living with your mother."

All thoughts of being patient with Aunt Lily went out of my head. I leaned forward until I was so close that I could see the tiny mole on her left eyelid clearly.

"How dare you talk about my mother like that! What gives you the right to mock her and belittle her the way you do? She was and is a great mother to me and she was a fine wife to your brother too. You're just jealous. You wanted your two brothers to stay here with you!"

I had expected an answering spark of temper, a bitter reply, a spate of cutting words. I did not anticipate tears. Not in Aunt Lily's eyes. The tears welled over. Aunt Lily seemed to dissolve, leaving behind an old, vulnerable, woman. I went to her and stooped down beside her, one part of me still alert to the possibility of the return of my familiar, bitingly sarcastic aunt.

"You're so wrong, Adele. I would have liked nothing better than to leave my two brothers, and this god-forsaken farm behind. Do you think I chose this excuse for a life, this isolation, this loneliness?"

I had never thought of Lily as having any emotions, any wants other than her need to dominate and bully.

"I'm sorry," I muttered. "I shouldn't have said that. But it wasn't Mom's fault. You shouldn't blame her for it."

"Yes, I can. It was all Sissy Robert's fault. She wouldn't let your father stay here on the farm. She insisted on having a house in the town."

"So what? They were entitled to buy their own home. I'm sure it can't have been too pleasant for them here with you and Uncle Noel."

I started as Lily suddenly snorted.

"Huh! You sound just like your mother now. Selfish. I wouldn't have stayed here under their feet. I could have made a life for myself if only they had taken over the farm."

"What about Noel? Surely he could have run these sixty acres? Why did you stay if you didn't want to?"

288

"Noel couldn't mind himself, let alone the farm. He was too fond of his drink. How could I have gone?"

Now I knew why Lily resented my mother so much. She felt cheated, trapped in this old house full of ghosts. I looked at her lined face and work-worn hands and pitied her.

"That's how your father got himself into debt," she said.

"Debt? What debt? Dad never owed anyone. What are you talking about?"

Lily sighed and sat back in her throne. She stared at me again but this time the look was softer. "He borrowed money from Michael Kirby. To buy the home you live in and to set himself up in business. He had no peace from Sissy Roberts until he did. Not much of anything else either, I believe. She refused to have a child until they were living under their own roof."

An ember sparked and spat a shower of ash onto the floor but neither of us moved.

"Your father sent the Kirbys money over the years until he had every last penny paid back. Michael Kirby sent the receipts here."

So the letters were receipts, not love notes. How had Sissy been aware of the letters and yet not of what was in them? She should have asked Dad. Maybe she did and then disbelieved his answer. Or more likely she had been too proud to ask and made the assumption that they were from Irene. Tortured herself at first and then pretended it wasn't happening.

"Did you tell Mom about the letters?"

"I wouldn't tell Sissy Roberts anything," Lily said with such bitterness that I knew she was telling the truth. "Noel probably told her."

That made sense to me. Unhappy Uncle Noel making sure everyone else was unhappy too.

"Did Mom know about the money Dad had borrowed?"

"I don't know. Although I don't think Sissy Roberts would have cared as long as she got what she wanted. God help everyone if she didn't. She does a great line in martyrdom, does Sissy Roberts."

This was true. Mom was an ace at silent suffering. But she was not an unreasonable woman. The story was not yet fully told.

"So are you saying there was nothing going on between Dad and Irene Kirby?"

"Like every other man, your father flirted with Irene. Whether it went further than that, only they know. "

"Irene told Mom that Dad could be the father of the child she was carrying."

"She would. That was the kind of troublemaking she revelled in. And Sissy is so gullible. But Irene was an ambitious woman. Michael Kirby had money. That's why she married him and that's why she never had any intention of leaving him. There was no way she was interested in your father other than having a bit of fun. And your poor Uncle Noel, God love him, she thought he was a fool."

So I still did not know. Not the full truth.

"The letters between Dad and New Zealand? They

were all from Michael, were they? Are you certain about that?"

"The letters that came here were in Michael's hand."

Mellow sunlight filtered through the net curtains. The day was passing and soon I would have to decide what to do about my date with Eoin Kirby tonight. I was more confused than ever. I stood up, stiff from my crouched position beside Aunt Lily.

"Maybe you should talk to him," she suggested.

"Talk to who?"

"Your young man. Eoin Kirby."

"He's not my . . ." I began to protest but then I stopped, wondering how she knew that I had been out with Eoin. Gossip had travelled fast, most likely given wings by Ned Lehane. I shrugged. Until Mom had said he was my half-brother, I had indeed considered Eoin to be "my young man." He was the man I had been hoping and praying to meet. I smiled at Lily. "I think you're right. I'm supposed to be meeting him tonight. I'll talk to him."

To my amazement, Lily smiled back at me. I saw a shadow of the girl she had been and in that shadow, I saw a reflection of the woman I now was. I shivered.

* * *

It was half past seven, I was dressed to go out, hair straight, make-up on and my stomach knotted with tension. I didn't yet know whether I was going to meet my half-brother or my boyfriend. Mom didn't help by hovering around me, asking questions, looking concerned and vulnerable. She was shrinking. I could look right down on the top of her head now and see where her hair was thinning. Maybe from age or maybe from too much hair lacquer. How could I ask her if she had nagged Dad into buying the house in which we were standing? If she had refused to have his baby until he had put this roof over her head? I could imagine her lips trembling and tears in her eyes. Some truths were best left unspoken.

I lied to her about where I was going. I was lying to myself so why not to her? She walked to the door with me.

"Don't be too late now. I know the way you and Jodi Wall forget the time when you start chatting."

"No, Mom."

"You should try that new bar near the Library. Tom said it's very swish."

"I'm not sure what we're going to do. Jodi might want to go for something to eat."

She stood there, her head to one side in that peculiar little way she had and I knew she was listening for the sound of lies. I drove away very quickly.

The bar of The Grand Hotel was busy. Looking around, I couldn't see any sign of Eoin. I found a seat and for an instant, I was relieved. I had a choice now. I could just run back home, tell Sissy that Jodi wasn't well, go to bed with Barry Bear and cry myself to sleep. As I was about to stand up, Eoin came rushing in the doorway, glancing around as he walked. He was wearing a white polo-shirt and jeans, his hair still damp from his recent shower. I quickly picked up a beer mat and pretended to examine it.

"Adele! Sorry I'm running late. I've had a busy day. How are you?"

He sat beside me and the scent of his aftershave stirred shameful feelings. I bit my lip. The sharp pain brought me back to the reality of our situation.

"We need to talk, Eoin. Seriously."

"Is this about Carla? Jodi Wall told me about your visit to the hospital."

"No. It's about us. Not us. Our families."

"Not again! Not the same old row. Are you ever going to let that drop?"

"I can't. Neither can you. And we can't talk here."

He frowned, staring at me in a bemused way. Then he shrugged.

"Whatever you want. The sooner we finally put this silly piece of history to bed the better. Where do you want to go?"

"Let's walk. On the strand."

It was that time of day when light still shone in the west but the eastern sky had begun to fade into darkness. The prom was packed with strollers; couples, families, people exercising their dogs. I walked ahead of Eoin, anxious to get to the privacy of the strand, say my piece and go. I was so intent on my mission that I did not notice him stop at Elliots' old shop until he called me back. He was standing in front of the big window, pointing at the sign and grinning.

"What do you think of that?" he asked.

I stared at the SOLD sign and felt my breath quicken in panic. Shit! He had really gone and done it. Eoin

Kirby would be in Cairnsure forever and ever, a constant reminder of how weak I was, how foolish. How desperate. My father's daughter.

"What do you intend doing with it?"

"For the time being, nothing. I have plans though."

"So I believe. Jodi told me she was going to meet you to discuss them with you."

"That's right. We had a useful conversation. She's a bright lady."

I was glad that he was now seeing the positive aspects of Jodi's character. He had witnessed her frailties first-hand.

We began to walk again, side by side this time. I had meant to ask him if he had gone to the Planning Department in Cork today as he had said he would but I was so focused on getting to the privacy of the now almost deserted strand that I stayed silent. Eoin obviously realised that I was not up for conversation because he walked along wordlessly beside me. We had almost reached the rocks, the scene of my rescue by Kieran Mahon, when Eoin caught me by the arm.

"This is far enough, Adele. Tell me what's wrong. Why are you still obsessing about some silly argument our parents had a lifetime ago? Has your mother been filling your head with more nonsense?"

"It wasn't a silly argument. It's potentially a very serious situation and I'm afraid it's still very relevant today."

His hand dropped away from my arm and I heard him release an impatient sigh. "I've heard enough about this, Adele. I told you I checked with my mother. It was just a misunderstanding. Your mother has obviously got it all out of proportion and you're following suit."

"I wish with all my heart that was true."

"Why do you say that? Do you know something I don't? Have you found out why they argued?"

The sun seemed to have suddenly dipped beneath the horizon. Night had fallen on Cairnsure bringing with it a darkness which seemed to permeate my mind, my soul. What was I to do? Unless Eoin Kirby was a gifted actor, he genuinely had no idea that there had been, at the very least, flirtation between his mother and my father. Did I dare tell this man, this stranger, that he might be my brother, that he was on a date with his sister? Could I ruin his life just as I surely knew mine had now been destroyed? I had been so certain coming here. I had no doubt that telling him was the right thing to do. Now, with the waves lapping gently on the shore and Eoin staring intently at me I was no longer sure.

"Did you put flowers on my father's grave?" I asked.

"Yes, I did. Is that what this is about? Shouldn't I have?"

"Depends on why you did it."

"My mother asked me to. She said that . . ."

He stopped talking then and took a step closer to me. I could see he was angry. "I think I see where this is leading, Adele. Are you implying that there was once some impropriety between my mother and your father? Is that it? Is that what makes your mother so unreasonable towards me?"

I nodded, unable to say anything.

"So what are you hinting at? That they had an affair?"

"They probably did."

"Really? My mother and a carpenter. I don't think so. Not unless she was a completely different woman thirty years ago."

"Thirty-five."

"Yes. She was pregnant with me when she left here, so . . ."

He stood stock still then, staring straight ahead. I could see the truth grab hold of him and shake him to his core. And with his dawning understanding of the situation, I felt myself let go of the last vestige of hope I had. Eoin had no new piece of information, no fact to tell me that would clear up the question of his parentage. No salvation. I realised with an even deeper sense of shock what I had not allowed myself to see until now. The man standing in front of me in the dimness could be my father. The fair hair, the broad shoulders, the height. I swallowed hard.

"Adele, are you trying to say that my mother and your father . . . that I'm their son?"

"Maybe. You could be. Your mother said so. She told my mother before she and Michael Kirby left for New Zealand. Now do you understand why Sissy is so upset? Why she didn't want me to see you?"

"That means so that you and I could be . . . Oh! Jesus!"

He began to walk, quick angry paces. I followed in his wake, counting my steps, listening intently to the scrunch of sand beneath my feet, sniffing the sea air, engaging my senses in everything but the awful reality of the situation in which Eoin Kirby and I found ourselves. Into which my mother had allowed me to fall because she did not warn me. Eoin stopped suddenly and waited for me to catch up.

"Bullshit!" he said as I approached him. "This is all bullshit. A fantasy of your mother's because she doesn't want you to meet someone. She wants you to stay at home with her."

"My aunt told me too. Did you know that your father, I mean Michael Kirby, financed the purchase of our house and set my father up in his business too? Why do you think he did that?"

"Because he was one of the kindest men I ever met. He helped a lot of people in his lifetime. I suppose you think it was a pay-off. A sweetener for your father to keep his mouth shut about the baby my mother was carrying."

"It could have been."

"One thing is sure, Adele Burke. You're your mother's daughter. No doubt about that. Same madness. Same badness. I'm proud to know Michael Kirby was my father. How dare you say otherwise!"

"I notice you're not near as proud to claim Irene as your mother. And I'm not surprised from what I've heard."

"Enough! God, but I was so wrong about you, Adele. I thought you were kind and warm. I thought we had a future."

I almost sobbed aloud. How precious those words would have been under different circumstances. "We have a past, Eoin. Not of our own making but we have to live with it anyway."

"If by that you mean you believe the slander about my mother, then I'm glad I learned so early on what type of person you are. Mum was right not to want to come back here. There's poison in the air."

"Why do you think your father pined for Cairnsure but never came back, even for a visit?"

A group of teenagers, pushing and shoving each other, laughing and all talking together, approached along the strand. Eoin glanced at them and then back to me.

"This is a pointless conversation. I don't wish to continue it or to see you again."

"Agreed. I certainly have no intention of seeing a man who could be my half-brother."

"Nor I a woman who thinks there's the tiniest jot of truth in that allegation. I'll see you to your car."

The group of young people were level with us now. They were carrying six-packs of beer. Off to a sheltered spot in the rocks, nothing more on their minds than getting drunk and maybe getting laid. I envied them.

"No need to escort me. I know the way myself," I said to Eoin.

He ignored me and fell into step beside me as I headed back to the car park in the Grand Hotel.

"I'll prove you wrong," he said as I put the key in the ignition.

As I drove home, I wished with all my heart that he

would. At least I would then know that I had not done the unforgivable and fallen for my half-brother. But if he was right, if all the talk about his mother was just jealousy, if my father had never slept with her, then I would also know that I had destroyed the best, and maybe the only, chance I ever had at true happiness. Whatever happened, Eoin Kirby would no longer be part of my life and that was the bitterest truth of all.

Chapter 22

Harry Selby rang early next morning. I forgot my self-pity the instant I heard his voice. I forgot everything except heart-stopping fear for Carla's life.

"Is there something wrong? Is it Carla?"

"Calm down, Adele. As a matter of fact, Carla is well today. She'll be going home this afternoon and that's why I'm ringing you now."

I let out a sigh of relief. Carla was well. Nothing else mattered. Not for now anyway.

"I was wondering if you'd mind going to see Finn? Vera says he's fretting and I must be at the hospital."

"Of course, Harry. I'll give him another computer lesson. Although, I'm sure he could probably teach me by now. How is he coping with his new computer?"

"No challenge to him at all. Isn't that the problem with Finn?"

It was and this was something I needed to straighten out with Harry.

"You know we discussed being honest with Finn about Carla's illness. How much does he know now?"

"I've already told him that Carla has cancer. He's thinking about that. I know this isn't fair on you but Finn trusts you and I ... well I'm having difficulty coping myself. My instinct is to protect him from the truth. But he must be prepared. We all must."

I didn't want to hear this. He had said Carla was well today, hadn't he? That was what I wanted to hang onto.

"I'll ring Vera now, Harry. See what's the best time to visit."

"Thank you. Carla is very grateful too."

When I put down the phone my hands were still shaking. Mom came bustling into the room.

"I heard the phone. Who was it?" she asked.

"Harry Selby. Carla is much better. She's coming home today."

"Thank God!" Mom said waving her hands rapidly from forehead to breast in her own inimitable way of making the sign of the cross.

I looked at her, lacquered hair, prim little mouth, the apron she wore like a badge of honour and I was very angry with Sissy Burke. Suddenly, I hated her smug faith, her total belief that her way was the only right way, her blinkered vision of what life was and how it should be lived, her arrogance in deciding that I could not be told the truth about my father. In a flash of insight, I saw through her pretended frailty, the little clasped hands and pursed lips, the huge hazel eyes. Underneath, Sissy Burke was as strong-willed as a mule and maybe her kick was as vicious.

I had never had reason to find out: I had always given into her, let her have her own way. And so had Dad.

The urge to shout at her, to tell her that she had ruined Dad's life and mine too, was so intense that I turned my back on her and ran into my bedroom. I locked the door and sat on the side of my bed, Barry Bear clutched tightly to my chest. I breathed deeply, trying to slow my pounding heart. As I sat there, rocking, holding my teddy bear, I realised that I was losing the control of my emotions on which I prided myself. Adele, the sensible one, the teacher. The pathetic one who had one boyfriend cheat on her and another turn out to be her brother. The one whose father had lived a lie and whose mother denied the truth.

The selfish one who was agonising over her own problems now when she should be thinking about Carla. Carla who had everything except time.

My heart-beat slowed back to normal. It was over, this mad fit of rage at my mother and at fate. For now. I put Barry Bear back on the bed, put my anger on hold and rang Carla's sister.

*　*　*

The children were very excited, even Finn.

"Mum's coming home!" they chorused. At least that was what they were all trying to say using their varying degrees of language skills.

"That's great news," I agreed and tried to match their broad smiles.

"I'm making a card for her," Liam said and showed me the page of paper and the stubby crayon he had in his hand. The twins waved crumpled pieces of paper too. As I was admiring the smudges of colour, Finn kept tugging at my hand.

"We must go, Adele. I need to make my card. I want to print it."

Vera was just about to correct Finn when I realised that I was mistaken about him being excited. The child was anxious. Even terrified.

"Finn and I have a lot of work to do this morning," I said. "The study again, is it?"

Vera nodded and then mouthed thanks as she shepherded the little troop of Carla's babies back to the kitchen and Finn went with me.

"Mum said I can use her computer for this. It's hooked up to the printer."

"Fine," I agreed as I sat beside Finn at the big oak desk. "Were you talking to her this morning?"

"Yes. She sounds different. Did you see her in the hospital?"

"I saw her yesterday and she looked very well. How do you mean she sounds different?"

Finn turned on the computer and stared silently at the screen as images flickered into life. He was dwarfed by the chair, the desk, the enormity of the situation he was facing. I saw frowns crease the still baby-skin of his forehead. He turned towards me.

"What's cancer?"

"It's a disease."

"Does it kill people?"

"People." Was this how early it started, this inability

of men to talk about their feelings? I believed a little girl would have asked if cancer would kill her mummy. That's what Finn wanted to know but the innate maleness in him would not allow him to personalise his fears. Or maybe it was just Finn's developed logic trying to make sense of the illogical.

"Sometimes," I answered carefully. "It depends on where the cancer grows and on how soon it is treated."

"Mum's is in her tummy. I was in her tummy too before I was born. And Liam and Dave and Lisa."

"Yes, that's right, you were."

He put his hand on the mouse and began to push it aimlessly so that the cursor skittered around the screen. I saw tears well on Finn's long eyelashes, teeter there and then plop onto the desk. I held my breath. He must ask the questions. And I, the person who could not manage her own life, hoped with all my strength that I could answer them for him. He turned towards me, his eyes wet and his bottom lip trembling.

"Was it our fault, Adele? Did Mummy get cancer in her tummy because she had so many babies in there?"

I sighed with relief. That question I could answer with honesty and with pity for this brave, confused little boy who thought he might be to blame for his mother's illness.

"Absolutely not," I said in my most authoritative teacher's voice. "Mummies carry babies in a special place in their tummies. It's called a womb and it's there specially to give babies a place to grow until they are strong enough to be born. Carla's cancer, your mummy's cancer, is in a different part."

He looked at me without blinking and I noticed that he had Carla's clear, violet-blue eyes. How had I not noticed this before?

"Where is it growing? The cancer."

"In her pancreas."

"What's that?"

I had a vague idea the pancreas was a gland that had something to do with digestion and with secreting insulin. I smiled at Finn.

"Tell you what, I'm not too sure. Why don't we log onto the Internet and find out."

"I can't. Not allowed. I haven't got the password."

"It's okay. Your dad gave it to me and he allows me to use it. I don't want you to look though while I'm putting it in. Turn your back."

To my surprise Finn turned around without argument. Once logged on, I Googled "pancreas" and came up with a plethora of websites. Eventually I found a site with a good colour diagram of the pancreas and its position in the body. There was some interesting information too. Just the right amount for Finn. And for me. We examined the diagram and then I read out some of the factual points to him. He soaked up the information like the sponge he was.

"So the pancreas helps us to take all the good things out of our food and it stops us having too much or too little sugar in our blood?" he said.

"That seems to be about it," I agreed, scanning over the information again and seeing that the complex enzymatic and hormonal function of the pancreas could loosely be described as Finn had done.

"And it has nothing to do with growing babies?"

"Not a thing. You can see that for yourself."

Finn looked from the screen to me. Then he suddenly grabbed the mouse and closed the page.

"Will you help me with my card now, Adele? I want to put a big 'Welcome Home' on it and a picture of roast potatoes. They're mum's very favourite thing to eat."

I smiled at him and tousled his hair. For one moment, one fleeting moment, Finn put his head on my chest and cuddled into me. I wanted to hold him close and to tell him everything would be all right. I knew I couldn't. His world would never be the same again but at least he knew now that he had not caused Carla's cancer. I wondered when he would ask how Carla could survive if she was unable to digest her food. I would have to talk to Harry again. I needed reassurance too.

* * *

A walk was imperative after my morning in Selbys'. Everything there was a reminder of how Carla had been. Her beautiful children, her artistic touches in the house, her four-by-four parked on the driveway. The sadness in Brigitte's and Vera's eyes was a painful reminder of how Carla was now. Especially Vera. On several occasions I saw her struggle for self-control as the children ran around in a welter of excitement because their mother was coming home. I had seen the same look of utter grief in Harry's eyes too and I needed to get away from it. It was ruining the hope onto which I was stubbornly clinging.

I had my trainers on, the ones with the pink laces.

Instinct had told me this morning that the longer I stayed away from my mother today, the better I would cope with my new insights into her complex character. Not new. Just recently acknowledged. The fleeting rage I had felt towards her and all she stood for had been tapped from a deep well. It would uncap and bubble up again. Just not now.

I drove aimlessly for a while. Where could I walk? I had no safe haven left. I didn't want to go out the hill road. That led to Aunt Lily's and Aunt Lily led to thoughts of my father and Irene Kirby. The beach was out of bounds too. Eoin Kirby could so easily be there, exercising along the shoreline or inspecting his new property on the prom. The fact that he had bought Elliots' shop probably gave him more right to be there than I had. So what did that leave me? A stroll around the town, an amble to the graveyard?

It was then I remembered the clearing in Glengorm forest. The place Eoin and I had found Jodi Wall. Having so recently been talking to Finn about wombs, the clearing seemed to offer that same warm, safe protection. I headed off towards Glengorm and parked my car in exactly the spot where Jodi had abandoned her mother's yellow Mini on the night she had almost OD'd.

It was cool in the woods. The sun, shaded by towering trees, did not touch the forest floor. I noticed as I walked along that briars and ferns had sprung back in the days since we had trampled them in our frantic search for Jodi. Nobody else had been here since. I was scratched and had a rip in my leggings by the time I rounded the corner to the clearing. My heart almost stopped. It was still there, sun-drenched, flower-strewn, a magic light-filled oasis in the midst of gloom. A symbol of hope.

I ran the last few yards, laughing as if I had finally lost my sanity. I twirled around, lifted my face to the sun and soaked in its warmth and energy. Manic phase over, I finally sat with my back to the trunk of an elm tree. The sun traced wavering patterns on the grass where it filtered through the oval, saw-toothed leaves. The dance of light and shadow was hypnotic, soothing. I had come here to mull over things. Bad things like my father's relationship with Irene Kirby, horrific things like the possibility that Eoin was my half-brother, confusing things like my anger with my mother. Unacceptable things like Carla's terminal illness. The sad and the bad thoughts shifted in rhythm with the rustling leaves and their dappled shadows. Tired, confused, I drifted into sleep.

My phone woke me. I jumped up, not sure at first what the unearthly sound coming from my pocket really was. I don't know why I ever thought the sound of a bull elephant trumpeting would be a good ring-tone. I glanced at the screen and saw that the call was from Jodi. A coincidence since I happened to be in the very spot where she too had found refuge.

"Hi, Jodi. How are you?"

"I'm confused."

"Really? Why?"

"What did you do to Eoin Kirby last night? He's like a bear with a sore head today."

"I did nothing to him!"

"That's it then. Maybe you should have."

"Jodi, for the last time, there's nothing going on between Eoin Kirby and me. And there never will be."

"So why are you seeing him?"

"I'm not. Not any more. How did you know I saw him last night? Did he say something?"

"He told me. Yesterday. It was all Adele this and Adele that. Today, he just goes pale at the mention of your name."

I leaned my back against the trunk of the tree and slid down along it until I was sitting on the grass. I closed my eyes. So, he was upset. Was that an aftermath of yesterday's anger or could it be because he had contacted his mother and extracted an admission from her? A confession that she had indeed had an affair with a lowly carpenter thirty-five years ago and that her eldest son was the product of that misalliance? Snob! Tramp!

"Adele? Are you still there? Are you all right? Where are you?"

I took a deep breath before I answered. "Yes, I'm fine. Just out for a walk. I was up in Carla's house this morning to see the children. She's coming home this afternoon."

"That's great and it's one of the reasons I want to talk to you. I have a plan and Eoin agrees with it. More than that, he's enthusiastic about it. I need to discuss it with you. Could you meet me for a coffee? In the Latte Bar?"

I looked around my secret retreat and wished I could stay there forever. But the mess that was my life would have to be faced. Moreover, plans hatched jointly by Jodi Wall and Eoin Kirby needed immediate attention.

"I'll see you there in thirty minutes."

Before leaving the glade, I stooped down and picked up a stone. A little pebble, grey and smooth. I put it in my pocket. I couldn't stay in the safety of this magic place but at least I could take something of it with me.

* * *

The Latte Bar was busy. Jodi was already seated at a corner table when I got there. She had a glow about her. An energy. I was suspicious as I sat down opposite her.

"Why are you staring at me, Del?"

I was going to make some excuse. Say that I was admiring her earrings or her hair. I decided not to lie. There had been too much lying.

She nodded her head. "I see. You think I'm on something. That I'm high."

She was right. "I'm sorry," I muttered. "The thought did cross my mind. You're buzzing a bit."

To my relief, she laughed. "I know. I haven't felt this good in ages. Eoin Kirby has offered me a job. Sort of Girl Friday for his proposed development. But I suppose you know all about that?"

I shook my head. Not just my head. I shook all over. Jesus! Development? Surely not here in Cairnsure? Was the man ever going to shag off back to New Zealand?

"Didn't he tell you that he went to the Planning Department? He checked out the proposal for the Marina. It seems the plan will soon be given the green light. Eoin has put in a bid on a fifty-acre site west of the prom. You know, it used to belong to that old farmer who always tied his coat with a length of binder twine."

310

"He's been dead for years."

"Yes and his son, his only child, fecked off to America and left the farm lie idle. Clever man. He just waited for planning permission."

"Planning for what?"

"So you were telling the truth about not seeing Eoin any more! I thought you were just being coy."

"For the last time there's nothing going on between me and Eoin Kirby. Now tell me about the planning."

"A shopping mall, golf course and really swish apartments on the fifty-acre site."

"And the developer will be Eoin Kirby. Right?"

Jodi frowned at me. I could see she was wondering just what had gone on between me and Eoin. I wanted to tell her. God, how I wanted to tell her! I began to let words rattle out of my mouth. Any words, just as long as they were not brother-and-sister secrets.

"So you're going to organise the set-up for him. Well done, Jode! Congratulations. You're more than able for that challenge. What does Kieran think of your new job?"

"He's a bit miffed to be honest. He offered me a job in *Cairnsure Weekly*. I turned it down because I don't think it's a good idea to work for the person you're living with."

"You've decided to move in with him permanently so?"

A waitress came along then and took our orders. I plumped for cappuccino and Jodi did too. When the waitress had gone, Jodi leaned across the table to me.

"I don't do forever and forever, Del. You know that. I've been independent for too long. I tried to explain that to Kieran but I don't think he understands. But I admit I've made a mess of things on my own. Maybe I do need someone to keep me on the straight and narrow."

"So you've decided that you do really believe in love, despite your cynicism?"

I had expected a mind-your-own-business reply or even a sneer. Instead Jodi seemed confused.

"I don't know. I'm sure that Kieran is a good person. He's kind and very supportive. That's enough for now. We'll see how it goes. Anyway I wanted to talk to you about something else. Something a lot more important."

It was my turn to frown now. Moving in with Kieran should have been the most important thing in Jodi's life. I thought of how intense Kieran's feelings for her seemed to be and I hoped that he would not live to regret them.

"What's so important?" I asked.

"Carla. Do you remember our conversation with her the night she told us about her . . . her illness?"

I thought back. All I could remember was devastating sadness. No words.

"Tell me."

"She was talking about Elliots', saying that she had wanted the three of us to work together. That she would have gone ahead with our café idea except that she got sick."

I immediately put up my hand to stop Jodi and again wondered if her thinking was chemically enhanced. "Enough, Jodi! It wasn't just Carla's illness put paid to

312

that notion. You know better than I do that it wasn't a good business proposition. Not for us. If you have any crazy thoughts about resurrecting the project, leave me out of it. Anyway, Eoin Kirby bought The Cabin. Isn't it up to him to decide what to do with it?"

"He knows what I want to do and he gives it his full backing. In fact he's being very generous about it which is more than I can say for you now."

I straightened my shoulders and felt my lips pursing. To my horror I realised I was doing a Sissy bristle. An image of myself in twenty years' time, hair lacquered, apron on and for good measure, leg bandaged like Aunt Lily, flashed into my mind and I coughed on the choking thought.

"Have a drink of water," Jodi said, pushing a water jug towards me. "Forget about the fact that Eoin Kirby owns The Cabin. Apparently that's a stumbling block for you. It's Carla we must think about. She wants a café and I'm going to make damned sure she gets one. And so are you when you stop feeling sorry for yourself."

I looked at the recovering cocaine addict sitting opposite me and I felt ashamed. Jodi had lost everything she had worked for – her job, her precious apartment, her status – yet she had the generosity of spirit to put Carla first now. Or maybe she was just being Jodi and getting the café she wanted come hell or high water. That thought made me feel ashamed too. I was in a welter of shame.

"Okay," I agreed. "I'll listen to your plan but I'm not saying I'll go along with it."

313

Jodi waved the waitress over and got two more coffees. Black this time.

"I rang Harry Selby. He said Carla will have a limited time when she feels well. Well enough to go out and about. When the enzyme supplements kick in, she will be able to eat more, maybe get a bit stronger."

"Then she'll have her radiation therapy."

"Maybe. That depends. Anyway, that's just a pain-relief measure. You must stop fooling yourself, Del. Carla is not going to be cured."

"Who said that? She might be."

"Harry said it and he should know."

"And he thinks your plan is a good idea?"

"'A wonderful thought,'" Jodi said in a very accurate imitation of Harry's plumby accent.

We were silent then, each of us dealing with the truth in our own way. Jodi taking it head-on and me letting it drip painfully into my consciousness. I lifted my head eventually and looked at Jodi. She was pale.

"Your plan," I said "What is it?"

"To open the café for Carla. For just one day."

There was no doubting Jodi's sincerity but I did think there was a big question mark over her sanity.

"Open a café for one day! How in the name of God could we do that?"

"With a lot of planning and hard work."

"Does Eoin Kirby know exactly what you intend doing?"

"Yes, he does. He's getting the electricity reconnected for us."

"Why?"

"Jesus, Adele! Because I asked him. Because he's a kind man. Because Carla is dying."

Unable to look at Jodi, I bowed my head. I couldn't question her motivation. She was doing something nice for her friend, something to make Carla forget her pain, her fate, if only for a day. But I had doubts about the wisdom of the whole idea. Would it not make Carla feel even sadder that she would not live to see a real café in Elliots' old shop? To know that it was all pretence because she was dying. I looked up at Jodi.

"Are you sure she'd want that, Jode? Would it not be more like a wake?"

"It will not! That's up to us anyway. We can fill the place with laughter and good food. And music."

"Not the Sound Bytes!"

We laughed then. Too much for such a silly joke. It was the release we needed from dour reality.

"C'mon," Jodi said, standing up. "I have the keys to Elliots'. Let's go and look over the old dump."

"And we'll look at Elliots' too," I said, setting the tone for the childish humour we needed to get us through today. I had no idea what would get us through the next few days, weeks, months, nor what I would do if Eoin Kirby walked into The Cabin.

*　*　*

Jodi flicked a wall switch as soon as we set foot inside the door of the old shop. Light flooded what used to be proudly known as The Cabin. Eoin Kirby certainly worked quickly.

I gazed from filthy floors to cobwebbed ceilings and swore underneath my breath. This was a mad enterprise.

"What about health and safety regulations?" I asked. "Even if we by some miracle got this place cleaned up, how could we serve food here? Wouldn't we need a permit or a licence or something?"

"Of course not. We won't be serving food to the public. This is a private party. Anyway we won't be cooking here. We'll be bringing the food in."

"I see. And what will we serve it on? That tatty old counter there? Or maybe if we took the sticky lollies and the musty papers off the shelves we could use them."

"Shut up, Del. Just give me a hand dumping that bag of stinking spuds outside. I don't know why it's still here."

I did as Jodi asked. She seemed to be working to a plan and I must admit, I was planless. We found an old bucket, mop and scrubbing brush in the back yard. By the time we had finished mopping up the last of the stinking potato residue at least the place smelt better.

"Money. How come you haven't mentioned it?" I asked. "Even a surface renovation is going to cost a lot."

"That'll be no problem," Jodi said airily. "We're all going to chip in. Harry and Kieran, my family, Sissy and Tom, Eoin Kirby. You too."

"Have they all agreed?"

"They will."

I gave up worrying about the details then. I was getting caught up in Jodi's enthusiasm and the more I thought about it the better I liked the idea. It would be our way of showing Carla how much she meant to us. How much she would always mean to us.

"How long do we have to do this makeover?" I asked, trying to make light of the fact that the question I was really asking was how long did Carla have to live?

"Harry said to get it done as soon as possible."

I had to lean against old Ma Elliot's filthy counter for support. There was no point in contradicting Jodi, in denying what she had said. The truth was etched on her pale face and in her tear-filled dark eyes. We stared at each other and allowed the awful reality to sink in. Jodi was the first to recover.

"C'mon," she ordered. "We're going to buy bin bags and rubber gloves and disinfectant. The sooner we start the better. And you're paying. I'm broke."

We raided the cleaning section of the supermarket and arrived back at The Cabin with every cleaner known to advertising. We dumped and brushed and scrubbed until the sun began to slant westward. Our backs were aching and we both looked as filthy as the shop had been when we had started the clear-up. We might have stayed longer, so desperate was our need to be doing something positive for Carla but Kieran rang Jodi to remind her that they were going out to dinner.

"Shit! I forgot, Del. I suppose we have enough done for today anyway. How about we meet here early in the morning. Say nine o'clock?"

We were dumping the last of the filled bin bags out in the back yard when the front door opened. I dropped the bag I was holding as I heard Eoin Kirby call out.

317

"I'm going, Jodi," I said in panic. "Just remembered something. See you in the morning."

I left an open-mouthed Jodi and ran past Eoin Kirby. He may have been shocked, surprised or amused. I didn't look at his face. I kept running until I reached my car. I arrived home in less than half the time it should have taken and was relieved to see that Mom's car was not there. I ran again, this time to the seat in the back garden – the one my father had crafted. I sat there, breathless, confused, and knew that no matter how far and how fast I ran, I could never leave behind the sadness, bitterness and burning shame which suddenly seemed to be the sum of what I, Adele Burke, had become.

Chapter 23

It was cloudy next morning. Big grey clouds which played hide and seek with the sun. I woke to the aroma of baking. Mom must have been up at cockcrow. When I got to the kitchen I saw scones cooling on a wire rack on the counter.

"Morning, Adele. I noticed you didn't eat the dinner I left for you last night. You can't keep going without your food. Sit down and have some of these."

She began to heap hot scones onto a plate for me and I tried not to feel manipulated. How could I be angry with her now after she had gone to all this trouble?

"Thanks, Mum," I muttered and obediently sat and began to butter a scone. The butter melted in golden puddles and soaked into the soft-textured centre. I took a delicious bite just as she placed a cup of coffee in front of me.

"You must keep up your strength for Carla," she said.

My physical strength was unassailable. It was my mental strength which was wilting. I swallowed a mouthful and looked into my mother's face and knew that scones or no scones, we must have honesty between us.

"This house," I began before I had really decided on what to say. "Do you know where Dad got the mortgage?"

Her eyes narrowed and she stood over me, hand in her apron pocket, a streak of flour on her right cheek.

"He had an arrangement with Michael Kirby."

"So you did know about it!"

"I bet you've been talking to Lily Burke. The vicious old woman! How your father paid for this house is not her business and certainly not yours."

"I'm sure!"

"Don't you take that sarcastic tone with me! The old biddy is just stirring up trouble, like she always did."

"Why should Michael Kirby put a roof over our heads? Was it a pay-off? A bribe to keep your mouth shut about Dad maybe being Eoin's father?"

"That's unfair! I'm disgusted you think either your father or I would stoop that low. It was a business arrangement. Every last penny of it was paid back through the bank. Plus plenty of interest."

Mom flopped onto the chair nearest to her and two red patches flooded her cheeks. I was gripped by fear.

"Are you all right, Mom?"

"How can I be all right when you keep dragging up the past? Can't you leave it where it belongs?"

"Can't you answer my questions fully? Then I wouldn't be annoying you about it any more."

She gazed at me in her doe-eyed way and I felt cruel. One part of me understood that Mom was trying to deny the awful events of thirty-five years ago. She had a right to her privacy but not when it affected my life. She took a deep breath and just when I thought she was going to talk she closed her mouth again. I gave up.

"Jodi and I are planning a party for Carla in Elliots' shop."

Mom sat bolt upright. "In The Cabin? How? I thought it had been sold? To Eoin Kirby. You've been talking to him! How could you?"

"I have not! I never want to lay eyes on him again. Jodi Wall is working for him. She somehow talked him into lending us The Cabin."

"How do you mean Jodi is working for him? You're not saying he's going to stay here, are you?"

"No, of course not. Jodi is just helping him out while he's here," I said, fervently hoping that what I was saying would turn out to be true.

"Anyway what are you thinking? A party is to celebrate. Poor Carla has nothing to party about. It's not suitable. You'll upset her."

"She really wanted to open a café, Mom. We're just making that wish come through for her. Showing her what we can do if . . . when she's better."

"Maybe. But why The Cabin? It's in an awful condition."

"You know that's where we had planned to open our café. It would mean more to her to have it there. You're right, though. The place is a mess. Will you and Tom give us a hand to clear it out?"

"Will Eoin Kirby be there? In The Cabin?"

I had only a split second to decide. Truth or lie? I took the easy option.

"No, he won't. He's too busy with other things."

"That's okay so. We'd be glad to do anything for Carla. Tom is very handy with painting and that kind of work. I'll bake for you and bring flowers too."

"Thanks, Mom," I said and continued with my breakfast while Sissy waffled happily on about what she and Tom were going to do. I passed no remark about the way she volunteered Tom without his say-so. That would be his problem to deal with. I had enough of my own.

* * *

I discovered a new talent that day. I was good at wielding a hammer. My toned muscles came into their own as I walloped the old shelves and knocked them from where they had sat snugly against the shop walls for many years.

"Shit!" Jodi breathed in disbelief as we stood in the middle of the wreckage. "What were we thinking? Were we mad?"

Looking at the apocalyptic scene, insanity seemed like the only explanation. We even looked crazy, me with tons of plaster dust in my hair and Jodi with a cobweb, complete with dead fly, clinging to the headscarf she had been clever enough to wear.

"This was your bright idea so stop complaining," I said more in panic than annoyance. "Just help me to dump all this rotten timber out in the back."

Thirty minutes later we were able to view the walls

of the shop in all their pock-marked glory. I had managed to tear out lumps of plaster with the wall brackets.

"We could paper it," Jodi suggested tentatively.

I shivered as I remembered a particularly vile paper Sissy had hung in my bedroom the year I made my Confirmation. It was brown with a lemon ivy design. There were tendrils on the jaundiced ivy and I had many nightmares about those tendrils strangling me while I was asleep.

"Think about it," Jodi urged. "We could get thick white paper. The type that looks like fancy plasterwork. Then we wouldn't have to paint the walls. It would save us a lot of time. It's made especially for walls like this."

Apart from the fact that there never were, and probably never would be, walls like this, she had a point. Besides, the sooner the holes and gouges were covered the better.

"We'll have to do something before Eoin Kirby sees it," I said. "He'll have a hissy fit when he realises we've almost demolished his latest purchase."

"You're quite the cover-up specialist, aren't you?"

I twirled around to face Eoin and realised that we had left the front door open.

"Hi, Eoin," Jodi said cheerily. "We're making progress, don't you think? Isn't papering a good idea?"

He shifted his angry gaze from me to let his eyes roam around the shelfless shop.

"You'll have to use a ton of filler first. But yes, I think hiding the damage is probably the way to go. That's the only thing to do sometimes. Wouldn't you agree, Adele?"

I didn't answer. I knew he was talking about damaged lives, not damaged walls.

"Well?" he prompted as Jodi looked from one to the other of us and frowned.

Eoin had taken a step closer to me. He stared steadily at me.

"Depends on the damage, Eoin. On how deep the cracks go."

"Are we still talking about the walls or is this a private conversation?" Jodi asked and there was a peevish note in her voice. She never liked not being the centre of attention.

"Why are you doing this?" I asked Eoin, ignoring Jodi. "You don't even know Carla."

"I know she's a young mother who is seriously ill. That's enough for me to want to help. Are you going to refuse that help just because it's coming from me? Are you that bitter?"

"Definitely private," Jodi said and stalked out to the backyard.

Eoin and I continued to eye each other.

"I think it's very good of you to want to do something for Carla. Thank you. It's just that . . ."

"Just that you'd prefer I stayed out of your life. Went back to New Zealand and forgot that we ever met. Is that it?"

"It's the circumstances for God's sake! You said you never wanted to see me again and I don't want to see you either. And now I hear you've bought up half of Cairnsure. We still don't know if . . . if we're . . ."

"Well, Adele. I've a surprise for you. In a few days'

time, you can question my mother in person. See if you're as willing to insult Irene Kirby to her face as you've done behind her back."

"She's coming here! But I thought she never wanted to come back!"

"You're wrong about that and a lot of other things too. I hope you'll have the grace to apologise."

I didn't get a chance to say anything else. Eoin swept past me and went to join Jodi in the backyard. I heard their voices but no words registered. I sat on Mrs Elliot's counter and tried to get my breath back. Irene Kirby was coming to Cairnsure. Back to the scene of the crime. I immediately thought of Mom. I would have to warn her. If there had been gossip about my father and Irene before it would be rekindled now and Mom would have to go through it all again. At that moment I hated the Kirby family with a passion.

Jodi and Eoin came inside again, Jodi smiling broadly.

"I told Eoin that Carla would like a barbeque area out in the back. Do you remember her suggesting that, Del? He said we can go ahead, didn't you, Eoin?"

Dispensing permissions for impossible makeovers hadn't seemed to improve his mood any. He was glowering.

"Give me a buzz, Jodi when you're through here. There are a few things I'd like to run over with you about the development."

Then he was gone, without even a nod in my direction.

Jodi hopped up on the counter beside me.

"That was heavy, Del. The air between the two of you was nearly on fire. Do you want to talk about it?"

I wanted to talk about it. God, how I wanted to unload the bitterness, shame and embarrassment! To bring it all out in the open, make excuses for myself, hear words of sympathy and understanding. But how could I tell the awful truth? Only some of the secrets were mine to tell. I shook my head and tried to smile at Jodi.

"Just a personality clash. That's all. I think we should take a break now anyway. It's almost lunch-time."

Jodi's "Hmm" told me that she didn't believe my glib explanation. I squirmed so much on the counter that I loosened a splinter of timber. I jumped up as it pierced through the deliberate rip in the seat of the designer jeans I had so foolishly worn for the demolition. We laughed as Jodi withdrew the long, narrow sliver and then we began to giggle as we had done yesterday. It was as if we had a tacit agreement to make silly laughter the antidote to all our problems. But my laugh went no deeper than my throat. My heart was not amused. And neither I suspected, was Jodi's.

* * *

Because Jodi was meeting Kieran for lunch, I found myself at a bit of a loose end. I rang Harry Selby to enquire about Carla. Harry was on his way to the hospital. He said Carla was very tired but happy to be home. I wasn't quite sure what to make of that. Was she not able to get out of bed? I didn't ask, knowing it was up to him to tell me as much, or as little, about Carla's condition as he chose.

"And Adele," he added, "I don't know what happened

between you and Finn but thank you. He seems a lot more at ease now."

"My pleasure. He's a great little boy."

"He is that. Most of the time. Before I forget, I must tell you I've opened an account in the DIY store. Get whatever you and Jodi need for The Cabin on that account. I really appreciate what you're both doing for Carla. She's going to love it."

"Thanks, Harry. Actually we may buy some wallpaper there, if that's okay."

"Go ahead. And no heavy work for you two. Hire whoever you want and send the bills to me."

"We'll manage. We really want to do it ourselves. Because . . . well, because it's for Carla."

Harry was quiet for a moment. Maybe he had hit some traffic. When he did talk again it was I who went into a silence.

"This Eoin Kirby person is showing extraordinary kindness. He doesn't know Carla and yet he's allowing us to use his premises. Do you know him, Adele?"

How could I know him better? He was probably my half-brother and for a very brief, heady period he had been my boyfriend too. How in the hell was I supposed to answer Harry's question? Not truthfully. Equivocate. I was getting good at that.

"I've met him, yes. It seems he's about to carry out some big development in Cairnsure and Jodi Wall is his assistant."

"Jodi, an assistant! That's not the Jodi I know. She'll be running Mr Kirby's development before he knows what hit him! Anyway I must meet him to thank him. Just pulling into the hospital grounds now, Adele. I'll tell Carla you rang and I'll let you know when she's up to a visit."

Then he was gone. Off to cure strangers while his own wife was dying.

* * *

Bitter from the irony of life I found myself drawn to the deepest source of bitterness I knew. I headed for Aunt Lily's.

After we had gone through the usual routine of curtain-twitching and a reluctant welcome, I followed her into the kitchen.

"You look disgraceful," she said over her shoulder. "You're covered in dirt, your hair is festooned with bits of plaster and your trousers is all ripped. Have you any pride at all?"

No was the simple answer to that but Aunt Lily was not an advocate of simplicity. I would have to explain The Cabin project to her and she would question and criticise every detail. She put on the kettle and two eggs to boil while I told her about our café party plan. To my surprise, she didn't interrupt me. When I finished she came to stand in front of me.

"Take Ned Lehane."

"Pardon?"

"Take Ned Lehane. He spends his days arsing around the bit of land here and pretending to work. I pay him good money. Let the lazy sod earn it. The Cabin project should shake him up a bit."

"Thank you, Aunt Lily. Are you sure you can manage without him?"

"I won't have to, will I? I didn't say keep him. Just use him for a few days."

I remembered the barbeque. Jodi was right. Carla would really love that. I smiled at Aunt Lily.

"I have just the job for Ned. How do you think he'll cope with slashing weeds and briars in the back garden of The Cabin and then doing a bit of paving?"

Lily's grin was wicked. "It will half-kill him. It's years since he did a decent day's work."

She cackled happily to herself as she made the tea, lifted out the boiled eggs and got bread and butter ready. When she served them up, we ate in silence. I enjoyed mine. Demolishing shops is a good appetiser. Finished, I sat back.

"My mother knew all along that Michael Kirby lent my father the money to buy our house."

I watched Lily closely for her reaction. A frown, a sniff, an eyebrow raised in surprise. Her face was impassive.

"Doesn't surprise me. I told you she wouldn't care as long as she got what she wanted."

"That's unfair," I said crossly. "You're very quick to judge. How do you know she didn't care? Maybe she was so unhappy living here that borrowing money from Michael Kirby seemed like the lesser of two evils."

"Maybe."

"I bet you didn't make it easy for her either."

"Sissy Roberts doesn't need anyone else to make things easy for her. She does that very well for herself."

329

I stood up. It was time to go. The walls of the dreary old kitchen seemed to be closing in around me and Aunt Lily's resentment was further souring my already bitter thoughts.

"Will you ask Ned Lehane to call to The Cabin tomorrow morning, please?"

"No. I'll tell him."

"Right. Thank you. And thanks for lunch."

She walked to the door with me, probably to make sure that I really was going. She looked so very self-assured that I was overcome with the idea of shaking her self-contained calm.

"Irene Kirby is coming to Cairnsure. In the next few days," I announced and waited for an explosive outburst.

Lily shrugged her shoulders and then smiled. I saw a shadow in her eyes and thought it was sadness. I was puzzled. I had almost reached The Cabin by the time I recognised the fleeting emotion I had seen. It was pity. The crabby, grumpy, bitter old lady pitied me. That knowledge made me pity myself.

* * *

My mother's car was parked outside The Cabin when I got back. For an instant, I was tempted to turn my car and flee. But where to? Maybe back to Dublin, the place I should never have left for this ill-thought-out, ill-fated and ill-timed sabbatical. Too late now. My shoebox apartment would be too small to accommodate me and all my new-found guilt.

Sissy was in full flight when I went inside the shop. Apron on, she was pouring tea from a huge thermos. Her beige tablecloth with a hunting scene stencilled on one corner was spread over the counter which had splintered my rear-end. She turned when she heard the door open.

"Adele, you're just in time. I brought something for you to eat."

"I had lunch, thanks, Mom."

"What did I tell you?" she asked Tom who was walking around tapping walls. "These young women are starving themselves half to death. Look at you, Jodi Wall, when was the last time you had a decent bite to eat?"

"About thirty minutes ago, Mrs Burke. I had steak and chips. I'd love some of that apple tart you brought though."

"I think we'll get away with filling these holes all right," Tom said. "I'll go get a few packets of filler."

"You'll have your lunch," my mother ordered. "You can't work on an empty stomach."

I went into the store, brought out one of the rickety chairs and sat down. Pointless trying to get any work done until Mom had satisfied her need to overfeed the parish. She handed me a plate piled high with sandwiches. I took the plate but left it untouched. A compromise.

"Aunt Lily is sending Ned Lehane down here in the morning. I thought he could start on the back garden, Jodi. What do you think?"

Mouth full of apple tart, Jodi nodded enthusiastically.

"What are you dragging Lily Burke into this for?" Mom asked.

"She offered. She wants to help too."

"She'll have some reason for doing that. She always has an angle."

"What about the floors? What should we do with them?"

Jodi's question made us all look down. It was difficult to see the flooring through the dust and dirt. I stooped and cleared a little circle. A cement surface shone through, smooth from years of foot-traffic. I remembered how Mrs Elliot used to keep it spotlessly clean.

"Floor tiles?"

"Big job," Tom said, now tapping the floor. I wondered if he had sensors on his fingers or if he had an ability to knock information out of walls and floors.

"The whole thing's a huge job," my mother said, looking around her and twitching her nose. "Is it worth it for one day?"

"Yes!" Jodi and I chorused together.

Tom did the wise thing then. He took my mother away with him to buy the packets of filler while Jodi and I went to work brushing and scrubbing until the last of the dust and dirt was gone. The shop seemed so much bigger now without the clutter of shelves and rubbish.

"How many tables do you think we can fit, Jode?"

She didn't answer. I looked at her and saw that she was biting her lip and staring at her feet. Lip-biting and foot-staring had always been signs that Jodi was worried about something.

"What's wrong?"

She raised her head and I could see confusion in her eyes, as if she had forgotten I was here.

"Kieran wants me to meet his daughter."

"Oh! Amy. Sounds like a real cutie. You don't seem too happy about the prospect."

"I'm not. What do I know about children?"

"What do you need to know? He's not asking you to look after her, is he? Her mother does that."

"Yes, the wonderful Norma Higgins, Solicitor and Supermum."

"Are you jealous?"

"I'm not! Did you ever notice the way she dresses? And she bites her nails. No, I'm not jealous, just a bit worried that Kieran is pushing things too fast. I'm not ready for a daughter-meeting."

I wondered if Jodi was ready for a relationship at all. She didn't seem sure of what she wanted.

"Maybe it's all a bit soon," I suggested. "After . . ."

"Yes, after losing my job and my apartment. Not to mention those fucking drugs. My head's in a mess, Del. I can feel myself going down into that black place I was before. I'd give anything now for the lift of a hit. Just one line, one half-hour of optimism and energy."

I leaned on the sweeping brush I was holding and for a brief but very intense instant I closed my eyes and prayed. Well, I wished very fervently and let the plea drift into the ether. To my mind that's a prayer. I needed guidance, wisdom, and an in-depth knowledge of psychiatry, psychology and any other discipline needed to cope with Jodi's present condition. I felt annoyance too. Why had she not got professional help? Carla had said Harry would organise it. Jodi shouldn't be scaring me half to death talking about black places. I knew the statistics. In this frame of mind, Jodi was in danger of self-harming. She was staring at me now, a very open and vulnerable expression on her usually inscrutable face. What if the wrong words came out of my mouth? What if my ill-advised comments drove her even further into her sudden black mood? I stopped thinking and the answer came to me. The proper words were none at all. I dropped the brush, walked over to Jodi and held her in my arms. I felt her slight body shake as she cried.

"Why isn't it me, not Carla?" she sobbed. "I would have been glad. It's not fair!"

I continued to pat her back and be silent.

"That's why I went to Glengorm Woods, you know. To think about ending it all. Why did you rescue me? I didn't want to be found until it was too late."

"I looked for you and found you because I care about you. So does Kieran Mahon and Carla and your family."

"My family! You must be joking. My mother said she was sorry she ever had me. I told her the truth about what happened in London. About the drugs and the money I took."

My arms dropped to my sides and I took a step back. What courage it must have taken for Jodi to confess to her self-righteous parents.

"There was a big scene, was there?"

"Jesus, Del, you'd swear I was after murdering somebody. I ruined my career, sure. I stole but I've paid that back. I'm trying, really trying to stay off the drugs. I haven't hurt anybody but myself. To listen to them you'd think I was the devil incarnate. Hypocrites! They threw me out of the house and told me never go back. Not that I want to."

"When did this happen?"

"Last night."

I had wondered at first if that was the reason she had moved in with Kieran but if the drama happened just last night, that couldn't be. Jodi was right. The Walls were indeed hypocrites of the highest order. Their ostentatious praying had a hollow echo. The substance of charity and forgiveness did not seem to concern them at all. The worst aspect was, whether Jodi consciously admitted it or not, she still craved their approval. Maybe much as I craved Sissy's.

"Unless I entered a convent or married and started producing little Catholics by the batch, my parents wouldn't approve. And do you know the funny thing, Del? The young ones, the sisters after me in the family, they shove two fingers up to Mam and Dad and they get away with it."

"More power to them! I hope the shoved-up fingers hurt."

Jodi smiled at that comment but I could see her struggle to hold back tears. The door-latch rattled. I heard Jodi take a deep breath.

"Thanks, Del. I feel better now. You're a brick," she whispered.

Sissy came trotting in. Tom, loaded down with packets of fillers and trowels, right behind her. She clapped her hands so energetically that I'm certain I saw her hair move. A little quiver anyway.

"C'mon, girls! No more gossiping. We've work to do."

I cursed myself for letting my mother know about The Cabin project.

* * *

After fifteen minutes of Mom supervising Tom as he worked I was struck by two thoughts. One, Tom Reagan was a saint not to apply plaster and trowel to my mother's ever-busy mouth, and two I just had to escape The Cabin before I did exactly that. I remembered something. An escape plan.

"Harry told me he's set up an account for us in the DIY store. I forgot to tell you, Jodi."

"Oh, great! We should go there now so and pick out the wallpaper," Jodi said so quickly that I knew she too needed to escape.

"Will I go with . . ." Mom said and then stopped, looking from Tom to us. What a dilemma for her. Should she allow us free rein with the paper or give Tom sole responsibility for filling the holes?

Jodi caught me by the arm and hauled me quickly towards the door.

"We're off, Mrs Burke. Thanks for the apple tart in case I don't see you again. Bye, Tom."

I allowed myself to be led through the door at lightning speed and jumped into Jodi's car. We didn't breathe a sigh of relief until we stopped outside the DIY store.

"You know I think your mom's a pet, Del, but she can be a bit too kind at times."

I laughed at that statement. Everything and everybody in the Sissy environment was under her control. So very cleverly done. My mother always appeared to be vulnerable, selfless. Even I, maybe under the influence of Aunt Lily, was just beginning to see that Sissy's magnanimous sharing of her time and opinions wasn't a sharing at all. It was a nudge, not always gentle, in the direction she wanted you to go.

"She is kind, yes," I agreed. "If only she could be silently kind, it would be a lot better."

"Well, you know she would never say she was sorry she had you like my mother did. No matter what you'd done. You should be grateful for that."

I got out of the car and began to head towards the store, head bowed, thinking about what Jodi had just said. If only I knew that to be true. But I didn't. If I told Mom that I had been out with Eoin Kirby several times, I was pretty sure she would disown me.

Jodi caught up with me, anxious now. "I'm sorry if you thought I was insulting your mother, Del. I didn't mean to."

I smiled at her, trying to reassure both her and myself. "I know that. It's just that I've got to tell her something I know is going to upset her a lot. I don't know how she'll take it."

"Oh my God! Don't tell me you're pregnant! You're not, are you?"

"Nothing that simple. You probably heard Eoin Kirby saying today that his mother is coming to Cairnsure in a few days' time. Maybe you already knew. I must tell Mom. Warn her."

"Warn her? Oh! You mean about the row you said they had in the dark ages. Surely not? Whatever it was must be well forgotten by now?"

"Not by Sissy Burke. Even the mention of Eoin's mother sends her into a tizzy."

We walked on in silence until we reached the entrance door. Jodi stood and caught me by the arm.

"Do you want me to ask Eoin to keep his mother away from yours?"

"No! Don't even mention my name to him. Or my mother's. Please, Jode. You promised. It's a complicated history and it's best not mentioned."

Jodi narrowed her eyes and squinted at me. I quaked under the gaze. I was so near telling her the truth. I had to bite my lips to make sure the words didn't come tumbling out. She gave my arm a pat.

"I'm here for you, Del, if you want to talk. Just like you are for me. Remember that."

Then she walked on, leaving me with the realisation that Jodi Wall knew I wasn't telling her the whole truth. I trailed after her and found her at the wall-covering section, her head buried in a pattern book.

"I've a few things to sort out first," I said. "Then we'll talk, Jodi. Okay?"

She shoved a pile of pattern books in my direction. "Wallpaper before everything else. We'll get The Cabin straightened out, the best party ever organised for Carla, and then, Del, you and I will talk."

I took her outstretched hand and squeezed it.

Then we turned our attention to the task of picking a paper for the pitted walls of Elliots' old shop.

Chapter 24

Aunt Lily would have been very pleased had she seen Ned Lehane next day. Sweat dripped from his forehead and he cursed quietly as he wielded a scythe through the overgrowth of The Cabin's back garden. The weeds and brambles were so tall I had barely been able to see the top of his flat cap as he walked through them earlier, his face getting paler with every stride he took. At least he had a colour by now, although the puce of his puffed-out cheeks clashed rather badly with his maroon work-shirt.

"Kettle on, Ned!" I called to him from the back door. "Tea up in a few minutes."

"You're slacking, Adele Burke," Jodi accused me when I went back inside.

She was perched on top of a stepladder, patting a newly hung sheet of paper with a cloth. Glamorous even in dungarees, she seemed quite perky and bossy this morning. One wall was almost finished now. The paper was wrinkled in places, bubbled in others but the overall effect was of smoothness and freshness. I felt a little thrill of excitement. The shop was beginning to take shape. Even the garden was unrecognisable from the jungle it had been earlier. No matter what Aunt Lily said, Ned Lehane was putting his back into this job.

"Get down off your high horse and go see the garden," I told Jodi. "You won't believe the difference."

She didn't need persuading. We were both exhausted from the bending and stretching involved in hanging wallpaper. I had managed to get tangled up in a sheet, pasted side in, and could now feel the paste drying into my hair. It had far better holding quality than Mom's hair lacquer. Even her industrial-strength firm hold. I should tell her. Maybe I should tell her everything. Mom, you must put wallpaper paste in your hair and by the way Irene Kirby is coming to Cairnsure and I . . .

"I thought you were making tea," came Jodi's voice. "No time for daydreaming, Adele!"

I turned around to see her and Ned Lehane staring at me. The kettle had gone off the boil. I flicked the switch down again. Ned drew out one of the little chairs and threw himself onto it. It groaned under his weight.

"By God, this is the maddest thing I ever heard of," he said, taking off his cap and scratching the top of his bald head.

"No. Carla Selby dying from cancer at thirty years of age is much madder than that," Jodi said, all her anger and resentment at the unfairness of Carla's death sentence resonating in her sharp tone.

"'Tis indeed. Is there no hope for her at all?"

"There's always hope," I snapped.

"I asked my sister's friend who's training to be a nurse," said Jodi. "She said the same as Harry. It's a matter of time for Carla. Probably a very short length since the cancer has spread to her liver."

I glared at her, not wanting to hear anything else she had been told second-hand by this trainee nurse. What could she know anyway?

"Better drink up our tea then and get back to work," Ned said, making me wonder why Aunt Lily had said he was lazy.

I smiled at him. "At least you have a break from Lily. Just listening to her is hard work in itself."

"She's all right, your aunt. Her bark's worse than her bite. She's had a tough old life. She's entitled to a moan every now and then."

"Every now and then would be acceptable. Every day is too much. And I don't think her life has been that tough, has it?"

Ned drained his cup and stood up, putting his cap back on. "Your aunt would be furious with me if she saw me sitting here drinking tea. I'd never hear the end of it."

He headed towards the back garden. I felt that he was annoyed with me for criticising Aunt Lily. Why? Didn't he know she spent a good portion of her life criticising him?

"Get a move on, Del. We're going to get another wall done today, come hell or high water. I must leave a bit early. Eoin wants me to do some work for him. His mother is arriving the day after tomorrow and he needs to have a business plan ready to show her. Apparently she's the major shareholder in their company. Have you told Sissy about the visit yet?"

I shook my head, remembering my failed attempts to bring up the subject last night. I never quite found the right moment.

"You must," Jodi insisted. "What if they meet by chance? Your mother could be very upset."

"I would have told her this morning except that she was rushing to go out. She and Tom were off to a garden centre in Cork to buy plants for the patio area here."

We had another sheet pasted by now and were negotiating the delicate process of lifting it off the counter and bringing it over to the wall. Jodi climbed the stepladder, holding the top end while I secured the bottom of the sheet down near the skirting board.

"Eoin seems to be very nervous about his mother's visit too," said Jodi. "I get the impression she's a tough lady."

"She's not a lady," I said before I had time to think.

Jodi stopped smoothing the paper and stood, cloth in hand, looking down at me.

"That sounds very bitter, Del. Not like you at all. What in the hell is going on?"

Hell! It was burning here, in my head. Suddenly, I could no longer contain my personal hell. The burning of it. The eternal punishment.

I told Jodi. Every shameful, grotty detail. I let it all pour out. Jodi came to stand beside me. She paled as I recounted my mother's story of Irene Kirby's revelation to her before she left for New Zealand. Her announcement that the child she was carrying might be Dad's. I was shaking by the time I got to the bit where Eoin Kirby spent the night on our couch and I had slept in his arms.

"Jesus, Del! If what Irene Kirby said is true then Eoin might be your brother. No, your half-brother. Fuck!"

"Exactly."

"Maybe it's not true."

"My father said it couldn't be. Eoin insists it's not true. But he does look a lot like Dad."

Jodi nodded. "Now that I come to think of it, he does. You can check it out. What about DNA testing?"

"How? My father and Michael Kirby are dead. What would be the point anyway?"

"The point would be peace of mind, of course. Maybe Eoin is not related to you at all. You could both be tested. Your DNA would indicate whether you are brother and sister or not. It's quite simple to get done. How about it, Del?"

I fiddled nervously with a loose thread on the old sweater I was wearing. I had thought of DNA testing. I had even looked it up on the internet and knew that I could get it done either here in Ireland or in England. I wouldn't even have to go anywhere. Just run the special sterile swab around the inside of my cheek and post off my sample in the supplied containers. But that would mean asking Eoin to do the same and that was a challenge too far.

"I can't, Jode. Eoin is furious at the suggestion that my dad might be his father. He wouldn't co-operate."

Jodi bowed her head and did some foot-staring. I knew she was biting her lip and I wondered if I should be biting my tongue. My situation seemed even worse now that I had shared the bald, shameful facts. Jodi raised her head and took my hand.

"Del, none of this is your fault. You must stop blaming yourself. Your mother should have told you. I'm so, so, sorry that it's worked out this way for you. Why don't you let me try to help? I could talk to Eoin, to his mother."

"No! You promised!"

"And what are you going to do? Spend the rest of your life feeling guilty because you fancied your brother when maybe that's not the fact at all?"

"I don't fancy him. I hate him!"

It was then we heard click of the back door. We both dashed in that direction in time to see Ned Lehane scurry out into the garden. How long had he been there? When I thought about it, I couldn't recall hearing the back door close when he had said he was returning to the garden. How much of my story had he overheard?

And me, I'd had enough of the whole agonising business. I put my head on Jodi's shoulder and cried until I could cry no more.

* * *

I threw myself into the task of wallpapering with total concentration. It did not really register with me that Jodi had left to meet Eoin Kirby or that Ned Lehane had sloped off home. Or maybe he had gone to the pub to spread the word about Adele Burke and her brother. The second wall was almost covered by the time my mother and Tom arrived in dragging a garden-centre full of plants and shrubs.

"Where's Jodi?" Mom asked. "Why has she left you all on your own?"

I climbed down from the stepladder and turned to face her. She rushed towards me in her busy, bustling way, a frown on her forehead.

"You were crying. What's wrong, Adele? Is it Carla?"

"No. I heard nothing about Carla today. I am upset though. I've got something to tell you."

Tom put down the potted palm he had been carrying and came to stand beside his bride-to-be. They both looked at me expectantly, Mom with her head tilted to the side. She seemed so vulnerable, so fragile, and yet I could now discern a calculating gleam in her eyes. I didn't know any more. The foundations on which my life had been based were sand beneath my feet. Dad had deceived Mom. Mom had deceived me. Irene Kirby had deceived us all.

"Irene Kirby is coming to Cairnsure," I stated baldly. There was no other way to put it.

Mom's eyes widened and her face paled. Tom reached for her arm and held it firmly.

"When?" he asked.

"In a few days' time. Soon. Very soon."

"The brazen hussy!" Mom said, a harshness in her tone I had never heard before. "Back to ruin more lives."

Tom let go her arm and brought over a chair to her. She flopped onto it, not even aware that the back was coated in paste. She was clasping her bag on her knee and I noticed her hands were shaking. Tom must have seen too. He placed his hands over hers.

"This could be the best thing that ever happened, Sissy," he said. "You can face Irene Kirby, tell her exactly what you think of her and then put the ghosts of the past to rest."

"They'll never be at rest. Not while my husband's child by another woman is walking around Cairnsure! Not while that trollop is here, invading my life again."

Her life! Always about her. I felt my temper flare and there was no stopping its meteoric rise.

"Will you stop thinking about yourself for one minute!" I shouted. "It's not just you. How do you think I feel? My life is turned upside down too. Jesus! You never even told me I might have a brother. How selfish is that?"

Mom's eyes widened at first and then narrowed as her whole face crumpled. She began to cry. I should have felt guilty but I had no more space for additional guilt.

"If you had been honest with me I would never have got myself into the mess I'm in. I'll have to live with the consequences for the rest of my life because of your pride and selfishness."

"What are you talking about? What do you mean?" she gasped between sobs.

"She means she and Eoin Kirby were romantically involved for a little while," Tom said. "She didn't know he might be related to her because you didn't tell her. How could she know? Neither you nor your husband ever told her the truth. You should have protected your daughter by telling her the facts."

Mom and I both stared at Tom in shock. I was angry

enough to want to hurt her with the shameful truth but it should have been my choice to tell her. Not Tom Reagan's. The words seemed to hang in the air, echoing around the half-papered walls of The Cabin. Mom was completely still, her face a ghastly colour. Tom turned towards me.

"I'm sorry if you think I'm interfering, Adele, but there has been too much deception and too much running away from the truth."

I nodded, seeing the common sense in what he said. "Ned Lehane knows anyway. He'll have the parish told by now. Your secret isn't a secret any more, Mom. Neither is mine."

Her face suddenly came to life, lit by an anger to match my own. "I kept my secret to protect you and your father's memory. I never believed for a minute, Adele Burke, that you would think so little of yourself. How could you have relations with a man you barely knew? A man you promised me you wouldn't have anything to do with?"

"Why did you not tell me that man was most likely my brother? Another week and I might have had sex with him. It's bad enough as it is. Don't you see, Mom? You've ruined my life."

"You've done that yourself. You're your father's daughter all right. His bad blood is in your veins."

She stood up then, settled her handbag on her arm, raised her head in the air and walked out of The Cabin. Tom stood uncertainly for a moment, looking from me to the door.

"At least everything is out in the open now," he said. "She'll calm down. Don't worry about her."

"I'm sure she will," I said with a bitterness Aunt Lily would have been proud of. "She'll pray, do a novena, bake some cakes and then pretend none of this happened. Sissy will continue on with her comfortable little life and leave the rest of us to bear the consequences."

"That's harsh, Adele."

"And her gibe about my father wasn't? She must have made every day of that man's life hell. A perpetual atonement for his affair with Irene Kirby. I'm sure he paid a high price for his falling from grace. Just as I know I will too."

"He cheated on your mother. There's a price to pay for that."

"He paid it. No wonder his heart gave out. It must have been broken."

"For heaven's sake, Adele! He had clogged arteries. Maybe some of that had to do with your mother's rich cooking but you can't accuse her of causing his death. You know she's one of the kindest people you could ever meet."

"I'm beginning to think I don't know her at all. Do you?"

Tom didn't answer. Instead he turned and walked after my mother. But not before I had seen a sudden shock pass over his face. I knew then that Tom Reagan would spend a restless night tossing and turning and wondering just who the real Sissy Burke was. I felt a base satisfaction as I returned with a vengeance to my wallpapering.

* * *

Measure, cut, paste, hang. Measure, cut, paste, hang. I kept up the relentless pace while the sun set. The prom became deserted and the sea shimmered with the reflected full moon. I imagined people in pubs all over Cairnsure talking about me. The teacher who was involved with a man who turned out to be her brother. I could see Ned Lehane, his cap on the bar counter, a pint of beer in his hand, whispering my story into the ears of anyone who would listen, the expression on their faces changing from shock to disgust to amusement. A joke. That's what I was now. I wondered if they were laughing at Eoin Kirby too or if his obvious wealth protected him from becoming a laughing stock.

I didn't turn around from my work when the door opened. I couldn't face anyone. I heard someone walk over to the storeroom where the paper was stacked and begin to open a new roll. The footsteps were heavy. A man's steps. Kieran Mahon opened up the roll and began to measure a length against the wall. I glanced at him and continued on with my work. Silently, side by side, we hung paper for another thirty minutes. Eventually my arms would not move another inch. Exhausted, I threw myself on the rickety, pasty chair abandoned by my mother.

"Are you all right, Adele?"

I thought I had no more tears left. I was wrong. They streamed down my face as I sat on the rickety chair, a broken woman surrounded by the remnants of a ruined life. I wondered if I was dying because images of my past kept flashing before my eyes. The day I graduated from training college and that red trouser suit I wore; the time

I found a wild bee-orchid growing in Lily's meadow field, its exquisite beauty isolated in the lesser glories of buttercups and daisies; my first pair of ear studs and the pain of my newly pierced ears; holding my father's hand, skipping along beside him, playing that game where he must take only one step to my three.

"Jodi told me about you and Eoin Kirby."

Kieran's voice seemed to come to me from a long way off. He was kneeling down beside me, the clear green eyes I had once dreamed about staring at me.

"Did you have a good laugh?"

"Don't be ridiculous, Adele! Of course I didn't laugh. It's an awful thing for you. I hope you don't mind Jodi telling me. She was upset about it and needed to talk."

"Everybody knows by now anyway. Ned Lehane will make sure of that. He heard me telling her – did she tell you that?"

He nodded.

Eyes clear of tears, I surveyed the mess around me. The floor was littered with sticky off-cuts of wallpaper. I got up with as much dignity as possible and went to get the sweeping brush.

"I'll do that," Kieran said. "You sit down and talk to me."

"About what? Do you want details? How much do you want to embarrass me?"

Kieran came to stand in front of me and there was sympathy, or perhaps pity, in his eyes. He caught my hand.

"Come on. We're going for a walk on the strand. You've been in here too long today."

I cleaned a small space on the white-smeared window and looked out. Everything was bathed in the silver light of the full moon. I would be seen, recognised. I craned my neck to see the strand. It appeared to be deserted. The thought of cool air and the soothing sound of the ocean tempted me. Unless I was going to live in The Cabin for the rest of my life I would have to leave it at some stage. Now, with Kieran for moral support, seemed like a good time.

"Right. A walk it is. I'm not sure about the talk though. I don't know what to say."

"You don't have to say anything. Just don't make me do any more wallpapering. I hate it."

He smiled at me then. His lop-sided grin. I smiled back and headed for the door.

We walked in silence along the prom. Several people passed by but none seemed to take much notice of me. Maybe they hadn't heard yet. I began to relax as we reached the strand. I felt protected by the sea and its comforting whisper as it lapped the shore.

"I had a terrible row with my mother this evening."

"I'm not surprised," Kieran answered. "She should have told you."

"I said awful things to her. She was very upset. I don't know whether I can go home now or not."

He stopped walking and peered into my face. "Why should you not go home? You've nothing to apologise for, Adele. You just got caught up in a set of circumstances that were of other people's making."

"True. I assume Jodi told you the full story."

"Yes, she did. But let me tell you, as a journalist, that it's a very patchy story. No evidence. All you have to go on is hearsay. I'd be sued if I printed it."

I looked at him in horror. "You wouldn't, would you? You couldn't do that to me!"

He began to walk ahead and I could see that he was angry. I caught up with him and apologised. "I shouldn't have asked that question. Of course you wouldn't."

"Glad you realise that. But I do think you should investigate further. I know Jodi suggested DNA testing. It's a good idea."

"I explained to her why I can't. That would mean asking Eoin Kirby and I don't want to do that."

"I could ask. I could talk to his mother too when she arrives. I know how to get information without arousing suspicion."

"I understand. For instance, you could ask Irene Kirby if her eldest son takes after her lover or her husband? She'd never guess."

Kieran kicked a stone ahead of him. It skittered into the darkness. "All right," he admitted. "Maybe that's not such a good idea. But you need to know the truth. You can't move on from this until you do. Even if that means finding out things about your father that disappoint you."

My father. The man who had an affair and borrowed money from the husband of the woman with whom he had the affair. That father was a stranger to me.

"I didn't know him at all, did I?"

"Do we ever really know anyone else?" he asked and I knew instinctively he was talking about Jodi.

The moon slid behind clouds. Our signal to turn back. The light breeze was in our faces as we headed for the prom. It teased my pasted hair into spikes. I didn't care. How I looked wasn't a priority any more. By the time we reached The Cabin again, some of the calm of the sea had seeped into my troubled mind.

"There's a couch in my apartment," Kieran offered. "You're welcome to sleep on it if you'd prefer not go home tonight."

I smiled at him and felt truly grateful for his kindness. I knew he was doing this mainly for Jodi but there was genuine concern for me too.

"No. I'll have to face my mother sooner or later. And, to be honest, I don't regret anything I said to her. Just the way I said it. Besides, I'm pretty sure she has run off to Tom Reagan's house again. Either that or she has blanked the whole incident from her mind. Pity I didn't inherit that trait."

"The offer stands anyway if you need it. And don't worry, there's a lock on the lounge door in case you're worried about me sleepwalking in your direction. Besides, Jodi keeps me in chains after midnight."

I heard myself laugh. The sound amazed me. Just an hour ago I had believed I would never laugh again. Kieran was laughing too and I heard the same hollow ring in his laughter. Jodi.

"She needs time," I said. "Jodi has a lot to deal with now."

Kieran's smile faded and he nodded his head. "I know that. Carla's illness is hitting her hard. And your problem

353

too. All that on top of her own struggle. It's just that I've waited so long. And now . . . well, now I wonder."

"She's lucky to have you, Kieran. She'll realise that as soon as she gets her life back on track. Her new job will make a difference. Even though Eoin Kirby is her employer."

"Kirbys seem to be centre stage in everyone's life at the moment, don't they? I know a few old-timers who would remember Michael Kirby. Would you trust me to chat to them? Very tactfully. See if we can at least fill in the background to this – this . . ."

"Fuck-up."

"Exactly! Well?"

I didn't hesitate for long. Everybody would be talking about it anyway but I didn't want Kieran stirring up even more interest.

"No, Kieran. Don't please. But thank you for the support."

He stooped, kissed me on the cheek and then waved me off as I headed home to the cottage and maybe, just maybe, another row with my mother.

Chapter 25

Mom had taken to her bed. She had been asleep when I arrived home late and she was still asleep as I left the following morning. I guessed that Tom had refused to let her run away again. Closed his door to her. Maybe she wasn't asleep at all. Just lying there, listening to me showering, pottering around the kitchen, rooting for a scarf so that I wouldn't have the job of de-pasting my hair again. I found a woolly hat, one I had bought for my ski trip to Salzburg a long time ago. It was red with earflaps and woollen plaits. I had thought it cute at the time. It suited my purpose now.

Ned Lehane was outside The Cabin when I drove up. He was sitting on the sill, squinting at the sea and pretending that he wasn't taking note of everything. I hadn't thought about how I should approach him. Should I face him head-on, accuse him of eavesdropping or should I just ignore him, not give him the satisfaction of seeing my upset? I still hadn't made a decision by the time I reached the door and put the key in the lock.

"Morning, Adele. Nice day."

"Morning, Ned. Yes, it's going to be a hot one."

Decision made. Just go on as if nothing had happened. I was more like Sissy than I wanted to admit.

"Before I forget, Adele, your aunt wants you to call to see her at dinnertime today. She says it's urgent."

A royal command from Lily. I knew she always had her dinner midday so that's when she wanted me to call. Had Ned repeated to her what he had overheard? He must have. Why else would she want to see me? She must be furious with me for shaming the family name. To hell with her. I was only sloshing through the mucky history my father and Irene Kirby had created.

"Right, Ned, thanks. I'll call to see her. What will you be doing in the back garden today?"

"I'll have to finish off the clearing and then I need to know about paving. Where do you want the slabs?"

"We'll wait until Jodi comes in to decide. You can just keep cutting the weeds and bushes."

Credit to Ned Lehane, he knew when he had been dismissed. He went out into the back garden. This time I checked the door after him to make sure it was closed. I had already started papering the third wall by the time Jodi arrived in. Breathless.

"Sorry, Del. Eoin was under pressure this morning. We had to finish the business plan because his mother has already arrived."

I let my paste brush fall to the ground. "Jesus! She's here!"

"Not here. Not in Cairnsure. Not yet. She landed in Dublin this morning. She's staying there overnight and flying to Cork tomorrow."

"How do you mean he was under pressure? Is he afraid of her?"

Jodi thought for a moment before answering. "Not afraid. More in awe of her, I'd say. He told me his father was a gifted craftsman, a master builder, but not a businessman. He was a soft touch and would have given away everything he earned had it not been for his mother's business acumen. She built the company to what it is today."

"And what's that?"

"Hasn't he already told you? The biggest property developer in New Zealand. They have overseas projects too in Nigeria, China, Australia, even Iraq."

"Don't forget Cairnsure. They must own half this little outpost by now."

"If they go ahead with the development, Del, it will be good for Cairnsure. It'll bring jobs and people here. Eoin sees it as a sort of monument to his father."

"Which father?"

"He's definite that Michael Kirby is his father."

"You asked him! For heaven's sake, Jode! Why did you do that? He'll know I was talking to you about it."

"No, of course I didn't. I just listened to what he was saying. And whatever the truth of the matter, Michael Kirby is the only father Eoin has known and they obviously had great respect and love for each other."

I stooped down to pick up my fallen paste brush. "I suppose we need a coffee," I suggested.

"Yes, put on the kettle and we'll ring Selbys' while it's boiling. See how Carla is."

I filled the kettle while Jodi rang. She spoke to Vera and from the one-sided conversation I overheard I gathered that Carla was in good form.

"One sec. I'll check with Adele," Jodi said.

She put her hand over the phone and asked me if I would go to Selbys' later in the afternoon. Carla would be up by then. I agreed, glad that Carla felt well enough to see us.

When she finished the call, Jodi had a huge smile on her face. "Vera says there's an improvement. Carla's eating again and has a bit more energy. As I told Harry, doctors don't know everything."

"Neither do you or your trainee-nurse friend. You were the one who was talking doomsday scenarios about the cancer having spread to her liver."

"Well, opinions don't matter, do they? It's in the hands of fate."

I said nothing. I had given up second-guessing fate. Elated now, showing no signs of yesterday's depression, Jodi grabbed my ski hat and plonked it onto her shiny hair. It looked fabulous on her.

"Keep it," I muttered. "Wear it with my blue sundress."

"Oops! I'm sorry, Del. I put your dress in a charity bag. You did say you don't want it any more."

I shrugged. I didn't want my sundress. I didn't want anything that reminded me of the time I had spent with

Eoin Kirby. I would probably never wear my burgundy dress again either.

Jodi picked up a roll of paper. "Come on. We'd better get going. We must finish this papering and get cleaned up before we go to see Carla. We don't want her to see us all covered in paste and bits of paper. No time for drinking coffee."

We chatted as we worked. About my argument with Sissy, about Eoin and Irene Kirby, about Carla and Harry and the children, about our plans for the café. About everything except Kieran Mahon and his visit to me last night. I began to wonder if Jodi knew about it at all. I could have asked. Some instinct told me not to. So we chatted and I wondered until it was time for me to go visit Aunt Lily. As ordered.

* * *

Lily was waiting for me. Keeping watch. A bad sign. Worse still, she opened the door before I had time to knock or to think about how I was going to defend myself against her onslaught. Believing attack is the best form of defence, I introduced the topic of Ned Lehane right there on the doorstep.

"I know Ned Lehane eavesdropped on a private conversation but . . ."

"I don't entertain people on the doorstep. Come in."

I followed her. Whatever else Aunt Lily did, on the doorstep or elsewhere, it wasn't entertaining people. Scaring them maybe.

"Sit."

I sat at the table as she had ordered. In front of me was a plate of corned beef, potatoes and cabbage. She pointed at it.

"Eat that. It's better for you than all the foreign foods ye eat now. They're not good for you."

I thought about the salt content of the corned beef but kept the thought to myself. Across from me, she had set a place for herself. She eased herself onto the chair and began to eat. Taking her cue, I followed suit and we ate our dinner in silence. I hadn't really thought about eating since yesterday and was hungry now.

"That was lovely, thank you," I said as I put my knife and fork together on my empty plate. "Will I make tea?"

"You can't. I'll make it properly when I'm ready."

I sat back and looked around the old kitchen. It was dull and dreary, even on this sunny day. But it was peaceful too. Solid and enduring, constancy in the ticking of the grandfather clock and the gleam of the willow-patterned ware.

Lily finished her dinner and swept both plates off the table. I knew I would have to wait now for the tea-making ceremony to be over before we could talk. I didn't mind. I was enjoying the soothing quiet. Eventually she put a cup and saucer in front of me.

"Drink that up. There's no cake today."

"Tea's fine. I'm full, thank you. Aunt Lily, about Ned Lehane . . ."

"That's why I called you here. We must talk about him."

"I know enough. He eavesdrops on other people's

conversations. He told you the full account of my conversation with Jodi yesterday. My confession. Am I right, Lily?"

When Lily reached across the table and caught my hand, I almost gasped. She had never voluntarily touched me before. Her skin felt dry and warm. Just like everyone else now, my aunt knew the depth of my shame. I bowed my head.

"I know you're worried that Ned will blab to the parish. That's why I wanted to talk to you. To put your mind at rest."

I raised my head and looked at Aunt Lily. I saw an old woman, wrinkled, withered but with a kind light in her eyes.

"Ned won't breathe a word of it to anyone else. Not after the talking-to I gave him. He lives in my cottage down by the copse. You know that, don't you?"

"Yes. He's lived there as long as I can remember."

"So, I put a roof over his head and I pay his wages too. He depends on me, you see. He doesn't have anyone else and God knows he can't rely on himself."

I could see where this was leading. Aunt Lily was threatening Ned. Keep your mouth shut or else . . .

"You're blackmailing him into silence," I said.

"What would you prefer? That I'd say nothing and let him blacken your name all over the town?"

She had a point.

"Besides, he's afraid of me. He knows I'd twist his scrawny little neck if he said anything."

That, coming from Aunt Lily, was not an idle threat.

Relief filtered through me. I had one problem less. Cairnsure wasn't rife with rumours about me and Eoin Kirby. The pubs weren't buzzing with the gossip, I wasn't the laughing-stock of the parish. Eoin and I still had our dirty little secret. Jodi and Kieran knew it too but they wouldn't talk. I squeezed Lily's hand and smiled at her.

"Thank you. I'm grateful, Aunt Lily."

She shrugged off my gratitude as if it felt like an uncomfortable weight on her shoulders. "Now what are you going to do about your situation?"

"I don't know. Somehow, I must find out whether Dad was Eoin's father. Mom says he was."

"Don't talk to me about Sissy Burke. She's no help to you. Ned says Irene Kirby is coming to Cairnsure. Why don't you ask her?"

"Maybe I should just let it go. I'll never be seeing Eoin Kirby again. I'll go back to Dublin and just try to get on with my life."

"And end up like me? Don't be daft. You'll never rest easy unless you find out."

The grandfather clock struck one. Lunchtime was over. I stood up.

"I must go, Lily. Jodi Wall and I are going to visit Carla Selby this afternoon."

"How is the poor girl?"

"Improved a bit. For now anyway."

Lily hauled herself up and shuffled around the table to stand in front of me.

"You know I have a low opinion of men. All of them. But I'm very sure of one thing. Your father was a gentleman. Irene Kirby turned his head. The same as she did with all the others, but I don't ever believe he would have been unfaithful to his marriage vows. I would have warned you off Eoin Kirby if I had that suspicion. I can't prove it though. You'll have to do that yourself. For your own peace of mind and for your father's honour."

I looked at the old lady, the aunt I had neglected and avoided for most of my life and I felt regret for never having taken the trouble to know this stubborn but kind woman. On impulse I hugged her. She smelt of lavender and old age.

"Go on with you now," she said gruffly. "Don't keep that sick girl waiting. And for God's sake get a trousers that fits you. That one is dragged across your backside."

I laughed as she glared at my jeans. She was right. They were tight. They were meant to be.

"I'll let you know if I find out anything," I said. "And thank you. For everything."

She turned her back to me and began clearing the table. I was obviously meant to let myself out. I drove back to The Cabin in a far more positive frame of mind than when I had left it.

* * *

Sissy was at The Cabin. I saw her car as I pulled in. Tom Reagan's car was parked beside hers. When I got inside the shop was empty. I heard voices coming from the garden. I opened the back door and it seemed the party had already started. Sissy, Tom, Jodi, Ned and Harry Selby were all talking together and waving their hands around.

"Del, the barbeque, where do we want to put it?" Jodi asked.

I looked around me in surprise. The back garden was unrecognisable. Dross removed, hedges cut back, clippings neatly bagged in refusacs. Ned Lehane had done a great job.

"We must buy the flagstones and sand before the builders' supplier closes for the weekend," Ned explained, "so we need to know now which area to cover."

I remembered the day Carla had been here with Jodi and me and the pompous auctioneer.

"Here," I pointed. "That's where she wants the barbeque. And over there she wants wrought-iron tables and parasols."

"You haven't gone and told her, Adele! It was supposed to be a surprise," my mother said in her what-have you-done-now voice.

So, she was speaking to me. I wasn't sure that I wanted to speak to her just now so I silently shook my head.

"We'll measure up so, Ned," Tom said and they began pegging out the area and making a big show of running the metre tape around it.

Jodi tugged impatiently on my arm. "We'd better go, Del. Carla will be waiting. We can't stay too long. She's still very tired."

"But she's improved, isn't she?" I asked Harry and noticed that he seemed to have aged in the last few days. Of course he was older than us. He was forty. Today he looked like a man who had lived through sixty rough years.

"She's more comfortable," he answered. "Could I have a private word with you, Adele, please?"

I led the way into the empty, almost-papered shop.

"I like the job you're doing on the walls," he said. "The place seems cleaner and brighter already."

He hadn't brought me in here to talk décor. He seemed to have lost track of his thoughts. He was standing at the window, gazing out to sea through the little porthole clearing I had made in the whitening.

"You wanted to have a word," I reminded him.

He turned around to face me and he was as pale as the wallpaper.

"I just want you to know that I explained the real situation to Finn. I don't know whether I did the right thing or not, Adele."

"How do mean 'the real situation'?"

"I mean that he can never expect his mother to get better. He kept asking. I couldn't continue lying to him. Giving him false hope. Or could I? Should I have? Bloody hell! Adele, I just don't know what's the right thing to do."

"What about the other children? How's Liam?"

"Settling very well with Vera. And of course Brigitte too. The twins and Liam are happy once they're fed and entertained. Finn's the problem. I just wish he was younger or less perceptive."

I walked over to the window to join Harry. Standing beside him, his upset was almost tangible. Or maybe it was my own heartbreak I was feeling. Harry's words were echoing in my head. "He can never expect his mother to get better." That was Carla he was talking about. My Carla. My friend. The girl I had grown up with and laughed and cried with. His wife. The mother of his children. I felt shame at my selfishness.

"How did Finn react when you told him?"

"Quietly. No tantrums. No boldness. He's withdrawn. He's a clever child but a child nonetheless. I should have protected him."

"That's what you're doing by being honest with him. You've given him a gift. Trust."

"But I can't give him back his mother, can I?"

There was no need to answer that question. We stood side by side, Carla's husband and her friend, both silently cursing the cancer which was stealing her away from us. How much worse must it be for the little boy who was blessed, or maybe in this case cursed, with an enquiring mind? He needed a distraction.

"How would you feel about Finn being involved in getting this place ready for Carla's party? Just a few hours here and there. It would make him feel he was doing something positive for his mother. Keep him from brooding too much."

Harry nodded. "That might be just the thing for him. He'd like keeping the secret too. Having one over on the others. Yes, if you're sure, Adele. You're doing so much here, wouldn't having a child tagging along be difficult?"

"One child! You're looking at someone who takes thirty in her stride."

366

Harry took my hand in his and stooped to kiss me on the cheek. "You're a good friend, Adele. Now I know why Carla has so much regard for you."

I couldn't answer him. Emotion choked the words.

"Must go. I have patients waiting."

Then head bowed, shoulders stooped, he walked out the door leaving me staring after him. Like Finn, I had nothing to say.

Chapter 26

The children were playing in Selbys' back garden. I could hear them squeal and laugh.

"They're out on their swings," I said to Jodi. "Let's say hello to them first."

Jodi grumbled as we walked around the side of the house. Something about having come to see Carla, not her brood. I ignored her. As soon as we rounded the corner, Liam saw us and leapt off his swing to run towards us. The twins, clambering all over their climbing frame, spotted us too and toddled over to meet us, Vera keeping a careful eye on them. I looked around for Finn. He was sitting alone at the garden table, dwarfed by the size of the huge timber seats. I left Jodi and Vera to chat and went over to Finn.

He didn't look up as I approached. I sat beside him and waited. He was fiddling with a piece of paper, twisting it into a tiny ball. When it was as small and hard as he could make it, he lifted his arm back and threw the paper with all the strength of his anger and frustration. It bounced harmlessly on the ground only feet away. Tears welled in his eyes. I longed to put my arms around him but knew he had created a defensive wall around himself which only he could scale.

Liam gave a particularly loud laugh as Jodi pushed him high on the swing.

"He doesn't know about Mum," said Finn.

I was relieved. At least he was talking.

"He's very young, Finn. Some things are hard to understand, even for grown-ups."

"Dad can't cure her."

There was a weariness in his voice, a sadness too profound for a little boy. I felt an inexplicable flash of rage against Sissy's God. Or maybe it was against Sissy. I buried it, somewhere deep inside with all my other resentments. I lowered my head and looked around, scanning the garden in an exaggerated way. Like the Mata Hari of Cairnsure.

"Why are you acting funny like that?"

"Because," I whispered to Finn, "I want to tell you a secret. A big surprise for your mum. I need help with it. Do you think you could manage not to tell the others?"

"Secrets are bad."

"Not surprise secrets. I'll tell you about it."

A glimmer of interest shone in his eyes. He leaned towards me. "Okay. Tell me."

I told him about the café. About how we had thought of working together, Carla and Jodi and I, how Carla couldn't do it because she got sick. When he heard what we were trying to do now, he laughed.

"Cool! Mum would love that."

"I know she would, Finn, but we'll have to work very hard to get it done. Will you help?"

"How?"

"Come to The Cabin with me. You can tell us how Carla would like it and there'll be plenty of jobs for you to do. I've got permission from your father so it's up to you to decide now."

Carla came out through the patio door. She was wearing one of the floaty, colourful dresses which were her hallmark. She looked very beautiful and, I thought, less jaundiced and healthier than she had been. I couldn't help the denial of facts and the hope which lifted my heart.

Finn smiled at me. "Okay. I'll help. Will you bring me there or Dad?"

"We can arrange that," I whispered as Carla walked towards us. I stood and hugged her.

"You look great, Carla. How are you feeling?"

"Much better than I was, Del, thanks. I don't believe what I'm seeing over there. Jodi Wall playing with the children. She's not sick too, is she?"

We both laughed as we watched a bored Jodi push the swing while Liam yelled "Higher! Higher!"

Brigitte arrived carrying a tray with iced tea and three bowls of fruit salad, a little container of Carla's pills beside the bowls. She clapped her hands and called out to the children.

"Who comes to the beach?"

In an instant the children, Vera and Brigitte were

370

gone. A noisy, excited gang on their way to the seaside. Even Finn had joined in the exodus.

We had our drinks and fruit salad sitting around the table. A picture-perfect setting. Large, well-kept garden, timber table, parasol, sun and three smiling women. Not a cloud in sight. No hint of ill-health, addiction or cursed bad luck. For a short sun-drenched spell, we were content.

Carla finished her fruit and pushed the bowl away from her.

"I want to tell you both something. Harry and I have agreed that when the time comes, I'll go to the hospice. It would be better for the children. And for me too. Hopefully that's a long way off."

There must have been some appropriate things to say. Denials, words of support or encouragement. Neither Jodi nor I could think of them. We just sat there in the sun, staring at our friend, our Carla, casually speaking the unspeakable. We were struck dumb.

"And that's all the talk of sickness I'm allowing," Carla said. "Tell me your news. I want scandal. Juicy gossip. How about you and Kieran, Jodi? How are things in your love-nest?"

"Just as well you mentioned that. I almost forgot. Adele, would you mind if I stayed at your house for tonight and tomorrow night?"

"Of course not, but why? Have you had a row with Kieran?"

"Not a row. Not really."

"But you're moving out because of a 'not really' row. Just as well you didn't have a 'really' one."

Jodi dropped her head. As I watched the sunlight play on her hair, I remembered her talking about Kieran's daughter

"Amy?" I asked and then began to explain to Carla that Amy was Kieran's daughter.

"I know her," Carla said. "Norma Higgins' daughter. Are you intimidated by a four-year-old? Surely not, Jodi?"

Jodi slowly lifted her head and, milking all the drama from the situation, kept us waiting for her answer.

"I tried to explain to you, Del. Kieran is moving too fast. Norma Higgins is going away for the weekend. Some hoity-toity legal conference in Killarney. Kieran has to look after his daughter. I don't want to play happy families. That's all."

"How does Kieran feel about that?"

"Not very pleased. He thinks he's the reason I'm staying off drugs but he's not. I'm the only one who can decide that. I won't fall asunder because he lets me out of his sight for two nights."

I felt annoyed by Jodi's casual dismissal of all the support Kieran had given her. She knew better than I that a few days, or even a few months, without drugs didn't make her a recovered addict.

"We all need support, Jodi. You're lucky to have Kieran."

"Yes, yes. I'll move back in on Sunday night when Amy has been reclaimed by Supermum."

"You are jealous of Norma Higgins! I knew it."

Jodi laughed in such a derogatory way that there was

no doubt about how low an opinion she had of Norma Higgins.

"Commitment phobia," said Carla. "That's your problem, Jodi. Looking after a child together, even for a weekend is too much like making a commitment."

"I'm trying to get used to living with someone else. Having to share a bathroom, a bed, a kitchen. I can't cope with a child as well. I like my own space. I hate having to ask before I change TV channels or feel obliged to tell someone else when I'm going out or where I'm going. And I detest the smell of cheese and onion crisps. Kieran eats them all the time."

"You went there of your own free will," I pointed out. "It seemed to me that you were glad to move in with him when you did."

"I was. And I'll be just as happy to go back. But no daughter. Anyway, it wouldn't be fair on the child. Things may not work out between Kieran and me. I don't want to confuse Amy by being there one minute and gone the next. That type of insecurity is bad for any child."

Carla sat back as suddenly as if she had been hit. She paled. So did Jodi who immediately realised how cruel and insensitive her remarks must seem. She began to stutter an explanation and apology. "I'm . . . I'm sorry, Carla. I didn't mean . . . I didn't think . . ."

I felt as guilty in the tense silence as if I had been the one to hurt Carla. I blushed – a rush of blood to my brain which resulted in a stream of foolish talk from my mouth. I was just a spectator as my words tumbled out, unfettered by any thought of consequence.

"Eoin Kirby, the man who is Jodi's new boss – remember, Carla – you saw him at Elliot's – he's going to build an apartment block and golf course down near the prom. He's from New Zealand but his family is originally from Cairnsure and his mother had an affair with my father. There's a possibility he may be my half-brother. I went out with him a few times before I knew."

My brainstorm over, I sat there, splotchy red and so ashamed that I felt smaller than Jodi and sicker than Carla.

"What in the fuck are you talking about, Adele?" Carla asked in a very small voice.

I knew now why I had my momentary madness. I had intended distracting Carla from Jodi's unfortunate remarks. I had succeeded. Carla was enthralled. More so by the time Jodi and I had explained the full story to her.

"Holy shit! How awful for you, Del. Why didn't your mother tell you? She could have saved you all this torment."

"She was trying to protect me. She knew how much I idolised my father. She didn't want me to think less of him. And it must be humiliating for her too. Did you know about Dad and Irene Kirby, Carla? Did you ever hear any rumours?"

"No, not that I can remember anyway. I never heard anything but good about your father."

Carla sat back and closed her eyes. Jodi and I looked at each other, worried that we had tired her out with the dramas of our mixed-up lives. She opened her eyes suddenly and looked at me.

"Sort it, Del. Do whatever it takes to find out the truth. Life's too short to spend it worrying about what may or may not be. Jodi's right. Get DNA testing. If Eoin is so certain that Michael Kirby is his father, he won't mind co-operating."

"It must be a shock for him too," Jodi said defensively and I wondered again if she had discussed it with him.

Carla stood up and leaned her hands on the table. "It was great seeing you both, girls. Sorry, I'm tired now. I think I'll go for a rest before the children get back." She turned towards me and I saw the sympathy in her eyes. "None of this mess is of your making," she said softly.

She took my arm then and I led her to a couch in her magnificent lounge. Her eyes closed the instant she lay down. For now, at least, Carla Selby was at peace.

* * *

Jodi made several excuses. She had to pack clothes for her weekend stay with me, she must meet Eoin Kirby to go over some figures, she must get her hair trimmed. She had millions of things to do but none of them involved coming back to The Cabin with me. I dropped her off in town and was secretly glad. And happier still when I arrived at The Cabin and saw that Mom's car wasn't there either. She, without a doubt, was gone to get her hair galvanised or whatever it was the hairdresser did to achieve the amazing steely effect that was my mother's hair-do.

I needed peace and quiet to think over what Carla had said, the comfort of the repetitive job of wallpapering to free my mind. I must, I would, sort this Eoin Kirby situation. I felt a mellowing towards Mom after the conversation with Carla, glad that I had instinctively wanted to defend my mother. It was the confirmation I needed that I truly believed she had not meant to deceive me. I felt more positive than I had in days. Until I opened the door to The Cabin.

Eoin Kirby was leaning against the counter, his arms folded across his chest, his huge feet firmly planted. My first thought was flight and my second that the seat of his pants would be covered in paste.

"What are you doing here?"

"I own the place, or have you forgotten?"

"How could I forget? You must own most of Cairnsure by now."

"Look, Adele, I appreciate that this is a very awkward situation for both of us. And yes, I do intend spending a lot of time and money here. We can't let this situation between us . . ."

I raced towards the back door and pulled it open. The back garden was empty.

"We're alone," Eoin said.

I shivered. Suddenly The Cabin seemed very big and very isolated from the world outside.

I went and stood near the window. Dust swirled in the narrow beam of sunlight which shone through the cleared circle on the glass. The dust-dance hypnotised me. I tried to focus on one particle and follow its graceful path.

"No point in pretending this didn't happen, Adele. We must face it."

I dragged my eyes away from the ugly dust made beautiful by a ray of light. Eoin had dark circles underneath his eyes. So he too had lain awake and cursed the fate which had led us to this situation.

"You've changed your tune," I said. "I thought you never wanted to lay eyes on me again."

"I didn't. Tantrum over. It's grown-up time, Adele. What do you want to do?"

"I want DNA testing," I said. "It's the only way we'll know. There's a sibling test. It will tell us with reasonable certainty whether we're related or not. At least we'll know."

Eoin reached behind him and picked up a package from the counter. He opened it and removed a leaflet.

"Here. Read this. The company is in Dublin. We can have our results back in under two weeks. They're very reputable. And the service is confidential."

I glanced through the document. I had seen this company's web page. I knew about the swab from the inside of my cheek, about the probabilities and possibilities.

"I've researched it. And it's what I want to do. I don't want to believe my father was unfaithful to Mom but if he was I'll just have to deal with it."

He picked up the package again and handed me a sealed box. "I've already ordered a test. Your swab and sterile container, Adele."

"Without asking me! You arrogant sod!"

"And you are a self-centred little madam, thinking you're the only one upset by this – this, disaster! I intended getting my own DNA profiled to compare to a tissue sample of my father's. Of Michael Kirby, that is. The hospital he attended before he died has agreed to release his biopsy sample from storage. I only offered this to you for your peace of mind. I'm sorry I bothered now."

"So, you have doubts too. Have you asked your mother? She's the one who claimed John Burke could be your father."

"Leave my mother out of this. Don't you dare mention a word of Sissy Burke's venomous backbiting to her. If you meet her, that is. I'll be doing my best to ensure that doesn't happen."

I frowned. I'd had an idea that the situation between Eoin and me was the reason for Irene's visit. It seemed I was wrong.

"Why is she coming here?"

"Business. Ours, not yours."

"So, she still holds the purse strings."

His eyes narrowed. I had hit a sore point. Good!

"Do you want to do this test or not?"

I nodded. I did. I must.

"I suggest we do it together here, witness the containers being opened and closed, witness the sampling. Then there can be no questions asked afterwards. Agreed?"

I agreed. He took his sample first, scraping the swab along the inside of his mouth in order to collect cells. I watched him seal his swab in the sterile container and then I repeated the process. I felt like laughing. What would Ned Lehane have made of it had he seen us waggling big cotton buds around our mouths? Some story he would have had for Aunt Lily. I knew the bubbling laughter was just a reaction. An antidote to the bitter knowledge that my fate now rested on the tip of a saliva-drenched swab.

"I've arranged for a courier. This will be fast-tracked to the company. I'll seal it all as soon as you sign the documents."

I scanned the pages. They were mainly about indemnifying the company and paying for expert opinion in the event of a court case. I scrawled my signature and handed the papers back to Eoin.

"I can arrange for a duplicate of the results to be sent to you. Do you want that or would you prefer I tell you?"

"I want my own copy, please."

"Certainly. And thank you for co-operating."

I wasn't sure what the etiquette for sharing a DNA test was, but I knew instinctively that the sharing was far too intimate for the cold, polite language we were now using. Yet how else could it be? I blamed his mother for leading my father on, he blamed my mother for not telling us. The only other alternatives were to blame my father, which I would not do, or blame ourselves, which was pointless. Eoin must have been thinking much the same thoughts.

"This is such a shame, isn't it? Things could have been... well, different to what they are now."

I didn't answer him. I was too full of regret, remembering our swim in the rain, our picnic in the clouds, the touch of his lips on mine, waking up on the couch and seeing his sleepy head beside mine. Then I was full of self-loathing. I went to the front door and held it open for him, as if I were the owner of The Cabin and he the interloper.

"Don't worry that I'll say anything to Irene Kirby. I'll be avoiding her like the plague she's been on my life. Make sure she doesn't upset my mother either."

Eoin stood in front of me, a white line of temper around his lips. I think at that moment he hated me as much as I hated myself. He gave me one last look full of suppressed anger, tucked the package with our DNA samples under his arm and strode past me.

I needed air. I went into the back garden. Ned had arranged a plank of timber across two barrels. It made a comfortable seat. I sat down and closed my eyes. I had done it! Now I would know. I would know if Dad had fathered a child with Irene Kirby, if Eoin Kirby was that child, if I was his sister. What I didn't yet know was how I would react to the results. My mind refused to allow me to explore the possibilities. I think I went into a kind of trance, a thoughtless state.

Banging on the front door roused me. Ned and Tom were outside, looking for a key to the gate at the side of the shop.

"It's the sand and slabs," Tom said, pointing at a lorry pulling up outside the shop. "We need to get them out to the back. It would be handier through the side-gate."

I handed them the key-ring, went into the little kitchenette and mixed a big bowl of paste. Then I got a roll of paper and began. Cut, paste, hang. Cut, paste, hang.

It was dark outside when I finished the papering. Ned and Tom had left a long time ago. I squinted my eyes and imagined tables and chairs in here, flowers, the smell of freshly brewed coffee. It was an illusion. A pretence. A play-café for one day. A two-finger sign to Carla's horrific cancer.

I dumped the last of the paste, scrubbed the counter and scraped off the stubborn little bits of paper which had embedded themselves into the grain.

My arms ached by the time I had finished. I felt unbalanced. I locked up and walked the strand until my legs ached with the same intensity as my arms. Something told me I was punishing myself but I hushed that voice and kept walking until I just couldn't take another step.

Neither Mom nor Jodi were there when I got home. I showered very quickly, put on my comfy fleece pyjamas and crawled into bed. Only Barry Bear knew that I cried myself to sleep.

Chapter 27

I woke to Jodi sitting on the side of my bed, shaking me.

"C'mon, lazy bones! We've loads to do today and I've no time to waste."

I was confused until I remembered that Jodi had slept in our spare room last night.

"You still have your teddy bear! I don't believe it! You're some baby, Adele Burke."

Barry Bear looked tatty and worn in Jodi's hands. I snatched him back from her and immediately recalled crying into his fur last night. My DNA test was probably in Dublin by now, being peered at, strands and spirals being noted and compared to Eoin's. I jumped out of bed.

"Go put on the kettle for me. I'll be with you in five minutes."

By the time I got to the kitchen, Jodi and Mom were wading their way through mountains of scrambled eggs and toast. I got my bowl of cornflakes and joined them at the table. I stopped, a spoon of cereal halfway to my mouth as I heard Jodi prattle on enthusiastically about Irene Kirby. Jesus! Why was she doing this? She knew any mention of Irene Kirby could only cause upset.

"Can we talk about something else?" I asked.

Mom looked at me and frowned. "You're dribbling milk from your spoon, Adele. And it's rude to interrupt. Go on, Jodi."

"Mrs Kirby will be here early afternoon. In Cork anyway. I think she intends meeting up with Michael Kirby's relations there before coming to Cairnsure."

"Staying in The Grand, I s'pose?" Mom asked.

"Yes. I booked the Grattan Suite for her. It's the only suite there and she had to have it. Not many takers at the price they charge."

"That's her all right. She mustn't have changed. Always demanding the best for herself. I'm warning you, Jodi, watch out for her. She's a Jezebel."

"What do you mean, Mrs Burke? Why don't you like her? From what Eoin says she's a terrific woman."

I was furious at Jodi teasing Mom like this, pretending she didn't know why my mother hated Irene. I frowned at Jodi but she ignored me and leaned forward to listen to Mom getting more and more vitriolic about Irene Kirby.

"Just take it from me she's not a nice person. And hold onto your young man. Unless she's changed a lot, no man is safe with her around."

"She's in her fifties now, Mrs Burke. A widow, mother and successful businesswoman. I doubt if Kieran Mahon would interest her in the least."

"A leopard doesn't change its spots," Mom muttered, nodding as if she had just coined the phrase specifically for Irene Kirby and was finding it very apt. I noticed her face begin to flush. It was time to call a halt to Jodi's games.

"Thought you might like to know the papering in The Cabin is finished, Jodi."

"Sorry I didn't get back last night. Eoin was busy in the afternoon. He couldn't see me until later."

Eoin Kirby certainly had been busy yesterday afternoon, rubbing a swab around the inside of his mouth. Jodi didn't seem to know. She would have dropped some hint if she had.

Not for the first time, I wondered about Jodi and Eoin Kirby. He knew her history, her penchant for cooking the books when it had suited her purpose and yet now he was her new employer. Not, of course, as his accountant but nevertheless he was placing a lot of trust in someone he had rescued from a drug binge. He must have an ulterior motive but I couldn't yet figure it out.

"Are we ready to think about flooring so?" Jodi asked.

"I've been looking up some catalogues. What would you think of floor paint?"

"Do you want everyone to stick to the floor, Adele? That's a daft idea," Mom said giving Jodi a conspiratorial, isn't-Adele-silly look.

I had been going to explain to her about floor paints but now I just ignored her.

"Are you ready, Jodi? We'll go to the DIY but I must collect Finn Selby first."

"Why? I came here to avoid children. What are you bringing Finn along for?"

"Because he wants to help. Because he wants to do something nice for his mother. Because his little heart is broken. Enough reasons yet, Jodi?"

Jodi had the grace to look contrite. A look she carried off very well.

I got my car keys and left. If Jodi turned up at the DIY great. If not, Finn and I would manage without her. I tried to figure out why she was making me feel so angry. By the time I had reached the DIY store, Finn in the seat beside me, I had given up searching for an answer. There probably was none, other than the fact that Jodi was at her smart-ass best this morning and I was teetering on the edge of one of my self-pitying moods. I glanced at Finn's face, so much sadness in his eyes, his mother's blue-violet eyes. I felt ashamed of my tetchiness. I smiled at him.

"Ready? Let's go find something fabulous for the floors."

"She ate her breakfast this morning, Adele."

"That's good, isn't it?"

"Vera was crying. And Brigitte too."

"It's good to cry sometimes. When you feel sad."

"I'm too busy now," he said and hopped out of the car.

I watched him run to Jodi who was waiting for us by the entrance door. She caught his hand and, smiling, waved over at me. I went to join them. Whatever had been wrong between us wasn't important any more. We were here for Carla's sake and for her son's. My feelings and Jodi's lack of them could not get in the way of giving Carla the best café-for-a-day anyone ever had.

* * *

We opted for a terracotta floor paint and bought a smaller amount of black as well at Finn's suggestion. He reckoned that a pretend café should have pretend tiles on the floor. It would mean more painting but since I had not much else to do for the weekend that didn't matter. We looked at some plastic garden tables too. Little round ones we could cover with tablecloths. Jodi kept checking her watch until I eventually asked her if we were delaying her.

"I really must go, Del. Eoin will be like a cat on hot bricks at this stage. He wants to go over the development plan, yet again, before his mother arrives."

I didn't comment but she took offence anyway.

"Well, he is paying me. And it's not as if anyone else is working on The Cabin today. It's the weekend. Get a life, Del."

"Don't mention Irene Kirby to my mother again. You know it upsets her. Amuse yourself some other way."

"Oh, for heaven's sake! I was only trying to protect her by letting her know where to watch out for her arch-enemy. I'd never deliberately upset Sissy."

"Fine. I'll see you at home, I suppose. You're staying again tonight, aren't you?"

"I'll be late back. I probably won't see you until the morning."

I looked at her suspiciously. Jodi was up to

something. I examined her closely. Whatever was making her jittery, I didn't believe it was narcotics.

"Right then. Finn and I will drop the paint off at The Cabin. Just go now. You're making me nervous fidgeting."

I was in The Cabin, Finn helping me to stack the paint cans, brushes and safety wear we had bought, when it suddenly dawned on me why Jodi had been so nervous. She would be meeting Irene Kirby later on today. I knew it. A royal command had been issued and Jodi would be there, probably in the Grand Hotel, looking stunning and being very clever. Why had she not said? I wished with all my bitter heart that Irene Kirby turned out to be more beautiful and more clever than Jodi Wall. That didn't work for me. I re-wished, this time that Jodi would be at her devious best and would make Irene Kirby sorry that she ever returned to Cairnsure.

Evil wishing done, I settled down to doing jobs around The Cabin with Finn until it was time to take him home to Carla.

* * *

The painting of The Cabin floor was a highly demanding operation. I was glad that it took all my attention. I liked the protective gear too: mask, goggles, gloves and paper overalls. I could hide inside them, like a scene-of-crime forensic detective. It took a lot of concentration and energy to prepare the floor and apply the degreasing solution. By the time the shop floor was degreased, I was glad we had decided that there was no need to do the kitchenette and store floors.

I took a break. To give the floor time to dry and me time to breathe properly. I thought of going to the strand but decided against that. It was packed on this sunny Saturday and anyway I didn't want to run the slightest risk of bumping into Eoin Kirby. Not while Irene was probably at this very minute flying her broomstick from Cork to Cairnsure.

I sat in the back garden on Ned's barrel seat, closed my eyes and raised my face to the sun. It was peaceful. I felt my skin tighten and prickle. It was burning. It always did without sun-block, especially my nose. When thoughts of Aunt Lily and how I should tell her about the DNA test began to nag, I opened my eyes again. Rooting around in the bag of goodies I had brought with me, I found the giant-sized chocolate bar. Milk chocolate with fruit and nuts. A slab of comfort.

I tackled the floor with renewed energy. The instant I dabbed on the first stroke of terracotta, I knew we had made the right choice. The colour was warm and rich against the starkly white paper. Beginning at the back of the shop, I worked my way slowly over the expanse of floor which I now realised was vast.

I sat back on my heels after two hours and surveyed my work. I had managed to cover just a quarter of the area. Irene Kirby was probably in Cairnsure by now, installed in the Grattan Suite, demanding room service, running her finger over furniture to check for dust. I frowned. What a biased picture I had conjured of a woman I had never met. I had done the thing I hated most in other people. I had judged her. I picked up my paint-roller again.

She deserved judging. And sentencing. If only for her brazenness in coming back here to the place where she had ruined so many lives. That thought led me to worry about my mother. Should I go home to her? Stay by her side until Irene Kirby was gone again? But Mom had Tom, hadn't she? And her unfailing facility to deny the truth. And what if Irene decided to stay here? I couldn't shadow Mom forever. I had other things to do. I must have. I couldn't think what. I attacked the painting again.

* * *

Mom rang at six o'clock. "Your dinner's ready, Adele. Are you coming home?"

"I can't, Mom. I'm painting the floor in The Cabin. I must get it finished so that it has a chance to dry overnight."

"Is Jodi with you?"

"No. She's busy."

I knew what Mom meant when she said "Hmm". It was becoming apparent that Jodi was leaving most of the heavy work to me. I didn't mind. I needed it and I wanted to do it for Carla.

"I'll bring your dinner down to you."

"No. Don't do that. Is Tom there with you?"

"Yes. We're going to evening Mass. I'm doing a reading from the altar."

"Good luck with that. I'll see you later. And Mom . . ."

"Yes?"

What could I say? Watch out for Irene Kirby? Be careful in case you meet her and she hurts you all over again? Whatever it was I meant to say it certainly wasn't the announcement I heard myself make.

"I've had a DNA test done. I'll know in a couple of weeks whether Eoin Kirby is really my brother or not."

"Right. I'll put your dinner in the fridge," she said and put down the phone.

I cursed roundly and then continued to paint the floor.

* * *

Even though I was wearing a face mask, I think I must have been high on fumes. Either that or I had gained manic energy from my bar of chocolate. Enough of the floor had been painted by now for me to judge the overall effect. I was pleased with it and that satisfaction drove me to even more heroic efforts with the roller. My energy didn't flag until I reached the last patch by the front door. I sat back and checked my pocket for keys. I heard them rattle as I patted. I had been planning this moment all night. Paint the last bit, lock the door, put paint tin, roller and protective clothing over the side gate, go home, shower, sleep. My knees felt raw and my back ached as I stooped over again.

"What are you doing down on your hands and knees? Praying?"

I started in fright, letting my roller fall. It was Kieran Mahon, camera slung around his neck. I pushed up my face mask and snapped at him.

"Now look what you made me do! Stay out there, don't walk on the floor. Anyway, you're working too or is the camera just for effect?"

"The prize-giving for the Athletics Club was on

at the hotel tonight. I had to line 'em up and shoot 'em."

"Where's Amy?"

"My mother's baby-sitting."

I turned back to my fallen roller and, pulling down my mask, finished the last piece while Kieran stood behind me. "This is an interesting view I have here. The overalls suit you. Not sure about the mask though."

"Kieran, just shut up. Or better still go away."

"I'll forgive you that bitchiness if you come for a walk with me."

Something in his tone made me look up at him. Something sad. Worried.

I gave the floor a last dab and tried to get up off my knees. I was stiffer than Aunt Lily.

"On the other hand, maybe you should come down here," I laughed. "We could go for a crawl."

Kieran took my arm and helped me up without making any smart remarks. He was definitely in a down mood. I knew just why by the time I had peeled off and dumped my painting gear. He had seen Jodi in the Grand Hotel, dining in style with Eoin Kirby and a strikingly beautiful older woman. My instinct had been right.

"That would be the infamous Irene Kirby," I explained to him as we began our walk towards the beach. "I thought Jodi would have told you. Irene was due to arrive here this afternoon. What does she look like?"

"She doesn't look old enough to be Eoin's mother. Very dark-haired, slim, beautiful brown eyes."

Eoin's eyes. His lustrous, dark-brown eyes. He had

probably inherited his curling black lashes from her too. The blond hair was from his father. My father. Our father.

"Jodi's getting very involved with the Kirbys, don't you think?" Kieran asked.

"She's just working for them. Isn't she lucky to have a job under the circumstances?"

"I would have given her work. She didn't want it. I'm not sure what she wants. Do you know?"

I didn't like the way this conversation was heading. I felt sorry for Kieran. I understood. God, how I understood his sense of rejection! But he should be discussing it with Jodi, not with me.

"Ask her, Kieran. To be honest, I don't think she really knows herself at this stage. She's been through a lot. It will take time for her to get her confidence back again."

The tide was in, lapping in gentle little ripples onto the sand. Kieran picked up a stone and skimmed it over the calm surface. It disappeared into the dark.

"You're wrong there, Adele. Jodi Wall has lost none of her self-confidence. All she's lost is an apartment and a job."

"And a big chunk of her life. She's still a very troubled woman. Can't you see that?"

I doubt if he did. I too had lost sight of that. Her brashness in recent days had made me so resentful that I had forgotten how vulnerable Jodi Wall really was.

"Remember the day Eoin Kirby and I found her in Glengorm Woods? Remember how very fragile she was then? She's still that fragile woman. It's just that she's building up a protective shell again."

We walked on in silence while we both thought about Jodi and her frailties. I tried to feel nothing but sympathy. I failed on that score. Resentment kept creeping into my thoughts. Why should she be sitting in the Grand Hotel with Eoin, looking all shiny and adorable, while I was on my hands and knees in The Cabin, doing a good impression of the Michelin Man in my overalls?

"Maybe you're right," Kieran said at last. "I'll talk to her. If she can take the time from Kirby enterprises. She could only spare me a few minutes tonight."

"You were talking to her?"

"Long enough for her to tell me your news."

"What news?"

"About your test of course. You and Eoin. It's the right thing to do. At least you'll know now."

I stood still and tried to remember my conversations with Jodi since I had done the DNA test. I raked over every word I could recall. I was certain that I had not told her. I was sure too that Sissy would not have said anything. Eoin Kirby! The git! He had no right! Kieran was justified in his concern about Jodi's relationship with Eoin. It was hardly employer–employee when they were sharing such intimate secrets. My secrets. Fuck them. What did it matter anyway? I would have told Jodi sooner or later. Sometime before the whole world knew.

I turned on my heel and strode back to my car. If Kieran thought my behaviour odd, he didn't say so. He had his own problems to think about.

Chapter 28

I saw Jodi Wall come and go a lot over the next few days. Coming to our house late at night, disappearing into the spare room and then going out in the mornings. Bit by bit her belongings arrived. Three cases of clothes. A box with shoes, a raft of make-up bags. I met her in the hall late Thursday evening, dragging a huge cardboard box. Glancing into it, I saw a portable television, a hairdryer and a printer. I had had enough.

"Looks like you're moving in, Jodi. Care to tell me what's going on?"

"Didn't Sissy tell you? She said it was all right. Do you have a problem with it?"

I tried not to let my surprise show. Mom hadn't even bothered to mention it to me. Her house, her decision.

"Why are you here and how long do you intend staying?" I asked.

"I thought Kieran would have told you."

"No. Kieran hasn't been saying much this week, although he's spent a lot of time helping out at The Cabin."

Stooping down, she grabbed the cardboard box and began to haul it again. I put my foot in front of it.

"Are you going to tell me what's going on? You haven't been near The Cabin since last week."

"That's not true. I helped with painting those silly imitation tile lines. The ones that Finn wanted. Actually, I'm surprised at how well they look."

"You spent a half-an-hour there, most of it drinking coffee. I'm not complaining about the work. Besides, it's almost finished by now. But the whole thing was your idea that we should do this for Carla. You haven't been to see her either."

"I rang. She's very well."

I felt like stamping on her fingers which were still clutching her precious box. I was tired, confused, and I think depressed. I had worked myself to a standstill, rushing and racing between the DIY store and The Cabin, painting, sanding, sweeping, scrubbing. It wasn't that I was alone. There were plenty of willing hands to help. It was just that none of them were Jodi's.

"I know you're busy with your new job. With the Kirbys and their big plans. But you could at least show some interest in what's going on in The Cabin, Jodi. You started it but now you seem to have abandoned it."

She pulled the box again. I moved my foot. It would have been too childish to play tug-a-box in the hall. I went to the kitchen, damned if I was going to help her move in.

I made coffee and then cut a big chunk of sponge cake.

Mom had been baking all day, experimenting with one recipe and another for the party. Tom and I were tasters-in-chief. As with all her baking, everything was delicious but she suffered agonies of indecision between flaky or short crust pastry, between egg or Victoria sponge. After two bites, I pushed the cake away from me. I wasn't hungry. I had been very tired but anger with Jodi made me restless now. Too agitated to sleep or read. I glared at the sponge cake as if it was to blame for the way I felt.

"Where's Sissy?"

I looked up from the cake to see Jodi stride into the kitchen. I frowned. When had Jodi Wall begun to call my mother Sissy?

"She's gone over to your mother's house."

"Jesus! Are you sure? What for?"

For one spiteful moment, I was tempted to say that Sissy was arranging for Jodi to go back home. When I saw her flop down on a chair, her face pale, I relented.

"They're planning the food for the party. Brigitte is there too. We've all agreed to hold it next Saturday. Carla is up and about now. It's getting harder to keep the secret."

"Do you not think it's getting a bit over-the-top, this fake café business?"

It all came together then. My feeling of betrayal, the hurt, the niggling resentment. It poured out in a torrent of bitter words.

"It was your blasted idea, Jodi. I told you it would seem like a wake but you wouldn't listen. Now you're sneering at the whole thing. You cynical little bitch! If anyone is over-the-top, it's you! Who are you, Jodi? Are you the pathetic junkie I scraped up off the forest floor, the one who lied and stole just to feed her habit? Or maybe you're the reformed addict, settling down to life as Kieran Mahon's partner? That didn't last long, did it? Not good enough for you. Now you're worming your way into the Kirbys' company and my home. What's next? Jodi the property developer?"

I stopped to draw breath and began to shake with shock and self-disgust. What in the hell was wrong with me? How could I have been so vicious?

Jodi's eyes were huge in her pale face. "You really did fall for Eoin Kirby, didn't you?" she said. "That's your problem. You think I've taken him from you. Just like I took Kieran Mahon. You've been pretty blunt with me, Adele. It's my turn now. Do you believe for one minute that either man has the slightest interest in you? Stop fooling yourself. I can tell you Eoin bitterly regrets ever having answered his phone the night you called him to comfort you about Carla's diagnosis."

I felt my skin go cold and clammy. I thought I might faint, suffocated by humiliation. They had discussed me. Eoin and Jodi had a sniggering chat about me, how easy I was, what a gullible fool. The swim, the picnic, the closeness I had felt to Eoin, had all been illusion. The imaginings of a needy woman. The delusions of a woman desperate for love. The source of Eoin's bitter regret. I tried to lash back at Jodi but my words were more whine than whip by now.

"You discussed my DNA test with Kieran. Who else have you told? I don't know why Eoin told you about it.

It has nothing to do with you. And I don't appreciate you discussing me with Eoin Kirby either."

"I didn't. I just listened while he talked."

"What about loyalty? Carla has cancer and you don't give a damn. You talk about me to a stranger."

"You spent the night with that stranger. Tough titty if he turns out to be your brother. And of course I care about Carla."

"You were always the same. Jodi first, last and in the middle. Nobody but Jodi, Jodi, Jodi. As if you're the most important person in the world. Well, you're not. Just look at the mess you got yourself into."

She sprang up from her chair. She was quivering with the intensity of her anger as she leaned into my face.

"You're a pompous, patronising, prig! You know nothing about me or my life. How dare you sit there and judge me!"

"I've known you since we were babies. I've never seen anything but selfishness from you."

"Did you ever wonder why I always looked out for myself? Why I don't depend on anyone else? Because I have to, Adele. I always had to. I had no one else to turn to."

"You had Carla and me. And your family," I said softly, afraid now that any loud word would drive her anger over the edge. I saw a light blaze in her eyes and knew she was already there.

"Family! My family! My father? The man who beat me until I blistered. My mother? The woman who watched him do it and never even tried to stop him?"

I stared at her in disbelief. She had her arms folded

tightly about herself, her eyes now blank, as if she was looking inward. Into the past.

"My mother said it was because I was the eldest. He expected a lot of me. And I was stubborn and cheeky. He had to teach me to behave. To conform. To cower before him. Bastard! He'd thrash me, she'd watch and then they would go to the church and bow and scrape to the clergy. Fuckers."

"Why didn't you say anything?"

Life flickered back in her eyes. She turned them towards me and I saw a despair in them.

"How could I? Who would have believed me? The holy Walls child-beaters! And it was only me. He never raised a hand to any of the others. I grew to believe that I deserved it. So I suffered in silence. And all the while I was so jealous of you."

"You — jealous of me! Why?"

"Your home, your mother and father. They adored you, Adele. Spoiled you. You were the centre of their lives. I used to watch your father make things for you, take you fishing, play with you while your mother clucked over you like a hen over her chick. They didn't expect results and achievements from you. They just loved you and I envied that."

I found that I too folded my arms around myself now. I needed the comfort, the security, the reassurance. I didn't doubt that what Jodi said was true. How had I not seen it before? How had I not guessed? Probably for the reasons she said. Who would have suspected quasi-saints like the Walls of such a despicable crime? Who could have known that the energetic, high-achieving child was being battered? Carla and I couldn't have known. We were children. Protected secure children with no concept of violence in the home. But I wondered about the adults in young Jodi's life. Her teachers, her uncles and aunts.

"Did anyone know?"

"He made sure the bruises and blisters were in places they wouldn't be seen."

Jodi shook her head and in that wordless movement I saw all the tragedy and isolation of her years of suffering. I remembered the little girl who wanted to be in my house or Carla's, but never brought us to her home; the child who would run away even in the middle of a game to do her homework; the teenager who spurned the company of boys; the woman who strove to be the best, to excel and surpass; the damaged soul who tried to find healing in drugs; the friend who often wounded with the sharpness of her words. I understood her now. Her defensiveness. Her need to succeed.

"I'm so very sorry, Jodi. I'm sorry you had to go through that cruelty and sorry I was no help to you. I wish I could take back the horrible things I said to you tonight."

Jodi sat down again. She looked drained. Small and defenceless.

"They were true, Del. Everything you said was true."

"No! I was just being . . . just . . . Oh, I don't know why I said those things. My head's all over the place."

"Me too. I didn't quite tell you the truth about Eoin. He's very upset about the situation you've both found

400

yourselves in. That goes without saying. But he never said one word against you, Del. In fact he told me you're one of the nicest people he has ever met."

"Really? I thought the same about him. Maybe our niceness is inherited from our common parentage."

"Maybe. You'll know soon anyway."

She smiled at me then and I saw a flash of the Jodi I was more familiar with. Making light of problems. Coping. It was up to her to talk about what her parents had done to her, to detail the beatings, the suffering. To take the memories from the dark corners of her mind. I could not, would not, permit her to bury all these memories again. To live a life poisoned by the toxic waste of the past. Nor would I try to force her to face things she was not yet prepared to handle. That would probably need professional guidance. I would just gently nudge her in the right direction.

"Have you ever confronted your parents about the way they treated you?"

"I did. That's really why they threw me out. That and the drugs and losing my job. Disgracing them. My father said he should have beaten me harder."

"The bastard."

"I played right into their hands. The way I messed up my life is their justification for what they did. They said they were only trying to save me from myself."

"How very considerate of them! I suppose they pray for you too. No wonder you . . . no wonder you lost your way."

Jodi leaned towards me and fixed me with an intense

stare. "If you're talking about my drug habit, Del, you're way off the mark. I'm not blaming them for that. I told you before. I developed the habit because I found it gave me so much energy. I could work endless hours and still not feel tired. I looked on my cocaine as a tool, part of my grand plan to outwork and outsmart everyone else. It was my own doing and I must take responsibility. I'll never recover otherwise."

I reached across and took her hand. It was cold. "You will recover, Jode. I know it. You're strong. And I think you're very generous to forgive your parents."

"I'm not forgiving them! I don't think I'll ever do that. I'm not blaming them for my drug addiction but I do believe they've ruined my life. I'm so lonely, Del. So fucking lonely. Nothing fills that empty space inside me. I can't let anybody get close. Every time I try, I start thinking they'll find out what the real me is like and then they'll hate me too. Just like my parents did. You and Carla are the nearest I have to family and now Carla . . . I can't face that thought. That's why I've been avoiding The Cabin. It's like we're saying goodbye to her and I can't. I just can't."

We both cried then. Arms around each other, our tears for Carla mingled.

We cried until we heard the key rattle in the door. Then we made a dash for the box of tissues. When Sissy came into the kitchen we were mopping our faces.

"Sad film or bad news?" Mom asked.

"We were talking about Carla," I answered.

"You can stop your crying so. I met her today. She

was in the supermarket with Vera and the children. She looked better than I've seen her for a long time."

Jodi and I exchanged glances. We knew Carla looked better. We had seen her too. We wanted to hope of course but Harry was still being very cautious about her progress.

"Well, how did the meeting go? Did you come up with a menu plan?" I asked in order to prevent Mom going into one of her God-spoke-before-man speeches.

"I have it here," she said taking out a sheaf of pages from her handbag. "Your mother was asking for you, Jodi."

"Really? How is she?"

"Busy with her prayers as usual. I don't want to interfere in any family business but all I'll say is that you're welcome to stay here as long as you want. Do you understand?"

Jodi's eyes flooded with tears again and she nodded her head.

I understood too. The Walls had spun some story about Jodi to Mom. I felt proud of her for not believing it. Or for believing it but accepting Jodi anyway. For a moment, deception, half-truths and half-brothers didn't seem to matter. I knew I was very, very lucky to have had Sissy and John Burke as my parents.

Chapter 29

I woke early to the white light of morning. I stretched, snug in bed, still sleepy enough not to be bothered by details of my increasingly complicated and busy life. Outside my window, branches of the big oak were swaying in a gentle breeze. I watched the play of shadows on the walls and ceiling and allowed the day to drift towards me. A knock sounded on my door and Jodi came in, clipboard in hand.

"I've just been talking to Eoin. He said I can have today off to organise The Cabin."

I pulled the duvet over my head. I wasn't ready yet for Jodi and the work in The Cabin and I would never be ready for Eoin Kirby and his blasted mother.

"Get up, Del. C'mon. It's Friday for feic's sake. The party's tomorrow afternoon. We've a million things to do."

A million wouldn't come near all the thoughts which began to disturb my peaceful waking-up. Taboo brother-sister relationships. Cancer and Carla. Chairs, tables, plants, the barbeque, flowers, burgers, salads. Shit! I threw off my duvet and jumped out of bed. Jodi looked wan but much better than she had last night.

"Are you okay, Jode?"

She dropped her clipboard on the bed and threw her arms around me.

"I will be. Thanks for the shoulder to cry on and thanks for listening."

I hugged her back and said nothing. There were no words to express my regret or the sympathy I felt. Besides there were different words in my head. Ones I had tried so hard to silence. I was spent now. Worked to a standstill. I couldn't run any more. I had to know.

"What's she like? Eoin's mother?"

"I wondered why you hadn't asked already," Jodi said. "You're not going to be very pleased with the answer."

"So? Try me."

Jodi looked out the window as if she didn't want to face me. "She's beautiful. But you knew that already. She has the most magnificent brown eyes and a fabulous figure for a woman of her age. A great sense of style too and —"

"Yes, yes. I had guessed all that. What's she really like? Her personality?"

"She's a nice person, Del. Assertive, certainly. She knows what she wants and expects to get it immediately or else . . . But she's kind. Understanding."

"She must have changed a lot so. Everything I've heard about her says that she's — well, that she's a bitch."

"Some people might think of her that way. She certainly doesn't suffer fools gladly. But she's fun too. She has a sense of humour."

I took my turn looking out the window now. I had difficulty trying to digest this new image of a funny, kind Irene Kirby. A sort of Mother Teresa in Claudia Schiffer's body. A paragon of virtue. A marriage-wrecker. I could see how Jodi might admire her. Irene Kirby was a successful woman and Jodi glorified success.

"How do she and Eoin get along?"

"He defers to her a lot. She calls the shots on the business. No mistake about that. Nothing happens in that company without her approval. Eoin says it was always like that, even when his father was alive. He's different around her."

"What do you mean? How is he different?"

"When I met Eoin, I thought he was very decisive. An in-charge sort of person. And he is like that too until his mother's around. Then he just sits back and lets her make the decisions."

I thought of how strong Eoin had been when Jodi had been missing. I had even thought him masterful. Maybe he was. It could be that giving in to his mother was the easiest option for him. A convenience. I understood that.

"Did she mention anything about living here before?"

"She said she was really bored by Cairnsure and the small-town life. That she was glad they left here."

"She is a bitch! "

"No, Del, she's not. She's been kind to me. Eoin told

her my history. About my problems. I was furious at first.
I thought I'd lose my job because I'm just on trial."

"What exactly are you doing for them?"

"I suppose you could say I'm Eoin's PA. I'm liaising
with the various government departments for planning
on the development, doing feasibility studies, costings.
That type of thing. And stop looking so worried. I don't
handle any money. Eoin made that clear when he took
me on and Irene has made it a rule."

There was a rustle by the bedroom door. We both turned
towards it and saw Mom standing there, apron on, the
heavy-duty Christmas one which covered her completely
from shin to shoulder and was decorated with a bleary-eyed
Santa. She had a wooden spoon in her hand, coated in a
creamy butter mix. I looked at her face for any sign that she
had overheard our conversation. She seemed calm. Even if
she had heard she was probably going to ignore it. Deny it.
Pretend it never happened.

"Will I put butter cream or fresh cream in the sponge
cakes?" she asked. "What do ye think?"

"You're the best judge of that, Sissy," Jodi said, grabbing
her clipboard and Mom in one movement. "You have two
minutes to get showered and dressed, Del. I must test your
mother's cakes."

They closed the door and left me alone in my sunlit
room of moving shadows. I thought of my father, maybe
because of what Jodi had said about him last night, or
maybe just because I felt raw and vulnerable this morning.
I wished he was here now to tell me why he had cheated
on Mom and if he really was Eoin's father. To tell me that

Carla's cancer was just a bad dream and would all go away as soon as I woke up. I wished I was six again and holding his hand.

I looked in the mirror and saw the face of a thirty-year-old. Forcing myself to smile at my reflection, I pulled my shoulders back and banished the six-year-old Adele to the past. Where she belonged.

I showered and dressed quickly and was already thinking ahead to lists of things to be done in The Cabin as I went towards the kitchen. I was brought to an abrupt halt outside the door of the spare bedroom. The one Jodi had commandeered. My feet were stuck to the floor in shock as I watched her through the half-opened door. Jodi was standing beside her bed, balancing a little plastic bag on her open palm. Concentrating on it as if in silent communication with the bag and its white, powdery contents. As if she was challenging it, willing it to do its worst. Where had she got this? Had she been lying about going off it? Had Kieran thrown her out of his apartment because he wouldn't have a drug-user around his child? Had all her talk about fighting her addiction been lies? I took a step forward, warnings, pleas, condemnations, on the tip of my tongue.

I saw her lips move. The bag appeared to take on a life of its own as her hand shook. A tear slid out of the corner of her eye and tracked down her cheek.

I suddenly felt like a voyeur. A Peeping Tom. Witness to a very private moment which I had no right to see. I tip-toed away, fervently willing her to make the right decision for herself, for her future. I wanted her to win the battle of wills against her lethal addiction. To be strong. But I vowed, as I went into the kitchen, that I would not judge her. Not any more. I had not been there for the child who was being beaten and terrorised. I would be there for the damaged woman she had become. Whatever her decision.

* * *

Ned Lehane and Tom Reagan must have been in The Cabin since dawn. They were on their first tea break when Jodi and I arrived, sitting side by side on the barrel seat, mugs in hand.

"I suppose there's panic in the kitchen of your house, Adele," Tom said. "Is Sissy still baking like a woman possessed?"

"Yes, she's working hard but not half as hard as you two have been."

I looked around the back garden. Hedges were neatly trimmed, grass cut so close that it looked like a carpet, patio area gleaming with the cream paving slabs Tom and Ned had laid. Potted plants dotted around the patio lent an exotic feel to the place which had so recently been a wasteland. I smiled at the two men who seemed to have forged a friendship over the clearing and paving. The Odd Couple.

"This is fabulous. Carla will love it."

"Yes, she will. I appreciate it too."

We all turned towards the back door where Harry Selby was standing. He looked exhausted. Haunted. I was afraid to ask about Carla but I had to.

"How is she?"

"Getting stronger by the day. Being able to eat is making a big difference. Ruth is taking good care of her."

I blushed as I recalled how snide I had been about Harry's ex-wife.

"Will Ruth be here tomorrow?" Jodi asked and I realised then we should have invited her.

"She'll try to make it," Harry said. "But she's putting in a lot of hours covering for me. We'll see."

"Where I'll put this?" a voice which could only be Brigitte's called. She appeared behind Harry, carrying a green and white striped parasol.

"Oh, very beautiful!" she said as she looked around. "Carla is going to get such a fright."

We all smiled, knowing that Brigitte meant surprise not fright. The next ten minutes were full of huffing and puffing as wrought-iron tables, chairs, parasols, and a huge gas barbeque were carted from Carla's four-by-four and Harry's car to the back garden. When they were all put together and in place it looked exactly like the barbeque area Carla had imagined.

"I must get back," Brigitte said. "Carla thinks I'm at the supermarket. She is probably worrying that I made an accident of her big car. Make sure you keep the windows not see-through. She wants to go to the sea today."

She dashed off. Just as quickly she came back in again.

"Adele, Finn he wants to talk to you about something. Important, he says. He's always important."

Harry and I exchanged glances. He shrugged. Finn

had seemed to be coping well this past week, enjoying helping out and keeping the café secret.

"I'll collect him and bring him here," I offered.

"Thanks, Adele. Thanks to all of you for . . ."

Harry didn't finish his sentence. Head bowed, shoulders stooped, he walked away.

"Anyone for a cup of tea? Coffee?" Tom asked.

Jodi grinned and went to her bag. She dragged out a plastic container stuffed with some of Sissy's cakes.

"I'm going to collect Finn," I told her. "Be ready for shopping when I come back."

She winked at me. It was a cheeky wink, full of humour. I could see no trace of her earlier suffering. Nor any trace of narcotics in her clear eyes. I winked back at her.

* * *

It had to happen sooner or later. In fact I had expected it to happen before now. Nevertheless I was shocked when I walked straight into Eoin and Irene Kirby at the door of The Cabin. Jodi had not been exaggerating. Irene was very beautiful. Much taller than I had imagined her. Younger too. Yet she was the mother of a thirty-four-year-old son. Botox and liposuction, of course. She could afford them.

"Good morning, Adele," Eoin said. "I know you're all very busy in The Cabin but I was wondering if we could look around now?"

"It's your building. No need to ask my permission."

"Exactly what I said to him," Irene said, stepping towards me.

No trace of the soft Irish accent remained in her clipped enunciation. Up close her skin was perfect, her teeth gleaming, her eyes stunning. She wore elegant high heels and a cream suit which hugged her slim figure. I was very aware of the contrast to my jeans, T-shirt and trainers. The ones with pink laces.

"Irene Kirby," she said, offering me her hand.

I hesitated before taking it. Had my father held this slim hand too? Had he been as in awe of her good looks as I now found myself to be? I took a deep breath and tried to convince myself she was only looking down on me because she was taller in her heels.

"Nice to meet you. I'm Adele Burke. I believe you knew my parents when you lived in Cairnsure."

"If you're Sissy and John Burke's daughter, then, yes, I did. You don't look like either of them though. More like your aunt who lived on the farm – Lily, wasn't it?"

"It still is. I suppose you know by now that my father died."

"Yes. I'm sorry. Your mother wrote at the time to let my husband know."

As I stood there letting her words sink in, my outrage grew. Mom had been so right. Leopards don't change their spots and neither do lying Irene Kirbys.

"That's a lie! My mother never wrote to you. She wouldn't have . . . she . . . she . . ."

Irene Kirby stood there unblinking as I stuttered, stammered and changed colour – from pink right through to crimson I was sure. I saw her lift one eyebrow, noticed a smile hover on her lips.

"Whatever makes you say that, Adele? Why are you so upset at the idea of her writing to let us know John had died?"

I glanced at Eoin. He was standing behind his mother, looking as uncomfortable as I felt. He shuffled from one big Burke-like foot to the other. There was a plea in his eyes now. A shut-up-and-go-away-plea to me. I knew then that he had been trying to avoid this meeting as much as I had. That made me angry. He might be afraid of his mother. I was not. Not really.

"Sissy may have written to your husband but I don't ever believe she wrote to you. You two didn't part on the best of terms, did you?"

Irene narrowed her eyes and fixed me with a penetrating stare. "I've changed my mind, Adele. You might look like your Aunt Lily but you have a lot of Sissy Burke in you. Eoin, come on."

She swept past me, leaving a trail of perfume behind her.

Eoin stooped towards my ear and whispered, "I asked you not to say anything. Do you get satisfaction from upsetting people?"

"If it's you and your mother, yes."

We stared at each other for what seemed like an eternity. His breath brushed my face, the scent of him engulfed me. I remembered the softness of his lips, the warmth of his touch. I wanted to lash out, to spit vengeance, but I was held immobile and wordless by the conflict inside me.

"Eoin. I'm waiting," Irene called impatiently.

"Leave my mother out of this," he whispered.

"It's all her fault! If she hadn't been flaunting herself around . . ."

He walked away from me. Left me standing outside The Cabin door, face red, laces pink and mood very black.

I was parking my car at the Selbys' house before my breathing returned to normal and my confused thinking came under control. I might yet need to crucify Irene Kirby but not now. Not until Carla had had her day in the café.

* * *

Finn was in one of his near hyperactive moods. He bounced up and down on a couch as I talked to Carla. Vera tried to take him away out of the room but he refused to leave. I could see that he was tiring Carla.

"Finn, you're in your bare feet. Go get shoes and socks and I'll take you for a spin somewhere."

"I know where I want to go, Adele. Stay there. I'll be quick."

He ran off, Vera rushing after him. Carla sighed.

"Poor Finn. He's trying to find answers to the questions the rest of us don't even dare to ask. I really worry about what's going to happen to him."

"Don't," I said with as much conviction as I could muster. "He'll certainly need extra help but that's all organised, isn't it?"

"I don't care how clever he is. He's still a child. He'll need his mother for a long time to come yet. I can't promise him the one thing he needs most."

I looked at her. The Carla I remembered was beginning to re-emerge from the yellow-tinged gauntness. The ghost of her blue-eyed, blonde prettiness was lurking behind the face which was slightly fuller, the skin a little less jaundiced.

"What you're talking about, Carla – being there for him always – is a promise nobody can make. None of us know, do we? Besides, you look so much better. How are you feeling?"

She smiled at me. A smile like a mother might give a vulnerable child.

"To be honest, Del, I'm feeling much better than I should. It can be a drawback knowing what's really happening. On the other hand, as a nurse, I've seen people beat the odds so often that I can't help but hope."

I reached for her hand, took it in mine, and gave her a smile which I hoped was full of reassurance. She didn't see it. She was staring at her smooth hand engulfed in my work-worn one.

"What have you been doing, Del? Digging up roads with your bare hands? Your nails are wrecked and you've calluses on your palms."

I withdrew my hand quickly and shoved it into my pocket. I shrugged.

"A little bit of DIY. You know me. One fad after another."

"So the cookery's put on a back burner, is it?"

"For now."

Carla stood up and walked over to the window. Turning her back to me, she looked out onto the front lawn. Standing, I noticed how big her stomach seemed in comparison to her very slim body. No longer fooling myself about a possible pregnancy, I knew the bloating had something to do with her disease. She turned around and looked at me.

"It would have been great, wouldn't it? The café, I mean. Great for all of us. You cooking like you wanted to, me having something to do outside home and Jodi organising us all."

I hesitated. Should I say that, yes, we could do those things: cook, escape and delegate, if only for one day. Or say that sometime in the future, it might happen. Carla spoke again before I could decide.

"Your situation, Del. The DNA test you told me about. You did the right thing. It's always better to face up to the truth."

Yes. She was right. She was facing her truth and I would very soon have to face mine.

"I met Irene Kirby this morning. Bumped into her just before I came here."

"And?"

And what? She was beautiful. A beautiful bitch. A manipulator and controller. I shrugged.

"I wasn't really talking much to her. Jodi seems to be getting along well with her though."

"How is Jodi? Is she driving yourself and Sissy crazy?"

Finn prevented me from answering. Shoes and socks now on, he came thundering into the room.

"I'm ready, Adele. Can we go now?"

"You behave yourself for Adele," Carla warned him.

He ran to her and hugged her, his little arms reaching around her.

"I must or else she'll shout at me."

"Finn! Enough of that silly talk. You're telling lies again."

"But honest, Mum. She has a huge cross voice. It's loud because her lungs are so big."

I grinned at him. Finn was enjoying his little game. I knew that I would probably have to use my "huge cross voice" today. The one I used for classfuls of fidgety children. He was really wound up about something in a very overexcited way.

"Come on, you little jack-in-the-box. How would you like to visit Lily on the farm again?"

"Great. But I don't want her tea. It's yuckie."

"Are you sure you won't come to the beach with the rest of us, Finn?" Carla asked. I could see she was torn between needing to keep her eldest son by her side and wanting the other children to have a few hours of fun without his disruptive behaviour.

"The beach is boring," he announced and then he ran out the door.

We passed Brigitte on our way out to my car. She gave me a thumbs-up sign behind Carla's back. I don't know whether it was because she thought the old Cabin looked great or because I was taking Finn away. He was hopping up and down beside my car, urging me to hurry. I strapped him in and then got in myself.

I turned the key in the ignition and glanced towards the house. Carla was standing at the front door, the twins on either side of her, Liam in front, Brigitte and Vera behind her, as if they were a little band of soldiers protecting the delicate woman in their midst. Carla lifted her hand and waved at me.

"Come on. Come on. First gear, Adele!" Finn ordered impatiently.

I filed the scene to memory, waved back to Carla and drove away. I had a lot of things to do.

Chapter 30

"I don't want to go here," Finn protested as I turned the car into the driveway of my mother's house. "You haven't been listening to me at all."

I turned to look at him, a small boy with a big anger. And rightly so. I hadn't been paying attention to his constant stream of excited babble.

"I'm sorry, Finn. I need to see my mom for just a minute. Then we can go to The Cabin."

"I knew you weren't listening! I need paints and brushes. We must go to the paint shop first."

"Why? All the painting's done. You saw it yourself."

If his feet had reached the floor of the car, I think he would have stamped them in fury. Tears welled up in his eyes. I leaned across to hold his hand and he immediately snatched it away.

"I must do a picture for Mum. Her own special

picture. The walls are all white. It looks like hospital. I want to make it nice for her."

I thought about The Cabin and what we had done there. The floors were terracotta, the walls sparkling white with the paper which seemed to be smoothing out very nicely. Everything else that could be painted had got a coat of white gloss, except the old counter which we had sanded and varnished. He was right. It was clinical.

"So what kind of picture do you want to paint?"

"I want to do a huge rainbow and butterflies on the walls. I have it all planned. "

I looked at the front door of my home. Inside, Sissy would be in the kitchen, the air filled with the warm aroma of baking. I needed to know if she had written to the Kirbys about Dad's death. If Irene Kirby had been telling the truth or if my mother had deceived me by omission. Again.

My gaze moved from the front door to the distressed little boy sitting beside me, special plans in his head and nobody to listen to them. I smiled at him.

"I think that would be brilliant, Finn. Carla would love it. Let's go get the paints and brushes. I'll talk to my mother later."

As I reversed out of the driveway, I knew in my heart that the conversation with Mom would have been a waste of time anyway. She would only have answered if she'd wanted to. More and more, I was beginning to wonder just what Sissy Burke was hiding underneath her steely grey, lacquered helmet of hair.

* * *

I scanned the prom for Eoin's car before I parked outside the Cabin. When I was certain neither he nor his mother were anywhere near the place, I went inside with Finn and opened up the little pots of paint for him. Jodi was horrified when he started by putting a streak of violet on the pristine wallpaper.

"It's going to be lovely," I assured her as I handed her the scrap of paper where Finn had outlined his master plan. She glanced at it and then shrugged.

"So long as he does just one wall. And of course that Carla likes it. But we have things to buy. Tablecloths, those checked ones I saw, and food too, and we have to organise ware and cutlery. Will I go shopping on my own and leave you to supervise young Michelangelo here?"

Jodi was anxious to get going. I didn't want to deal with her impatience now.

"Go on. I'll catch up later."

We both turned when we heard a knock on the door. Kieran Mahon pushed his head in.

"Need a hand here? Amy and I have some time to spare."

He pushed the door open and came in, holding Amy by the hand. She was a dark-haired child, serious, like her mother. She and Jodi exchanged looks and I could see that neither had much affection for the other. Amy walked straight across to Finn and stared at him. He pretended not to see her. Grown-up behaviour from two four-year-olds.

"That's lovely, Finn," Kieran said. "The place needed a bit of colour."

"Mum loves butterflies and I'm going to give her a rainbow too."

"You'll need a stepladder so. Rainbows are up high, aren't they? I'll get it for you."

I opened my mouth to object but Kieran put up his hand to silence me.

"You two go do your shopping. We'll stay here. What do you know about rainbows and butterflies anyway?"

"More than you know about tablecloths and ware," Jodi snapped. "How come Amy is with you today? Another crisis conference?"

"Her mother's gone for a few days' holiday. Not that it's any of your business."

I grabbed Jodi by the arm and began to haul her towards the door.

"We won't be too long, Kieran. Just give me a ring if you need me. You behave yourself, Finn."

Totally absorbed in his work by now, Finn continued painting without raising his head.

* * *

Jodi and I soon got swept up in a flurry of buying. Wine-and-white checked cloths to cover the plastic tables, little white vases as centrepieces and six trays to give an authentic café feel to the converted shop. When we got to the supermarket, I pushed the trolley as Jodi raced around the aisles, list in hand and a very determined look in her eyes. I got bored at the ketchup stage and went into a mini-trance but snapped out of it when I saw her load about twelve packs of serviettes.

"Do you realise there are fifty serviettes in each pack? How many people are you expecting? Six hundred?"

She stopped long enough to glance at her list. "Twenty adults plus or minus five very messy children," she said before she dashed off again to get something else. I glanced at my watch. We had been away from The Cabin an hour and ten minutes by now. If we finished here quickly, we would just about have time to grab a coffee before going back.

"Enough, Jodi. Gas cylinders for the barbeque and we're finished. I'm going to throw a tantrum if I don't have coffee soon."

My tantrums must be more awesome than I realised. She led the way to the check-out without protest, then stacked our purchases into the car as I rang Kieran to check on Finn.

"We're doing fine here. Take your time."

We walked to the nearest pub and ordered two cappuccinos. While we were waiting for them, Jodi leaned towards me and stared into my face.

"Well? What do you think? I know you bumped into her outside The Cabin. Elegant, isn't she?"

She could only be talking about Irene Kirby. Cairnsure had not seen such elegance since she had emigrated. An elegant cow. A viper in designer clothes. A cheat.

"She looks well for her age, I suppose. She's a trouble-maker though. Watch your back, Jodi."

"Why? What did she say to you?"

"That Mom wrote to tell her when Dad died."

"So?"

We stopped talking then as our cappuccinos were brought to the table. I had nothing to say anyway. Jodi knew the history so why was she jumping to the defence of a woman whose cheating in the past was destroying my life now? I stirred my drink and watched as the sprinkled chocolate powder dissolved in the white froth.

"Well, Del? If your mother was courteous enough to contact Irene when your father died, surely you can at least talk civilly to the woman now."

"How in the hell can I be civil to her? It's her fault I'm in this position, waiting for some stranger to examine my spit to find out if I've slept side by side . . ."

Jodi grabbed my hand and squeezed it, almost knocking over my cappuccino in the process. As she did, I became aware that three of the four other customers in the pub were staring at me. The fourth was too drunk, even at this early hour, to focus his eyes but I think he too was trying to steady himself to look in my direction.

"Calm down, Del," she whispered. "You don't want the town knowing your business. If I'd realised you'd react so hysterically, I wouldn't have invited Irene and Eoin to the party tomorrow."

"You didn't! You knew Mom would be there! And me. Why have you invited Irene Kirby? How could you have done that to us?"

Jodi sat back and glared at me. I saw anger as intense as my own reflected back at me.

"Just get over yourself, Adele. Remember we're doing this for Carla."

"Irene Kirby never even met Carla."

"Eoin doesn't know her either but he's allowed us to use his building. Doesn't that tell you anything about the Kirbys? It would be rude not to invite them. And while you're agonising over your own problems, remember my mother and father will be there too. I'll have to face them."

I pushed my cappuccino away from me. It wasn't having the usual uplifting effect. Fiddling with my spoon, I thought about what Jodi had just said. I was terrified at the thought of another confrontation with Irene Kirby, hated coming face to face with Eoin and the things I had done with him. Hated admitting that the man I had briefly thought to be my perfect partner might be my brother. Might be. That was the difference between Jodi and me. However improbable, I still had hope. The DNA test could yet prove that Eoin was not my brother at all. Jodi did not have that get-out clause. Nor did Carla. Jodi had been a battered child and would have to face her abusers. Carla had cancer and there was no escaping that. Of the three of us, Carla, Jodi and me, I held the best hand. I looked across at Jodi and smiled.

"You're right, Jode. I'm sorry. If you and Carla can cope, then so can I. And I know Sissy is stronger than she looks. She'll be okay. We all will. Carla too once her treatment is finished."

"She really is improving, isn't she? Even Harry seems more positive."

"It must be awful for him. We're only feeling a fraction of what he's going through and you know how devastated we are."

I looked at my watch and drained the last of my cappuccino. "Come on. We'd better get back and see what Finn's done to our lovely white paper."

Three pairs of eyes followed us with interest as we left the pub and the fourth pair was trying but again not succeeding in focusing. I wondered for an instant what they thought of me and my spit. Then I suddenly realised that it didn't matter what these strangers thought of me and my very attractive dark-haired friend. Nothing mattered except that tomorrow would be one of the happiest days Carla Selby ever had.

* * *

We were almost back as far as the prom when Kieran rang. I immediately anticipated disaster when I saw his name flash on my screen.

"Carla has just driven by with Vera and the other children," he said. "They're gone to the beach now but be careful. She had a good long look as she passed here. Just as well the window is blanked out."

I sighed with relief. Finn had not fallen and hurt himself or gone berserk with one of his temper tantrums.

"We'll park a bit away from The Cabin just to be sure. She thinks Finn and I are gone to my Aunt Lily's farm."

"Quite the plotter, aren't you? Is Jodi coming back with you?"

"We'll both see you in a few minutes."

As Jodi and I walked to The Cabin, I wondered if I should talk to her about the tension between herself and

Kieran or just leave it to her to work out that she was jealous of Norma Higgins. I kept my mouth shut as I scanned the beach area. In the distance I could see Carla's four-by-four parked near the dunes. It was at an angle and had an abandoned air about it. I shivered.

When we opened the door to The Cabin, Jodi and I just stood there, mouth open, staring. To our left, the terracotta pretend-tile floor space was dotted with tables and chairs. To the right the counter glowed with the patina of aged timber. Elliots' old shop gave a good impression of a rustic café with a French feel about it. Except for the wall opposite the door. The one where Kieran and the two children were so busily painting that they didn't even notice us when we came in. Kieran was standing on the top of the stepladder, Finn and Amy on the floor at either side of him. A rainbow spanned almost half the wall, glowing with colours even nature would envy. Underneath it butterflies, or at least good imitations of them, fluttered and flew in all directions. Finn had achieved what he had set out to do. He had given his mother something special.

"Jesus Christ!" Jodi muttered underneath her breath.

"Not a word!" I whispered. "Not one word!"

Finn heard us and turned towards us.

"What do you think, Adele? Mum's going to love it, isn't she?"

I moved nearer to the mural and examined it. Up close I could see the pencilled outlines of butterflies which the children were filling in with colour. The outlines were so realistic I knew they were Kieran's handiwork. I wondered how Finn had allowed Kieran to have so much input in his special wall. They must have forged a very trusting relationship.

"It's very beautiful," I said and I meant it. Finn had been right. I could see that now. The old Cabin had suddenly come to life with rainbows and butterflies. And that's what Carla was. A butterfly. Delicate and very beautiful. The café had become a Carla space, a place of magic.

"This is going to be her best surprise, Finn. She'll be so proud. Her very own magic wall."

He gave me one of his calculating looks. The look that said this woman is stupid.

"Told you before there's no such thing as magic."

"Is too," Amy said.

"Not."

"Is too."

This to-ing and fro-ing could have gone on for ever except that Kieran said he and Amy had to go.

"I mightn't get all the butterflies done, Kieran," said Finn. "Would you finish them if I'm not here?"

I looked in surprise at Finn. It was so unlike him to allow anyone else interfere in something he was doing. Kieran Mahon seemed to have a way with children. But not with women. At least not with Jodi. She was busily tearing open packets and putting cloths on the tables, so studiously ignoring Kieran that it drew more attention than if she had been fawning over him. Several times she glanced from her tastefully discreet wine-and-white checked cloths to the riot of colour on the wall but had the sense not to complain.

"I'll see you both later so," Kieran said. "I shouldn't be too long. Just a book launch and a prize-giving to cover."

"I won't be here," Jodi announced. "I'm going out tonight."

She didn't have to say any more. Kieran and I exchanged glances. We both knew she would be meeting the Kirbys. Not in an employer-employee way but in an out-on-the-town sense. Just what was going on between Jodi Wall and the Kirbys? And why? Eoin had been good to give her a job. More than good. He knew her story. Knew she could be a liability as much as an asset and he was generous to give her a chance. But had generosity been his motivation? If the horrible spectre of his possible blood relationship to me hadn't arisen, would he still be taking me for picnics and swims or would he, just like Kieran had done, have fallen prey to Jodi's fragile beauty?

"Have a good time then," Kieran said so lightly that I envied his control. "See you tomorrow. See you later, Adele. Unless of course you're going out too."

"I'll be here. I cancelled all my dates."

"Me too," he laughed and then winked at me.

I couldn't help winking back. I can never help myself from reacting and responding. And that, I thought, as I picked up a narrow little paintbrush to help Finn with his butterflies, is Adele Burke's main problem in life.

* * *

When we were sure that Carla and her gang had left the beach, I drove my car back to the Cabin and unpacked the shopping. Jodi decided then to go check with the people who were supplying ware, cutlery and food for tomorrow. My mother, Carla's Mom and Jodi's own mother.

"I'll call to your parents' house if you don't want to go there," I offered.

Jodi shook her head and smiled at me. "Thanks, Del, but there's no need. The hypocrites are in the church as usual. My sisters will be home. The girls are doing the work anyway. I have them making coleslaw and potato salad. I'd better run. I must make the calls and still be ready for six thirty. We're going to the Opera House in Cork."

"We?"

"Eoin, Irene and myself. Must rush. I'll let everyone know six tomorrow evening is kick-off time. Harry's going to tell Carla he wants to bring her out to dinner so that she can rest in the afternoon if she needs to. See you at nine in the morning."

Then she was gone. On a date with the two Kirbys. She would probably wear one of her barely-there dresses and sit beside Eoin in a cloud of fragrance, her shiny dark head on his shoulder. Maybe not. Not with his mother seated on the other side. What did I care anyway? If she wanted to shag the man who was my brother, she had every right. If she wanted to shag the man who had, so briefly, been my boyfriend, then I suppose she had that right too.

I picked up my paintbrush again and joined Finn in painting butterflies' wings. I needed to be a child for a while. I needed the fantasy of Carla's magic wall.

* * *

When I brought Finn back home I was happy to see Carla

look even better after her day out on the beach. Finn ran to her and threw himself into her arms. Carla hugged him close to her. When I saw the two blonde heads so close together I felt hope. I had faith. I knew that nothing, not distance and certainly not illness could separate these two, mother and son. No disease, no matter how lethal, would be strong enough to break their powerful bond. Carla was stroking her child's hair, pushing the fine strands back from his forehead.

"Did you enjoy the farm, Finn? What did you see?"

"Butterflies. Loads of them."

"Oh, you lucky thing! Wish I'd been there. You know I love them."

"That's what I told Adele," Finn said as he smiled slyly at me from the circle of his mother's arms.

I left them then, telling them I'd let myself out. I took with me the new hope I felt in Carla's future.

* * *

Mom rang with a dinner alert as I was driving away from Selbys'.

"I've a nice roast done, Adele. You can't keep working the way you are and not eating properly. Come home."

She was surprised when I told her I was on the way. And I had more surprises in store for her. Sissy was going to tell me whether she had written to Irene Kirby or not. I'd drag the truth out of her, whatever it took.

Tom Reagan was seated at the table when I went in. Sissy was fussing between cooker and table, heaping plates with meat and roast vegetables. Tom looked tired and little wonder. The work he and Ned Lehane had done on The Cabin would have been an effort for men thirty years their junior.

"Carla's in great form," I told them. "I've just been talking to her. She seems to be responding really well to whatever treatment she's on."

"What did I tell you? God is good."

I let that remark from my mother pass. I was too hungry to argue with her now. Dinner was delicious but I noticed that Tom wasn't eating much. I examined his face again. The lines I had thought to be from exhaustion seemed far deeper and sadder than just overwork. He was quiet, no trace of his usually ready smile.

"What's wrong, Tom? Have you been working too hard in The Cabin?"

"He's sulking," Mom said. "He wants to get his own way all the time."

I pushed my plate, now scraped clean, away from me and laughed. "Tom, if you're going to marry Sissy Burke, you'll have to learn her way is the only acceptable one."

I had meant my comment to be funny. An amusing aside. Tom didn't laugh. Neither did Mom. I now picked up on a frosty atmosphere between them. I should have noticed earlier. I began to feel uncomfortable stuck in the middle of a lovers' tiff, made even more uncomfortable by the fact that the lovers were my elderly mother and her fiancé. I felt in the way and wondered if I should just go and leave them to sort out their differences. But I had come here to find out about the letter to Irene Kirby and I wouldn't go without doing so.

"You must have a cup of tea and cheesecake, Adele." Mom said. "You're getting haggard-looking."

I had lost weight – I knew that from loose waistbands – but I was a long way from haggard.

"I met Irene Kirby today, Mom."

She was cutting huge wedges of cheesecake and putting them on plates. I wasn't sure whether she had heard me or not.

"She's pretending not to hear," Tom said sourly. He was obviously getting to know my mother very well.

"She said you wrote to her to tell her Dad had died. Was she telling the truth?"

Mom walked to the table and placed cheesecake smothered in cream in front of me. Then she just stood there, her hands joined, her eyebrows drawn together.

"You should have seen the get-up of Jodi Wall this evening. I've never seen so little material in a dress. I don't think she was wearing any undergarments. I don't know what the world is coming to."

I stared up at her. She wasn't going to sidetrack me, no matter how hard she tried.

"Eoin and Irene Kirby will be at Carla's party tomorrow. Do you want me to ask her in front of you about the letter or are you going to tell me now?"

Her hands fell to her sides and her eyes opened wide. "Sweet Mother of God! What have you done, Adele? Why did you invite them?"

"It's their shop," Tom said. "They've more right to be there than anyone else."

Mom went back to the counter in a flounce. She

came back to the table and slapped a plate of cheesecake in front of Tom.

"Next you'll be telling me the siren is really a nice woman. A saint."

I saw what she was doing. Avoiding the letter issue. I stood up and looked down on her, as determined that she answer my question as she was to avoid it.

"Did you write to Irene Kirby? Have you been in touch with the woman you say you won't even speak to now? The woman you said you've never had contact with since she left Cairnsure thirty-five years ago?"

Mom lowered her eyes. I had my answer. She had indeed written to Irene.

"I had to let her know the man who might be father of her eldest child had died, didn't I? I am a Christian."

I felt a wave of resentment against my father. How could he have done this to Mom? And now to me? How could he have been so kind and gentle, so caring and yet so deceitful? I hadn't known my father at all. And that's what hurt the most. But I knew Mom and all her peculiar little ways. As I looked down at her bowed head, I felt a love for her which was tinged with pity. My father had put her through humiliation and suffering. I would not do the same. I put my arms around her and hugged her close to me.

"Did she write back to you?" I asked.

"No. Not a word. I didn't want to hear from her anyway. I just wanted to do the right thing."

That statement had a ring of truth about it. Sissy always wanted to do the right thing. The decent thing. But it had to be her concept of what was right and proper. Black and white. And yet she looked anything but certain now.

"I don't know how I'll cope with meeting her again," she said and her voice shook with an emotion I suspected was fear.

"It'll be okay, Mom. You won't have to talk to Irene tomorrow. I'll make sure she stays away from you. Anyway, she may not even come. She doesn't know Carla and we're not sophisticated enough for her."

"She'll be there. Irene Kirby wouldn't miss that opportunity to lord it over everyone. What she's doing in Cairnsure after all these years, I don't know."

"It's got to do with all the property they're buying. She's the boss in their company."

"She always was. And the boy, Eoin. Does he take after her in personality?"

I thought about that. Eoin had no trace of his mother in him except his brown eyes and height. He was gentle. Kind. Fair-haired. Just like my father.

"He's like Dad," I said and then regretted my honesty as tears welled in Mom's eyes.

"That's why you have to move out of here when we marry," Tom said. "You must finally put all this behind you, Sissy. You'll never do that while you're living in John Burke's house."

Now I knew what the frosty atmosphere was about. I agreed with Tom but had no intention of saying so. That was an issue only they could work out. I kissed Mom on the top of her lacquered hair.

"I'm going to see Aunt Lily, then I'm going back to The Cabin. I must paint butterflies and rainbows."

It was a measure of how upset both Mom and Tom were that neither asked had I gone completely mad.

* * *

"I was watching the News," Aunt Lily grumbled as she led the way reluctantly into her sitting room. I noticed a footstool in front of her armchair and wondered if her sore leg was paining her.

"I won't keep you long, Lily. I just wanted to make sure you have a lift to The Cabin tomorrow evening."

"What would I want to be going there for?"

"Why not? It's because of Ned Lehane the garden looks as well as it does now. I want you to see Carla's face when she goes out there. Anyway, you'd enjoy the evening. You'll know every one. Even Irene Kirby."

"Is Sissy Roberts going?"

"Of course."

"Then I'll go to see what happens between the two of them."

"Aunt Lily! I hope you come for Carla's sake and mine but don't go causing any trouble."

"The trouble was caused a long time ago, young woman. Long before you were born. I wasn't the trouble-maker then and I'm not now. Remember I've lost two brothers before their time because of those two women. I'd love to see them finish each other off."

She eased herself onto her chair then and slowly raised her bandaged leg onto the stool.

"Any results yet of that test you were telling me about?" she asked.

"No. But I'm preparing myself for the news that Eoin Kirby was my father's son. He's probably my half-brother and I'll have to live with that curse for the rest of my life. That would make him your nephew, sort of."

"How can you know for certain without the science thing? Surely you're not depending on someone else's word. Especially not Sissy Roberts."

I was torn between trying to understand Aunt Lily and wanting to murder her. Flight was my best option.

"I must go. You never said whether you wanted a lift or not."

"Ned Lehane will drive me."

"Stay there. I'll let myself out."

She sat staring at the screen, obviously having no intention of moving.

"Bye, Lily."

"Has she kept her looks, Irene Kirby?"

"Yes. She's very attractive. Even now."

"That was always your mother's problem. Jealousy. Sissy had lovely hair but not much else going for her except her determination to best Irene Kirby. I hope she's happy with herself now."

I walked away, trying but failing to remember how close I had felt to Aunt Lily recently. I had a bellyful of these old people and their secret pasts. I needed butterflies and rainbows to restore some peace to my confused mind.

* * *

Kieran Mahon was already in The Cabin when I got

there. He was up on the stepladder again, carefully filling in colours more intense than any rainbow that had ever graced a moisture-laden sky.

"You're on butterfly duty," he said. "Try to fill in the spaces the children left and put designs on where they daubed paint."

"But it's meant to be their work. Do you really think we should interfere with it?"

"Why do you think Finn asked us to finish it? He wants it as perfect as possible for Carla."

He was probably right. Finn the perfectionist would want a rainbow with the seven colours and butterflies that could flit from flower to flower. I picked up a brush and began the intricate job.

At some stage I had to turn on the lights because the sun went down leaving The Cabin bathed in eerie dusk. Silently, Kieran and I dabbed and daubed until at last a fluorescent rainbow and beautiful butterflies decorated the wall. We stood back and admired our work.

"Bloody brilliant, even though I say it myself," Kieran said as he examined the rainbow.

"The butterflies make it."

Then we both laughed at our childishness.

"Come on, Adele. We need a walk on the strand. Nothing left to do here except the food tomorrow."

"Jodi has that well in hand. I can't believe we got it all done so quickly. It doesn't look anything like Elliots' old shop now, does it?"

"Carla will love it." He paused. "Do you know where Jodi's gone tonight?"

438

I turned to look at him, my hand on the key of the door I was locking. He was anxious. Sad.

"She's gone to Cork."

"With Eoin Kirby?"

"And his mother."

We walked to the strand in silence, each involved in our own thoughts. I was pretty sure that Eoin Kirby was as central to Kieran's thinking as to mine. We reached the rocks and stood listening to the sea lapping on the shoreline. When Kieran caught my hand, my fingers curled around his. We needed the contact.

"There's something I must tell you, Adele."

I waited, hypnotised by the rhythmic sound of the ever-busy sea. It was a while before I realised Kieran was looking at me, a worried frown on his forehead.

"Yes? What is it?"

"Nothing. Nothing really."

"That's a lot of fuss about nothing. Is it Jodi?"

"Yes. Yes, it is. She's not the girl I thought she was."

"Give her time, Kieran. She's had a lot to cope with."

"I've given her too much time. Years too much. I was in love with a myth. I should have known. Jodi is driven to success. What's happened to her, the drugs and the fallout from them, is just a glitch. She'll pick herself up and be off climbing the ladder again."

"Not as an accountant."

"No. Maybe as a property developer. Or the wife of a property developer."

Wife? Of Eoin Kirby? Jodi? Whatever made Kieran say such a stupid thing. I let go his hand and began the

439

walk back along the strand. He caught up with me and held my arm.

"I'm sorry if I've upset you, Adele. But you should realise by now that Jodi Wall has her sights set on Eoin Kirby. Or rather on his business."

"Don't be ridiculous, Kieran. She barely knows him and, besides, the company belongs to his mother, not him."

"She's courting the mother as well. Don't you see? Your problem is that you're too nice. Suppose Eoin turns out not to be your brother after all? Do you really think Jodi would let him go back to you?"

His patronising tone was too much for me. As was the rubbish he was talking about Jodi. I stood, forcing him to stop and face me.

"How dare you, Kieran Mahon! In the first place, I would never, ever want Eoin Kirby back and, secondly, just because Jodi left you doesn't give you the right to call her a gold-digger! Maybe Eoin's a nicer person than you. More dependable. Stronger. Did you ever think of that?"

He stared as if I had slapped him across the face. Then I turned my back on him and walked away. I didn't want to be angry with Kieran. I had no right to be. He had, after all, saved my life. As I drove home, I remembered him throwing the lifebuoy to me, hauling me across the vicious channel of water, being there for Jodi when she needed him most, painting rainbows with the children. And yet he had really hurt my feelings tonight by implying in the first place that I would ever want to get back with Eoin and that, even if I did, I would have to take second place to Jodi.

I got into bed and cuddled Barry Bear close to me. It seemed at that time that the teddy bear was the only friend I had left in this big, two-faced, deceitful, cruel world.

Chapter 31

I didn't make The Cabin for nine o'clock the following morning as planned. It was nearer ten by the time I managed to drag myself in there, tired and embarrassed at the thought of meeting Kieran Mahon. A quick look around assured me that even though the whole town seemed to be here, Kieran was not. Jodi had taken charge, while her army of sisters, Carla's mother and aunts, my mom and Brigitte, were all following orders. Mom was arranging flowers in the little white vases while the others were unpacking ware and cutlery and stacking it on the counter.

Jodi looked fresh. I hadn't heard her come in last night. Maybe she had stayed over in The Grand Hotel. Right on cue I heard my mother ask her what time she had got back.

"It was late, Sissy. We went for supper after the Opera."

I walked out to the back garden. I needed the air. Tom

and Ned were sitting on their barrel seat again. I carefully avoided meeting Tom's eyes.

"Is the sergeant major still there?" he asked. "We're dying for a cup of tea but it's banned by order of the management."

I assumed he was talking about Jodi. It could have been Mom, of course, but she would have been more likely to be forcing tea on them.

"Stay there," I said. "I'll get it for you."

I went into the little back kitchen which was by now all gleaming white. Even the old Belfast sink sparkled like it hadn't done since it had been new a whole lifetime ago. I put the kettle on, rinsed the mugs Tom and Ned had claimed as their own and stood with my back to the sink waiting for the water to boil. It was nice to hear the buzz of conversation and the clatter of ware from outside. Old Mrs Elliot was probably pirouetting in her grave at the idea of what we had done to her shop.

"There you are! What are you doing hanging around here when there's so much to be done?"

Jodi had her ever-present clipboard in her hand and a frown on her forehead. A pretty frown, complementing her orange top and jeans very well. She could wear anything with style, even a frown.

"Tom and Ned want tea. I'll be with you in a minute."

"That pair do nothing but drink tea and talk about long ago."

"'That pair', as you call them, have broken their backs to clear the garden. Look at the job they've done. They deserve a cuppa."

"Who got out the wrong side of the bed this morning? I keep telling you get a life, Del. You wouldn't be half as moody. Give me a shout as soon as you're ready. We must get meat, milk, cream and loads of other things. Hurry on."

The kettle clicked off just as she left. As I got tea bags, I heard Harry Selby's accented tones. He was admiring the painting his son had done and from what I could hear trying to give a big wad of cash to Jodi to buy the groceries we needed.

"No. Put your money back in your pocket. We've all chipped in. We want to do it for Carla," Mom said and everyone agreed.

Except Jodi. Like Mom, I tilted my head to one side to hear better but Jodi didn't add her voice. I imagined her accountant's brain ticking over and longing to take the offered cash. A taker Jodi was. Of cash and boyfriends. And brothers.

Ashamed of my pettiness, I made the tea, gave it to the odd couple and called Jodi. We embarked then on a frenetic shopping expedition from greengrocer to butcher and every shade of food store in between. When the shopping was finally done and stacked into my car, we realised there was no fridge in The Cabin.

"Shit! We'll have to buy one."

"Like hell," Jodi said. "We'll take the food to your house now. That will do. It'll only be out the few hours of the party."

"No way! I wouldn't leave anything perishable out in this weather."

As we stood arguing in the street, the *Cairnsure Weekly*

van pulled up beside us. Kieran pulled down the window and grinned at us.

"Who's winning? I'd put my money on you, Adele. You've a way with knock-out words."

I looked at his grinning, open face and felt very ashamed of myself. "I'm really sorry about the way I spoke to you last night, Kieran. I don't know what came over me. I didn't mean to . . . I shouldn't have . . ." I trailed off, belatedly realising that Jodi, who was standing beside me, had been the subject of our dispute.

"This is very interesting, Del," she laughed. "What have you done now that you shouldn't have?"

Kieran's smile faded quickly. He shot Jodi a very cold look. "She did most of the work on The Cabin while you were swanning around. That's what she did."

"Oh, shag off, Kieran! There's no need to insult me just because I moved out of your apartment. Anyway, Adele has a lot more time on her hands than I have. I'm working, you know."

"I realise that. After hours too. It's a tough job."

People passing by were beginning to stare. Jodi usually attracted attention, but for her looks, not for bad temper. In an effort to calm things down I asked Kieran if there were any second-hand fridges in the *Cairnsure Weekly* "For Sale" column.

"As a matter of fact, yes, there is one. I know the couple selling it. They've just put in a new kitchen. Do you need one?"

"For The Cabin. We should have thought of it earlier. A small one would fit in the back kitchen."

"Jump in. I'll take you to the house. It's only minutes away. We'll see you at The Cabin, Jodi."

Before I had any more time to think, I found myself sitting in the *Cairnsure Weekly* van beside Kieran Mahon, on my way to buy a second-hand fridge, while Jodi Wall fumed on the pavement, the car keys I had thrown her dangling in her hand. She still looked beautiful.

* * *

When we got back to The Cabin, it all seemed worthwhile. All the scrubbing and sanding and painting. I stood at the door and looked around. The tables were perfect with their checked cloths and Mom's flower arrangements in the centre, the counter had trays and cutlery wrapped in serviettes laid out, while Finn's wall added a touch of magic to the café-for-a-day. I knew of course that the storeroom in the back was now piled high with leftover wallpaper, paint, tools and everything else we had used to achieve this result. It was a mess but it was out of sight. The old shop was transformed into the new café.

I could hear a lot of roaring and shouting from outside as Kieran, Tom and Ned made heavy work of bringing the fridge in the side gate. Jodi was still running around, ticking off items as she checked our shopping. Everyone else had gone home to bake, mix or peel the food they had arranged to bring for the party. The Three Wise Men finally got the fridge plugged in and, when it was cleaned, we stacked it. There just didn't seem to be anything else to do.

"What about the window? Are we going to leave it with that awful white gunk on or are we going to clean it?"

"Leave it, of course. We don't want strollers on the prom staring in at us," Jodi snapped.

"A net curtain," I said. "We should have thought of that too."

I was really annoyed with myself. That was two essential items I had overlooked. Kieran was already measuring the window and Ned had started to clean it. It took me all of fifteen minutes to buy a curtain, wire and hooks. We were just standing back to admire the finished effect when my phone rang. I answered impatiently, knowing it was Mom with some last-minute drama. I was wrong. It was Eoin Kirby.

"I need to see you urgently, Adele. Where can we meet? I'd prefer somewhere private."

I was paralysed with terror. Private. Urgent. It must be the results of the DNA test. What else could it be? But there was no postal delivery in Cairnsure on Saturday. How could Eoin have his results? Courier of course. Money made things happen quickly.

"Adele? Are you there? Can you meet me?"

I glanced through the now clean window. The tide was out. Where else could I meet Eoin Kirby except in the spot that had so recently almost claimed my life.

"Over near the rocks on the East Beach. Do you know where that is?"

"I'll see you there in ten minutes."

He cut off the call without another word.

"Jesus, Del! You're like a ghost. What's wrong? Not bad news, I hope."

"I hope not," I answered Jodi and walked out of the Cabin, not caring that they were all staring after me in puzzlement. They couldn't have guessed at a fraction of the confusion I felt as I went to meet Eoin Kirby.

* * *

Because it was Saturday and also sunny, the beach was packed. Not the privacy Eoin had asked for. The sand seemed to suck my feet down as I walked through it. Even my normally strong calf muscles were aching. I wished the sand would swallow me. I even imagined it dragging me down, burying me, choking the life out of me. I knew. I didn't have to see the results or talk to Eoin. Beyond reasonable doubt. Two different mothers but the same father. John Burke. That mild-mannered, kindest of men who had been a cheat and a liar. My father, Eoin's father. Carpenter, husband, father and philanderer. A weak man. As my knees shook and my heart thumped, I admitted I had inherited that weakness from him. I was always the one to agree, to take the least line of resistance. I had none of my mother's strength. It must have been so easy for Irene Kirby to entice Dad. He wouldn't have known how to say no.

When I reached the rocks, I sat down to wait. It was quieter over here, most people preferring to stay on the strand. I saw Eoin stride across the dunes. He was rushing towards me and I longed for him to slow down, to put the awful moment off. The only thought that kept me sitting there was that we had not fallen foul of the ultimate taboo. We had not had sex. Maybe that would calm his anger too when he took time to look at it that way.

"Thank you for meeting me, Adele."

His speech was clipped. Polite. Cold. He sat down beside me, reached into the pocket of his trousers and handed me an envelope.

"That's your copy of the DNA test, as requested."

The envelope shook in my hand as if a strong gale was blowing it.

"Tell me. What's in it? What does it say?"

"Read it yourself."

I read my name on the envelope and the large block print which said PRIVATE & CONFIDENTIAL. My fingers trembled as I slit the envelope and took out several sheets of paper. The top sheet was a letter headed with the testing-company logo. I looked at the words and they meant no more to me than if they had been written in Chinese. I tried again, this time breathing deeply to calm myself. I knew, of course I knew. Irene Kirby had warned Sissy and Sissy had warned me. But that had left room for doubt. For hope. Now there was no escaping the biochemical analysis. No hope in the cold black letters.

Words began to emerge from the blurred jumble. Analysis ... criteria ... no match ... not sibling ... I squeezed my eyes shut and then opened them quickly. Those precious words were still there. "We can state beyond reasonable doubt that the samples do not indicate any of the characteristics of sibling DNA. See attached for . . ."

I began to cry then, my tears falling in big drops onto

the letter. Eoin put his arm around my shoulder. I moved away from him. This was too new, too unexpected. Part of me still felt he was my brother and I did not want him to touch me.

"Now you see why I didn't want you to involve my mother in this. She would have been so upset. And for no reason."

"Heaven forbid that we'd upset Irene Kirby, especially since this is all her fault anyway!"

Anger blazed in Eoin's eyes. How had I ever thought him to be like my father? I had never, not even once, seen John Burke lose his temper.

"You can let the vendetta drop now, Adele. John Burke is not my father. My mother did not sleep with him."

"You don't know that. Just because he's not your father doesn't mean they didn't sleep together. Cheating on my mother and your father. Sissy has gone through hell for years and years. You know Irene told her John Burke might be your father. My mother didn't make that up. Why should she?"

"Money? Maybe she thought it worth her while."

I realised then I should be slapping Eoin Kirby across the face now. But I could not tolerate violence and I didn't want any contact with him. Even the briefest of touches.

"Go away. I don't ever want to see you again."

He didn't go. He moved closer to me. "I'm sorry, Adele. I should never have said that. It was unforgivable."

"It was."

"I'm very sorry. Your mother is a good person. I'm sure your father was too. The whole episode has been a nightmare. Neither of us is behaving normally now."

"Let's just leave it at that, Eoin. I need some time on my own."

"It could have been different, couldn't it? We were getting on so well until . . . well, until the whole question of our parentage came up."

I thought back over the last times we had been on this beach together. The wonderful swim in the rain, the after-dinner stroll at the water's edge. The gentle kiss. Even now, with the DNA results in my hand, my stomach heaved at the thought of the kisses we had shared and the night I had slept in his arms. The night I found out Carla had cancer. I looked at him and noticed that he seemed thinner, a little older. We had both suffered through this not knowing. I smiled at him.

"You were there when I needed you, Eoin. When I was so upset about Carla. When Jodi was in trouble. I appreciate that. I'm sure in time we'll learn to be friends. It's just all so raw now."

I saw his shoulders relax and heard a little sigh of relief escape him. So! Eoin had feared that I would want to take up where we had left off. Flirting, cuddling, exploratory kisses. Getting to know each other.

I read my letter again. Just to be really sure. Then I tucked it back into the envelope and stowed it safely away into my pocket.

"I hope we can see our way to being friends, Adele. I'll be visiting Cairnsure a lot over the next few years.

My mother has given the go-ahead for the development so I'll be keeping an eye on it."

"Will Jodi be your agent here? Your PA or whatever?"

He looked out to sea. Avoided eye contact. "I'm not sure yet what position Jodi will have in the company."

Of course. She was on trial, wasn't she? They were just waiting to see if she would rob them blind or go on a drug spree. I opened my mouth to warn him, to plead with him to handle Jodi carefully, to respect her fragility. I closed it again very quickly. I had no right to interfere like that. Eoin Kirby had shown Jodi nothing but kindness and understanding so far. There was no reason to believe he would not continue to do so. The rest was up to Jodi. And of course, Irene Kirby. She would be the one to decide.

He stood up and I was relieved. He looked down at me, his brown eyes so dark now that it was hard to read any emotion from them.

"I hope you don't mind my mother and me being at the party this evening. Mum wanted to go so I couldn't say no."

"Not at all. You must be there. You made it possible, didn't you? Besides, I need to have a word with Irene Kirby."

"Please, Adele. It's all over now. Just let it go."

"What about my mother? Are you telling me forget that? How can I?"

"It's between your mother and mine. Let them sort it out if they want to. We have no idea what really

452

happened all those years ago. It's their business. Not ours. No point in you interfering."

Interfering! Had he any idea at all what Sissy and I had suffered because of his mother? Why could he not see the trouble Irene had caused? As I sat there, staring at the man I had so recently believed to be my brother, this handsome, kind, sensitive yet weak man, I realised that he would never admit Irene Kirby had done wrong. Nor would I openly apportion any blame to Sissy Burke. Stalemate. Perhaps the best, the only choice, was to try to get on with life as it used to be. I was ready to wave the white flag.

"As long as your mother never upsets mine again, we'll agree to leave the past where it belongs. Agreed?"

"And ditto. My mother has more important things to concern her anyway."

Bitter replies sprang to mind but I held them back, reminding myself that the DNA results were all that mattered now. I managed to smile at him.

"See you later then."

He stood awkwardly for a moment, as if not sure how to say goodbye to the woman who was no longer his half-sister. Then he turned his back and walked away.

I watched him for a little while and then I closed my eyes. I was waiting for the elation. All I could feel was sadness. So Dad had not fathered a baby with Irene Kirby but did he have an affair with her? Why else would Irene have told Mom that the baby she was carrying could be John Burke's? The shadow of the events of thirty-five years ago hung over my head, blocking out the relief I should be feeling. I kept hearing Eoin's words repeating over in my head. "We have no idea what really happened all those years ago."

"Are you all right, Adele?"

I started in fright and opened my eyes to see Kieran standing over me, a very concerned look on his face. I felt it then, the elusive elation.

"He's not my brother! I'm not his sister. John Burke was not his father!"

"That's great news, Adele. You must be relieved."

I stood up and straightened my shoulders, proud again to be Adele Burke. I smiled at Kieran.

"Relieved is putting it too mildly. I'm ecstatic!"

"Do you think then you and Eoin will get back together?"

"Never. I was telling you the truth last night. In fact, I'm off men for life. This time I mean it."

Kieran took out his reporter's notebook and began to scribble.

"What the hell are you doing?" I asked.

"I'm writing down what you just said about being off men for life. I want to remind you when I see you arm in arm with someone."

I gave him a push which was meant to be playful but it caught him off balance and nearly knocked him off his feet. I began to laugh and run, chased by Kieran. People looked askance at the adults playing chase along the beach but I didn't care. I was again, as I always had been, my father's only child.

* * *

The Cabin was locked up when we got back there, window sparkling, net curtains gleaming and a sign on the door which said CLOSED.

"You got a sign?" I asked Kieran, wondering what we would have done without him.

"Yes. It should keep all the would-be customers away. The rest of the gang are gone to get ready. We're back here at five to get the barbeque going. Harry's bringing Carla along at six. Scram now and make yourself beautiful."

That's when I began to wonder what I'd wear. Glancing at my watch I saw that I would have time for a quick visit to town. Cairnsure at that stage had four boutiques and a chain store. Surely I could grab something which would fit and flatter.

"See you at five, Kieran. And thanks."

I jumped into my car and headed for the town. Forty minutes later I had bought a red sleeveless dress and red sandals. The dress was V-necked, dipping low at the back, nipped in at the waist and fitted like a second skin. I twirled in front of the boutique mirror and noticed how toned all the walking and wallpapering had made me. I rushed back to my car and headed home as fast as speed limits allowed me go.

* * *

Mom was in a tizzy. Every available surface in the kitchen was taken up with carefully wrapped baking.

"Sit down for a minute, Mom. I've something to tell you."

"I've no time for sitting around, Adele. What is it?"

455

"It's good news. The best. But you'll definitely have to sit to hear it."

She sighed impatiently but sat anyway, perched like a bird on the edge of her chair.

"The DNA test results are back. Dad is not Eoin's father."

Her eyes and mouth opened wide and the colour drained from her face. I don't think she understood what I had said.

"Eoin and I are not brother and sister, Mom."

She began her rapid signing of the cross, her hands flying and her lips moving silently. I wondered if she had gone into shock. Jesus!

"Are you all right, Mom? Say something!"

She looked up at me, tears in her eyes. "Are you sure? Did the scientists say you are really not brother and sister?"

"Without a doubt. We couldn't be related to each other."

I should have pointed out to her that the results did not mean that Dad had not slept with Irene Kirby. That Dad could well have cheated. Looking at her tear-filled eyes and pale face, I knew Mom had gone through enough. And she would always, always, no matter what, believe what she wanted to anyway.

"Irene Kirby did a terrible wrong," she said.

"Just try to put it out of your mind now, Mom. Irene Kirby isn't worth getting upset about."

"She never was. But at least it's over now. Your father can rest in peace."

I made a cup of tea for her, worried about how pale her face was and how red the spots on her cheeks.

"Why don't you go for a rest, Mom? You could have an hour or so before the party. Will you be able to cope with Irene Kirby being there?"

"I'll just ignore her. She's a tramp. She always was and always will be. I don't want to have anything to do with her. Or her son."

"She probably won't stay long. Our little barbeque won't be her style. Maybe you could slip away for a while to avoid her."

"I never ran away from anyone in my life and I'm not going to start now. Go and get yourself ready. You're a show in those running shoes and sports pants."

I smiled at her, relieved. She was going to be okay. I hugged her, being careful not to disturb her hair, and then went to get ready.

* * *

The Cabin was bedlam by quarter to six. Mom, dressed in her special-occasion lilac silk suit, kept moving things around and Carla's mother kept putting them back. Jodi was counting everything that stood still and her sisters were teasing her by hiding things and then making them reappear. Outside in the garden, Tom and Kieran had the barbeque heating up and judging by the appetising smell they were doing a trial run with some steaks and burgers. The other men had escaped the flurry inside and congregated there, Jodi's father dominating the conversation. I brought my CD player out to them and told them to organise the music.

I was in the back kitchen, Kieran's daughter helping me to fold serviettes, when Brigitte and Vera arrived with the children. Amy abandoned me immediately to go to Finn. They didn't speak. Just stood side by side in front of their rainbow and butterfly wall and studied it. The twins were shy in the crowd, clinging onto Vera. Lisa was wearing a yellow dress and had her fine blonde hair in a wispy little topknot. I promised myself I would get to cuddle her before the evening was out.

Just as I was about to bring the folded serviettes to the tables, I noticed a peculiar smell. I sniffed. Gas! Definitely gas. In a panic I made for the back door. The cylinders were there. The smell got stronger but it was coming from behind me now. I turned to see Ned Lehane and Aunt Lily. Lily was solemn-faced and surrounded by a cloud of noxious fumes. One look at her suit told me the cause of the smell. It was the same suit she had worn for my Holy Communion. Twenty-three years ago! It must have spent the intervening years swaddled in equally ancient mothballs. The camphor whiff was overpowering.

"I'm just taking Lily out to the garden to give her an airing," Ned said as he winked and passed me by.

"Thank you for coming," I said to Lily as she neared me, head in the air.

"I didn't come for you," she said.

I put my hand on her arm and got as close to her as I could tolerate.

"I got the results of my test," I whispered.

"Well?"

"Eoin Kirby is not related to me at all."

Her chin lifted even higher. "What did I tell you?

458

Your father was a decent man. You should not have doubted him."

Aunt Lily had never learned the art of whispering. I looked around me in panic to see if anyone was listening. Noticing that Ned had somehow slunk off and left her to me, I brought her out to the back garden. The mothball smell was less overpowering there. At least we wouldn't be bothered by insects.

I heard Jodi call my name, urgency in her voice. I ran back inside.

"They're here! Carla and Harry. They're just parking outside. Everybody quiet!"

We gathered our little group together in our café-for-a-day and lined up inside the front door. There was a gentle tap on the door from outside.

I nudged Finn forward and he opened the door. Carla just stood there, looking from face to face, from the tables to the counter. She seemed confused, even a little shocked, until her eyes were drawn to the rainbow wall. A broad smile lit her face. "Butterflies! I love butterflies! And rainbows."

Finn tugged her by the hand until she was standing in front of the wall, near enough to touch it.

"I did it for you, Mum," he said. "I wanted you to have it for your special day."

Carla stooped down to hug her son. "It's beautiful, Finn. Thank you so much."

"Amy helped me a little bit."

"A big bit," Amy said, quite loudly for her.

Jodi tapped the counter with a spoon for silence. She

took centre-stage as Eoin and Irene Kirby arrived in the door, apologising for being late.

"Just a small speech, Carla," Jodi said. "Your friends and family want you to know how much you mean to us so we've opened this café especially for you today. On one condition. That you get better soon and open a café for real! There's loads of food and the boys are barbequing out in the garden. Everyone, most of all you, Carla, have a good time. Enjoy."

There were tears in Carla's eyes as we clapped. Her smile was radiant. She had never looked more delicately beautiful, the white linen pants and pink chiffon top softening the angular thinness of her body.

"Thank you. Thank you all so much. I can't believe the trouble you've gone to. The least I can do after all this is to get better as quickly as possible. I promise you I'm fighting every step of the way."

There was a pause, a moment when everyone one there was silenced by the thought of Carla's lonely fight. Harry clapped and we all followed suit.

"Burgers and steaks shortly on the patio," Kieran announced and suddenly everyone sprang into action. Minerals were opened and poured, wine decanted, plates and cutlery handed out.

I heard music coming from the back garden. It was ABBA. A good choice I thought for the mixed group.

And so we wined and dined in Elliots' old shop, laughing, singing, and all loving Carla Selby and wishing her well in what lay ahead. I saw her at one stage, a plate of Sissy's sponge cake in her hand, her head thrown back as she laughed at something Aunt Lily had said and I sensed a new energy in her, a new determination to beat the horrible disease which had threatened to leave her husband widowed, her children motherless and her friends without her. I squeezed my eyes shut and wished as hard as I could that the positive feelings generated this evening would carry her through to victory.

"Taking time out, Adele, or are you in some kind of discomfort?"

I opened my eyes to see Irene Kirby in front of me, an eyebrow raised, her son one respectful step behind her.

"Just thinking about Carla and hoping she'll be well soon," I answered, trying desperately to maintain calm. I felt so gauche beside her sophisticated coolness. I couldn't help glancing at her exposed arms in her sleeveless dress. Not one trace of cellulite. Not even a pucker. How in the hell did she do it?

"You look stunning, Adele. Red suits you," Eoin remarked.

I examined his face for signs of sarcasm. I couldn't see them. He looked sincere.

"Yes. You do clean up rather well, I must agree," Irene added. "The colour is flattering with your dark hair. I notice your mother is here too. I barely recognised her. Amazing what the years do to some people."

Bitch! How dare she sneer at Sissy! I couldn't let her away with that.

"I find it more amazing when the years don't make any changes. Some people never learn."

Jodi, from the other side of the room obviously sensed some bad feeling. She came rushing across.

"Irene, Eoin. I'm sure Adele is thanking you for the use of the shop. I'm very grateful too. Let me introduce you to Carla. Come on."

She shot me a filthy look as she led them away. I shrugged at her and then went to find Mom. I would stand guard over her until Irene Kirby was gone.

The mistake I made was in not keeping an eye on Aunt Lily. I realised that when I heard her raised voice from the garden.

"You've a cheek showing your face in this town again after the way you carried on," she was saying in a very loud voice.

I peeped out the back door to see Lily four square in front of Irene Kirby. Irene was leaning back as if afraid of my aunt. I knew Irene was not afraid of anyone. She was just being overcome by the strong mothball smell. I ran and stood between the two women.

"We're making tea, Lily. You'd better make your own. You won't drink it otherwise. Come on into the kitchen."

"No need to coax me," Lily said crossly. "I'm moving away from here anyway. There's a bad smell around this woman from New Zealand."

Lily stared at Irene Kirby while everyone stared at her and a few, including me, smothered a giggle. Could it be possible Aunt Lily didn't know that Irene smelt of Chanel while she herself reeked of camphor? I led Lily into the kitchen and managed to fit both of us into the tiny space together. By the time she was finished scalding a pot and straining her tea with the strainer she fished from her bag, Irene Kirby had slipped quietly away.

Kieran turned the music up louder and a few began dancing in the garden. Soon everyone was out there, laughing, all joining in the fun. I saw Ned Lehane and Lily take to the grass and do what I think was a tango. Bandaged leg or not Lily could move. I borrowed Lisa from Vera and waltzed her around as she giggled in my arms. When I handed her back I looked for Carla but could see no trace of her. Harry was talking to Kieran, her parents were there but no Carla. I went inside to search. Carla was standing in front of the rainbow wall, Jodi's mum close beside her.

"You must pray, Carla." Mrs Wall was saying. "You must have faith in the power of God."

Carla reached her hand out and gently touched the wing of a butterfly. "I'm putting my faith in magic."

"Your husband wants you in the garden, Mrs Wall," I lied.

She scurried off. Carla looked tired now. Glancing at my watch, I realised it was already after nine o'clock. Time for the children to go home.

"I hope you enjoyed your party, Carla."

"I loved it, Del. Thank you so much. Now I know why your hands were in such a state. Some DIY! Tearing Mrs Elliot's shop and garden asunder."

"Everyone helped. Besides, it was good therapy for me. Especially when all the Eoin Kirby drama was going on. I hadn't a chance to tell you earlier but the DNA results are back. Eoin is not my brother."

"That's great news! Are we going to see the blossoming romance continue so?"

I shook my head. "No. For two reasons. One, I don't think I could ever again see him as a boyfriend, no matter what the DNA said. I believed for a while that he was my brother and I won't forget that awful time in a hurry. And secondly, he's not the man I thought he was. He's handsome and very kind, yes, but he's too much under his mother's thumb for me to respect him."

"Pity. You seemed to be getting on so well."

"There could be a third reason. I'm not sure but I think he and Jodi are getting very cosy."

Carla looked surprised. "Really? I was hoping Jodi and Kieran Mahon would sort out their differences."

"Did I hear my name?" Kieran called from the doorway. He had a camera in his hand and Jodi just behind him.

"All good," I laughed, praying they hadn't heard the rest. "Are you going to take our photo?"

"I want a shot of the three of you lined up under the rainbow."

Jodi joined us in front of Finn's wall. Carla, Jodi and me stood, our arms around each other, the rainbow above us and butterflies all around.

"Magic," Kieran muttered as he focused the lens.

And it was. I felt Carla's bones underneath my hand but I also felt a new strength in her, a determination to beat cancer, a belief that she could. Finn jumped into the frame, beaming proudly.

"Everyone! In here!" Kieran called and the whole group trooped into the picture, smiling, surrounding

Carla with laughter and love. Even Aunt Lily smiled as Ned Lehane, his cap at a jaunty angle stood beside her.

"I'll always remember this," Carla said. "I'm so grateful. But I'm tired now. I'll say goodnight. And thank you. This is the best café in the world."

She hugged each person, and then turned to Jodi and me. "I know everyone helped but you two did the lion's share. Thanks, girls. And thank you, Del, for understanding Finn. I'll see you tomorrow for the post-party gossip. Just like the old days."

Harry took her by the arm then and led her away. She stopped at the door and glanced back at her magic wall. She smiled. A smile full of wonder. Full of hope.

* * *

By eleven o'clock most people had gone. Even my mother had given up on trying to force more food on people. The night was mild, the heat of the day lingering on in the warm breeze. Eoin and Kieran, sitting in the garden at a wrought-iron table, a bottle of wine between them, seemed to be chatting easily. Mom gathered up what was left of her baking and packed it away.

Jodi's sisters decided to go to a club. The only one in Cairnsure. They issued a half-hearted invitation to the rest of us. "All ages go there really. Even older people."

Jodi and I looked at each other and laughed. When had we become the "older people"?

"Off you go. We'll probably have some cocoa here and go to bed after taking out our teeth and hearing aids."

Sissy and Tom went at the same time but only after Sissy had embarrassed me by asking Kieran to see me safely home. Eoin Kirby, Kieran Mahon, Jodi and myself stayed behind, seated at the wrought-iron tables under the silver wash of moonlight. We moved indoors when the breeze began to cool and insects, free of the Aunt Lily exclusion zone, began to bite. We lit candles and drank more wine, laughed, congratulated ourselves on how successful the night had been, how much it had meant to Carla.

Eoin was very good company. He spoke a lot about New Zealand. I sensed pride in what he said. He liked Ireland but it was very clear he loved New Zealand with its sweeping landscape and great swathes of natural beauty. I noticed how Jodi hung on his every word and how Kieran watched her watching Eoin. After at least five glasses of wine I reminded them all that I was there too and I needed someone to look and to listen.

"I'm calling a cab, Adele," Kieran said. "Time I brought you home to your mother."

I stood up then and made my way to the magic wall. The wall of rainbows and butterflies. I leaned in close and saw the brush strokes, each one a labour of love from a son to a mother, from a friend to another precious friend.

"She's going to be all right, isn't she? Our Carla will be well again."

Kieran put his arm around my shoulder and he too looked up at the rainbow and the butterflies.

"You made her very happy tonight, Adele. I wouldn't be surprised if you cured her too."

466

A car hooted outside. The cab. So soon. I was reluctant to go. Slow to leave the warm feeling of Elliots' old shop. Eoin and Jodi were still sitting at a table with its chequered tablecloth and a flickering candle. Jodi seemed at peace in the wavering light. As if she too was cured. The car hooted again and Kieran caught me by the hand.

"C'mon, Adele. It's time to go."

That reminded me of a poem, a quotation, something I had heard a long time ago that I could not quite recall now. Not surprising since walking was proving to be a challenge. I fell asleep in the cab on the short journey home. Kieran shook me awake and walked me to my door, just as he had promised Sissy. I think he kissed my cheek. I remember his head close to mine. Maybe I staggered against him. I fell into bed, make-up on, still smiling, happily drunk.

I slept soundly until the phone rang at thirteen minutes past four.

Chapter 32

The ringing reached me through a fog of alcohol and sleep. I reached out my hand to pick up the phone without opening my eyes.

"This is Harry, Adele. I'm at the hospital."

My eyes flew open and I sat up, my heart drumming. "What's wrong? Is Carla all right?"

"I've bad news."

"Oh, God! Was the party too much for her? Is she sick?"

"Carla died thirty minutes ago."

No! Why was he saying this? Carla was getting better. She was stronger. She said she was fighting. No!

"An embolism. There was nothing we could do."

I didn't want to hear any detail that would make what he was saying true. Not Carla. Not my Carla with the blonde hair and violet-blue eyes. Not Carla with the welcoming smile. Not the children's adoring mother. Not

468

Harry's beloved wife. Harry, with the devastation echoing in his voice. I felt an icy cold wave envelop my body.

"I'm so very sorry, Harry. How can I help?"

"Would you let people know in the morning, please, Adele. I can't face it. Her family know of course but nobody else as yet."

"I will. Don't worry about that. Were you with her when . . . when . . ."

"Yes, I was. She didn't suffer. It was quick and dignified as she would have wanted it."

I gripped the phone so tightly that my knuckles were white. Stupid man! There was no dignity in the decay of death. Why didn't he know that? Carla didn't want to die! She wanted to live for him, for her children. For me. She promised. She wanted to open a café. Damn him!

Realising that shock and hysteria were imminent, I took a deep breath.

"Just ring me, Harry, if there's anything else I can do. The children. Anything."

"Thank you, Adele. I'll contact you in the morning."

Then he was gone, leaving me shivering and cold. Shocked. I got out of bed, slipped on my dressing-gown and headed for the spare bedroom. Jodi would know what to do. I tapped on her door, pushed it in and flicked on the light. The room was empty. She must be in The Grand Hotel with Eoin Kirby. I didn't care. What did that matter now? I continued down the corridor to Mom's room. She opened the door before I could knock, a net on her hair, her lips sucked inwards because her teeth were in the container beside her bed where they spent every night.

469

"I heard the phone," she said. "It could only be bad news at this hour of the morning. What is it?"

I couldn't say the words. I opened my mouth but no sound came out.

"Carla? Is it Carla?"

I nodded. Mom lost all colour from her face. She understood that Carla was gone without me having to say the awful words. I took a step towards her. The movement seemed to trigger my shock. It ripped through me from head to toe, bringing a rush of memories, images of three little girls playing together, planning their future, swearing to be always there for each other. I wailed. Dry-eyed. Without the release of tears. Mom led me to her bed, the one she had shared with Dad for so many years. She sat me down, wrapped her arms around me and rocked me like she used to do when I was small.

"The children," I whimpered. "Finn! Poor Finn."

"They have their father and plenty of help. They'll be grand."

"They need their mother. Harry needs his wife, the Gills need their daughter. I need Carla, Mom. It's not fair. It's not right."

"God was good to her, Adele."

I pulled away from her embrace, so furious that I could have shaken her. "Don't, Mom! Don't give me any of your pious claptrap! How could you say that? Was he good to give her cancer? Is that it? Good to end her life so cruelly when it wasn't even half-lived? Good to take a young mother from her children?"

"We don't understand the ways of God, Adele. But

470

I'll tell you, He spared her wasting away, didn't He? She was young. She could have survived a long time and who knows what suffering she would have gone through."

"So he puts her husband and children through the suffering now instead. I'm glad he's your God, not mine."

She crossed herself quickly, a pained expression on her face. I wasn't being fair. I knew it. But fairness did not belong in this terrible night.

"You're upset, Adele. And angry too. I understand. Why don't you ring Jodi?"

"How do you know she's not here?"

"I saw the way she and Eoin Kirby were looking at each other. I'll make us a cup of tea while you ring."

Quite inappropriately, I laughed. Sissy Burke would never cease to amaze me. So astute in some ways and yet so childlike in her misplaced faith in a cruel God. As soon as I heard the sound of my own laughter, I began to cry. Mom held me as the tears gushed and a huge ball of pain stuck in my throat. I remembered the feel of it. It was the physical manifestation of grief. It had almost choked me when my father died and here it was again, pressing on my gullet, preventing me from breathing. Sissy produced a bundle of tissues for me and then kissed me on my chin.

"You've things to do now, Adele. You can cry later. Go ring Jodi."

I did. Her mobile was switched off. I had to ask the reception desk at the hotel to put me through to Eoin Kirby's room for an emergency call. As soon as I heard his sleepy voice, I couldn't think what to say.

"Hello. Who's there? Hello."

I took a deep breath to steady my voice. "Eoin, it's Adele Burke. I need to speak to Jodi. Do you know where she is?"

I heard a rustle in the background and immediately heard Jodi's voice.

"What is it, Del? Don't tell me you're spying on me!"

"It's Carla."

"How do you mean? What about her?"

My instinct was to shout down the phone at Jodi, to roar as loudly as I could that Carla was dead. That by saying the word I would somehow come to believe it.

"She was taken to hospital tonight. It's not good news, Jode."

"No! It couldn't be. It's not! No!"

Jodi was uttering the same words of denial I had but I knew she had grasped the awful truth a lot more quickly.

"Harry rang. An embolism. She died in the hospital. Some time after three."

I had expected shocked silence, maybe hysterical crying. Instead Jodi sounded efficient and in charge when she spoke.

"Where are you, Del?"

"At home."

"I'll see you soon. I'll get a cab."

When I went to the kitchen Mom was standing by the cooker, her frail shoulders shaking and her face buried in a tea towel. I held her while she cried just as she had me. Her tears were no less bitter because she had a God to thank for sparing Carla from prolonged suffering.

472

Sissy's mourning was as deep as mine and, on that early morning in our kitchen, it was every bit as angry and unforgiving of the fate that had robbed us of our Carla.

Jodi came in and tried to control the situation. Tried to make sense of it, to organise it, to put it on a list of things to do. Then she too cried in my arms. Jodi and me and a cold, painful gap where Carla should be. Like we would always be. Jodi, no Carla and me.

Chapter 33

I went into a trance over the next few days. It's all a dark, murky fog in my memory with just a few splashes of vibrant colour to pierce the gloom; the red butterfly I helped Finn cut from the magic wall of The Cabin, holding the blade for him as he gently peeled off the painted scrap and then bringing it with him to his mother's coffin to place beside her waxen face – "Now she'll always have butterflies," he said; the yellow of dandelions dotting the fields as the funeral wound its way to Cairnsure cemetery; sun sparking golden highlights from the name plaque on her coffin; the piercing blue of the summer sky as Carla was lowered into the grave.

And then it was over. Carla was dead. And buried.

There was a reception after the funeral in The Grand Hotel. The children, who had not attended the service, were there. Little bits of Carla. Lisa, a miniature of her mother. Liam looking up at me with Carla's eyes. And

Finn. Gifted, cursed Finn, asking me if ice can turn into water, and water into steam, steam into rain and back to ice again, why can't his mum go on for ever. Just like water. I asked myself the same question and told him I didn't know the answer.

Brigitte, red-eyed and pale-faced, sought me out in the crowd.

"You were very good friend to her," she said.

"I loved her," I answered from my heart and deeply regretted that I had never told Carla this truth.

"She knew that," Brigitte said. "After the party she say she was the luckiest woman in the world to have such family and friends. She say she love you and Jodi very much."

Perhaps Brigitte was lying. I didn't question what she said. I just took it to my heart and let it be the seed for the healing which I knew would be slow, never complete but inevitable.

"I think the family must be alone with their crying for a little. I'm going home to Hungary to see my people. I come back then after one week to help Selbys get on with their lives."

I smiled at Brigitte. So warm and wise. So kind.

"Lake Balaton must be beautiful at this time of year."

"Yes, it is always. Why don't you come too? My family would be very welcome to you."

I opened my mouth to refuse politely but then I thought of the days stretching out ahead. Brigitte was right. Carla's family would need privacy to mourn. I wouldn't be any help to them now. They would have to come to terms with the reality in their own way. And in their own time. Sissy didn't need me either. She had Tom Reagan and her God. I looked across the function room of the Grand Hotel and saw Eoin Kirby hover behind Jodi, watching her, protecting her. Irene stood aloof, watching them both. Kieran Mahon was talking to Carla's father, Amy by his side. Everyone had someone. Even Aunt Lily had Ned Lehane. I had just my grief. That big black cloud of suffocating sorrow. At that moment I felt as isolated in the crowd as Carla was in her grave.

"Are you sure your family wouldn't mind, Brigitte? I could book into a hotel."

"No. You must stay with me. Carla, she was going to come when I go home. You make the journey for her now. Then you know you do something good for her."

"When do you plan on going?

"Tomorrow. You could get a flight on the internet and if not for the day after."

"If you're sure."

She took my hand and squeezed it. "For Carla," she whispered. "We walk by the Lake and remember the happy time."

I saw Kieran and Amy approach, the little girl looking very lost.

"Finn won't talk to me," she said.

"He's sad today, Amy. We all are. He just wants to be quiet for a little while."

She looked to her father for confirmation of what I'd said. When he nodded agreement, she seemed more content.

"I check on the internet so we be together. I ring later," said Brigitte and then with a wave of her hand she went over to Vera and the children.

"Are you all right, Adele?" Kieran asked.

"No, but I will be. And you?"

"I'm angry. Such a terrible waste. It's so wrong."

He was staring across the room. I followed his gaze to where Harry was now standing, a twin in either arm. He looked old. Drained. More like the twins' grandfather.

"I'm going to Hungary with Brigitte. To Lake Balaton."

"What? For how long? Are you sure that's a good idea?"

"For now, it's the only one I've got. It's just for a week."

"I see. Have you told Jodi?"

"Not yet. I think she'll be fine, don't you?"

We both watched as Eoin Kirby slipped his arm around Jodi's shoulders. She leaned her head against him. She looked so tiny beside him. Irene was still hovering over them. Concerned. They were a family. An alliance of a physically strong man and two mentally strong women. I saw a new depth of sadness cloud Kieran's green eyes. I had reached my limit of sadness.

"I'll see you when I come back, Kieran."

I had run out of capacity for goodbyes. I slipped out of the Grand Hotel, scene of my first Holy Communion lunch, my dinner with Eoin Kirby and Carla's funeral reception. I drove to the prom and parked my car at The Cabin. I kicked the door with its closed sign outside and the memory of Carla's party inside. Then I walked the beach, not caring what carefree day-trippers thought of the woman in the black trouser-suit and high heels as she stumbled through the sand, tears pouring down her face.

For the first time in my life I hated the sea. Hated its playful little ripples that tickled the shore, the gleeful sparkle of sun on the waves. I hated the life, the energy of the sea when inside I felt nothing but death. And not just Carla's death. Part of my childhood had died with her. Memories that only she and I had shared. Those times when Jodi had run home to study and Carla and I had played with my doll's house. The one my father had so lovingly crafted. He was gone too. Only me and the doll's house, now covered in cobwebs in the shed, remained of a childhood which had been so safe and protected. Of the three little girls, Carla, Jodi and me, only Jodi had known how cruel the grown-up world could be. But we all knew now. We knew about drug addiction and cancer and death and loss.

I passed the spot where I had last seen Carla on the beach. So thin in her bikini, the children playing around her. That had been the day we first discussed the idea of opening a café. Stupid idea. The thought that the party had contributed to her death came to the fore again and I walked faster. Harry had assured me it had not been a factor but the thought still haunted me. It rolled in now on every slurping wave. I turned quickly, almost falling much to the amusement of onlookers, and headed back to my car. I had packing to do and a plane to catch. I had an escape to plan.

Chapter 34

Balaton by the lake was a place of drifting days. They melded lazily, each into the other, marked only by sunrise and sunset. It was a place too of healing. We did as Brigitte had known we would: we cried for Carla and for the pain of her passing and then, gradually, as the thermal waters of Lake Balaton shifted ceaselessly in the breeze, we smiled at our happy memories of her.

I spent some time alone too. Brigitte's family were just like her. Warm and welcoming. But I knew she needed time with them and I needed time alone. I walked by the lake, listening to the water splash gently against the stony shores, watching the birds dive and swoop, the boats sail, the couples who walked hand in hand along the surrounding pathways. I began to feel the sun on my face again and the breeze in my hair.

When I looked around me in this lakeside town

called Balatonfüred, I noticed how beautiful the buildings were and how unique the goods on sale in the craft shops. I bought a hand-embroidered dress for Lisa and T-shirts for the boys. I remembered Amy and her serious little face so I bought her a traditional Hungarian doll. For Jodi and Mom, hand-painted glasses. For Aunt Lily a fine wool pashmina. When I saw a ceramic butterfly, its wings etched with splashes of gold, I knew it would be perfect for Carla. For an instant, one wonderful moment of forgetting, I believed she was still alive and waiting for her gift. I left that shop very quickly.

Mom rang. I thought she sounded subdued.

Jodi rang too. "I miss you, Del," she said. "Eoin and Irene are very kind but only you understand."

I knew what she meant. Only we understood just how close the relationship between the three of us had been. Carla and Jodi and me. Three children who together became women and then became two.

"Is Mom okay?" I asked." I thought she sounded a bit down when I talked to her."

"I don't know. She didn't get her hair done this week. That's weird, isn't it? I thought at first it was because I brought Eoin to meet her."

"You what!"

"Oh, stop fussing! They got on very well. They spent ages talking about Michael Kirby and forgetting I was there. She made a Dundee cake specially for him."

I shifted the phone to my other hand to give myself time to think about that. What had brought about Sissy's change of heart towards Eoin Kirby? Could she accept him now because she knew he was not her husband's son? Or was it because he was so obviously with Jodi and not with me?

"Promise me you won't bring Irene Kirby anywhere near her, Jodi. That would really upset her."

"Too late. Irene has invited Sissy to dinner and Sissy accepted. In fact they're in the Grand Hotel as we speak."

Jesus! My mother had not mentioned a word of this to me. I was glad now to be going home the following evening. I wondered if there would be anything of Mom left after Irene Kirby had chewed her up and spat her out.

"Just look after her until I get home, Jodi. Be there for her. I'll see you tomorrow night. Around eleven."

Brigitte's family had cooked a beautiful meal for our last night in Balatonfüred. They plied us with goulash and wine. I looked around the table at the smiling faces and wondered how Brigitte could bear to leave them. Then I thought of Carla's motherless little family and knew why Brigitte felt she had no choice.

* * *

I was exhausted by the time we were driving back into Cairnsure the following evening. The flight from Balaton to London had been on time and comfortable but there had been a long wait in Stansted for our Cork connection and then it was raining as we walked around the airport car park, trying to remember where I had parked my car.

I dropped Brigitte at the house which to me would always be Carla's. The big house was in darkness except for one light from the back. It, too, seemed to have lost its life when Carla left.

I almost crashed into the back of Eoin Kirby's car in our driveway. I hadn't been expecting to see it there. It looked as if he and Jodi had taken over the house. Taken my place. Annoyed, I grabbed my suitcase from the car and went into the kitchen. Mom threw herself into my arms and hugged me tight. I could see she hadn't yet had her hair done. It was flat and lifeless. I squeezed her small frame to me, panic-stricken. Of course Mom was getting old. She would die. But not now. Not while my heart still bled for Carla.

"How have you been, Mom?"

"I missed you."

"I missed you too," I said. I meant it. I had missed her fussy little ways and her constant caring for me. She moved away from me and patted her flattened hair.

"You must be starving. I've dinner made for you."

I smiled at her. However down Sissy was, she certainly wasn't out.

Jodi took her place in my arms. "I'm so glad you're home, Del. It's been awful."

Over her head, I glanced at Eoin. He was sitting comfortably at our kitchen table, his long legs stretched in front of him. He nodded to me.

"Nice to see you back, Adele. I hope the trip did you some good."

We all sat around the table then as I told them about Balaton and they told me about a Cairnsure shocked by Carla's death. I felt a ripple of guilt for running away when

I did. When so many people were sad and lonely. But I knew I had to cope with my own sadness and loneliness before I could be of help to anyone else. I forgave myself my flight into selfish oblivion.

"I've had The Cabin cleared out," Eoin said. "Jodi thought it was too painful a reminder of Carla's party."

"What are you going to do with Elliots'?" I asked because I did not want to think of the wall with butterflies and a rainbow, Carla standing in front of it, smiling.

"Probably build a house there. I'll be visiting Cairnsure quite a lot so I'll need a place to stay. I like that site overlooking the sea. It's where my father would have loved to end his days."

My heart gave an automatic leap of fear when Eoin mentioned his father. I felt momentarily confused until I recalled the DNA results. Those glorious pages which confirmed that Michael Kirby was his father. Not John Burke. Not my dad.

"Can I tell her my news now?" Jodi asked him and I noticed she flashed him her most wheedling smile.

"You're going to anyway. Why ask?"

"Guess what, Del. I'm going to New Zealand."

"No! When?"

"Next week. I'm going back with Irene and Eoin to the head office in Auckland. For training, she says, but I know she just wants to keep an eye on me."

So that was finally it. The trio of Carla, Jodi and Adele torn apart by death and distance. Jodi read my thoughts. "I'll be back here often. Working on the new golf-course development. We'll see each other as much as when you were in Dublin and I was in London. And we'll always be on the phone."

"Not while you're working, you won't. My mother wouldn't tolerate that."

"Oh, lighten up, Eoin! Irene isn't half the ogre you think she is."

"You'll learn," Eoin said and I could hear a warning as well as a promise in his tone.

The battle between Jodi Wall and Irene Kirby should be an interesting one. I put my faith in Jodi because she seemed to have Eoin wrapped around her little finger. Also because I knew this would be Jodi's last chance to straighten out her life. A chance she was lucky to get. A battle she must win.

Eoin stood up.

"Come on, Jodi. We still have work to do. Thanks for tea, Sissy."

"You're welcome, Eoin. I'll be making rice pudding tomorrow."

Mouth open, I listened to this exchange. Just what had gone on while I had been in Balaton?

"We'll have hot chocolate now and then we're going to talk," Mom said as soon as they went out the door.

I was tired and longed to go to bed, Barry Bear on the pillow beside me, but I sensed a determination in my mother. Something which just had to be said.

"Where's Tom?" I asked as she heated the milk.

"At home. His home."

So, the argument about where they would live once they married was still raging.

She brought the two mugs to the table and sat opposite me. Her face looked tiny, her eyes huge.

"What is it, Mom? You're worried about something. Tell me about it."

She lifted her mug to her mouth but her hand was shaking. Hot chocolate dribbled down the front of her blouse. She put the mug back on the table with a bang.

"I'm not going to marry Tom Reagan."

"Ah, Mom! Surely you could have come to some agreement about which house to live in. Tom is lovely."

"He is. A good man. A nice companion."

"Is it Dad you're thinking about? You know he'd want you to be happy."

"I know that. It's all he ever wanted. He was a very good husband to me. But I was not a good wife to him."

I stared at her. What had got into my mother in the week I'd been strolling around the balmy Lake Balaton shores? There was only one answer.

"This has something to do with Irene Kirby, doesn't it? Why did you go to meet her last night?"

"We needed to talk to each other."

"What in the hell for?"

"Language, Adele!"

"The truth, Mom!"

"I wanted her to know the trouble she had caused to your father and me. And to you and Eoin too."

I nodded waiting for Mom to go on. She was silent so long I had to prompt her.

"What did she say? Did she apologise?"

"God, no! She hasn't changed that much. She did point out though that I was equally to blame."

485

"Cheek! How can she say that? It was she came to you saying –"

Mom put up her hand to stop me.

"She did it for revenge, Adele. It was her way of getting back at me before she and Michael took off for their new life in New Zealand."

My mother bowed her head. I could not see her face but there was shame in the droop of her shoulders and her reluctance to look me in the eye.

"Revenge ? For what? What did you ever do to Irene Kirby?"

"I – I was very taken with her husband. I couldn't help myself. I –"

"Stop! Stop now!"

I got up and opened the patio door. A cool draught of air wafted into the kitchen. I breathed in deeply, counted to ten and then exhaled. The horrible words were still in my head. How could this prim and prissy woman, this paragon of virtue, be talking such utter nonsense? Who was this little person with the flat hair and the name of another woman's husband on her lips? A sudden gust shook the leaves of the big oak. I had the notion it was Dad, angry at Sissy's betrayal. Then I believed that maybe he was angry at me. For judging. For condemning. That fleeting, irrational thought made me take control.

I sat again and tried to speak calmly.

"Why are you telling me this? I don't want to know."

"Lily Burke will tell you sooner or later. I'd prefer to tell you myself while I still can."

I remembered things that Lily had said now. Confusing things. Hints.

"Tell me what, for God's sake! All you've said so far is that you fancied Michael Kirby."

I heard my mother draw in a shuddering breath, as if she was about to cry but when she spoke her voice was clear and strong.

"I didn't fancy Michael Kirby, as you put it. I loved him. I still do."

My heart must have continued to beat, my lungs to breathe, seconds slip by but I was unaware of my body or time as Sissy's words hung in the air between us. "I loved him," she had said but she hadn't been speaking about Dad. She had been talking about Eoin's father. About Irene's husband. About Michael Kirby. The branches of the oak shook again and this time I knew Dad was definitely angry and I was angry for him too.

"Jesus, Mom! First Dad and Irene and now you and Michael Kirby What were ye up to? Wife-swapping? Gang bangs? I thought your generation was so moral that you wouldn't even mention sex and now I find ye were like dogs on heat!"

"Don't be so vulgar, Adele! When I say I had feelings for Michael Kirby that doesn't mean I did anything improper with him. Nor, according to Irene, did your father with her. I bitterly regret not believing him. Irene was just teasing me in a very cruel way when she told me my husband could be her child's father."

My exhaustion had dipped to a new low by this stage.

Holding my head up was an effort, let alone working out the rationale behind this saga.

"Did you tell Michael Kirby?" I asked. "If you believed what Irene told you was true, her husband had a right to know as well, didn't he?"

"It wasn't my place to tell him. I thought that was up to your father or Irene. Both of whom knew of course that what she had said wasn't true. Michael wouldn't have believed it anyway. He idolised her. She could do nothing wrong in his eyes. That's why she had no fear saying what she did."

A shadow of something cold and calculating insinuated itself into my thinking. Something I did not want to acknowledge but had to voice.

"There was the loan for our house and Dad's business to be considered too, wasn't there? You wouldn't have wanted to jeopardise that either, would you, Mom? You couldn't have a vengeful Michael Kirby demanding immediate repayment of his loan."

She didn't answer. Her silence was a reply in itself. She kept staring at me but I didn't know what to say. What did she want? Absolution? Forgiveness? For me to say I understood? I didn't.

I stood up, went to the sink and rinsed my cup. I needed to do that mundane thing, to hold onto some reality. Something I could understand. My head was reeling with exhaustion and confusion.

When I turned around she was standing behind me. I saw tears glistening in her eyes. She reached her hand towards me. I moved away from her touch.

"Did you ever love Dad? Ever?"

"I grew to depend on your father. To need him. That's a kind of love, isn't it?"

I went to bed then. I didn't want to hear any more.

* * *

I lay on in bed next morning, the duvet pulled over my head to block out the daylight. To block out all thoughts of my mother's revelations last night. When I eventually heard the front door bang, I got up. I would have to face Sissy sooner or later but not yet.

After breakfast and shower, I put on my best jeans and runners. The ones with the pink laces. I started out on the hill road at a brisk pace but slowed as I neared Aunt Lily's, not sure now what I would say to her. Not really sure that I should say anything at all. From her yard, I could see Ned Lehane mending a fence in the hill field. I knocked on the front door and waited as Lily came slowly to let me in.

When we got to the kitchen I handed her the pashmina I had bought for her in Balton. She glanced into the bag but passed no remark about it.

"You look exhausted," she said. "All that flying isn't good for you. It's unnatural."

She too looked tired but I realised that hers was the tiredness of old age. Of having lived too long. Of coming to the end of a trying journey. I sat in the chair by the range and felt bound to the seat by the weight of tragedies past and those yet to come. She pottered around with her tea-making ritual as I wallowed in a depression as deep as any I had ever before experienced.

"How did you like that foreign country?" she asked as she handed me my cup.

"It's beautiful. I'll go back there again some time."

"Don't be silly. Life's too short for going back anywhere."

She was right. Forward was the only way to go but how? How could I move on from missing Carla, from the residual terror of believing Eoin Kirby to be my brother, from my mother's confession which made a mockery of the childhood I had thought perfect. I put down my cup and looked Lily in the eyes. For once I didn't flinch. I needed her brutal honesty.

"Mom. Did she . . ."

I stopped then. What did I want to know? Had Mom been telling the truth about not sleeping with Michael Kirby? Had she made Dad unhappy? Had he died of a broken and not a diseased heart?

"What about Sissy Roberts? Ridiculous little woman."

"Did she have an affair with Michael Kirby?"

Lily threw back her head and laughed. I was too puzzled by her reaction to say anything.

"She tried. My God! How Sissy Roberts tried, making a show of herself following him around, giggling and smiling at him. She never gave the man a minute's peace. I always believed he brought Irene back from Galway just to get rid of your mother. It didn't work like that though."

"What do you mean?"

"Well, Sissy didn't give up, did she? Irene tried to give her some of her own medicine by flirting with your father. And your Uncle Noel too, God help him. A floosie that one was. Poor Michael Kirby had to emigrate to free himself of Sissy Roberts."

This didn't sound right. Not like the Sissy I knew. Mom had dignity. And pride.

"You're lying. Mom wouldn't carry on like that."

"Don't believe me if you don't want. But ask any of the old-stagers here. They'll remember it. The battle of Sissy and Irene was high entertainment in this parish thirty-five years ago."

I blushed with shame for my mother. I remembered myself, young and so obsessed by Kieran Mahon that I had followed him around until he told me to go. It must be in my genes, this falling for unattainable men. This lack of self-respect.

Lily was leaning close to me, peering into my face now.

"What are you reddening up for? You did nothing to be ashamed of. And if I wasn't such a cantankerous old woman, I'd probably say the same about Sissy Roberts. All she did was make a laughing-stock of herself and your father. There was no carry-on, only in her head. She was young. Naïve. I did my own fair share of falling for the wrong man too."

"Really? I never knew."

"Of course not. You thought I was born a wizened old spinster, didn't you?"

I laughed, enjoying the sound because it was so unexpected. Only minutes ago I had felt I would never again smile let alone laugh.

"You survived it well, Aunt Lily."

"Be sure I did. Your mother did too. She and your father had a good life together. They looked after each other."

"She didn't love him. Not really."

"Don't give me that piffle. Of course she did. She just never let go of her unrealistic dream. Michael Kirby was a weak man. Easily swayed. He needed Irene Kirby and, make no mistake about it, Sissy Roberts needed John Burke."

I sat back in my chair and closed my eyes. It was peaceful in the old kitchen. Dad's childhood home. He had forgiven Mom. She had forgiven him. As the clock ticked and I heard the dogs bark outside, I knew that the time had come for me to forgive them both. Sissy had been a good mother to me. I had no right to judge her now. Or Dad.

Lily touched me on the knee to get my attention.

"How are the Selbys? Do you know?"

"I haven't been up there yet. I think they're better left alone for the time being."

"You mean it's more comfortable for you to leave them be."

Lily was, once again, right. I didn't want to go near that house. To see Carla's children, the rooms she had furnished in her tasteful way, the garden where we three had held our thirtieth birthday party. Carla, Jodi and me. I hauled myself out of the chair.

"I'm going up there now. See if there's anything I can do to help."

Lily got up too. She took a step nearer to me and put her hand on my shoulder.

"You're a good girl, Adele. A lot more of your father in you than your mother. Try to remember Carla the way you last saw her. Smiling and laughing in The Cabin. She was so happy with her buckshee café. And thank you for the shawl. I'll wear it with my good suit."

I wanted to tell Lily I was sorry for not visiting her more often, for never having got to know the soft heart in the iron-clad shell. I knew she would be embarrassed by the words so I just hugged her instead.

* * *

The walk across town and out to the Selbys' house took almost an hour. As I approached the boundary wall on their property, I could hear the children laugh and shout at each other. I stood, concealed by a pillar of their gate and watched as Harry Selby played football with his children while Vera looked on, keeping a careful eye on them. Brigitte was there too, holding Lisa's hand as they ran after the ball, a huge smile on the child's face. There were goal posts dug into the grass. Carla wouldn't have liked that. Not on the front lawn. Finn was standing at one end, fiercely concentrating on the game, while Liam guarded the opposite goal area and Dave just toddled around. It was a happy scene until I looked more closely at the adults' faces. Their teeth were bared in parodies of smiles but their eyes were blank, their shoulders sloped downwards. Their hearts broken. A private grief.

I turned and walked back down the road. I needed to see Carla now. To tell her the children were well and that Harry was looking after them for her. I could almost hear her ask who was looking after Harry.

493

My legs ached as I climbed the hill to the cemetery, retracing my steps of just over a week ago when I had followed Carla's coffin. The dandelions were still yellow, the sun still shining and Carla was still dead.

Just as I opened the cemetery gate, my attention was caught by a sound, a little whimper. It was coming from over near the wall where Dad's grave sheltered from wind and rain. I heard the sound again but had to follow the curving path before I saw anything. Mom was kneeling on the kerbstone of my father's grave, a tissue held to her face, her shoulders shaking. I ran to her and knelt beside her.

"Mom, come on! Stop crying. You shouldn't be upsetting yourself like this."

She lowered the tissue and looked at me, her eyes red and swollen.

"I've been a terrible mother and a terrible wife to your father. You both deserved better."

I stood, caught her by the hand and pulled her to her feet. She was wearing a heavy cardigan even though the sun shone. I felt a surge of protective love for my mother, this little bundle of bones wrapped in wool.

"Don't ever say something like that again. You goose! You're the best mother in the world and you know Dad adored the ground you walked on."

She shook her head and a new spate of tears washed down her face. "No. I've wasted my life and almost destroyed yours. If John had been Eoin Kirby's father, that would have been my fault. I drove both him and Irene to it with my carry-on. I chased Michael Kirby, you know. Neglected your father and pined after another man. How could that make me a good wife?"

"Dad did his share of flirting with Irene Kirby too, didn't he? You weren't the only one to blame."

"That's not what you thought last night, was it? You couldn't even look at me, could you? You were disgusted."

She was right. That's exactly how I had felt. But today, in the solemnity of the graveyard and the warmth of the sun, I didn't feel as judgemental. They had all made mistakes: Dad had his head turned by Irene; Mom had nurtured dreams of Michael Kirby she never should have dreamt; Michael Kirby, from what I could see, had been naïve, spellbound by his young and beautiful wife; Irene had been manipulative and spiteful, playing with all their emotions just because she could. Perhaps she had been bored. Their games of thirty-five years ago had cast long shadows. I put my arm around Sissy's drooping shoulders.

"I can't say I understand, Mom. I probably never will. But you and Dad were happy, I saw you. I remember the way you laughed together and looked out for each other. It was what Dad wanted. You made him happy and me too. Irene and Michael made a good life for themselves in New Zealand. It's time to leave it all in the past where it belongs."

She stopped sniffling and put her head to one side. "Do you think so? Really?"

"Yes. Really."

She looked at Dad's grave again. I knew she was on the way to recovery when she stooped and tugged at a stray weed. "We should really put down stones here. Those little white ones. I'll ask Tom."

Illogical maybe, but my mother had seemed to shrug off thirty-five years of jealousy, deceit and guilt in an instant. All it had taken was a word from me and a tug at a weed. Sissy was back and so apparently was Tom in some capacity. I made up my mind then that I would never understand Sissy Burke and I would never, ever stop loving her. I smiled. I know Dad was smiling too, wherever he was.

I didn't go to Carla's grave. She wasn't there. She was in her children and in our hearts. She always would be. Instead I walked back to the town with Mom, now complaining that her cardigan was too hot.

"I'm parked near the Library," she said. "Do you want a lift home?"

"No, Mom. I'll walk."

"Dinner will be a bit late. I'm going to get my hair done now. I'm sure they'll fit me in."

I was sure they would too. Sissy would sit in the hairdresser's, doe-eyed and flat-haired, until they shampooed, dried and lacquered excessively. I watched as she toddled off, a spring in her step. Dad would have been so proud of her. I was too.

* * *

I had learned my lesson. I checked that the tide was out before climbing the rocks on the East Beach. Every stride seemed to fill me with new determination. I was going to decide my future. Today. Now. Just as soon as I found a comfortable place to sit. The spot I eventually found wasn't so much comfortable as convenient. It was a flat-topped rock, battered into smoothness by thundering winter tides.

I gazed out to sea and tried to bring discipline to my thinking. I had almost a full year of my leave left to fill. What should I do? Travel? Look for a part-time job? Stay in Cairnsure or run as far as I possibly could from the scene of Carla's passing and the near-disastrous consequences of the tangled past relationship between my parents and Eoin Kirby's? Sissy was getting frail. Her will was as strong as ever but I saw old age begin to shadow her. Aunt Lily was even more strong-willed but older yet. I smiled as I thought about both of them. How had I, with such a background of strong females in my family, grown into the indecisive woman I now was? Or perhaps that was the reason I was sometimes too slow to decide, too anxious to please, too accommodating.

I heard the excited call of gulls and watched as they swooped and dived on an area of bubbling water. Silver flashes told me they had detected a shoal of mackerel. Early for them yet but there they were, breaking the surface of the water and glinting in the sun. I took a deep breath of the sea air and knew at that moment that I could not go back to the city. I didn't want the smoke, smog, traffic, the rush and hurry of city life. The smallness of it.

So what did I want? To be by the sea. Near the people I loved. I could move to Cork, only twenty miles from Cairnsure. To do what? To teach? To wear my patience thin in front of a class of children who would rather be listening to their iPods than to me. The answer to that was yes. Every day in the classroom, there was one minute with one child, when you knew that you had taught them something they would carry with them for the rest of their lives. Yes, I wanted to continue teaching. But where? And I yet had the problem of the rest of my leave to solve.

Jodi would be going away shortly. Poor Jodi. Such success and failure all wrapped up in the one beautiful package. But I was hopeful. Eoin, and Irene also, would take care of her. In this time of honesty I whispered Eoin's name and then shouted it to the waves. Eoin! Eoin Kirby! I waited for my heart to pound. My knees to tremble. Nothing. Except a titter when I examined the madness of shouting at the sea. I wished that Jodi would find peace and that Eoin would help her find it.

"Are you all right there? Don't move! I'll get you."

I started in fright. I looked towards the direction of the voice and saw Kieran Mahon scrambling along the rocks towards me. It happened then. Just like it used to do when I had been a teenager. The heart pounding. The knee trembling. I was Sissy's daughter after all. Spending a lifetime pining after the unattainable.

"What are you doing here, Kieran?"

"You were shouting. I thought there was something wrong."

"There is. I want to be on my own."

"I see. Push over."

He squeezed himself into the space beside me, so close that I was sure he could feel the heat from the blush which flooded my face. I tried staring ahead, counting the waves, following the flight of the gulls but I was still aware of him beside me. I thought of how he had hurt my feelings so badly when I had been little more than a child. That did the trick. My voice was steady and I was pleased by how coolly sarcastic I sounded when I spoke.

"Do you spend your time patrolling these rocks? What a sad life you must have."

"Sissy told me where to find you."

"Why? What do you want?"

"I want to offer you a job. Badly paid and very busy but I think you'd find it interesting."

"In *Cairnsure Weekly*?"

"Yes. The girl at the front desk is going on maternity leave next week. Jodi was supposed to take over but, as you know, she's found something more suited to her."

I glanced at him trying to gauge if he was upset about Jodi. He was in profile. I'd have to ask if I wanted to know.

"Do you mind, Kieran? I mean, about Jodi and Eoin Kirby."

He picked up a pebble and threw it. It bounced off the rocks before skittering to a halt. He turned towards me.

"I thought I would. Now I realise I don't."

He kept looking at me as if waiting for me to comment. I didn't know what to say so I looked at the laces on my runners, liking the way I had double-knotted them.

"Well, Adele? The job? Are you interested?"

It could be the answer for me. A temporary job to tide me over while I decided what I wanted to do next. But then how would I cope with Kieran as my boss? Heart pounding and knee trembling did not belong in the workplace.

"All right, Adele. I'll up the pay."

"No. It's not that. It's . . . It's . . . Do you think we could work together?"

"Why not? We get on well, don't we?"

"I suppose. Okay then. It's a deal."

Kieran jumped up and held his hand out to me. I noticed the tide was beginning to head towards the rocks. Time to go.

"There's one other thing you might like to think about," he said as I tried to swing myself up without holding too tightly to his hand. "One of the teachers is due to retire from Cairnsure National school next year. Just thought you might like to know."

I had managed to get myself into a standing position and immediately let go Kieran's hand. I was interested in what he had said. It was like pieces of a jigsaw slotting together. A temporary job in *Cairnsure Weekly*, then back to teaching but in my local school. What more could I want? I looked up into his crystal clear green eyes and admitted that I wanted more. A lot more. I decided it was time I left Cairnsure behind. Otherwise I could end up like my mother, spending a lifetime lusting after a man who had no interest in me.

I led the way across the rocks, Kieran following on behind. He said something to me as I jumped a narrow gulley. I stood still and let his words play over again in my head. Then I wondered if he had said them at all. If I had conjured them up out of the soft breeze and whispering tide. I turned towards him as he too crossed the gulley.

"Can you repeat that? I didn't hear."

"You did. You just want to make me say it again."

"Well?"

"All right then. I missed you when you were away in Hungary. I don't want you to go again. Please stay here. For a while anyway. It took me a long time to realise how I felt but now I know. I – I need you."

I'm not sure which one of us moved first. Maybe we reached for each other at the same time. I'm very sure though what happened next. We kissed. A tender, satisfying kiss. A beginning. A fulfilment. We clung together, holding tightly to the happiness we had just found. We might yet be there had it not started to rain. A sudden spattering of a light shower. Laughing, arms around each other we headed back towards the beach.

We had just reached the dunes when we were both brought to a sudden standstill. Our eyes were drawn towards the horizon where a rainbow shimmered. Delicate. Beautiful. Ethereal.

"Carla," I whispered.

We stood there, our arms around each other until the rainbow faded. I knew, in the part of my soul where logic doesn't apply, that Carla had given Kieran and me her blessing. She had let me know that she would always be there in the refracted colours of the rainbow. Always watching over us. Always caring.

"Will you come to dinner in my house?" I asked him.

"Sissy has already asked me. Roast, rice pudding and you by my side. What more could I want?"

There was more. A lot more. And it all happened under the watchful eye of the rainbow.

THE END

If you enjoyed *Under the Rainbow* by
Mary O'Sullivan why not try
Inside Out also published by Poolbeg?
Here's a sneak preview of Chapter One.

inside
out

MARY
O'SULLIVAN

POOLBEG

CHAPTER 1

The thump, thump from upstairs was incessant. Meg felt as if the ceiling, the whole room, was vibrating to the rhythm of the awful noise her son called music. But at least she knew where Tommy was tonight. A headache was a small price to pay for that peace of mind.

Pressing the volume on the remote control, she turned up the sound and sat back to watch the TV news. War, drought, floods, poverty, wealth, power and powerlessness. Not what she needed now. Flicking through the channels she found a reality show.

When she heard the front door open she checked her watch. Nine thirty. John was home early tonight. He came into the lounge and threw himself into an armchair.

"How are you?" Meg asked.

"I'm whacked." He glanced at the screen. "Why are you watching this rubbish?"

She stood and handed the remote control to him, too tired to take up the challenge he was offering.

"Are you hungry? There's some cooked salmon in the fridge."

"I've eaten. Just a cup of coffee, please. And tell Tommy turn that racket down."

Kettle on, she went upstairs, tapped on Tommy's door and opened it. Her son was sitting in front of his computer, jiggling around in time to the music which was rocking the whole room.

"Your father's home!" she shouted over the noise. "Put on your earphones, please!"

Tommy turned around to stare at her. She looked back at her seventeen-year-old son and tried to see the child he had been up to a year ago. He was in there somewhere behind the studs and piercings. Somewhere underneath his mop of orange-streaked hair.

"So, the Führer's here."

"Just do as you're asked," she said and closed his door before he could answer.

By the time she brought coffee into the lounge, John was asleep in his chair. He seemed vulnerable in sleep, the normally stubborn line of his jaw relaxed. She put the cup on the coffee table and went to wake him. Her hand on his shoulder, she hesitated. Maybe he needed rest more than coffee. But then she didn't really know what her driven husband needed. Success? Money? Promotion? He had all that but his ambition was still as honed as it had been when he'd started out as a handyman in the storage company he now managed and part-owned. He continued to drive

506

himself forward, working impossibly long hours, fretting over contracts, second-guessing competitors. She touched his hair, silver-streaked but yet thick and strong.

Her hand slid from his hair onto his shoulder. She must talk to him about Carrie. She shook him gently.

"John. Your coffee."

For an instant he looked at her sleepily without any recognition in his eyes. Meg had to consciously control her resentment.

"Tough day?" she asked quietly, not really wanting to know. According to her husband his working life was a series of tough days, tough decisions, tough deals. A tough man. Strong, decisive.

He rubbed his hands over his eyes, then reached for his coffee and swallowed a long draught.

"Anything that could've gone wrong today, did. And we've got problems with the CCTV again."

Sitting across from him, Meg nodded and waited for the litany to start. Competitors were ruthless, tax prohibitive, profit margins dwindling. He never asked for her opinion. All he needed was an attentive audience and the odd nod of agreement. Meg had perfected the art of appearing to listen. It would be pointless trying to talk to him about his daughter until he had gone through his complaining routine.

Then Meg noticed the silence. There were no complaints from John. In fact, he had not said another word. She glanced across at him and saw that he looked drawn. Weary. His tie was loosened and his normally healthy colour had a tinge of grey.

"Are you feeling all right?"

Draining off the last of his coffee, he stood up. "Just exhausted," he said. "I'm off to bed. Tell Tommy I want him in my office at nine o'clock tomorrow morning. We're clearing out Bay 6 and I need extra manpower for a few days."

Instructions issued, he turned and left the room. No goodnight kiss. Not even the peck on the cheek which had lately become their only form of physical contact. And no chance to talk about Carrie. Meg looked at her watch and did some quick subtraction. What time would it be in Maine now?

Going into the hall, Meg picked up the phone and tapped in the international dialling code. She knew the whole sequence of numbers off by heart at this stage. She listened as the line crackled and hissed. Eventually Carrie's phone rang on the east coast of the USA. Across the tumbling breadth and dark depths of the North Atlantic. It rang and rang. The voicemail greeting clicked in. Meg's hands began to shake as she listened to her daughter's familiar voice. Sweet and serious. A deep voice for such a young girl. "Please leave a message after the tone and I will get back to you as soon as possible." Meg tried and failed to keep the panic out of her voice when she spoke: "Carrie, this is Mom again. Please send me a text or call. It's a week since I last heard from you. You know I fuss. Love you."

When she put down the phone Meg just stood where she was, eyes shut, watching a stream of horrific images flash past. Her daughter lying in some back street, throat slashed. Carrie bound and gagged, kidnapped by gangsters, crying out for help, calling for her mother.

"Is this one of your new fads, Mom? Transcendental Meditation or something?"

Meg opened her eyes to a sight almost as frightening as her mental images. Tommy was dressed to go out, a silly little black bowler hat perched on top of his orange-streaked hair and eyeliner around his eyes.

"Where do you think you're going? It's after ten o'clock."

"Out."

"No! You're not. Come into the lounge. We need to talk."

"What about? I haven't time. I'm meeting Breeze in five minutes."

"Breeze! That says it all. What kind of a person would call himself Breeze?"

Tommy moved towards the front door but Meg got there before him. She stood with her back against the door, blocking his path.

"I'm serious, Tommy. You're not going out now. It's too late."

"For Christ's sake! I'm nearly eighteen. Stop treating me like a child!"

"Stop acting like one!" Meg shot back but that wasn't what she meant to say. God! How she wished with all her heart that he would act like the child he had been. Funny, co-operative, kind, bright and intelligent. A little stubborn but then he would have got that from John. Except that in Tommy the stubbornness had been tempered by a willingness to listen not very apparent in his father's make-up. The pre-Breeze Tommy.

"You're not eighteen yet. You'll do as I say until you learn to behave responsibly."

"You mean until I become the nerd you and the Führer want me to be. Degrees pouring out my ears. Big deal!"

Meg had to clasp her hands tightly together. She wanted to slap her son's face, to see his defiance turn to shock. But the shock was hers. How could she ever want to hurt her child? What was happening to her? To the family.

"We really need to talk, Tommy. I don't want to argue. Please don't go out now."

Maybe it was the despair in her tone or maybe it was just the innate decency in him. For whatever reason Tommy lifted his hand and took off his silly hat. A capitulation. Taking out his mobile he began his impossibly fast texting. Meg guessed that he was cancelling his arrangement with Breeze.

"Do you want a cup of coffee?" she asked.

"Too late."

"Hot milk?"

When he nodded agreement Meg went into the kitchen and put milk for two into a saucepan. Tommy followed her in and sat on one of the high stools at the breakfast counter. His eyeliner looked even weirder in the bright kitchen light.

"If you're going to wear that stuff around your eyes you should learn to put it on properly," she said and instantly regretted making yet another criticism.

"Is that what you wanted to talk about? All-important appearances?"

"As a matter of fact I wanted to talk about Carrie. When did you last hear from her?"

Meg caught a hesitation, a beat of fear, before Tommy replied.

"It's odd," he said quietly. "I haven't heard from her for over a week. She's not answering her phone and she hasn't picked up any of her emails either. I wonder what she's up to that she doesn't want us to know."

Standing at the cooker watching the milk start to bubble, Meg felt her heart pound. Turning around, she caught the concern on Tommy's face. Her heart beat even faster. Tommy and Carrie were close. The strongest bond in the Enright household. Carrie was the caring older sister and Tommy her adored young brother. Meg had often noticed them share a silent communication. Just like twins even though Carrie was the elder by four years. One always knew when the other was feeling down or sick.

"Is she all right, Tommy? I haven't heard from her either. I'm worried."

He shrugged his shoulders. "She's twenty-one, Mom. She doesn't have to report in to you every day. Anyway, she's not on her own in Portland. You'd have heard if anything bad had happened."

The sudden hiss of milk boiling over onto the hob brought Meg's attention back to the cooker. By the time she had mopped up the spill and poured out the two mugs of milk the closed look was back on Tommy's face. But Meg felt better able to cope with it now. He was right. If

Carrie was missing or if her mutilated body had been recovered, either the Maine police or one of Carrie's friends would have contacted home. Her friends were a nice group. All second-year university students on a working summer holiday in America. Nice people. Just like Carrie. They would look out for each other. Especially Trina. Carrie and Trina Farrell were best friends. Meg smiled at Tommy.

"You're a sensible lad, Tom. You're right. I worry too much. Carrie will be home next week anyway. Which reminds me, you're back to school then too."

"I don't want to talk about it!"

"It's your last year in secondary. You've done so well up to now it's not worth throwing it all away. Remember our agreement?"

"Agreement? Is that what you call it? You and the Führer laid down the law and left me no choice."

"Stop calling your father by that awful name!"

"It's a description, not a name."

Ignoring that comment, Meg lifted her mug and swallowed a mouthful of hot milk. She had put some nutmeg and vanilla into it. The flavours melded at the back of her tongue. While she savoured the warm tang Tommy stared at her defiantly. More relaxed now, she tried to reason with him.

"The deal was you wore whatever you liked for the summer holidays but you know well you won't be allowed back to St Martin's looking as you do now."

"Whatever," Tommy said, shrugging his shoulders.

All Meg's frustration and resentment rushed at her in

an unstoppable wave. Banging her mug onto the counter she got up from her seat and stood in front of her defiant son, her face flushed and her throat almost choked with a flood of angry words.

"How dare you! Do you think it's easy for your father and me? We've worked hard to give you a good education. St Martin's isn't cheap. We've paid your fees there for the past four years and you're going back next week whether you like it or not. And that means complying with their dress code. No studs or piercings, no outrageous hairstyles and definitely no orange streaks! Understood?"

"You can't make me. And what is it with you? You're beginning to sound like the Führer."

Meg knew she was handling this situation badly. Of course they couldn't make him go if he really didn't want to. The fact was, he did. Carrie had told her. By next week his studs and hoops would be removed and his orange streaks would be covered by a dark dye until they grew out. No point in arguing about it now. This was just his way of asserting himself. Looking for attention. And her way of expressing her worry. Looking for reassurance. She took a few steps back from him and let out a long sigh.

"Suit yourself," she said. "You'd better go to bed now. You must be up early in the morning. Your father wants you in EFAS. Some bay or other needs clearing out."

"More slave labour."

"He pays you."

"Not the going rate."

Meg managed to keep her mouth shut. Tommy was telling the truth. John paid his own son less and worked him harder than anyone else. "Character building", he called it and refused to budge from that position. Everyone was refusing to budge from their entrenched positions. John was determined to work endless hours for EFAS. Tommy seemed equally determined to go down a ruinous path. Even Carrie, gentle Carrie, was doggedly refusing to answer her phone.

"I'm going next year."

Meg looked at her son. What was he threatening now?

"Going where?"

"To America to work next summer. I'm not spending another holiday slaving in EFAS. Or maybe I'll just backpack around Europe. Anyway I'll be eighteen then. I can do what I like."

He picked up his hat and walked out of the kitchen. Meg listened. When she heard him climb the stairs she sighed with relief and picked up the mug he had left for her to clear away.

Kitchen tidied, Meg locked doors, closed windows and put on the alarm. She waited until the "alarm on" sign flashed. The Enrights were protected from the outside world for tonight.

But as she climbed the stairs Meg had to fight the feeling that she had locked the threats to her peaceful existence in rather than out. Guilty at such a thought, she leaned over and kissed her sleeping husband on the forehead. He muttered in his sleep and turned, taking most of the duvet with him.

Snuggling into his back, she slipped her arm around

him. She listened to his breathing for a little while and thought about Tommy and what he might become, about Carrie and what she might be doing. Meg drifted uneasily from drowsiness to restless sleep.

• ◆ •

If you enjoyed this chapter from

Inside Out is by Mary O'Sullivan

why not order the full book online
@ www.poolbeg.com

See page 518 for details.

• ◆ •

PUBLISHED BY POOLBEG

Ebb and Flow

MARY O'SULLIVAN

Heavy rain, a narrow road and a violent car crash changed Ella Ford's life forever. Until that impact, she had a wonderful life, running a successful auctioneering business with her husband Andrew.

A year later, Ella is still trying to pick up the pieces – terrorised, both waking and sleeping, by images of Karen Trevor who died in the crash with her little son.

When Ella is asked to handle the sale of the dead woman's home, Manor House, she seizes the opportunity. By confronting Karen's history, she hopes to put an end to the horrific memories. But as Andrew embarks on an affair and their business is threatened by the ruthless Jason Laide, she begins to believe that Manor House is central to every event in her life and is exerting a powerful influence over her and those closest to her.

Has Ella finally lost touch with reality? Will she ever again be the confident woman she once was? Can the ghost of Karen Trevor be laid to rest?

ISBN 978-1-84223-305-5

PUBLISHED BY POOLBEG

As Easy as That

MARY O'SULLIVAN

Kate Lucas is happy. She's married to businessman Fred and works as P.A. to the leading trial lawyer in the country. A member of the smart set, Kate believes that having a baby is all she needs now for total fulfilment.

That is until a tragic accident reveals her friends in a new and shocking light. As proof of immoral and illegal behaviour unfolds, Kate is forced to find answers to some very difficult questions. Her quest for the truth leads her from Ireland to Budapest.

Along the way her relationship with her husband weakens while that with her boss grows into something far more than just loyalty to her employer.

Has Kate's chance of complete happiness slipped away from her, never to be recaptured?

ISBN 978-1-84223-270-5

Poolbeg wishes to

THANK YOU

for buying a Poolbeg book.
As a loyal customer we will give you
10% OFF (and free postage*)
on any book bought on our website
www.poolbeg.com

Select the book(s) you wish to buy
and click to checkout.

Then click on the 'Add a Coupon' button
(located under 'Checkout') and enter
this coupon code

POOLBEG

USMWR15173

POOLBEG

(Not valid with any other offer!)

WHY NOT JOIN OUR MAILING LIST
@ www.poolbeg.com and get some
fantastic offers on Poolbeg books

*See website for details